The Cain File

Max Tomlinson

Copyright © 2016 Max Tomlinson

All rights reserved.

ISBN: 1522995978
ISBN-13: 978-1522995975

DEDICATION

To my wife, Kate, the ultimate beta reader, who has been enduring rough drafts ever since we met.

ACKNOWLEDGMENTS

One of the rewards of sitting in a dark room, banging out stories about people who never really existed doing things that never really happened, is connecting with readers. So thank you, dear reader, for coming along for the ride. I hope you enjoy it. You are the reason I do this.

And a huge THANK YOU to all of those who nominated THE CAIN FILE for Amazon's Kindle Scout program. What can I say? It would not have happened without you.

Likewise, my stalwart fellow workshoppers and beta readers who plowed through drafts and helped whip the book into shape. They are, in no particular order: Barbara McHugh, Dot Edwards, Heather King, Cara Black, Stan Kaufman, Kathleen Murray, Nanette Asimov, Phil Laird, Townsend Wright, Andy Fraknoi, Ross Pudaloff, and (drum roll, please) my wife, Kate (aka Deb).

Please check out my Amazon Author Page for more about me and my other books and to keep tabs on THE DARKNET FILE, the follow-up to THE CAIN FILE, due out in 2016.

http://maxtomlinson.wordpress.com/

-1-

"Four guards," Maggie said to John Rae. "And that's just on the front gate."

Two limos idled in front of theirs, tailpipes puffing in the cool night air, waiting to enter the minister's Spanish colonial mansion over a mile and a half above sea level. The lights of the capital twinkled in the narrow, mile-long valley below. A river of fog poured down into the city from the Andes.

Maggie de la Cruz could see all the guards through the limousine's tinted window clearly now. Two were obvious, moonlight reflecting off their silver helmets as they checked the papers of guests attending the oil minister's party. Two more soldiers waited in the shadows behind the tall wrought-iron fence, the outlines of submachine guns visible.

Flashlight beams bounced as one guard examined underneath a vehicle. Another instructed occupants to get out, so they could be patted down.

Maggie's heart rate sped up. "They're searching the guests," she said.

"Don't y'all worry," Agent John Rae Hutchens said, sitting next to her in the roomy back seat. "With the international guest list Minister Beltran has, it's no surprise. Besides we've got nothing to hide."

"Except that we're here to arrest him." Maggie snapped open her chain-mail clutch purse, extracted her lipstick. She had requested more people on this operation. But the Agency knew better. She was just a bean counter. "There will be more guards out back, too," she said. "Behind the mansion."

"Don't sweat it." John Rae brushed his thick sandy-colored

hair behind his ear. "The National Vice Squad will be here to make the actual arrest. All we need to do is set it up for them."

"If they can make it through the gate," Maggie said.

"They're the top police force in this country."

"A country known for its corruption."

John Rae checked his cell phone, reading a text. "On their way. Once the documents have been signed and the payoff confirmed, they'll come in and arrest Beltran and his two cronies."

Wasn't it pretty to think so? But she had to remind herself that distrust was part of her job and sometimes it could get the better of her. This was a quarry that wanted to walk into a trap. Two million dollars was one hell of a honeypot.

The pearl Mercedes 500 in front of them motored up to the guard shack. A soldier checked papers, waved them through with his white-gloved hand, then beckoned their car forward. Achic, their driver, a small-framed Indian in a voluminous suit who was also an undercover SINE agent collaborating on the op, put their car into gear.

"Got the official invitation, Achic?" Maggie asked in Spanish.

He held up a heavy-weight bond letter in one hand. "I do, ma'am."

"A little less on the *ma'am*," Maggie said. "I'm younger than you are." She caught a smile in the rearview mirror. "Ten to one they pat us down."

"Just remember, Maggie," John Rae said. "Y'all are along for the ride."

"And the fact that I handle the electronic bank transfer? And collect everyone's signature?" The hard evidence would seal the fates of a corrupt Ecuadorian oil minister, a Chinese minister of energy and—tonight's star prize—a vice president of a company owned by Commerce Oil.

"This is a milk run, Maggie," John Rae said. "Let me take care of the heavy lifting—if there is any. And there won't be."

"That's good—because none of us are armed."

Two million could generate a lot of potential resistance.

Maggie nudged John Rae to one side with a bare shoulder and used the rearview mirror as she freshened up her lipstick. She had her mother's looks: dark, Indian, striking. She was lucky in that respect. John Rae leaned to one side in the leather seat to give her an appraising glance as he took in her figure, more Latin than American, firmed by the miles pounded out in her ASICS on San Francisco's hills. Her long raven-colored hair gleamed. Her soft skin practically glowed with Christian Dior.

"I'm speechless," he said.

"I doubt that will ever be the case." She shot him a wink as she put her lipstick away, sat back, admired her new black Gianvito Rossi toe pumps. With the single-shoulder black evening gown, she looked a lot more confident than she felt.

This was only her second field op, a departure from her regular gig as a forensic financial analyst for the Agency. She needed to branch out, climb up from the rut she was stuck in. John Rae was the lead, and a seasoned pro. But the criminal world was a technical one anymore and being able to crack a firewall was often more valuable than kicking down doors. It was Maggie who had caught the irregularity in the oil worker's paystub that led them all to being here in the first place.

The driver's window whirred down and Achic addressed the guards softly, as his nature demanded, despite the fact that he was a decorated Ecuadorian Coast Guard vet with three tours of the Amazon, where *los cocainistas* ran rampant, under his belt.

"Where are *your* papers?" the guard snapped at Achic, using the *tú* form of the verb and pronoun. Informal, insulting—the way one would talk to a servant, or a child.

"What for?" Achic said, nodding back at Maggie and John Rae. "I'm their driver."

"Get out of the car, boy."

"*Oye!*" Maggie leaned forward, catching the guard's eye, shooting daggers into the coarse face of a big Mestizo. His eyes narrowed in return from under the shiny brim of his helmet.

"What's your problem, *chapo*?" she said in the local dialect.

"You saw the letter. It's signed by the Oil Minister's secretary. Or can't you read?"

The guard was clearly taken aback, but there was no mistaking the angry folds creasing either side of his mouth. In a different setting, Maggie would be begging his understanding.

John Rae's hand touched her arm. "Settle down, darlin'."

She swiped his hand away. "Don't call me *'darlin'* unless we're in bed together. And that's *not* likely to happen." Maggie continued to trade stares with the guard. "And what's *your* name?" She annunciated the *tú* clearly, the way he had done with Achic. "I need to make sure Minister Beltran knows what kind of people he has working the gates. Or should I say 'used to work'?"

"I meant no disrespect, *señorita*," the guard said, clearing his throat. He stepped back, stood to attention, waved them on.

"Okay, Maggie," John Rae said as they drove through the gates, which had clanked open. "I'm impressed. Look, I didn't mean anything I said back there. That's just the way we talk where I come from."

"I know," she said. "I just don't like shitheads who bully Indians." It ran a little too close to home.

"But you know—you did just say not *likely* to happen. About us being in the sack? That means I've still got a fighting chance."

She shook her head and laughed. They stopped inside the gates where a guard ran a flashlight under the wheel wells, then asked them to get out of the car for a search. Maggie grabbed her leather briefcase containing the sting documents and a svelte MacBook.

"Hopefully, the Vice Squad will be here soon," she said as she got out.

John Rae checked his phone again. "I'll let them know we're almost inside the target."

~~~

A *sonidera* band was playing a subdued *cumbia* at the far end of a ballroom the size of a *fútbol* stadium, where the high-coved ceiling flickered with moonlight shimmering off Minster

Beltran's swimming pool out back. Beyond that, the moon broke through clouds over the jagged Andes.

Faces Maggie recognized from Agency files dotted the room. One or two men chatted with the tightly clad escorts who seemed to be trying to outdo one another for alluring companion of the year. It wasn't unheard of for a local girl to be taken up as a mistress by an important figure and have her life change dramatically. All ethnicities of men were represented, some in suits and ties, and the occasional red-and-white-checked keffiyeh.

"Kind of like the National Geographic." John Rae handed Maggie a glass of burgundy-colored punch. "But with clothes and money."

"*Lots* of money," she said, taking a sip of sweet sangria. Not bad. "Oil money. Drooling to tear up what's left of the Amazon. For the nine hundred million barrels they just found under the Yasuni Rainforest."

"That Arab over there with the blousy woman," John Rae said. "He's drinking a highball. I didn't think they were allowed to do that."

"What—speak to women? They generally don't. Unless it's to order something to eat or tell her he wants sex. Or both."

"*Drink.*"

"The kind of cash he has buys all sorts of free passes."

Back by the bar stood two Latin men in dark suits and ties, wearing sunglasses indoors. Hands behind their backs, as if at attention, they had matching gun bulges under their left armpits.

"What about Abbot and Costello over there?" she asked.

"Yeah, I noticed them when we came in."

Maggie sipped sangria, pretending to relax. "Anything to worry about?"

"At an event like this?" John Rae frowned and took a drink of Heineken beer from a long-neck bottle as he weighed things up. "With half the criminal world south of the equator in attendance? They're probably just here to make sure no one walks off with the silver."

"They keep looking this way."

"You mean; they keep looking *your* way. That's because you're the most interesting thing to look at." John Rae gave Maggie a smile, held his bottle out for a toast.

She blushed slightly, clinked her glass cup on John Rae's bottle, caught Achic's eye by the door where he stood dutifully with the servants, holding her briefcase. Achic gave Maggie a careful nod, indicating a biggish man wearing a hand-embroidered Quechua shirt under his Armani jacket who had just entered the huge double doors. His well-combed hair offset a pock-marked face and a cruel-looking mouth. Armand Beltran: Ecuador's oil minister. He stopped and spoke to a smallish man with a thin mustache and glasses.

"There's our victim," John Rae said. "One of them, anyway."

Beltran noticed Maggie, gave her an open leer.

"Doesn't have a clue who I am," she said to John Rae as she smiled back at Beltran. "Thinks I'm one of the paid escorts."

"Don't take it too hard. There are some pretty high-end hookers here."

"Ha ha."

"How did a clown like that ever become oil minister anyway?"

"Started as a foreman with a little oil driller in Colombia, chiseling the workers, taking a cut from their pay packets if they wanted to keep their jobs. Worked his way up to be pals with all the people no one else wanted to be seen with: drug dealers, organized crime—you name it. The president of Ecuador gave him a ministerial slot so he doesn't have to sully his hands with anyone dirty. Look at him. Wouldn't be caught dead talking to an Indian, but wears the shirt, now that they're in fashion. Doesn't know a potato from a pumpkin."

"Well, he'll get his soon enough. Once Velox and Li show, we can get started."

"Have National Vice confirmed yet?" Maggie asked.

"Stuck in traffic."

"Ai."

"Don't sweat it, darlin'. Not that ladies sweat in the first place."

"I'm going to check in with Achic."

"Looks like we ordered some class tail for this party," she heard Beltran say in Spanish to his companion in what was probably meant to be a discreet tone as she strolled past on her way to Achic.

"An oil deal ultimately worth billions?" his partner said. "What surprises me is that she's wearing any clothes at all."

"With an ass like *hers*, the gringos'll pay double. But then, I'm an ass man, from way back."

They snorted laughs.

"Want something to drink?" Maggie said to Achic, drinking sangria.

"Not while on duty, thank you. Are Vice here yet?"

"On their way—or so they keep saying."

Achic grimaced and she knew what he was thinking. Anyone in law enforcement in a country like this was suspect of being on the take or incompetent at best, no matter how high up they were. Achic, however, had been thoroughly vetted by the Agency. "Thank you, by the way: for telling that *tombo* out on the gate where to go. I took a bullet on the Napo River when I was in the Coast Guard, but to them I'll always be a *caiman*—a lazy Indian."

"I know what it's like," she said, sipping her drink.

"With all due respect, *señorita*, I don't think you do."

"We'll see: Where are you from?"

"A little village called Cotacachi," he said. "Just outside . . ."

"Otavalo," she said. "I went there when I was six years old. For Fiesta del Yamor."

A look of surprise crossed Achic's face. "But you're from San Francisco, California—"

"Born in Zuleta," she said in Quechua. "My father is a *yanqui*. I was sent to the U.S. when my *mami* died."

"Lucky you," he said.

"In some ways." She turned, traded glances with John Rae,

on his phone again. John Rae gave a shrug. Nothing yet. Maggie sauntered over to Beltran the ass man, all wet smiles and ogle eyes. His companion was at the bar.

"Well, hello there, *chica*," Beltran oozed in Spanish. "And what's *your* name?"

"Kristina Marin. From Star Bank?" She put her hand out in a businesslike manner. "Representing Commerce Oil. For the document signing? A pleasure to meet you, Minister Beltran."

Beltran coughed into his drink. "I'm so sorry," he said, immediately changing his tone, shaking Maggie's hand. "We weren't properly introduced."

"Not a problem," she said. "Where are the others? Velox and Li?"

"Just arriving." Beltran nodded at two men entering the room, a *norteamericano* with silver hair and sideburns and a severe-looking Asian wearing a dark suit and a wide tie. Earnest Velox, regional vice president with Five Fortunes Petroleum, a Chinese shell company fronting Commerce Oil, and Hong Li, the Chinese minister spearheading the Amazon deal in exchange for two billion dollars in loans.

The two men joined Maggie and Beltran. Once introductions were out of the way, Velox was quick to get to the point.

"Did you bring the documents, Miss Marin?" Velox smiled warmly, but Maggie knew him to be ruthless when it came to anything that got in the way of drilling for oil.

"I did, indeed," Maggie said, trying to snag John Rae's eye. He was on his cell phone again, not smiling and looking at his watch. "Did you bring a pen?"

Velox patted the breast of his suit coat. "Should we get started? I have a red-eye later tonight. Back to Beijing."

Frowning, John Rae put his phone in his pocket, smoothed the flap over it, then came striding over, hand out, brandishing a smile. "Well, hello there, gentlemen—and I do use the term loosely." Laughs all around. "JT Owens—Star Bank, on behalf of Commerce Oil. How y'all doin' anyway? I see you've already met my lovely assistant."

Hands were shaken, backs slapped.

"Now we're in business," Velox said. "I believe we're meeting next door. Correct, Minister Beltran?"

"Yes we are."

"What's your rush?" John Rae said. "You just got here. This promises to be one hell of a party, eh, Minister?"

"My parties are never anything less," Beltran said.

Velox looked at his watch. "I wish we could, but . . ."

"Anybody want a real drink?" Maggie drained her sangria, winking at Beltran. "I'm ready for something stronger. And I bet twenty-five *centavos* your barman makes a terrific *pisco* sour."

"I have verified that to be true," Beltran said with a grin, giving Maggie bedroom eyes.

"Now you're talking," John Rae said, taking Maggie's empty glass. "Anybody else? Come on, gentlemen. Where I come from it's bad luck to sign a deal without wetting it first."

John Rae stopped a waiter in a white jacket, ordered drinks. They arrived, far too soon for Maggie's liking, and everyone drank.

Velox, Li, and Beltran were now checking watches regularly.

"I hear your pool table was built in Spain in 1792," John Rae said to Beltran. "I do love the game, but it doesn't love me. I promise to lose gracefully."

Beltran lost his smile. Velox's was non-existent. Li's face turned to vinegar.

"I was telling your assistant here that we have to get to the airport tonight," Velox said to John Rae. "With the traffic in Quito, we need to leave soon."

"I agree," Beltran said.

"JT," Maggie said. "Can I have a quick word with you?"

"Sure, darlin'," John Rae said. "Excuse me, gents." He and Maggie moved off to one side, well away from Velox, Li, and Beltran.

Maggie said: "I'm starting to smell a rat."

"I hate to say this." John Rae maintained a devil-may-care smile, but his words were the opposite. "But I'm thinking we better bail."

"Yes." Maggie gave a deep sigh. "We'll never get another shot at it."

"No, we won't. You had to beg to get this, Maggie. And they were reluctant. This was your shot to make good. But, I'm sorry to say, it's starting to look a little funky. I'll make up some excuse, tell them we can't go through with it."

In her mind, Maggie saw the bulldozers tearing up ancient trees and the topsoil of the Amazon blowing away. That would only be the start. Entire tribes would be rendered homeless, made extinct. There were two pristine fragments of Amazon rainforest—the lungs of the planet. The Yasuni was one of them. With it gone, that left one lung. And seven billion people needing to breathe through it.

"Christ, John Rae—it's not just about me. I want to nail those guys. I want Commerce Oil."

Their eyes met. More than a little electricity. "You and me both. But you know the protocol: if Vice fails to show, we can't move forward with the arrest. We're not armed. We'll just have to give 'em the money, regroup, and report back home. Convince the guys up top to think this warrants another stab down the road."

Maggie felt a year's work slipping away.

"John Rae, you didn't come all the way down here to give those bums two million and go back home without a fish. And Commerce Oil is a whale."

"I knew you and I were cut from the same cloth."

"We can string them along, right up to the signing. If National Vice aren't here by then, we'll cancel. I'll pretend the access codes don't work."

John Rae drank. "You got it."

Maggie saw Velox marching over. His smile had a twitch to it.

"Is there some kind of problem?" he said. "Li's starting to get antsy. We all are, quite frankly."

"None at all," John Rae said.

"We had to notify Star Bank and let them know we're going

to be entering the access codes in the next fifteen minutes," Maggie said.

"We'll be right over, Mr. Velox," John Rae said. "Thank you so much for your patience."

Velox huffed mildly and marched back over to Li and Beltran.

"How am I going to know if Vice are on their way?" Maggie said. "How are you going to communicate that to me?"

"Right hand on the chin means it's a go," John Rae said, demonstrating. "Left means *no*."

"And if we get right up to singing, and it's still a *no?*"

"Give Beltran the damn money."

"That's about the worst plan I've ever heard," she said.

"Me too," John Rae said. "But it's the official line from head office. No one wants to see anyone get hurt over two measly million."

"Two measly million of U.S. taxpayers' money."

"Bottom line, this is a milk run. And I'm not just a pretty face, either." John Rae flashed one of his winning smiles, patted Maggie's arm. "Roll with it." He turned, looked over at Velox, Beltran, and Li, waiting. Velox tapped his wristwatch and raised his eyebrows.

"Let's get signing," Maggie said.

~~~

In a grand office next door, the five of them sat around a table the size of an aircraft carrier, while the two humorless men in aviator glasses manned the door, hands behind their backs. One man was about fifteen pounds heavier than the other, but apart from that, they were clones. The ceiling high above dazzled with elaborate rococo plasterwork with gilt highlights. The far end of the room, overlooking the pool, gave out onto a huge leaded-glass window of dozens of frames. The murmur of the band and party was muffled through the thick stone walls.

Li leafed through the documents to be signed, while Maggie booted up her MacBook.

The first thing she did was to activate the web cam and

position the computer so that she had Beltran, Li, and Velox nicely framed. She hit *record*. All of this would be documented, whatever transpired.

Li passed the papers to Velox and eyed Maggie. "I hope Star Bank understands the discretion this transaction requires." His voice echoed in the room.

"It's all been made very clear, Mr. Li," Maggie said, speaking clearly so the microphone would catch everything. "None of us wishes a high profile. Commerce Oil wants complete discretion as well. That's why Star Bank is representing them. The two million will be transferred to Minister Beltran's private account."

Maggie saw the suspicion in Li's face. No one trusted a man like Beltran. But there was plenty of cash for everyone down the road once Five Fortunes started pumping oil out of the Amazon for Commerce. The two million was penny ante compared to what these men stood to make for their respective interests.

"It all looks kosher to me," Velox said, reaching into the breast pocket of his suit jacket, retrieving a gold pen. "As soon as Miss Marin here finalizes the electronic payment, I'm good to go." He clicked his pen a couple of times with his thumb.

Beltran smiled as well and Li even divulged what might have been called a non-frown.

John Rae had his phone out and was checking texts.

Maggie kept one eye on him while she accessed the Agency's global IKON network, looking for any indication that National Vice might not show.

John Rae rubbed his chin with his left hand. Vice were still en route.

Maggie took her time logging into Star Bank Online, the front that she had set up. The USB connector flickered green as an hourglass on the laptop's screen stopped spinning.

"What is taking so long?" Beltran said in a stony voice that bounced around the big room.

"Slow satellite connection," Maggie said. She gave John Rae a sideways glance. He rubbed his chin with his right hand, gave her an almost imperceptible nod.

Brigada del vicio nacional were in place. She could move ahead. Relief flowed through her otherwise acidic stomach.

She selected as payee the Amazon Wildlife Restoration Fund, a front owned by Beltran, and, while another hourglass spun, retrieved her digital-access key fob, a small device the size of a keychain, typed in yet another password, and was presented with a one-time use digital key. She entered that hexadecimal number onto another screen, stepped through more authentication, and landed on the main account page.

There it was, waiting to be kicked off: an electronic payment from Star Bank to Beltran's façade account, based in the Isle of Jersey, British Isles: $2.1 million.

And when the documents were signed and the transaction completed, arrests would be made.

How very little money powerful men could be bought for.

Powerful weak men.

"Here we are gentlemen," she said. "*Finally.*"

Just then, the *vip* of a text popped up on Maggie's screen.

msg pending from Blackhorse:

Blackhorse was Ed, her Agency supervisor, back in San Francisco.

Maggie typed a quick response: *?*

Blackhorse: NVC is 10-7

Maggie stared in disbelief. 10-7 was old CB-radio code for "out of service." NVC was obviously the National Vice Squad. The vice squad wasn't going to show after all. John Rae must have gotten some bad information. Or someone was leading him on.

She typed a quick response: *r u sure?*

10-4

so no go? she typed.

go ahead and authorize but no pending action will be taken

Beltran must have found out about the arrest. Cancelled it. But she was supposed to go ahead and give the rat two million dollars of U.S. taxpayer money anyway, and then let him, Li, and Velox go off and trash the Amazon at will.

k, she typed to Ed. *will do*

"Is there some problem?" Beltran said.

Maggie looked up at the attentive faces watching her.

"I'm so sorry, gentlemen," she said. "But I seem to be having problems with the access code. I'm afraid we'll have to reconvene while I look into it."

John Rae squinted at her, trying to read her words.

She rubbed her chin with her left hand.

He did a double take, as if to say—really?

She gave a curt nod.

"What the *hell* is going on?" Velox said, bordering on a screech.

Li and Beltran drilled her with unpleasant stares. John Rae was looking at Maggie with his eyebrows raised.

"We can't proceed," she said to him. Meaning, *I'm* not going to proceed.

"I see," John Rae said, nodding sagely. Then, to Beltran, Velox, and Li: "I hate to say it, gents, but Ms. Marin needs to sort this out. Damn computers, anyway. We were better off when we used a shopping bag full of cash. Can we circle back tomorrow?"

"No," Beltran said, his voice rising. "We can't. I demand an explanation."

Li was panic-stricken. Velox was gulping.

"Make that bank transfer," Beltran said to Maggie.

"I wish I could," she said.

"I don't believe you for a moment," he said. "You've been stalling us for an hour. Now do as I say or I'll have you placed under arrest."

"What?" Velox said to Beltran. Li was looking more than uncomfortable.

"They're trying to back out of the deal," Beltran said.

"Now relax," Maggie said. "I just need to get another access code. That requires several approvals. I'll start contacting people, but it's late. It won't be ready until tomorrow. Say first thing?"

Beltran snapped his fingers at the two men by the door.

They drew their pistols and came forward. Beltran stared at Maggie with slitted eyes. "Make the transfer," he said between his teeth.

"Gentlemen," John Rae said, drumming his fingers calmly on the table. "And I use the term more loosely than before, because you ain't gentlemen at all now, are you? What we have here is what is commonly called a Mexican standoff. Sorry for the political incorrectness and all."

"Do you really think the National Vice Police are waiting outside?" Beltran said with a smirk. "Who do you think runs this country?"

John Rae nodded, taking everything in.

"I'm not sure I like this," Velox said to Beltran, eyeing the two men with their pistols drawn. "Maybe we do need to make alternate plans."

Corruption, Maggie knew, was one thing, but being part of something that involved guns wouldn't fly with someone like Velox, a well-known American businessman with connections to Commerce Oil. Li, a political figure in China, would probably be less fazed, though he was much less easy to read.

"They have no intention of making any transfer," Beltran said to Velox and Li. "Can't you see that?"

"Then we need to resume at some other time," Velox said. "Or cancel altogether. I didn't authorize anything like this."

John Rae said, "We're not paying you a thing, Beltran. Not tonight."

"I beg to differ," Beltran said and Maggie saw what he was thinking. The payoff slipping away. A drastic change to the oil deal. Quite possibly failure. What would that mean for him? He had scrabbled his whole life to get where he was.

John Rae stood up. "Pack up, Ms. Marin," he said to Maggie. "We're out of here."

Beltran signaled one of the men with guns to come closer. Then he pointed at John Rae. "Sit down. If you don't, you'll regret it. So will she."

John Rae nodded as if he had been asked whether he wanted soup or salad. He straightened his jacket, sat back down.

Beltran spoke to the gunman: "If she doesn't authorize that bank transfer, put a bullet in one of her pretty little knees. She can decide which one."

The gunman approached the table.

John Rae was leaning back in his chair, not looking rattled at all. He said to Maggie, "Just go ahead and send the money, then, or whatever it is you do with that damn thing. We'll deal with these *people* when we get back home."

"Are you sure?" Maggie pressed the power button and held it down until the MacBook's screen went black and the laptop powered down. "Ai, *mierda!* That's 'shit' for you non-Spanish speakers, by the way."

"Why, you damn *puta!*" Beltran growled.

John Rae leapt up, swinging a fist so fast the gunman's face hadn't fully dropped in surprise before John Rae clocked his jaw with a crack that sent the man's sunglasses flying, skidding and spinning across the polished floor. His gun went off, thunder echoing off the high ceiling, and John Rae was on top of him, punching in short, sharp blows, suit jacket ripping at the armpit as his arm moved like a piston.

Li, Velox, and Beltran jumped up from the table and dashed for the door.

Plaster dust rained down as the other gunman came forward, pistol in both hands now, moving to and fro as he tried for a shot that wouldn't take out his partner.

Maggie sprang up, folding her laptop shut. Reaching back with it, she took aim.

"Hey, *boludo!*" she shouted at the gunman leveling his weapon on John Rae.

The gunman looked up at Maggie just as the laptop caught him directly in the face. He jerked, stumbling backwards. He dropped his gun and fell. The laptop bounced off the floor. John Rae saw this, leapt off gunman number one, secured number two's gun. He jumped up, gun in hand.

Gunman one scrambled to his feet, fired, hit John Rae in the leg. John Rae swore calmly, hopping on one foot, bringing the pistol up, firing twice, hitting gunman number one both times. The man staggered and fell, the back of his head hitting the floor with a thump.

John Rae grabbed his leg, already blossoming red, swung the pistol on gunman number two, who was climbing up off the floor.

"Get the hell out of here, Maggie!" John Rae yelled.

Beltran, Li, and Velox were long gone.

Achic came rushing into the room, saw what was going on, ran over to pick up the gun that gunman number one had dropped.

"Will you get her the hell out of here?" John Rae said to Achic while he held his pistol on gunman two. "On your knees, pal. Hands above your head."

The man blinked in confusion.

"*¡Sobre sus rodillas!*" Maggie shouted at the gunman. "*¡Manos encima de la cabeza!*"

The gunman got on his knees, put his hands up.

"Go on, Maggie," John Rae said, gripping his bloody leg. "You and Achic—out of here."

"Don't think we're leaving you here," Maggie said. "There are at least four guys outside."

"What the hell do you think it is I do for a living? Go on—git."

Maggie collected her laptop off the floor.

"Come on, Achic," she said. "Help me get him out of here. He's wounded."

Voices shouted outside the door. Two guards charged in, wearing camouflage and military caps, holding the submachine guns Maggie had seen outside. Just as Achic raised his weapon, one of them turned on him, sprayed wildly with a short *pap-pap-pap* that dropped Achic to the floor like a puppet without strings. He lay there, gasping.

John Rae turned, both hands gripping his pistol, firing repeatedly, the pistol jerking three times. The guard crumpled over his gun and fell.

The other guard stood there, his gun on John Rae, John

Rae's gun on him.

"Now this is a real standoff," John Rae said, then shouting at Maggie. "Maggie! Out the damn window. There's a swimming pool. I'm right behind you."

Maggie turned, saw the flickering swirls of the pool on the ceiling. In her heels, the polished wood floor was a skating rink. She kicked them off and, laptop in hand, bolted for the huge leaded-glass window, a work of art containing dozens of panes, centuries old. She built up her speed, running hard, bracing herself for the crash about to happen. She could hear John Rae behind her taunting the guard, the guard not fully understanding, but getting the gist of his words.

Maggie took a deep breath, closed her eyes, raised her arms in front of her face with the laptop as added protection, jumped for the window.

~~~

Kacha's first look at the American woman was when she crashed through the enormous first-floor window of the mansion. Leaded-glass panes burst apart as the woman came flying out, her long hair trailing behind her, and Kacha noticed, in the moonlight, that she was wearing a tight black dress. She looked like something out of a fashion magazine in flight. She seemed to have something in her hand, a handbag, something like that. She hit the water of the pool with a mighty splash that sprinkled Kacha's face, even back where she stood behind the wrought-iron fence, keeping a lookout while her sister entertained a guard in the bushes.

The woman surfaced, gasping for air, paddled to the end of the pool, favoring one arm.

"*¡Ayúdame!* They're trying to kill me."

She needed help.

Kacha brushed her bangs out of her face and shouted to Suyana, her sister. The soldier, a young Mestizo boy, not much older than she was, thrashed his way out of the bushes, pulling up his fatigue pants in a hurry, gun slung haphazardly over his shoulder. The dent of an erection seemed to be slowing him down.

Kacha grabbed the half-meter length of iron rebar she had stashed, held it down by her side.

"What's going on?" the soldier shouted. "Who broke that window? Is someone in the pool?"

The voices of men shouting wafted through the broken window upstairs.

"Looks like the party got out of hand," Kacha said.

"Jesus Christ!" The guard zipped up his pants. "I'm screwed."

"Yes, I think so." Kacha clubbed the boy across the side of the head. He expelled a painful sigh and sunk to the ground.

Suyana peered out of the bushes, eyes popping in astonishment. She emerged, yanking her tight jeans up her round butt. "What did you do *that* for? I haven't been paid yet!"

"We need to get that woman out of here." Kacha dropped the iron bar and dashed to the back gate the guard had left open when he came out to buy a quick favor. "They're trying to kill her."

"You do that," Suyana said. "I'm going to get his wallet."

Kacha was soon on her knees at the swimming pool, helping the American woman out. Soaking wet, her long hair hung like a dripping mantle. She gulped air as she climbed out onto the Spanish tiles, the laptop computer still in one hand.

"*Gracias, gracias, gracias,*" she said, stepping gingerly in her bare feet as Kacha led her through the gate in the fence. "*Please* get me out of here. I will make it worth your while."

"Sounds good to me," Kacha said.

The two women disappeared into the shadows.

Men appeared at the far side of the pool, from under the house. Machine guns were pointed.

"Who goes there?" one yelled in a booming voice. "Halt!"

"*¡Vámonos!*" the American woman shouted.

-2-

"Thank God—whoever She is."

Wrapped in a scratchy blanket, sitting in damp bra and panties on a blue plastic chair in the corrugated-iron shack Kacha shared with her sister Suyana and Suyana's baby, Maggie shook with the cold. Not to mention the scratches and abrasions from bursting through the window. But she breathed a sigh of relief as she tapped the space bar of the MacBook resting on her frozen knees and watched the thing come to life. The hard drive ground, but she kept her fingers crossed. At her first tech job, she saw machines getting taken apart and literarily scrubbed down. Computers were generally hardy enough to survive occasional abuse, even a dunking in chlorinated water.

Kacha sat cross-legged on the dirt floor, jiggling her infant niece in her arms, boiling a dented pan of water on a camp stove. The heat from the blue flame teased Maggie's frozen shins as they vainly fought the night air from one of the world's highest cities. A candle in a tin can flickered, lighting up Suyana's face as she slept fitfully against the metal wall in the windowless hut. Her head tilted to one side, her mouth open, a crust of dried spittle in the corner of her lips. Her breath came and went in shallow puffs. She didn't look well.

"Are you contacting the people with the money?" Kacha asked Maggie.

"The reward money's going to take a while. My purse is back at that party from hell."

"Oh."

"I *will* get some cash to you, though, Kacha," Maggie said.

"But right now I'm flat busted."

"I see." Kacha gave a sigh. The girls hadn't only been helpful, they'd taken a huge risk, and deserved to be rewarded.

While Maggie waited for her grating machine to connect to the Agency network, she pondered what could have gone wrong with what John Rae had called "a milk run." It was supposed to be a simple sting, no weapons required. Two agents, one American, one local. And Maggie, of course. Her second field operation. But someone had tipped off Beltran and he'd compromised the National Vice Squad.

Who?

At least Beltran hadn't managed to get hold of the two million.

She was supposed to have just handed it over. But she couldn't see doing that at the time. Now people were dead. Where was John Rae? And Achic? Had he survived?

What a mess. What a damn mess.

The IKON network finally connected and Maggie thanked her lucky stars. But her digital access fob was back at Beltran's mansion, so any truly protected communication was out. With the power of IKON's satellites providing access even in a shanty on a mountainside in the slums of Quito, though, she had the World Wide Web at her disposal. She just had to be discreet.

Maggie opened Skype and pulled up Ed Linden's number from the contacts list. The shimmering screen bathed her face in blue light while the voice-over-IP connection dialed him. White animated bubbles rose sluggishly under the blurry photo of her boss, showing him to be disheveled and overweight. She prayed he was online.

Thankfully, Ed answered right away, even though it was well into the wee hours. She suspected he would be standing by, anxious to hear from her. The live video stream kicked in, choppy and buffered over the miles, and a bleary Ed appeared through a haze of cigarette smoke. His dark hair hung over his forehead, tousled; his Buddy Holly glasses sat crooked on his wide face—how he looked most days. Only tonight he had an excuse. He was no doubt aware that the operation had ended poorly.

"Hey Maggs," he said in a husky voice. "How's your vacation?"

"Well, the weather sucks."

"Yeah, I heard you had a real soaking last night. You dry now?"

"More or less." *Meaning she was safe for the moment.*

"What hotel are you staying in?" *Where are you?*

"The Marriott." That was the code word they'd picked for La Mariscal or old town, the colonial city center.

"OK." She saw Ed chew his lip as he consulted papers on his desk. "OK."

"Hey," Maggie said. "How's your uncle? I was actually thinking of stopping by, since I'm here." *Should she go to the embassy?*

"You know, he's just come down with a cold." *Stay away. The embassy was off limits.*

Ed knew something she didn't. "What about that friend of yours," she said, "the cowboy?" It was their private joke about John Rae, their verbal cipher. "Whatever happened to him?"

"Oh, him. He got bored. Took off." *John Rae managed to get away.*

Good. But she wondered how. When she had jumped for the window, he was facing down a man with a machine gun.

"Where'd he go?"

"To the movies." *Ed didn't know.*

An ICE alert popped up on Maggie's computer screen: ATTEMPTED GPS PING. Someone was trying to map her location. She clicked DENY. "I'm getting bored here, too," she said. *She needed to get out ASAP.*

"You know, a buddy of mine wouldn't mind meeting you. I told him you were single and could hook up for coffee. Hope that wasn't out of line. Maybe you could show him around? You never know. He might like you." *Someone would pick Maggie up, take her to safety.*

She felt a blast of relief. "Why not? I got nothing else to do.

What's his name?"

"Frankie." *Plaza San Francisco, one of their pre-arranged spots.*

"What's he like?"

"A real hoot. He's in finance. A go-getter. Make sure he picks up the check."

The code phrase her contact would use would include the word "check." Call it arcane, but their simple code worked. A team of analysts could no doubt crack it, but by the time they did, it wouldn't matter. Ed had been around and was a survivor. Old school.

"When does Frankie want to get together?" Maggie said. "For coffee only, mind you."

Ed forced a laugh and puffed on a cigarette. "Can he call you tomorrow at this time?" *As soon as possible.*

"Sure, why not?" A second ICE alert popped up: ATTEMPTED GPS PING. Again, she clicked DENY. "I've got a bad connection, dude. See you."

"Send me a postcard." *Call Ed back within twenty-four hours.*

She shut down her computer, feeling more settled, although the GPS pings bothered her. Maybe they were nothing. Then again, someone had outed their operation.

Kacha pressed a steaming cup of tea into Maggie's hands while she hefted her sleeping niece in one arm. The hot mug radiated heat into Maggie's cold fingers. She had to meet her contact. But first she needed dry clothes, a change of outfit. "I have to get out of here, Kacha—before the barrio wakes up. You and your sister *cannot* be associated with me. Not after that fiasco up there." That GPS ping was making her more and more nervous. "I'm sorry I don't have any cash," she said. "But I will see you're paid." She set her cup down on the dirt floor and grabbed her damp cocktail dress from the back of the chair. It would have to do.

"How?" Kacha said, eyeing Maggie's slim black Evelin Brandt that, although wet, stood in stark contrast to Kacha's ripped jeans and purple-sequined T-shirt. The infant in her arms cooed and she gave it a kiss on its tiny nose.

Maggie sized Kacha up. She was a 2, a 4 at the most. They

could be sisters. She held up the dress. "It's wet, but it'll survive. It cost a small fortune. Want to call it a down payment? You could sell it for a tidy sum. But we'd need to swap."

Kacha's face lit up. "You think I'm going to *sell* it?" She placed her niece down gently on a folded blanket on the floor and snatched the dress from Maggie's fingers, then quickly stripped. The baby gurgled and flubbed her tiny fingers over her wet lips.

"I could sell *that* if you like," Kacha said slyly, nodding at the chunky engagement ring on Maggie's finger.

"I hate to tell you, but it's the best glass money can buy."

"A fake engagement ring? What kind of cheap *novio* do you have?"

"Keeps the wolves at bay," Maggie said, pulling Kacha's warm jeans over her damp undies and slipping her torso into the tight top. It reeked of flowery perfume, but provided more warmth than a wet dress. Moreover, it allowed her to blend in. The police would be looking for a woman in a black cocktail dress.

"I could sell that computer . . ." Kacha eyed the MacBook.

"No can do," Maggie said quickly. There was sensitive information on it, not to mention photos taken with the webcam at the meeting before things went bad.

Kacha pulled the dress over her head and straightened the damp garment over her curved hips. Her face broke into a grin.

Maggie said, "I know it's beautiful, girlfriend, but don't hang onto it."

Kacha touched her midriff. "I suppose."

"Doesn't quite go with the sneakers, anyway." Maggie studied the black high tops next to Kacha's bare feet. "I left my shoes back at the mansion . . ."

Kacha gave a sigh. "Take them."

Maggie slipped into Kacha's warm Keds, lacing them up. Without socks they were a bit loose, but beat the hell out of bare feet. She now felt like the world's oldest teenager. She wished she had a jacket, but she wasn't going to ask for any more clothes from these poverty-stricken girls. They'd done more than enough. She pulled her long hair back with her fingers, tied it into a quick loose braid, Indian style. It was as different as she could muster up on short notice. Walking around with a laptop wouldn't work. "Do you have anything I can hide this thing in?"

"Here." Kacha handed her a thin blue *lliq* carrying blanket from the floor, the size of a large square scarf. "It needs a bit of a wash."

Maggie took the blanket. It smelled of baby barf. She tied her laptop up in it, slung it over her shoulder. She flipped her ring around on her finger so that the stone didn't show. Now she was an Indian girl, on her way to wherever.

"If anyone asks anything, you know nothing." Maggie drank the last of her coca tea. It might be the only thing she would have for the foreseeable future. A warm, mild narcotic glow began to seep into her. It had served her people for centuries as they fought fatigue and hunger and now it would serve her. "We never met."

"Why are you flying out of windows in the first place?"

"It's a long story." Maggie set her cup down, glancing at Suyana, comatose against the wall. "What is your sister *on* anyway?"

Kacha shook her head in disgust as she hugged her niece. "Devil's Breath."

Scopolamine. Many of the working girls and thieves in this part of the world used it on unsuspecting clients, putting the powder in their drinks in order to liberate them of their wallets, not to mention their memories. But rarely did they use it themselves. "You've got to be kidding. That stuff is mighty dangerous."

"It grows wild back home in the jungle. There are borrachero trees everywhere. We brought some Breath with us. When things are tight, well, sometimes we need to get by—you know?"

"And your sister's taking a liking to it herself," Maggie said, shaking her head sadly. "We have to put a stop to it."

"It's not easy for Suyana. She needs to get away from it all sometimes."

Maggie cleared her throat. "Do you think you could see your way to giving me a dose or two?"

"What for?" Kacha squinted. "Do you have someone you need to knock out? Follow you around like a helpless puppy? Give you the card and number to his ATM machine?"

"You never know."

Kacha let out a sigh. "My sister doesn't need it anyway. We can always get more. But don't let it touch your skin. You'll end up walking the streets in a daze."

A few minutes later, Maggie had a folded paper packet of white powder safely in the pocket of her—Kacha's—jeans. Before she turned to leave, one hand on the opening of the hovel, Maggie said, "Why can't you and your sister go back home?"

Kacha nodded sagely for such a young woman as she swayed her niece to and fro. "Sis is no longer welcome in my village—not since she came back with a swelling in her belly and no man to own up for it."

Things hadn't changed much in this part of the world. Maggie's own mother had gone through the same ordeal with Maggie in her womb, almost thirty years ago. "So you came here to the big city to make your way. And you ended up turning tricks. Hanging outside rich people's parties to pick up the leftover men."

Kacha gave a shrug. "Little Irpa needs to eat." She wiggled the baby again. "But we really came looking for my cousin. Tica. She was arrested."

"Arrested?" Maggie let go of the door, turned back around. "What for?"

"Protesting the bulldozers. The oil companies. Plowing up our village. In the Yasuni."

The Yasuni. The part of the Amazon Beltran's cronies were itching to tear apart.

"You're Kichwa?" Maggie asked.

"We are."

"How long ago did this happen?"

Kacha stared off in thought as she toddled Irpa. "Over a month ago now. We were released. But Tica wasn't. We've tried to check the prisons. But no one will tell us anything. No one will even talk to us. So here we are, looking for her."

"And you haven't seen your cousin Tica since she was arrested?"

Kacha shook her head.

"What's her last name?"

"Tuanama."

"Tica Tuanama. Do you have a picture by any chance?"

Kacha jostled her niece. "Tica's sixteen. Slender. Fair-skinned. Long hair. Pretty hair, shiny and black. Tribal tattoos on each cheek." She indicated under each eye.

Maggie had gotten involved with this operation to stop Commerce Oil and men like Velox. She thought it was just about them breaking the law, denuding the land, and fouling one of the two lungs. But that wasn't all of it, she realized. It was also about the people who got in their way.

"Let me look into it, Kacha. Don't make any more enquiries. Be careful. How can I get in touch with you? Where can I send you a letter?"

"There is no mail here."

"Anyone you can trust?"

She shook her head no.

"Do you ever go to the Internet cafes?"

"Sometimes."

"And do you have an email address?"

"Doesn't everyone?"

"Tell me what it is."

Kacha recited it and Maggie repeated it to herself three times. "When I get back, which might take a few days, I'm going to email you from an address I'll get from one of the free services. I'll send something made up around Jennifer Lopez—the singer? It'll look like spam, so check your spam folder. Do you know what I mean?"

Kacha nodded once.

"Good. The email will be full of rubbish. Reply to it with just a phone number and a date and time to call you. But here's the trick: add ninety-nine to the phone number. Got that?"

"Add ninety-nine to the phone number you are to call."

"Right, and add one digit to the hour and one day to the date. So if you want me to call you on June second at seven p.m., you say 'June third at eight p.m.' Got that?"

"So if anyone is watching they will be too late. Very clever. What about time zones?"

"Just use your time zone. It's the same as mine."

"OK. I think I have it."

"Sure you do. You're a smart girl. No one will be watching you, but they might be watching me. What we're doing is burying our conversation, so it's hard to track. But not impossible, eh? Be careful. The free email addresses you get are scanned regularly."

"I didn't know that."

"Well, now you do."

"Right. Thank you. I am so anxious to learn what you find out about Tica."

"It's the least I can do. I'll wire money when I get a chance. Might take a couple of days—until I get back home."

"I'll be happy if you just find Tica."

"I'm going to do that too," Maggie said, although she didn't want to say whether Kacha's cousin would still be breathing. "You know—I'm a lot like you."

Maggie felt Kacha's eyes scour her and could tell that she didn't believe a word of it. "That must have been a very long time ago," she said.

"I was born in a small village in the Andes. My mother was Quechua. So we're both Incas. Although my father is American. I was brought up in the U.S."

"And now? You're flying through windows? Men with guns chasing you?"

Maggie gave a sad smile. "I have to run. Take care of your little sister and niece. They need you. I'll be in touch.

Tupanachiskama."

Outside, in the shantytown, dogs barked as the coming dawn crept over the Andes to cast its first light over Quito. Maggie walked briskly down the steep dirt road into town.

-3-

three weeks earlier...

The guards came for her just after the sun came up. The cell block was still quiet, except for the hacking cough of a woman who had been up all night, pacing the rough cement floor. The guards were gentle, which made her suspicious right away. One even helped her up from her mattress, as if she was already an invalid.

She was sixteen, Indian, and she'd been arrested for standing in front of the bulldozer plowing up the rainforest leading to her village. Six others had been arrested too.

A doctor had examined her in the jungle, and given the sergeant a nod. They sent her to the prison outside the capital. Young soldiers, barely older than she was, sat with her in the back of the truck. In the capital, the morning fog crawled across the cobblestone streets, and she saw the statue of the Virgin on the hilltop. It seemed as if the Virgin was looking down at the city, looking at her. In the mist, it seemed as if she might be crying.

Early in the morning when the guards woke her, they wouldn't look her in the eye. She was thirsty and asked for water. Not until afterwards, they told her.

When they got to the hospital, she was led down a white hall into a room that hummed with machines. Two nurses there wouldn't look at her either. One doctor had a beard and smiled, the other wore a facemask.

They laid her down gently and gave her an injection and as she drifted off, she thought of the Virgin, crying on the foggy mountain.

present day . . .

The city awoke slowly as Maggie passed people heading off to the markets carrying bundles, starting their day. A pig trotted by in the opposite direction, grunting. The Virgin of El Panecillo watched from the early-morning mountainside, her sad gaze locked onto the capital.

Maggie needed to meet her contact, be on her way. The police, and God knows who else, would be on the lookout for her.

As she headed into town, the tin and cinderblock shacks turned to buildings built with permits, the dirt roads transformed to paved streets that became cobblestones by the time she reached Plaza San Francisco, with its huge white rococo church and monastery taking up one entire side of the long square. Vestiges of fog floated across the center. A glimmer of early daylight pulled back the shroud of night.

Although many people weren't out yet, four heavily armed National Police *tombos* in olive drab fatigues and black lace-up boots stood on the church steps, scanning the square. Head down, Maggie walked by them at an even pace, resisting the urge to cut a wide arc that would have only raised suspicions. A few hardened faces hovered in the shadows at the far end of the plaza, where Old Town continued into the narrow capital huddled in the long valley nestled between the mountains. At the end of the plaza, across the street, she stood under a colonnade. Adjusting the blanket containing the laptop over her shoulder, she eyed the few cars trolling by. One of them would hopefully be her ride to safety.

A beat-up red Toyota pickup with a crushed fender pulled over, two *campesinos* in the bench seat. The passenger window squeaked as it rolled down. A grizzled man with a face full of stubble squinted out at Maggie. He drank from a bottle, turned to his companion, got a nod, turned back.

"How much, *chica*?"

"Ten million dollars?"

He laughed, drank. "If I had it, gorgeous, it would surely be yours. Come on—how much? For both of us?"

No reference on his part to a check, the coded exchange word. These two were just what they looked like—losers.

"What do you think I am?" Maggie said.

"That's pretty clear. What we're doing now is haggling is over the price."

"No one's haggling with you, *boludo*. On your way."

"Stuck-up cow." The window squealed back up and the pickup rumbled on.

More cars passed by. A lot of men looking for women. Love never flagged. Church bells rang six times. More people were crossing the plaza, some in suits.

A white Ford Fiesta slowed down. A chubby businessman in a suit at the wheel. Promising. Maggie went over, bent down as the electric window whirred open.

"Speak English?" the man said in a heavy Germanic accent.

"A little."

"How much?" He wore glasses and his eyes were bugged out behind the lenses. Too nervous to be an operative picking up on-the-run agents perhaps. Car-rental paperwork sat on the passenger seat.

"How much for what?" She'd give him one chance to use the coded exchange word.

He looked about nervously. A car whipped around them, horn blaring, echoing across the plaza.

"For coffee," he stammered. "How much for coffee?"

"Coffee."

"Do you want to have coffee with me? You're beautiful."

"Ai." She stood up, sunk back into the shadows as the Ford drove off. Across the square, she saw one of the *tombos* staring at her. He spoke to his partner. His partner looked her way as well.

She needed to get away before she was arrested for soliciting.

A red BMW sedan pulled up smartly. The driver, the only

occupant of the vehicle, leaned over. Latin, in his thirties, nice-looking. Shirt and tie. He gave Maggie a questioning look, raising his eyebrows.

She returned an affirming nod and dashed over as the window slid down. Two cops were strolling across the square toward her.

"I'm sorry to bother you, but you don't know where I can cash a traveler's check at this hour, do you?"

This was her ride. Thank God.

"Yes, I do, as a matter of fact." She opened the door, got in the car, heaved the door shut. "*Vámonos*. The *chapos* are headed this way."

The man behind the wheel confirmed with a single nod, threw the car into gear, took off. Speeding around a corner they headed into the narrow flagged streets of Old Town.

"Are you OK?" he asked, gunning the engine as they shot by the grand Plaza de la Independencia.

"Good enough," she said. "And aren't you going a little fast? You'll attract attention."

"Not fast enough. It's all over the news. Gunfights at international events tend to do that, you know. Even in this country."

Maggie let out a breath of air. "Where are we going?"

"Airport," he said. "You're on a morning flight to Houston. But we have to move, fast."

Maggie's insides unwound a millimeter or two. "Do you have a new passport for me? Mine's in my briefcase, along with my purse, back at that so-called party."

"We're having one made as we speak."

Her heart jumped. "You didn't bring the passport with you?"

"We need a headshot of you. Won't take long."

Her heartbeats bumped up. "You don't have my photo on file?"

"You're with Forensic Accounting—a new department. The authorization process hasn't been set up. We couldn't get your photo at such short notice."

He spun the BMW out of Old Town and up into the hills overlooking Quito.

"Where are we going now?" Maggie asked.

"The Embassy."

Maggie's nerve endings tingled. Ed's instructions had been pretty clear: *Don't* go to the embassy. "You sure about that?"

"Absolutely. All we need do is take that photo of you, have the passport finalized, and we're on our way. No worries, eh?" He shot around a curve as rubber skidded.

She hadn't done her seatbelt up. She did so now. He wasn't wearing his. Typical Latin male.

Maggie noticed a pack of Marlboros on the console. She picked the package up casually, slid a cigarette out, stuck it between her lips. Punching the cigarette lighter in on the car's dash, she ran her fingers nervously together, flipping her ring back around so that the stone pointed outwards.

"Relax," the driver said, navigating around another hairpin turn as they climbed toward an upscale part of Quito. "It will all be over soon."

That's exactly what she was worried about.

The cigarette lighter popped out, ready. She pulled it from its socket. It glowed red and pulsed with heat.

"Stop the car," she said calmly. "Now."

"Stop the car?" He gave her a quick turn of the head. "What are you talking about?"

A note of falseness in his voice confirmed what she had suspected. Gunning the BMW around a tight bend, they got to Avenida Avigiras, the top of the hill.

"I'm going to be sick," she said. "Pull over."

He ignored her, headed for a modern white building on the right, overlooking the summit. There were barricades out front and a huge satellite dish on the roof. The U.S. Embassy.

"Stop the car," she said. "I won't ask you again."

He turned and she saw his eyelids flicker. His smile became a furtive sneer.

She jammed the glowing red cigarette lighter into his cheek. A sizzle of burning flesh filled the cabin.

He screamed, clutching his face with one hand, trying to maneuver the car with his left.

"Stop the damn car!" she yelled. "Now!"

Howling in agony, he tried to steer the wobbly vehicle toward the barricades. Two U.S. Marines in dress uniforms were backing away, raising their rifles.

She jabbed his face again, the crackle of skin drowned out by his banshee-like howl. Both of his hands came off the wheel as he clutched at his face. Maggie reached over, grabbed the steering wheel with both hands, losing the cigarette lighter in the process. She gritted her teeth and navigated the BMW back onto the two-lane road, her mysterious contact's foot still on the gas. But now she was in the oncoming lane. At this point she would just keep going, get as far away from the embassy as possible.

They flew past the guards. One shouted for them to slow down in Americanized Spanish.

Another sharp turn lay up ahead. Worse, a truck was barreling toward them. Its horn blasted.

"You damn *puta*!" her driver screamed, striking Maggie's chin as she wrangled the car back into the right lane. Again he punched her. She lost control and the car lurched toward the truck. She heaved the wheel just in time to pull the car back to the right. With a whoosh of air, they narrowly missed hitting the truck head-on. But not entirely.

The BMW banged off the side of the cab in an ear-scraping screech. Maggie fought the wheel as they spun into a 180. The driver finally took his foot off the gas and they came to a complete stop, facing the embassy. The stink of scorched rubber and burned flesh filled the car.

She sucked in air, fighting to control her thoughts. *Get away.*

Her driver was twisted up against his window, having been flung from his seat. His left cheek bore two large red welts that oozed blood.

"Get out of the car!" Maggie shouted.

Her attacker came to, eyes blazing, and threw a wild punch. She blocked it, grabbed his flailing hand with her right, and struck him repeatedly across the temple with her left, gouging him with the ring. She twisted and dug. His hands went slack as the cuts on his face ran with blood. She kept whipping him with the ring, clenching her teeth, willing herself to see this nightmare through.

"¡*Bastante!*" he gulped. "Enough!"

She slammed his head against the window. "Get out of the car!"

The Marines were running toward them, rifles up. She needed to put some distance between them and her.

The car's console blocked her from stomping on the gas pedal with her foot. She reached down with her left hand and pushed the accelerator to the floor, clutching the steering wheel with her right. She could just see over the dash. The plan was to get out of range of the guards, then leap from the car and hoof it down that hill that lay up ahead.

The car took off but the flap of a flat tire caught her by surprise. She had no control. The BMW swayed from side to side for fifty yards before it spun, and fishtailed. Her driver was thrown back into the rear seat, his leg smacking Maggie's face. They flew off the road into a bank of trees. The BMW leapt into the air, then slammed onto the dirt between two tall pines. She glimpsed the city far below: Quito in the mile-long valley.

The car rolled toward the precipice.

She jerked the wheel hard, all the way left. The car twisted, flipped on the passenger side, skidded on the dirt, then came to a stop.

Maggie panted with desperation.

But she wasn't injured—or if she was, she didn't know it yet. She found herself pressed against the passenger window, staring down at pine needles packed against the glass. The car lay on its side, pointing downhill.

Behind her, crumpled up in the rear, was the driver. Motionless. His head jutted out at an unnatural angle. If he wasn't dead, he was incapacitated: a broken neck or worse. Nausea gripped her stomach.

Maggie reached over to the dash, stretching to press the

moonroof button. Couldn't quite reach it. She grunted and pulled against the seatbelt and finally made contact. The moonroof slid open. Struggling, she released her seatbelt and thumped against the passenger door and window. Taking deep breaths, she calmed herself, then clambered onto her hands and knees and climbed out of the moonroof, dropping down onto the layer of pine needles.

She stood up, her legs shaking with adrenaline. She was in one piece.

"¡*Alto!*"

Turning quickly, she looked up the hill, through the trees.

One of the Marines stared down at the crashed vehicle. And at her. His weapon was at his side and he was obviously trying to assess the situation. Was it an attack on the embassy or simply an auto accident?

Maggie looked down the steep hill at the capital. She broke into a slow jog, trying to keep herself low. Her legs were wobbly, but they were moving. She was okay.

"¡*Alto!*"

The laptop. Damn! Head spinning, she turned around and slogged back up the hill, slipping on pine needles.

The driver was still where she had left him, crumpled up in the back. Frozen in death.

Maggie got on her hands and knees and searched. There it was. The blue *lliq* blanket containing her silver laptop. Under his shoulder. She reached back, pushed his twisted arm to one side, got hold of the blue blanket. She pulled. The weight of the man's body made it tough.

The thin blanket began to rip.

"Hey you!" she heard the Marine shout in gringo Spanish. "Stop right there!" His voice was closer. She peered through the rear window.

He was coming down the hill now, negotiating the slippery pine needles.

She tugged while she shoved the driver's shoulder out of the way with her free hand. He was heavy and still. She had to move slowly, tease the thin blanket and laptop free.

It finally came loose. She got a whiff of baby spew.

"You!" the Marine shouted again. "Stop!"

Blanket containing laptop in hand, she retreated on her hands and knees back out of the moonroof.

She stood up. She could see his face. He was young, with pink acne and blue eyes.

Bag over her shoulder, she spun and scurried down through the trees, toward the fog-shrouded valley of the city.

-4-

At the bottom of the hill, Maggie stopped to catch her breath, loosening her impromptu braid and fluffing her long tresses loose with her fingers. Change your hairstyle, change your appearance. She broke into another run. Despite the altitude, despite Kacha's cheap sneaks with no socks, Maggie's daily five-mile jogs were paying off.

By the time she got back to the Plaza San Francisco, she was filmed with perspiration and the narrow streets were clogged with morning rush-hour traffic that she suspected lasted all day. Bitter auto exhaust hung in the cool morning air, stinging her nostrils. The long square was now marked with stalls being set up, and people were crossing en masse, heading into Old Town.

One part of her said it was insanity to come back here. But another knew she needed money to get back to the U.S. Any way she could.

Over by the large white church now stood a half-dozen national police officers. As of yet, no one seemed to notice Maggie so she resumed her position under the colonnade, jutting her chest out in the tight sequined T-shirt Kacha had given her. An old woman in black clucked as she waddled by, giving Maggie a disdainful shake of the head. Maggie eyed the cars crawling by. Most were simply stuck in the snarl of morning-commute traffic, but she noticed one or two telltale stares from men desperate to satisfy last night's leftover cravings.

The booming of church bells filled the plaza and beyond. Nine a.m. Time was running out.

Then, amidst the creaking stream of traffic, the polite tap of a car horn caught her attention. The white Ford sedan—the same one she'd encountered a couple of hours ago. The same pudgy Nordic man exploring her with his eyes, magnified by glasses. He pulled over.

She hurried over as the passenger window rolled down.

"I thought you'd gone," he said with a trace of relief. His English was stiff and halting.

"I was waiting for you," she said in deliberately accented English, yanking open the car door and hopping in. She pulled the door shut before he could change his mind or anyone could spot her. She gave him a sly sideways smile and took in a deep breath and puffed her chest out. "I was hoping you'd come back."

His attentive eyes were immediately drawn toward her constricted cleavage.

A horn honked behind them: *shave and a haircut*. Her new partner released a taut smile and they lurched out into traffic. Although he had to concentrate on cars mere inches apart, he kept stealing glances at her. "Do you live nearby?"

"We can't go there," she said. "My mother . . ."

"Can't you ask her to go out for a little while?"

"There are my brothers and sisters. You really don't want to go to the part of town where I live, anyway. Why not your hotel?"

"Can't we just go park somewhere? Surely you must know a place."

"At this hour? There's no privacy." She gave him her best *come-hither* look. "Don't you want to *relax* properly? At your hotel? Hmm?"

"Yes, of course . . ." He eyed her T-shirt, dirty jeans and Keds. His temples pulsed. "It's just that . . . I'm not sure the Hilton . . ."

. . . Wanted low-rent street hookers at nine in the morning? Whyever not?

"Who cares?" She gave him an animal stare. "What about what *you* want?"

He took a deep breath as he tried to focus on the truck directly in front belching fumes. "I'm worried my fellow conference attendees might see us. I have to give a talk at eleven this morning, you see."

But he obviously wasn't *that* worried. He couldn't keep his eyes off her. And he had taken foolish risks. Picking up a street hooker in one of the iffier cities in Latin America. He hadn't even asked for a price.

"Maybe we should just say *adiós*, then," she said. "What a shame. I *was* in the mood to get to know you better. Loosen you up for your conference. Oh well. Can you stop here, please?" Maggie reached for the door handle.

"Wait!" He chewed his lip as he blinked rapidly behind his glasses. "You think it will be okay? Going through the hotel lobby, I mean?"

"Absolutely."

The car reeled into the grand Plaza de la Independencia, its neat white classical government buildings softened by tall palms in the elegant square. At the other end of the plaza stood an Indian woman wearing a fedora, with a baby slung over her back in a blanket similar to the one Maggie's laptop was in. She was hawking brightly colored shawls out of a cardboard box.

"Pull over there," Maggie said.

"Why?" he said nervously.

"Just pull over."

He stopped at the curb. Maggie rolled the window down, caught the woman's attention. "Something not too garish," she said.

The woman adjusted the baby on her back as she searched her box and produced a smart-looking gray-and-black hound's-tooth checked shawl. She held up the neatly folded wrap, letting it unfurl with a bit of panache. The finest polyester China could produce.

"*Buenazo*," Maggie said. "I'll take it."

The woman's mouth parted in surprise. Maggie wasn't even going to haggle. "Five dollars?"

Maggie took the garment, turned to her new beau. "I need five dollars."

He looked taken aback, but produced a ten-dollar bill quickly enough. Maggie handed it to the woman. "Keep the change." They set off, Maggie modeling her new shawl.

"Better?" she said. "A little more grown up? For your hotel lobby?"

"Yes!" He gave an unctuous smile as he pushed his glasses up his shiny pug nose. They headed over a hill into downtown traffic. "You know, you don't seem like a local."

"Is that what you want? A local girl? An Indian girl?" She ran a finger up his plump thigh. "One who is grateful? One who will do *anything*? I am grateful. You'll see."

He gulped as he drove, his hands shaking visibly as they gripped the wheel. "What's your name?"

"Suwa."

"What a beautiful name! It's Indian, is it?"

"Yes." It was also the Quechua word for thief.

"Indian girls are beautiful."

"Well, thank you," she said. "And what's your name?"

"Ulfric."

"Ulfric," Maggie said, pronouncing it carefully. "Such a strong name."

"Umm . . . we haven't discussed . . ." He couldn't seem to finish his sentence.

"Discussed what, Ulfric?"

"Um . . . how much . . ."

She sat back, wrapping the shawl around her coyly. "What do you think I am—some girl who does these things for *money*? I'm just desperate to buy food for my brothers and sisters. I only ask that if you are pleased with me, that, when we are done, when you are satisfied, of course, that you give me a gift. Forty dollars."

"*Forty?*" His voice rose. "Isn't that a lot of money down here?"

"It's not *that* much."

"Twenty." He nodded as he drove. "Twenty is plenty.

Don't try to take advantage of my good nature."

"Twenty, then. Whatever you have." Twenty was just the start.

He cleared his throat and drove. "Indian girls are beautiful."

"Yes we are," she said. "And we'll do anything."

Anything.

~~~

"What a view," Maggie said. Ecuador's long narrow capital stretched out from the hotel window, stories below.

"I have to give a talk in less than two hours," Ulfric said, his voice still quivering.

Maggie turned from the window. Ulfric, her German, or whatever he was, stood by the table in his corporate cookie-cutter hotel room. His laptop was out on the table, binders were open, pages of notes scribbled over in red were scattered here and there.

"I thought you could hop in the tub," Maggie said. "Hmm?"

"But my talk. We need to hurry."

"Don't worry. We'll be quick." She peeled off her wrap, threw it on the back of the chair. "But not too quick, eh?" Then she pulled off her sequined T-shirt slowly and languorously, revealing her firm torso in lacy black bra. "I'm going to have you nice and unperturbed for your lecture."

"How do you know a word like . . ." He pushed his glasses up his nose again as if to get a better look. Her breasts caught his eyes like magnets.

"How about a drink?" she said.

"A *drink*?" A little screech in his voice. "It's not even ten in the morning. Tea. I'll have tea. It's over there."

"Tea, then," she said, noting the coffee maker and materials on the nightstand by his bed. She also saw some questionable reading material: a shiny paperback with a teenage girl on the cover in bra and panties. A hotel bottle of hand lotion and a box of paper tissues sat next to it. "I'll make you some tea while you get in the tub," she said, kicking off her black Keds and peeling off her blue jeans. Down to her underwear, she grabbed the coffee pot, darted into the bathroom, turned on the taps to the Jacuzzi bathtub. She filled the pot partway with water from the sink and dimmed the bathroom lights on her way out.

Ulfric stood puffing as he watched her make tea. He was probably wondering how an Indian girl got hold of such classy underwear, she thought. At least her lingerie seemed to be occupying his thoughts. "Sugar. I like plenty of sugar."

"Go on! Into the tub with you. I'll bring it in."

"Right," he said, turning like a robot and heading into the bathroom. "Right." The door shut behind him. She heard him sneeze.

Maggie removed the filter from the coffee maker and fired it up, making hot water. She heard Ulfric getting into the bathtub, splashing. He started humming a German tune.

She made a paper cup of tea and while it seeped, she tapped quietly on the keyboard to Ulfric's laptop. His screensaver appeared and prompted her for a password. She picked up the cell phone lying on the table. It required a security gesture to get in. She set it down quietly, retrieved the packet she had gotten from Kacha from her jeans. She opened the paper slowly, so as not to touch or spill any of the white powder. There was perhaps a half-teaspoon. A lot, it seemed.

"Suwa?" Ulfric said in a theatrical whisper from the bathroom. "It's getting late!"

She dumped all of the Devil's Breath into the cup and stirred it with a plastic spoon. She added two packs of sugar, mixed that in too.

She pushed open the bathroom door with her foot and entered.

He was sitting in the tub, naked, his glasses off, looking at her with his mouth agape. His clothes lay in a pile on the floor. She held up the spiked tea.

"Plenty of sugar," she said. "You'll need your energy." She winked.

"*Ja*," he said, pawing at her leg with a wet mitt. "Come here!" He swiped at her breast as she bent over to put the cup down next to him. She had to maneuver so she didn't spill any tea.

"Hey! Go easy, Ulfric."

"Indian girls have big ones."

"Drink your tea."

He picked up his cup, toasted her, giving her an evil little grin. "*Skol!*"

"Come on," she said, picking up a bar of soap, unwrapping it, as she sat on the rim of the tub. "I suspect you need a bit of a rubdown."

"Yes." Laughing like a schoolboy, he gulped tea. "Rub me down like a good girl."

She stood up. "I'm just going next door to slip out of my underwear. I don't want to get them wet. Any wetter than they already are, hey?" She gave him an evil glint.

"Hurry back!" he said, slurping his tea. "I'm really excited, you know."

"Yes, I can see that."

She went into the bedroom, shut the door, picked up her jeans and T-shirt, and dressed quietly.

~~~

"*Messtechnik?*" Maggie said, sitting at Ulfric's laptop. "And how do I spell that?"

"*M-e-s-s-t-e-c-h-n-i-k.*" Ulfric stood in the middle of the hotel room wearing nothing but a towel, dripping on the carpet, rubbing his bulging white stomach absent-mindedly as he stared at the wall with wide, unfocused eyes.

Maggie typed the recited letters into the password field of his laptop and was granted access. The desktop screen showed a mousey Asian woman with a forced smile, partially hidden behind two overweight preteen Nordic boys. So Ulfric had a mail-order bride. She probably doubled as his maid, nanny, cook, and whatever else he demanded.

Maggie fired up the email program. "Same password for email, Ulfric?"

"Messtechnik," he repeated in a monotone, blinking at the wall.

Maggie typed in the password, waited for his email to connect and download.

From Ulfric's email account, Maggie fired off an email to a clandestine account Ed had set up, giving him Ulfric's cell number and the phrase: *the next time you think you have power and influence, try ordering someone else's dog around.* It was one of Ed's favorite quotes and he would know who had sent the email. She hit *Send*, then went to Ulfric's *Sent Items* folder, where she deleted the sent copy of the email, for whatever security was in it.

Ulfric stood staring at the wall in his towel.

"Ulfric," Maggie said. "I have a few more questions for you."

"Yes?"

Within minutes Maggie had access to Ulfric's cell phone and hotel safe. Soon she had four hundred euros, several hundred U.S. dollars—the base currency in Ecuador—and a German passport. "Ulfric, where's your wallet?"

"Under the mattress."

The wallet contained seven dollars, an ATM card, and several credit cards. Another jackpot.

She left Ulfric the seven dollars and slid the wallet back under the mattress.

While she waited for Ed to call, Maggie nudged Ulfric over to the bed where she sat him down like a stoned Teddy Bear and continued to question him. Eyes open wide, twiddling his pudgy toes, he answered like a dutiful child, one with a German accent. She jotted down his pin and access numbers on a pad of hotel notepaper.

She turned on the TV, found Canal 13, the Quito station. "Las Noticias" was on, the breaking news, a serious man in a tie with a microphone standing in front of the U.S. Embassy she had sailed by not a few hours ago. A collection of police cars flashed behind him. "Police are on the lookup for a young woman, wearing jeans and a purple T-shirt, and an American man with fair hair."

Reasonable identikits of her and John Rae appeared.

"The two are wanted in connection to a shooting at an event last night in Guapalo. The woman is believed to be the same one who tried to run the barricades this morning at the U.S. embassy, resulting in the death of her driver. She is considered armed and dangerous."

Maggie *wished* she were armed. And she hadn't run any barricades.

She switched to TeleAmazonias, the national station. Students were marching in Guayaquil, protesting the agreement with the Chinese to continue oil exploration in the Amazon. Footage showed bulldozers cutting a road of rust-red dirt through pristine rainforest, natives demonstrating there as well. In their painted faces, bare torsos, and native dress, they looked vulnerable and undermanned. Maggie was reminded of Kacha's cousin, Tica, under arrest somewhere. The red dust blew around the ankles of the demonstrators in swirls. Without the ancient growth to keep it in place, the precious Amazon was blowing away. Maggie shook her head.

But there was nothing on the national news of a runaway Indian girl in jeans and purple T-shirt, wanted for causing havoc in Quito. Yet.

Ulfric's cell phone rang.

Maggie answered. "Did you order a pizza?"

"What the hell is going on, Maggs?" Ed Linden said.

Street noise in the background. Ed was calling away from the office. Playing it safe.

"I'd sure like to know," Maggie said.

"I thought I said to steer clear of the embassy."

"Well, that's not what the driver thought. How did he know the *check* passphrase?"

"We don't have a profile on him yet. The local police won't let us near. He wasn't one of us. And whoever he was, he's dead."

"Yes, I know." She had never been responsible for the death of another human. She could argue it was in self-defense, but it didn't make her feel any better.

"The guy who was supposed to pick you up just missed

you."

"Minister Beltran thought he could get over on us, Ed. He stopped the arrest. Who alerted him?"

There was a pause while traffic honked in San Francisco. "All good questions."

"Sounds like we got a mole."

"Maybe."

"Who else knew about the passphrase?"

"The usual channels. But we'll have to deal with that later. Right now, there's an alert out for you. Everybody and anybody is searching."

"What about John Rae?"

"He made it out."

"The guy is good."

"He's a field op. That's what he's paid to do. Unlike you. I was nuts to let you go on that."

"I badgered the hell out of you," she said. "I wanted to play op." Truth was, she needed to switch her career path in order to survive in the Agency. "Where is John Rae?"

"We don't know exactly where. Yet. But he'll be fine. I'm not worried about John Rae. He's not my department. You are."

"I've accessed some funds. A German passport. I can try to find someone, get it cobbled. With a U.S. visa. But it might take a day or two. I'll use the name Melanie Kirsch. Can you get me papers and a flight to the States?"

"No, it's too hot there. Get out of Quito. Get out of Ecuador. Can you get to Lima?"

"Peru?"

"I have a person there in the embassy I trust implicitly."

"Less than a thousand miles," she said. "OK. Next stop, Lima."

"He'll get you to the U.S.," Ed said, puffing on a cigarette. "Email contact info when you get there. Leave now. And I mean *now*. Stay off the main roads."

"OK," she said. "Wish me luck."

"Good luck. Leave." Ed hung up.

Maggie steered Ulfric into the bathroom.

She slung her MacBook over her shoulder in the smelly blue *lliq* blanket, gathered up Ulfric's credit cards and pile of cash, the list of pin numbers and access codes, and nabbed the keys to Ulfric's rental car on her way out the door. She left the passport. She wouldn't need it. But she took his phone, since there was a call from Ed on it. She'd dump it in the trash somewhere. She headed out into the hall, pulled the door shut.

Down the hall the elevator dinged. Two men in suits appeared and marched her way—Ulfric's business associates no doubt, wondering where he had gotten to. He was supposed to give some talk. Well, it was going to be an incoherent one now. Maggie kept her head down as the men passed, one man's eyes hard upon her. She pushed open a stairwell door, stealing a glance before she entered.

The other man knocked on the door. "Ulfric? Are you there? We're waiting for you downstairs. I hope you haven't forgotten about your presentation."

Maggie entered the stairwell and took the stairs two at a time. In the parking garage, she located Ulfric's white Ford Fiesta wedged up against a cement wall, blocked in by a grey sedan on the left. The only way out was a narrow L of space behind her to her left. A hunter-green Jag was nosed in to her rear, on the other side of the L. She'd have to reverse out, cut it tight. She eyed the clearance. Not much. But the Ford was a compact and she could make it. Maybe.

Unlocking the car, she squeezed herself in, inadvertently dinging the gray sedan. She threw her laptop in its blanket onto the passenger seat and wrapped the shawl around her shoulders, so she didn't look like such a hussy. Fumbling the electronic key into the slot, she started up the Fiesta with a rattle and whine.

She put the car into first, tapped the car's bumper in front. Hand on the wheel, she turned in her seat, gauging the room between her and the Jag again. Like getting ten pounds of potatoes into a five-pound bag. Someone was going to get a bit of a repair bill.

"Excuse me?" A voice echoed through the garage in heavily accented English. A rapid clip of heels followed and she saw the tall dark-skinned attendant who had parked Ulfric's car when they arrived an hour ago, running up, his tie flapping. He stopped in the space behind her.

"Let me do it, please!" But his smile disappeared when he saw that the driver was not the German guest he obviously expected, but the young woman the man had snuck into the hotel. "Yes?" His eyes narrowed as he scanned Maggie's face. "This is not your car?"

"I'm Herr Müller's secretary," she said in English, smiling wonderfully. "He needs overhead transparencies for his presentation." She had a ten-dollar bill ready and held it up between her index and middle finger. "Can you move that Jag, please? Thank you so much."

The attendant smiled as he squeezed in and the bill disappeared into his pocket. Then a flicker of recognition crossed his face. "Wait! I know *you*. You're the one on the news. The one wanted by the *tombos*. Stop the car. Get out. Now!"

"Sorry, *amigo. No hablo español.*"

"Don't give me that!" he shouted in Spanish. "Out of the car!" He reached for the door handle.

"Best get out of the way, *cabrón*." She threw the little car into reverse as he pressed himself back against the gray sedan. She cut back around the L in an attempt to miss the Jaguar. Unsuccessful. The long scrape resonated through the garage as she left a pricy white graze along the driver's side of the Jag, setting off a piercing auto alarm. Her tall attendant crouched down fearfully. Tires burning, she fought the little car out.

One more *smash* and she was finally clear. Gunning the engine, still turned in her seat, she reversed with alacrity down the row of parked cars.

The attendant sprang up, came sprinting for her car, shouting.

She swung the car around in a tight reverse churn, bolted forward, headed for the daylight of the exit.

A barrier arm on the exit booth blocked the way between her and the street behind the hotel. Maggie stomped the gas pedal. The barrier snapped over the windshield and clattered off behind her. The attendant shouted colorful curses. In the rearview mirror, she saw him, still after her. She jammed the car into second, bumped over a curb, fishtailed out of the hotel, swerving around an Indian family pushing a cart full of melons. She whipped past cars in a direction she'd committed to memory on her way to the hotel, taking a right practically on two wheels. A park lay on the left, the hotel opposite. The Pan-American Highway, which cut through the center of the capital, lay ahead. She shifted into third, swerved around a groaning bus listing to one side, straight into oncoming traffic.

Horns blared.

Maggie yanked the car back into the appropriate lane.

Snaking through traffic, she caught E35—the Pan American Highway—bouncing the little Ford onto the onramp and heading south. Lanes weren't empty but it was manageable. She stayed to the right where she could exit quickly if need be.

Lima, Peru: only twenty-fours away. With a pesky little border stop in the middle. She'd figure that out.

Suddenly, the howl of a siren floated up behind her. Then: a flashing yellow beacon filled the rearview mirror. A white-and-green pickup closing in.

The *tombos*. Ed had told her to stay off the highway. But what choice did she have? She jerked the wheel right, pulling off onto the shoulder abruptly, speeding past queued up traffic waiting to get onto the highway.

The police pickup did the same.

She banged the car off the shoulder, onto trash-strewn grass, over a curb, thumping the roof of the car with the top of her head, into a rough street jammed full of traffic. She was in a part of town the tourists never saw: cheap ad-hoc construction, ceramic-brick and cinderblock storefronts, garish hand-painted signs. And people everywhere.

The truck was tight behind her, siren wailing, having

negotiated the off-road jaunt better than she with its four-wheel capabilities. A crew cab, multiple occupants. Maggie charged into a log-jammed intersection, horns shrieking all around. At the last possible moment before a collision, she veered around a truck laden down with lumber, leaving the larger police truck stuck in traffic. She shifted down and buzzed up a side road into the hills surrounding Quito. Engine screaming, chickens squawked as they flew aside, on road now made of dirt. Older buildings changed to shacks and shanties. Kids playing. Dogs. She didn't want to hit one. At the top of a hill, she swung around a corner into a vacant lot where a group of preteen boys were kicking around a soccer ball.

The ball whacked against the windshield, making Maggie jump, and causing much merriment with the boys.

"Can you boys park that for me, please? I'll be right back." Grabbing the laptop bundle, she leapt from the Ford, left the door open, the engine humming. With any luck, someone would take off with the vehicle and divert the *tombos*. Maggie raced across the lot, computer swinging in the blanket. Across a narrow dirt street, and a patch of ground to where the ragged neighborhood ended and the steep slopes of the Andes began.

-5-

"Very nice, *señorita*," the portly woman with a tape measure dangling around her neck said. "*Very* nice."

Maggie admired her new dark purple fedora in the smudged mirror hanging off the stall in the busy street market. Along with the black-leather bomber jacket that was as soft as chamois, she had to admit she looked *muy chido*. Very cool. She handed over a small wad of dollars. There was no time for haggling and besides, Ulfric could afford it.

"How far to the bus terminal?" Maggie asked the stall assistant.

A kilometer. Maybe one and a half.

Then she was back with *la gente*—the people—walking through the busy streets on market day, to Quitumbe Bus Terminal with her laptop in a proper shoulder bag now, which also contained a new toothbrush, hair brush, even a clean pair of underwear. The barf blanket had been relegated to the trash, along with Ulfric's phone. As she strolled, she bought a pair of dark sunglasses and a *salchipapas*—french fries with a butterflied hot dog on top, onion, and special salsa—from a street vendor, which disappeared in no time. It had been hours—well over a day—since she had last eaten.

She stopped at an outdoor ATM and withdrew three hundred dollars from Ulfric's bank account using the pin he had given her. It would leave an electronic trail, but she needed as much cash as she could withdraw while he was still under the influence of the scopolamine and wouldn't alert his bank.

In Quitumbre, the airy modern bus terminal, she lined up to buy a bus ticket to Lima, Peru. They wanted a passport. She bought a ticket to Baños instead. Baños was high in the mountains of central Ecuador, near the active volcano Tungurahua. She also picked up tickets to a couple of small jungle towns on the border with Peru. She'd find a way to cross there. While she waited for her bus, she accessed another bank ATM inside the terminal and, under the watchful eye of an armed guard, took a two-hundred-dollar advance on one of Ulfric's credit cards. She did the same with his American Express.

She'd have to get rid of the cards, now that she'd exhausted the cash-advance limits.

She bought a badly needed coffee at a stall and sipped the steaming brew on the way to a restroom, where she left Ulfric's bankcards by the sink after she washed her hands. The cards would be gone in no time.

Fedora tilted over her eyes, Maggie slept much of the way up to Baños, despite the blaring Sylvester Stallone movie dubbed in Spanish. She woke to see the jagged Andes twist around her with precarious turns of mountain road. Maggie was pulled back to her childhood, walking along roads just like these, barefoot with her mother, on the way to market, the two of them carrying dishes *Mami* had made and sliced democratically into even pieces in their dented pie pans, carefully draped with gay red-checked tea towels. The slices of meat pie sold out quickly, because *Mami* made the dough with cornmeal and lard and fresh butter and the diced beef was carefully trimmed and blended with olives and onions and red peppers. They'd share a bar of chocolate on the way home, sauntering back to their village, *Mami* rattling coins in a bunched-up tea towel to keep the rhythm as they sang mountain songs.

Thinking of those days hurt so much sometimes.

She never spoke of it, but Maggie loathed her father for leaving *Mami*. And her. She hadn't talked to him since graduation, five years ago now, and then only barely, when he showed up at Stanford to her ceremony with his pretty, sensible, blonde wife with her freckled inoffensive nose, who probably slept in 600-thread-count sheets that some maid ironed, a maid who looked a lot like *Mami*, with her copper skin and thick mane of gleaming raven-colored hair and deep-set llama eyes, stopping conversations and turning heads as a matter of course. Father was with the U.S. State department in Ecuador when Maggie was young and *Mami* was his Indian mistress, and the reason he was sent back home. Not proper. And it wouldn't have done for him to bring her back. Especially with a child he had spawned. Yes, he provided for them when Maggie was young—small random checks arriving now and then, and he did bring Maggie to the U.S. when *Mami* died of malaria, and put Maggie through school, but Maggie knew that was gringo guilt at work.

She wondered if he would chat with the maid in his perfect Spanish, using all the slang to let her know just how much in the know he was. She imagined him flirting with her, maybe more, when his wife wasn't around.

Grief was the real reason *Mami* gave up the fight.

In Baños' bus station, a small facility with more dirt than asphalt, Maggie noticed a battered green dump truck with yellow Peruvian commercial plates, parked by a hole-in-the-wall eatery. The driver was an old soul, badly in need of a shave and a comb, wearing sandals and baggy dungarees with his threadbare shirt hanging out, half-buttoned. Leaning against his rig, he scooped his way through a mess of *menestra* beans in a clear plastic container with a plastic spoon. His table manners left something to be desired but he looked friendly enough. The bleats and grunts of farm animals emanated from the back of his truck.

"*Hola*," Maggie said. "What's all that racket? Sounds like goats."

"Goats it is, pretty one." He shoveled more beans into his mouth, standing back to drip sauce on the gravel, missing his dusty toes.

"My *mami* and I raised a goat or two. Taking them to market, are you?"

"I am indeed."

"And where might that be?"

"Tarapoto."

"Peru."

"The very same." He licked the back of his spoon.

Maggie got out her wad of money, peeled off enough twenty dollar bills to make him lose interest in his beans, then added a couple more, folded the stack in half, and strolled on over, giving him a sly grin.

"I'm looking to go to Tarapoto myself," she said.

~ ~ ~

Just outside Hurango, inside Peru, past the border stop, the truck pulled over and Maggie climbed out of the back. Reeking of goat, she brushed herself off, clambered back up into the cab, the old driver grinning at her moxie. As suspected, the border guards hadn't been the slightest bit interested in inspecting goats. She rolled the window down and the warm, moist, jungle air rushed in as the driver ground the rig up to cruising speed, which meant tolerable kidney jarring. The driver flipped on the radio, found a lively *cumbia*, bouncing accordion and Latin horns over thick African rhythms. It was an old one, played at all the weddings and family gatherings, about taking life as it comes. He started thumping the wheel in time and singing in a raspy voice and Maggie joined him on the second verse.

¡Oye! Abre tus ojos…

They didn't sound half bad singing together.

In Tarapoto, Maggie scrabbled down from the cab, shifting her bag up on her shoulder. She tilted her fedora back and waved goodbye to her chatty driver.

At a *Movistar* shop, she bought a new mobile and a SIM card. She had the clerk, a bookish boy with a serious frown, unlock the phone and replace the card.

Anonymous. For a little while anyway.

She rented a room in a cheap hotel, on the second floor, fired up the clattering laptop. Still some battery left. She emailed Ed the phone number. Another GPS ping alert popped up. She hit DENY, powered down. Who—or what—

was trying to sniff her out?

She took a badly needed shower, propping the phone up on the gurgling toilet tank so she could hear it in case it rang. By the time she was toweling off, it did.

"Did you order a pizza?" She had the receiver cradled to her neck as she pulled on undies.

"Is your husband home?" Ed said. *Safe to talk?*

"Nope." *Yes, it was.*

"How's your trip?"

"A few miles from home." *Still a ways.* "But I'm in the neighborhood." *She was in Peru.*

"When you get there, call." *Call the embassy when you arrive.* Ed hung up. He kept the call short, even though she was supposedly in the clear.

She thought about that nagging GPS ping again. Who? Or what? Human or digital? Even if it was a bot, a program, behind every automatic crawler was a person. Ed? *No.* If she couldn't trust Ed, she couldn't trust anyone. How about any one of those creatures at that so-called party?

She ran a brush through her wet hair and finished getting dressed. Then she put her new jacket on, hat, got her laptop in a bag, checked out, walked down to the main drag. A line of beat-up taxis waited in front of a cinema. She strolled up and down and found the friendliest face.

"Yes, missy?" He was a wiry-looking guy with a bit of a stoop. But he had a nice, dilapidated smile.

"Do you know the way to Lima?" Maggie said.

"Lima? You mean the capital? *That* Lima?"

"Is there another one I don't know about?"

"No, but it's a good twelve hours. And that's without stopping."

"Will five hundred U.S. dollars get me there in ten?" It was over a month's salary in this country.

He cracked a wide grin, made lopsided by a missing tooth. "Only if you wear your seatbelt, missy." The cabbie came around with alacrity and opened the door for her. "Only if you wear your seatbelt."

~~~

As the sun rose next morning, the taxi whirred up Avenida Encalada, a stark wide street below the hills in Lima that resembled an office park, its only saving grace being the tall palms swaying in the median of the road. The early light flattened on the U.S. Embassy, big and blunt, the size of a factory, with small square windows and topped with cement. She was finally here. Her driver was happy to get the seemingly never-ending stream of twenty-dollar bills. As soon as Maggie got out of the cab with her shoulder bag, the tall embassy door opened and a lean man in suit and sunglasses came jogging out, talking into a Bluetooth clipped to his ear.

-6-

"And what prompted the investigation in the first place?"

Maggie took a deep breath and considered her response as she looked around the SCIF—Sensitive Compartmental Information Facility—a lead-lined conference room in the Agency's San Francisco headquarters on Golden Gate Avenue. Two of the Agency higher-ups, flown in from D.C., sat at the far end of the long, polished, conference table, along with several local Agency executives. A woman with heavily sprayed hair, wearing a red polyester pantsuit that fit better ten pounds ago, typed meeting notes into a laptop. As if to complete the post mortem on the failed Quito operation, the more prominent U.S. presidents stared down impassively at Maggie from the walls in the despondency of fluorescent light.

The man asking the question was Robert Houseman, deputy director of West Coast Operations, even though he was based in D.C. He wore a gray suit, white shirt, and dark blue striped tie, along with a severe glower. His distrust of the fledgling Forensic Accounting team Ed had forged was no secret; he saw it as a threat to his control. He brushed his thinning brown comb-over into place.

Sitting next to Maggie was Ed, her boss, gulping from a twenty-ounce Starbucks cup. A brown splash already decorated his blue shirt, first thing in the morning. His wide yellow tie was loosened down his substantial neck and his brown-bear beard needed trimming. He looked like an unmade bed. But behind Ed's horn-rimmed glasses, his eyes were sharp and focused.

And he was the only one taking Maggie's side.

Straightening the mandarin collar of her royal-blue suit jacket, which matched her nail polish, Maggie said, "As I detailed in my initial report—over a year ago—I discovered suspicious payments into an offshore account belonging to a foreman at one of Five Fortunes's exploration sites in northern Ecuador."

Houseman frowned. "And why were you focusing on the bank account of an employee of a foreign oil company in the first place?"

"Because that employee was getting kickbacks from an American corporation," Maggie said. "Five Fortunes received those funds directly from Commerce Oil, an American . . ."

"Everyone knows what Commerce Oil is, Agent de la Cruz."

"Yes, sir."

"Are you on some kind of crusade? Against Commerce Oil?"

Maggie glanced over at Ed. On the phone, before she'd left her apartment in the Mission this morning, Ed had instructed her to keep her comments to one of two options: yes or no.

"I work on the accounting side," she said. "I'm not concerned with what an American company actually does—until it breaks the law." She looked around the room at the impassive faces.

The next to speak was Eric Walder, director of the clandestine Field Operations, a slender man with frizzy hair. His face was cradled in one hand propped up on the arm of his swivel chair. He'd been taking everything in with half-lidded eyes. "Two men were killed," he said in a New York accent. "Two of our people wounded."

Maggie thought of Achic, out of the hospital now, thank God. John Rae had yet to surface. Two people had been killed: one guard and the mysterious driver Maggie had encountered. "I'm aware of that. One of the deaths was related to the fact that I was almost killed myself." She was still coming to terms with that.

"Yes, you were. And none of it was warranted."

Maggie folded her hands in front of her on the conference table and made a conscious decision to control her words. She was furious. But she was lucky to be alive. She'd spent the last three days getting back from South America. She was exhausted and her body hurt. "It was deemed justified when I first submitted my report, showing Five Fortunes, a Chinese company, to be a front for Commerce Oil and that political manipulation was taking place in Ecuador. The operation was approved by the Agency. Signed off, funded, and Field Ops-supported. And it wasn't until the very last minute at the meeting with Beltran, Velox, and Li that I found out Ecuador's National Vice Squad had been compromised. It looked like we were going to simply give away two million dollars. I just couldn't see doing that. And I still haven't been given an explanation—"

"An explanation? You're an employee of the Agency. You follow orders. And your orders were to continue with the transfer."

Ed was next to speak: "Sir, under the circumstances, it made sense for Agent de la Cruz to stall the transaction, as it was clear that Minister Beltran had gained prior knowledge of the sting and manipulated the police. His men drew weapons on our agents."

Walder stared at Ed. "It was your responsibility to make sure your agent did as she was told."

There was a pause. "Yes, sir," Ed said.

Maggie cleared her throat. "I take full responsibility for . . ."

Walder held his free hand up to silence Maggie, but maintained his lazy lean position, head in hand. A taut hush stifled the air in the windowless room. "This is not the first time you've disobeyed orders, is it, Agent de la Cruz?"

She cleared her throat. "No, sir."

"You went over your director's head when you filed that report."

Did she? Yes. "A prominent American corporation breaking the law in an international setting? I have a duty to stop that."

Director Walder smirked. "Where did you get your information that started the original investigation? On the kickbacks going to the foreman at Five Fortunes?"

"Through an anonymous tip," she said.

"One of the one-eight-hundred numbers?"

"No, it wasn't through one of the whistleblower numbers."

"Who then?"

"I can't say."

"You certainly will if you're subpoenaed."

"I can't, because I don't know. It was anonymous."

"An email?"

"No. That I could trace easily enough. Snail mail. A note. Two notes actually. They came a few days apart."

"Really?" Walder said. "And where did you get these two notes?"

"Delivered to my apartment in San Francisco. They arrived several days apart in USPS postage-paid envelopes—the kind you buy at the post office. The first one contained a yellow Post-It with a single word: Ecuador."

The woman with helmet hair typed that into her computer.

"It's all in my report," Maggie said to her. "Central Records."

The woman blushed as she continued to type.

"And the second note?" Walder asked, giving an impatient sigh.

"Just five words, which, on their own, read as pure gibberish, until I realized they were encrypted using the word in the first note—Ecuador—as a cipher text to encode them."

"A *what* text?" Walder said, clearly annoyed.

"A cipher text—basic plaintext encryption. The code word is used to shift the standard alphabet and form substitutions.

"The five words boiled down to two names: 'Ryan Morris' and 'Five Fortunes Petroleum.' I started researching—in my own time at first. That's when I found that Ryan Morris, a foreman with Five Fortunes Petroleum on a site in northern Ecuador—clever how the whistleblower used the actual cipher word itself as an additional clue—had over eighty thousand in his checking account. His paychecks were building up. That's a classic sign he's getting funded somewhere else. I put a trace on his activity—authorized—and it turned out Morris was getting a lot of cash dumped into an offshore account. A lot. It was coming from a payroll company contracted out by Commerce Oil. Morris and half his team were getting paid to forge oil-contamination reports, make them look clean, so they could acquire drilling rights in the Amazon. What's more, Ryan Morris worked for Commerce Oil at one time. It kept leading back to Commerce Oil."

Walder nodded, while Helmet Hair typed. "And you still have these anonymous notes? Evidence to support your case?"

"In the files—Central Records. The case number is C39A4001A."

Walder smiled, but it wasn't a nice smile. "Any idea who could have sent these notes?"

"A disgruntled former employee? The foreman's ex-wife? A jealous co-worker?" Maggie's eyes met Walder's. "A concerned citizen who has it in for Commerce Oil? Take your pick."

"Well, it's still sounding like you have it in for Commerce Oil yourself."

"If I have it in for anyone, it's for American companies that think they can cheat the system—and the American taxpayer. I don't care what their name is—just how they do business. That's why I took this job. That's why you pay me—I hope."

Ed kicked her shin gently.

"That will be enough of that," Deputy Director Houseman said. "Our job is not to police the environment, or U.S. companies—"

Director Walder interrupted again. "Let me make something clear—and this comes from the top. There will be no more witch-hunt missions like this in the future. This was a simple sting that turned into a bloodbath—one that we now own and must explain—to the Ecuadorian government. I'm spearheading an investigation into why this operation was ever approved in the first place. Commerce Oil, the supplier of much of the world's energy and a major employer in this country, if not the world, being hounded by an intelligence agency?"

Maggie looked at Houseman, then Walder. "Our transfer was meant to look like a donation to Beltran's Amazon Wildlife Restoration Fund. It all looked good. I set it up myself. But Beltran knew it was a sting. Shouldn't we be asking *how*? Along with *who* was the contact who picked me up? Shouldn't we be asking *why* that happened?"

Ed leaned over and whispered quietly, "Maggie. Shut up."

Walder gave Maggie a furious eyebrow-twitching glare. "All of this because of a payroll inconsistency. Two deaths, two wounded. A major humiliation."

"Two million dollars saved," Maggie said. Along with the Amazon, for the time being. But she kept that to herself.

Walder spoke to Ed and Maggie both. "Cowboys—and cowgirls—forensic accounting analysts. What's clear is that this department overextended its reach. Your job is to provide analysis. Why Agent de la Cruz was even allowed to go along is a matter of concern. And she should have simply transferred the money when the situation turned south. This has made it to CNN and Fox News. All over an employee of an oil company taking a kickback. Good lord."

Don't bring Her into it, Maggie thought, running her tongue under her lip. But she said, "Understood. It will not happen again."

"No, it certainly won't," Walder said, standing up, buttoning his jacket. "And if it does, Agent de la Cruz, you'll be looking at more than simple dismissal. Do I make myself clear?"

She absorbed that. "Yes, sir."

"This meeting is over. I don't expect to ever attend another one like it." He left the room.

Houseman rose while the woman in red packed up her computer. On the way out the door, he approached Maggie. "I'll take that laptop."

"There's still some data I need to catalogue. Evidence we can use against Commerce Oil—if need be."

He put his hand out. He'd been overshadowed by a director and wanted to look tough. Agency politics. "I said, 'I'll take that laptop.'"

Maggie shut down the MacBook and it died with a rattle and whiz. She closed the lid and handed it over. She wanted to ask if he even knew what to do with it.

Luddite. She'd already backed everything up anyway.

~~~

"What did you expect, Maggs?" Ed stuffed a thatch of wiggling noodles into his mouth with throwaway chopsticks and slurped the food down before he continued. "You should never have gone over Houseman's head on the op to begin with." Wiping his beard with a white cloth napkin, he gulped tea from a cup without a handle. "Oh, but that's freaking hot." He set the cup down and shook his fingers.

Moshi's was packed with a lunchtime crowd and the voices, many of them speaking Japanese, clattered off the walls at a level that would keep any conversation private, as waiters bustled to and fro, delivering steaming bowls of food to crowded tables.

"That report sat on his desk for months," Maggie said, sipping from a bowl of miso soup. The salty broth felt restorative after her ordeal in South America, which was finally beginning to subside.

"Well, it was a noble effort. But it didn't happen. I hope you learned something. About going over a deputy director's head."

"Is this the 'impulsive' speech again?"

Ed shrugged. "It's gotten you into trouble before. Learn a lesson. Before it learns you."

"Thanks for supporting me in that meeting, by the way."

"Lot of good it did."

The crash of dishes back in the kitchen added to the din for a moment.

"We're not really finished, though, right, Ed?"

"On this? Ed picked up a blue-and-white ceramic bowl with fish patterns on the side. "As far as you're concerned—*ja*.

Finished. Most definitely. Half of Washington is getting their pockets lined by Commerce Oil. Why do you think they sent Walder and Houseman out to stamp on our toes?"

"For not giving away two mil like it was chump change. How did Beltran know about the sting?"

Ed set his bowl down, belched softly, said *sorry*.

"How did you know National Vice weren't going to show?" she asked.

Ed shook his head.

"Meaning you're not going to tell me?"

"Meaning I can't. Department protocol. But it was on the up and up. John Rae's intel wasn't as good. Sometimes having distance from an op is better. Not generally, but sometimes. And in this case, it was."

"Where *is* John Rae?"

"Just made it back. Getting debriefed as we speak."

"Well, I'm glad to hear that."

"Held them all off until you got out of there, and then managed to diffuse the situation so no one else died. Talked his way out."

Yeah, he was pretty good at what he did. Maggie had to agree.

"Rumor is, he says not giving Beltran the money was *his* idea. That he pushed you into it."

Well, she had to admit she liked John Rae a whole lot better. And she liked him enough to begin with. "That kind of makes him a real gent, doesn't it?"

"They're not going to nail an op as good as him for making a cowboy decision."

"Any update on the guy who picked me up? And how he knew about me in the first place? The 'check' code?"

"You mean the guy whose neck you broke? He's not really in a position to tell us."

"Yeah, but you've got your finger on the pulse."

"The authorities down there aren't releasing any information on him and are blaming us for the incident. Standard."

"Throw me a bone."

"I don't have a clue, Maggie. But I'm going to try and find out."

"*Try?*"

"Were you at the same meeting I was just at? The one with Walder chewing us out? Houseman? We have to keep out noses clean. Snot free."

"Thanks for the lunchtime image." She set her bowl down, pushed it to one side. "How many people knew you and I were in contact that day on Skype? When you told me not to go to the embassy?"

"Yeah, that bothers me." Ed rested his elbows on the table. "The usual channels. The communication was logged."

Maggie nodded slowly. "So a lot of the Agency knew. Maybe the same person who told Beltran about the sting. But get this, you said not to go to the embassy, and my mysterious pickup with the broken neck was planning on taking me there. Thought I'd go along with it. Thank God he got it wrong."

"Whoever She is," Ed said, quoting Maggie.

"So how did you know? Not to go to the embassy?"

Ed took a deep breath. "Now that's something else I'm not going to tell you. Just be happy you got out of that car alive. Because I am."

"I think what I'm saying is don't tell me to just drop this, Ed. Not something this big."

"This is the game that moves as you play, Maggie. You're the one who wants to be a field op."

"Only because I'm dead where I am."

"Because you go over people's heads."

"I appreciate that, but . . ."

"Believe me, Maggs, I'm looking into it. But you—you're not looking into anything." His piercing eyes focused on Maggie through his glasses. "You heard Walder. Can you say: 'jail time'?"

She sat back, drummed her blue nails on the Formica tabletop. No one wanted to know the op existed. Or was it that Commerce Oil didn't want anybody to know the op existed?

"Got it."

"Good."

"One small thing, though."

"Jesus. It better be small at this point. I'd like to make it to retirement."

"Those kids who guided me to safety. Kacha. And her sister. Whatever is going on in the Yasuni is more than dirty money looking for a pocket to hide in."

"No doubt. But I just got done saying that's not your job."

"These girls—a cousin of theirs was arrested and imprisoned. A young woman named Tica Tuanama."

Ed drank tea. "Arrested for what?"

"Protesting the oil companies . . . out in the Yasuni. I said I'd help try to find out what was going on . . . maybe get her out . . ."

Ed stared at Maggie.

"Ed, Kacha saved my ass and I said we'd help find her cousin and try to get her out. I know we can do that sometimes."

Ed stared at her over his teacup. "Ask me again next week. When this has died down to a dull roar."

"I also said we'd get her some reward money. I'd like to do *that* soon."

"Jesus H., Maggie. I can just see the response that's going to get."

"Those girls are living in a shack. The sister is turning tricks so they can eat. She's got an infant. Want me to describe little Irpa living in the slums while you scarf down your lunch?"

"Look, I'll do what I can. But I can tell you now it's not going to be much. And it's not going to be soon. Anything that smacks of this op will get shit-canned and put you—and me—under the microscope."

"Ed, she stuck her neck out for me."

Ed gave a deep sigh. "Write it up," he said. "Submit it. Then take a day off, rest up. And when you return to work, get stuck back into the Acorn probe. You've been overdue on your forensic analysis on that for some time now."

"We both know Acorn is nothing but a keep-busy project. Half the people are already indicted."

"I'll look forward to reviewing your notes. You go back to forensic analysis. NCIS without the bodies." Ed picked up his bowl, dug more noodles out, forced them into his mouth.

It was a good thing he was a cute slob, otherwise it would be even more difficult to eat with him, Maggie thought. It already was kind of hard to eat with him.

"But now there *are* bodies."

Ed sucked down the last of his noodles. "When you're on a losing streak, you walk away. You don't keep doubling down."

"This isn't blackjack. This is some kid scared shitless in a South American jail. I won't ask for anything else. I promise."

Ed raised his bushy eyebrows. "Why not call your old man to pull a few strings? He must know people."

"Don't talk about my father, Ed." Maggie said. "You know better than that."

"A lot of ops don't work out the way they should. That's why I went for a desk job."

Truth was, Ed got out of Field Ops to marry an Irish girl with green eyes and jet black hair. Who dumped him once she moved to San Francisco and saw that settling for a giant Teddy Bear with atrocious table manners in a town where pretty people were the norm wasn't, perhaps, what she wanted after all. After Ed had paid her way to the U.S., got her a work permit, taken the job transfer.

The waitress bustled by, dropped a plastic tray with a bill on top of it unceremoniously on the table.

Ed got his wallet out. It was beat up and falling apart. "Acorn is your focus. Find the facts. That's what you're good at: finding facts."

But facts were people, when you got right down to it. And people wound up hurt. Sometimes worse.

"Take a day off," Ed said, leaning back, extracting a credit card. "Take two. Decompress. That's an order. You look beat."

"Thanks."

"Beautiful but beat. You didn't get any sleep on the plane?"

"In between getting questioned by Field Ops? As much as one can sleep on a C-one-thirty." She'd had to wait for the better part of a day in a sweltering hangar outside Lima for the military transport to be dispatched. She tapped the toe of her dark blue Lanvin scrunch loafer. Her feet were still killing her after her sprint across Quito in cheap Keds.

"Might not be a bad idea to lay low for a while. Take a couple of days, come back refreshed, and work on Acorn." Ed raised his thick eyebrows. "Acorn."

"Acorn. Got it."

She could say she was off the hook having to worry about Tica. She had tried. She could say that. Couldn't she?

She remembered her *mami* saying: If someone needs your help and you're in a position to, then what you must do is obvious.

Ed crossed his big arms, motioned at a plate of calamari in front of her, in a tangy red sauce. "You gonna eat those?"

"Knock yourself out."

~~~

On the way home, Maggie stopped at Civic Center, the cherry blossoms opening up over the homeless encampments around City Hall. She stood, wondering what time it was for a moment, then dialed John Rae Hutchens' phone number on her cell. She had a good head for numbers and remembered it from looking it up earlier that morning.

She got the standard Agency voicemail blurb. At the beep, she said, "Heard you just got back. Checking that you made it in one piece. And to say *gracias* for going to bat for me. What a ride. Give me a call when you've settled." She left her landline number, and not her name, and took the Muni metro back home.

"The president's office," Oil Minister Beltran said. "And step on it."

His chauffeur shut the rear passenger door to the 750Li, ensconcing Beltran in black-padded leather and soft classical music. He ran around to the driver's side, his pistol bouncing in its holster under his arm, got in, started up the luxury sedan with a throaty rumble. They set off through the gates of the mansion on the top of the hill overlooking Quito, the silver-helmeted guards saluting as they sailed by. Morning fog was burning off, which meant Beltran was running late. But the call from *el presidente's* office had only come a little over an hour ago. Unexpected.

Unwanted.

Beltran had been on tenterhooks since the disastrous reception for the oil coalition. Things had gone horribly, disastrously, wrong, but at least he'd had prior knowledge of the intended trap. Thanks to his connection. And been able to foil it by *not* signing the documents. And saved Li and Velox from scandal as well. Were they the least bit grateful? People like them never were. No one acknowledged dirty work, the necessary pain, digging the trenches the foundations of enterprise were built upon. Even when done on their behalf. *Especially* when done on their behalf. Right now they were no doubt scrambling to cover their tracks. Velox and Li were masters of coming out of steaming piles of manure smelling like roses, thanks to people like Beltran. While Beltran took all the risks.

No one valued what the guy on the front line did.

His biggest regret, however, was that he'd lost the two million. With what he'd squirreled away, he could have said goodbye and moved to Madrid with that money. Spain. The mother country. Now *that* was the place to be. But that damn woman, the good-looking *norteamericana* accountant, had foiled his plan, risking all of their lives, when she could have simply transferred the money and been done with it. Everyone could have gone their separate ways without a single shot fired. What were two million little *pavos* to the Yanquis? She was as bad as that uppity agent who talked like a cowboy—sounding like John *Pendejo* Wayne. Before she jumped through the fifteenth-century window he'd scoured Andalusia for and brought back at considerable expense.

Although he did have to acknowledge the woman's nerve. And her shapely figure.

Well, he wasn't going to worry. Not too much. Beltran didn't get where he was today by being a worrywart. He'd grown up in a slum without a pair of shoes to his name until he could liberate some from a quivering schoolboy in a uniform on his way to class. He hadn't eaten three meals a day until he was conscripted into the army. Where he finally got some respect and met the people who could help him up the ladder. That was all he needed. He'd dealt with far more dangerous types in his checkered past than the president and his privileged, half-assed cronies. Beltran wasn't going to jump like a frantic rabbit just because *el presidente* was unhappy with the outcome of the oil party. He'd jump. High enough. But no higher.

But now that the oil rights had been signed over to the Chinkies, Beltran needed a new angle. He'd lost some leverage. But he still had his connections. He just had to find a new direction and then lead *el presidente* by the nose to it.

El presidente had a pretty big nose.

The 750 glided along the high road and down toward Quito. The trees and open space flew by and he savored them, as he always did, before the descent into the smoggy city of two million.

A lone figure on the road up ahead caught his eye—mostly because she was female and bent over the open hood of a tiny blue Honda that was more rust than blue.

Her fine derriere was encased in tight blue denim. A poncho of orange, yellow, and black was draped over it, the tail of which danced tantalizing back and forth in the breeze over her not-just-above average, but quite exquisite heart-shaped ass. He pictured her buttocks without jeans, which were on the floor of his mind now, well-honed cheeks twisting against each other in fine cotton panties.

And in his mind, he pulled those panties down with his teeth. Along with the Mozart playing on the car's loudspeakers, a moment to take note of. The little things.

Why did a man become the hound when it came to a luscious behind? Because he'd always been an ass man. But not an ass.

Beltran smiled to himself. No matter what the pressures, he always took time to appreciate life. Smell the roses. And the beautiful women. Life had its pleasures. One needed to seek them out, make the most of them. It was his secret for success. Along with the subterfuge, of course.

The woman stood up from the hood of the car, brushed her long black hair back as Beltran's vehicle approached, and started waving frantically.

A beautiful smile. And her thumb out now. Life was good.

"Pablo, slow down for our lovely damsel in distress."

The chauffeur turned as he drove. "Are you sure, boss?"

"Why do you constantly doubt me? You've done that ever since we were boys. I pay your salary. And call me *Minister*."

"My apologies, your highness. It's just that I don't want my meal ticket endangered by being late for a meeting with the president. All for a piece of ass. This is a reoccurring situation."

"But Pablo, did you see that *culo?*" Beltran pointed a finger. "The juiciness. Don't you just want to rub your face between those fabulous butt cheeks?"

"It is quite exceptional, boss. You do have an eye. But as I recall, you're the one who said to s*tep on it. El presidente* being pissed off with you and all that."

Beltran turned in his seat as they whipped by the girl in the poncho, back over the hood of her tiny econobox. He needed a better look.

"You just drove right by that gorgeous creature, Pablo. I'm beginning to question your sense of chivalry. Not to mention sexual orientation. Now stop. Stop or I'll send you back to Manaus where you may immediately resume your life of poverty and squalor."

"Yes, boss." Pablo pulled over to the side of the road, the luxury sedan's tires crunching in the dirt.

"*Minister*," Beltran said.

"Minister."

Beltran turned in his seat, peering eagerly out the back window. The woman was jogging to catch up. Her poncho swung to and fro and Beltran imagined her full brown breasts heaving from side to side as she rode on top of him, constrained in a lacey bra of some sort that would match the panties, which would still be in his teeth. "This is a fine country, Pablo. The women. It's the altitude."

"Yes, but the meeting with *el* . . ."

"You can make up the time."

The woman got to the door of the car.

Woman? Hell, she was a goddess. Rich caramel complexion. He could practically smell every part of her. Taste them. She was salty and tangy and sweet at the same time, like some concoction mixed just for his wild, randy mind. He wondered what else lay beneath the peasant poncho. He had a pretty good idea, but one had to be thorough.

Hang *el presidente*. He would only keep Beltran waiting for hours anyway, to teach him a lesson. He was nothing but a phony populist.

Beltran pressed the window button. The glass whirred down.

She had eyes like a llama's, big, round and moist. Her lips were full. He imagined them wet with passion. All of her lips.

"Your auto has malfunctioned on you, I see," Beltran said.

"Yes, sir. I need to get it to a garage."

"It would be my privilege to offer you a ride."

"Why, thank you, *señor*," she said shyly, batting long lashes, casting her dark eyes down to the ground.

"Pablo, you sloth! Kindly open the door for this young lady."

"Yes, b—Minister." Pablo hopped out and came running around the front of the sedan, holding his tie in place as he reached out to grab the door handle. "Here you go, miss."

As he pulled open the door, Beltran moved over to make room for his enchanting guest—and saw the orange, yellow, and black stripes of her poncho fly up. And a squat MAC-11 pistol appear in her hand.

Beltran's heart jumped.

The gun went off—*pap, pap, pap*—jerking in her small brown fist. And Pablo, stumbling back, face crumpled, hit the open door, slumped down, was dragged down. Hit the ground like a sack of potatoes.

Kidnappers!

Beltran scooted over to the driver's side of the car and with shaking hands fought to open the door. He bounded clumsily from the 750Li. Into the middle of the road.

Must get away!
Head into the trees on the other side of the road.

"Don't move, pig," the girl growled right behind him, "or you're dead, see?"

Beltran froze.

"I mean it," he heard her say.

Slowly, he turned back around.

She squinted at him over the top of the black sedan, her arms resting on the roof, holding the weapon in both hands. One eye shut. Again, she smiled that wonderful smile. "Hands above your head, etcetera."

Beltran took a deep breath, praying for a vehicle to come along. But in this country, where roadside abductions were commonplace, it probably wouldn't stop anyway.

"Quickly now," the woman said, motioning with the gun for Beltran to raise his hands.

He did so, heart thumping, but not too badly. He had been through these things before. This would make it three times. A lucky number. It was money they wanted.

"Fine," he said. "How much is the *bite*?"

"Shut up, you smug bastard. You're nothing but a traitor."

The last word set off an internal alarm that raised his pulse to a skittering pace. A word like *traitor* belonged in a particular vocabulary. One not interested in just a fistful of dollar bills. One intent on revolution.

Tree branches behind the girl moved and rustled. And here came her friends. *Terrucos*, several faces covered in kerchiefs, one man wearing a camouflage jacket. All with weapons. Pointed. This was serious.

Beltran's hands shook above his head. The sound of a large engine groaned in the distance. A bus? A truck? Did it matter?

The *terroristas* approached, weapons raised, formed a circle around him. Their eyes. Intense. Eyes of madmen.

"Let me just say this. I am worth far more to you alive."

"For the time being, anyway," the man in camouflage said, jabbing Beltran's gut with the perforated barrel of a submachine gun. "Into the car, Minister."

The vehicle in the distance was getting closer, grinding at high speed, and Beltran caught the view of the bus as it whooshed around the sedan. The *terrucos* holding him at gunpoint, breaking away for a second, shaking their fists imperiously at the passengers of the bus, shouting out their slogans of victory.

"*¡La venganza es la justicia!*"

Vengeance is justice.

The passengers shouted back in encouragement as the bus roared off.

This was more than simple money trouble.

"How much?" Beltran said, attempting to quell his trembling voice. "I have money, boys. And girls," he added, to placate the women, of whom there were two. "Quite a *lot* of money, eh?"

"I'm tired of hearing about your fucking money," a woman in a red neckerchief seethed. She had passionate eyes, black with hate. "To you, that's all there is—*money!*" She said the word as if it were the vilest one she could think of, then reared back and struck Beltran across the face with her TEC-9 pistol. The blow knocked him sideways, onto the ground. His head spun.

"That was uncalled for, Comrade Lita," the man in the camouflage said. "Now get him into the car."

Beltran sat up, rubbing his face. It dripped, wet and warm, and began to throb with pain.

He saw the girl with the fine derriere throw her machine pistol onto the dash of the car and get in behind the wheel. She flipped up the back of her poncho and adjusted the driver's seat forward as she positioned herself. The line of her white panties hovered above her jeans. It failed to arouse him now. The other *terrucos* hustled Beltran up and into the middle of the back seat, one on either side, the man in camouflage climbing into the front passenger seat. One of them slammed the hood on the rusty blue Honda and jumped in, starting the engine with a tinny whine.

Car doors were thumped shut.

Mozart prattled away on the loudspeakers.

"The call from the president's office . . ." Beltran said. "The meeting?"

"You fell for it," the man in camouflage said, shaking his head. "Too hasty to please your boss."

"Lackey," Comrade Lita said, sitting next to him, her TEC-9 gripped tightly in her hand.

"What is it you want from me?" Beltran said, wary that she might hit him again.

"The Amazon," she said. "The Yasuni."

"That should do it," the man in camouflage said. "Free from your filthy oil exploration. In exchange for your miserable life. Or we kill you and take a bigger prize. But let's see how this works out first, shall we?"

They set off and Beltran stared into the rearview mirror, at Pablo lying face up by the side of the road. Pablo. They'd chased tires with a stick together, then girls, then money, then power.

Would they both die by the same hands?

-8-

In the hallway of her apartment building on Valencia Street, Maggie stood at the line of mailboxes, fishing out junk mail, bills, a postcard reminder from her dentist with a smiling tooth on it.

And, curiously, a padded 5x7 prepaid USPS envelope with a small oblong item inside. She didn't recall ordering anything. She felt the packet. Whatever was in it was about half the length and thickness of a pack of gum. But hard. On the envelope itself, in neat blue ballpoint, her name and address were neatly centered in a generic, but familiar, handwriting. No return address. Outside, the honking of San Francisco city traffic filled the gray air.

Maggie locked the mailbox and trotted up the old staircase with its ornate carved banister. On the third-floor landing, a basketball game boomed from her apartment. Maggie stopped, took a breath, braced herself. All she wanted to do right now was crawl into bed and turn the disastrous Quito op into a faded memory. And this morning's lousy meeting.

And she wanted to do it alone.

She unlocked the door to her apartment.

"You're home early, *chica*," Sebastian said, his voice raised against the TV.

Maggie's boyfriend, or whatever he was these days, held the refrigerator door open in the small kitchenette, gazing inside, scratching his muscled abs. Seb had his jeans hanging low on his hips, no shirt, not looking at Maggie as she tossed the mail on the hallway table, along with her keys and purse. Incandescent light from the fridge cast a bluish glare on his tattoos. It was impossible not to be overwhelmed by the blaring flat-screen TV on the living room wall beyond the kitchen area.

"Ed gave me the rest of the day off!" Maggie shouted, dumping her briefcase by the table. The basketball game switched to a commercial and grew even louder as someone bellowed about car insurance. Once again, Maggie regretted giving Sebastian a key to her apartment. But he'd needed a place to stay last year, in between apartments, and . . . it was OK. At the time.

Now it was damn awkward to ask for it back.

The basketball game returned with a vengeance.

Maggie stifled the disappointment at not being greeted with a kiss and marched into the living room thundering with basketball, found the remote hiding on the floor behind a couple of empty Corona bottles, one with a wet cigarette butt in the bottom. The room reeked of smoke, not just tobacco. Seb knew how she felt about smoking and the impact drugs might have on her career, but she wasn't going to make an issue out of it at the moment. Another time. She clicked off the television, tossed the remote onto the black-leather sofa next to Sebastian's Gold Top Les Paul guitar. The guitar case was open on the floor and a couple of pieces of sheet music were laid out, propped up here and there. Seb's socks and black boots with the big buckles were scattered by the window, along with a black T-shirt and a leather jacket that could have been classified as falling apart twenty years ago. She walked to the bay window, wrenched it open, and let cool fresh air billow into the room. The sheer white curtain fluttered.

"I thought you had rehearsal," she said, turning back around to face him.

"Gave it a pass." Sebastian slammed the fridge door, the way he always did, opened a long neck Corona, tossed the cap into the kitchen sink with a tinkle that told her it contained dirty dishes. Taking a long swig, he finally acknowledged her with a wink of lashes that any woman would have killed for, ran his fingers through his jet-black undercut. Then he strode into the living room in that manner that first caught her eye two years ago when he came out on stage at El Rio with his band *Los Perros de Caza* and tore the place up.

"Don't you have an important gig coming up?"

"Hey, I'm cool," Sebastian said, scratching his six-pack stomach, eying her in that way when he hadn't seen her for a few days. She flushed inside, despite the exhaustion. Seb was a good-looking guy to be sure, trim and sexy, with his stubble shadowing his lean cheekbones, accentuating his dark eyes.

Now if you could just do something about that personality, she thought, and said: "Aren't you the one who told me even Black Sabbath rehearsed every day, ten hours minimum, back when they were getting started? No matter what they got up to the night before?"

He knocked back a mouthful of beer. "What's the matter with you? That Ed still trying to get into your pants?"

"Ai!" she gasped, walking back to the hall closet, slipping out of her Burberry Brit double-breasted trench coat. She brushed off the collar and straightened the coat on a hanger before she found a spot for it in the cramped hall closet, full of her many other coats and jackets—not to mention one or two of Sebastian's. She kicked off her blue scrunch loafers and wiggled her toes.

"What does that mean?" Seb said.

"It means a man and a woman can have a relationship that doesn't involve sex."

Seb gave a sly grin. "Not the way *you* look. No man alive could be within six feet of you without wanting you. Unless he was a *castrato*. Or gay. And maybe even then. You should be pleased with that fine body God gave you. Now come over here and let me tell you all about it."

She ran her fingers through her hair, actually considering it. She was one big knot of tension and frustration. And Seb was no slouch when it came to relieving that kind of stress.

"When you get back from rehearsal," she said, checking her little gold wristwatch. "You still got time. You can get that solo the way you want it. The Eric Clapton rip you're working on?"

"It's not a *rip*. I'm paying homage." Seb thumped down on her black-leather recliner, slugged beer. "Clapton copied it from Albert King. *Note for note*. Because it's a kickass solo."

"But I can hear you – when you *do* practice – trying to get that little vibrato thing right. Isn't that what it's called? Where you wiggle your little finger?"

"Come here and I'll wiggle something. It won't be so little, though."

"Hey. You really know how to sweet-talk a girl."

"Come on, baby. *¡Ven aquí!*"

"After rehearsal. Go wiggle your little finger."

"Why're you being such a tease?"

"Because you don't rehearse, Seb. And I paid for that damn guitar."

"You mean you *lent* me the money for that damn guitar."

Two years ago, she almost said. Wave bye-bye to five grand. She wouldn't really give a damn if he'd just knuckle down.

She was beat. Her ears were buzzing. If she closed her eyes, she was still rolling over in a BMW outside the embassy. Running across Quito like a deer in those crap sneakers. And she couldn't stop thinking about Kacha's cousin, Tica, in some prison cell, some dank little hellhole outside Quito. And nothing getting done about it.

"I'm going to get a couple hours shut-eye," she said, heading into the living room, collecting the empty bottles. "See you *after* rehearsal."

His long arms stopped her, wrapping around her leg.

"Yeah, I'll see you after rehearsal," he said, firm bicep pressing up against her thigh, his hand cupping a butt cheek. "And I'll see you *before* practice too. You need it. I can tell."

Laughing, she pushed Seb away, but not quite hard enough. "Not any more. I banged a homeless guy on the way home from work."

"On the *street*?"

"What do you think I am—some kind of tramp? No, a doorway of course."

"Oh, OK. And his buddies, too? I hope."

"Just the one who let me drink from his forty-ouncer."

"Oh, so you're all warmed up, huh? Cool. Saves me some time." Seb's strong fingers climbed her leg. Slid up underneath her dress and found that spot on her hip. The divot. He stroked it with his thumb and she could feel the edge of his guitar player's callus moving gently up and down. Slowly, his hand glided down onto her *montículo de venus*.

She responded. Things were getting warm.

Seb pulled her down onto his lap. Bottles tumbled from her arms onto the Persian rug, clattering off onto the hardwood floor. Seb was already hard. She responded to that too. Moistness. He pushed his lips to her ear and started whispering in Spanish. Not the way he spoke to her in English. Calling her *Chichi*, nibbling her earlobe.

She ate it up.

Found herself spooned on him in the leather recliner. His hands all over her. And his mouth. Then her dress was quickly pulled up around her midriff and her panties down to her knees. Seb kneeled on the floor, lips on her thighs, making a lazy path for her *concha*.

"I need a shower," she said in Spanish. It was their language when they were making love.

"No, you don't," he said. "Not at all."

"Promise me you'll go to rehearsal afterwards," she said, tousling his hair.

"Yeah, sure," he said, as he pulled her panties down her calves and off. "God, you're beautiful. I'm crazy about you."

"I mean it," she said, settling in, gripping the armrests of the chair, getting ready.

"So do I."

~~~

Maggie woke in a tangle of sheets, the curtains to her bedroom drawn tight against the Valencia Street racket several stories down. The antique clock on the nightstand told her it was late afternoon.

"Hey, Sebi?" she shouted. "You there, *amor*? Make some coffee, will you?"

No response. Cool. Maybe he'd actually gone to rehearsal after all.

She was alone, in that delicious dreamtime, which she seemed to remember from her childhood, but knew was time more imagined than anything else. It had only been a few hours, but the coma-like sleep felt luxurious and illicit, stolen from work, and on the tail of wicked lovemaking. She got up, wrapped her black-and-white kimono around her naked body, slouched into the front of the apartment to make *café cubano*.

And felt a little angry fire glow inside her when she saw Sebastian's Les Paul still lying on the sofa, untouched, exactly where it had been when she came home that morning.

While coffee brewed, she set about picking up the living room. Cleaning out the full sink, flinging Seb's dirty dishes into the dishwasher.

There were a couple of wine glasses already in the top rack. She'd been out of town, hadn't left any dirty dishes. She could not stand the smell of a rank dishwasher, always ran it on a regular basis, especially before she left for a trip. She specifically recalled running it before she left for Ecuador. Maggie extracted a wine glass in front, brushed her hair out of her eyes to inspect it. She put the glass back.

Mami always told her never to distrust her man. Lot of good it did *Mami*.

Maggie picked up the other wine glass. When did Sebi start wearing lipstick? Pink in this case.

She opened the cabinet door under the sink and tossed the glass into the trash with an angry flip.

God. Damn. You. Seb.

The doorbell rang, making her jump. Fastening her robe, she thought of pink lipstick as she stormed to the buzzer, where she leaned on the intercom. "You didn't go to rehearsal, you lazy bastard."

"No, I did not," a recognizable southern voice said. "And I'm very sorry about it, too, ma'am."

Maggie flinched. It wasn't Seb. But she knew that voice. John Rae Hutchens.

"No," she said, laughing. "I'm the one who's sorry—for making a freaking idiot of myself. Come on up. Third floor." She thumbed the buzzer until she heard the front door slam down in the lobby. She pulled open her apartment door an inch and realized she was wearing her kimono and nothing else. Well, the two of them had practically died together—what was a little familiarity? She gave the living room a quick once-over while John Rae hurried up the flights of stairs. Scooping up her crumpled blue-satin panties from the recliner, she stuffed them quickly under a sofa cushion, then went into the kitchen and pulled out a box of brown-sugar cubes.

She heard John Rae reach the top of the stairs and stride up to her door. "It's open!" she yelled.

His hand appeared around the door. Slowly it opened and John Rae entered, shut the door, stood in the hallway. He wore a slim, powder-blue poplin suit that fit his tallish frame well, with a crisp white shirt done up to the collar, no tie. Signature cowboy boots, gray and embossed with a curlicue pattern. His right thigh was padded, no doubt from a bandage over his bullet wound. His hair was slicked back behind his ears today and a serious bruise on his left cheek was turning an ugly purplish-yellow. More residue from the Ecuadorian oil party. But he looked pretty good, considering. He brandished a beaming smile. "You're alive," she said.

"Yeah, I think so. You too. Good to see you."

"How's the leg? Last time I saw you, it had a bullet in it."

"I made it up the stairs." He didn't seem to be in any pain. She was impressed.

"And you know where I live."

He hooked his thumbs in his belt loops. "I'm not really a stalker," he said. "I was getting debriefed over in Oakland. Decided to take the liberty after your voicemail this morning." He noticed her kimono. "Hope I didn't wake you up."

"Just catching up on my sleep. After that fiasco. But I was already up. Just made coffee." She held up the pot. "High-octane."

"Perfect." He seemed to be averting his eyes, from looking

at her legs. A gent? Who woulda thought?

"Make yourself at home," she said. "I'll be right back."

In the walk-in closet of her bedroom that she had constructed at some expense, she tossed her kimono on the floor and slipped on a pair of ripped and faded jeans, going commando to save time. She topped it off with a soft loose gray alpaca sweater. No bra. She fluffed her hair as she strode back into the living room in her bare feet.

John Rae was standing by the sofa, hands in his pockets, gazing down at Seb's guitar. Maggie poured coffee into demitasse cups.

"Les Paul Gold Top," he said, giving a low whistle, then looking at her with interest. "Do you play?"

"Belongs to a friend," she said, bringing in cups of coffee from the kitchen.

He gave a quick nod at the word *friend*, took the coffee, sipped it. "Excellent."

Maggie set her cup down on the glass top of the coffee table, picked up Seb's guitar, leaned it against the wall, making room on the sofa.

"You're allowed to sit down," she said, taking her spot on the recliner.

He did so. They both drank coffee for a moment, while a bus groaned by on Valencia Street.

"So when did you get back?" She was beginning to wake up with the rich dark coffee flowing through her veins.

"Last night. Had to go through Colombia. What you did, though—with that goat truck? Creative."

"Me and goats just go together. Took you longer than me, though."

"Complications," he said. "I felt a whole lot better when I heard from Field Ops that you got out. The last I saw of you, you were flying through a leaded-glass window in a dress that cost a week's salary, into Beltran's swimming pool. But I needn't have worried, by the sound of things."

"*I* was plenty worried, if that makes any difference."

"Good way to be in a situation like that. But you can

obviously take care of yourself. That little stunt in front of the embassy in Quito, for another example. Ditching that car the way you did. The Marine guards said you run like a gazelle."

"Five miles a day," she said, sipping. "Rain or shine. But do you have any idea who the hell my kamikaze driver was?"

He sipped coffee, shook his head. "It raises a few concerns."

"More than a few. Are you suspecting a mole?"

John Rae gave a slow nod. "Somehow connected to Beltran."

I killed him, she thought.

"Don't let it bug you too much," John Rae said, obviously reading her face. "It could have been you. But you were faster."

"How did you get out of that party from hell, anyway?"

"Once I got hold of that gun, I held them off for as long as I could, to give you time to get away. Then it was a genuine standoff. There was no reason for them to shoot once you were gone. What was the point? Beltran wasn't getting the money. So Achic and I walked out. Limped. Quickly. With guns on us." He shook his head. "That op was my responsibility. And it went south."

"You know, I've been told to stay away from this subject. I got my hand smacked. Pretty damn hard."

John Rae drank coffee. "I can imagine."

"I've been told it's done, finished."

He nodded.

"That I could face legal sanctions if I continue to pursue it."

John Rae took another sip of coffee. "That's what I wanted to talk to you about." He raised his eyebrows. "If you still want to hear."

A quick thrill shot through her, making her as nervous as it did excited. And they couldn't put her in jail for listening. Maggie set her cup down on the floor by the recliner, sat up, met John Rae's blue-eyed, steely gaze. "I'm all ears."

"This is completely confidential. You can't say a word.

Whatever you decide."

"Yes."

"Even to Ed."

"Got it."

John Rae set his cup down on the glass coffee table, leaned forward, elbows on his knees, and folded his hands together. "I'm going back."

-9-

"Going back? To Ecuador?" Maggie asked, more than a little surprised. And more excited, even though the subject was off limits, as far as work—and her future—were concerned.

"Not exactly," John Rae said. "But close enough. I could really use your help."

"Help you how?"

"I can't say exactly until you've been officially cleared. But it would involve your financial expertise. Working your electronic magic. Another payoff. This time, though, you can manage your end remotely—from here. No physical risks." He gave her an encouraging smile.

A ripple of disappointment washed through her. If she wanted to have an effect on what happened to Kacha and Tica, she'd be much better served down there. And besides, she didn't like the idea of unknown assailants trying to pick her up and get away with it.

"What's the matter?"

"I thought you'd need me to go along."

"Hell no." John Rae picked up his coffee. "With your photo burned into the brain of every *poli* in the country?"

"You know, the remote computer thing looks great in the movies—but it doesn't work that way in real life."

"We're getting ahead of ourselves." John Rae checked his watch. "You need to meet my handler."

"And who might that be?"

John Rae shook his head. "I've already told you too much, Agent de la Cruz. I'd like you to meet him. Tonight. Eight o'clock. I'll even let you pick the restaurant."

The doorbell buzzed.

"Just a minute." The doorbell droned three more times before she could set the coffee pot on the tile counter and get to the intercom. "Who is it, already?"

"Your little *lique*, baby. Ready for round two."

Seb. Half in the bag by the sound of his voice. Maggie let out a sigh, then saw more red—a shade darker than the pink lipstick on the rim of the wine glass in her trash. "What happened to rehearsal?"

"Hey, *chichi*, I wanted to see *you*."

"Well, *chichi*, I wanted *you* to go to rehearsal."

"What's your problem? Let me in, already."

"I'm busy."

"Busy how? Let me in. I'll get my ax, go to rehearsal."

"Like they're going to be waiting for you, after all this time? Just go away, Seb. I'm not happy with you today. Not at all."

Then she heard Seb talking to someone downstairs over the intercom. "Can you let me in?" she heard him say. "I forgot my key."

Jesus H. She pushed the buzzer, left the door ajar, went back into the living room.

"Bad time?" John Rae said.

"Maybe," Maggie said.

John Rae stood up. Seb's boots stamped up the stairs.

"What do I have to say to change your mind, Maggie?" John Rae said. "About helping out on the op?"

"Take me along."

"Besides that?"

The front door opened.

"Hey," Seb said, a little breathless, obviously surprised to see that Maggie had company. Male company.

"Seb, this is John Rae."

Seb sauntered into the hallway, eyes narrowing, looking tight around the shoulders. He jammed his hands in the pockets of his beat-up leather jacket.

Maggie saw their eyes meet, a little too long. Two dogs, out on the street, one about to lose it.

"Nice guitar," John Rae said.

"Yeah," Seb said. "What's it doing, leaning up against the wall like that?"

"Not much, by the looks of things."

"It's bad for the neck." Sebastian slurred the *it's* and *bad*.

"Sorry about that," Maggie said, heading over to the window. "That's my fault."

"I've mentioned that before," Seb said. "That it's bad for the neck."

"I guess I didn't hear you." Maggie picked the Les Paul up by the neck, deliberately, strings tinkling in a haphazard thrum. She brought the guitar back, still holding it by the neck. Held it out to Seb. "Here you go, sweetheart."

Seb glared at Maggie, took the guitar, leaned it against the wall by the entryway. The guitar slid a centimeter or two to one side.

John Rae drained his coffee, plonked it on the coffee table. "I better run."

"Where do you know Maggie from?" Seb said to John Rae.

"I'll let Maggie explain that to you."

"I'm not asking her."

John Rae suppressed a smile.

"Through work," Maggie interrupted. "Now lighten up, Seb."

"Oh, the stuff you can't ever talk about?"

"Seb. Enough. You're drunk. Or whatever."

John Rae strolled over to the doorway. Seb blocked his path.

"No, I'm not," Seb said, not budging.

"Thanks for the coffee, Maggie," John Rae said, obviously waiting for Seb to move aside.

"You bet," she said, not taking her eyes off Seb.

Seb's hands were still planted in the pockets of his leather jacket.

"I need to get by," John Rae said.

"What do you think I am?" Seb said.

There was a moment of tense silence. Somewhere out on

Valencia Street, the sounds of a truck backing up were audible by an incessant beeping.

"I don't really know," John Rae said to Seb, not smiling. "And it's really none of my business."

"Damn straight."

"Seb," Maggie said. "Take your damn guitar and get out. We'll talk when you've had your sixth birthday."

Seb said to John Rae, "You take me for some kind of fool, man?"

John Rae's mouth flattened into a line. "I think you might have gotten your chain wrapped around the axle. I worked with Maggie on a project. I stopped by to ask a favor."

"What kind of *favor*?"

"Really?" John Rae let an irritated laugh flutter from his lips. "It's work. And it's confidential."

"You mean it's pure *bullshit*. I know what kind of favor you're after."

John Rae rubbed his face. "If you think she would even give me the time of day, you're crazy. Besides, she's got class. And you've just insulted her about nine ways. Now, how about you move aside and let me out of here before you really do make a fool of yourself?"

Seb stood rooted to the spot, feet apart, in a ready stance. "What is that little outfit you've got on? Seersucker? You going to the Kentucky Derby?"

"Good one." John Rae turned to Maggie. "You OK here?"

"Yeah," she said. "Sorry about all this. I'll talk to you later."

John Rae nudged Seb gently to one side, patting him on the arm.

Seb erupted, shoved John Rae against the wall. "I asked you a question, pal."

John Rae regained his balance, stood back up. "*Pal?*" He straightened his jacket. "I don't think we're quite pals yet. But want some advice? Go home, sleep off your liquid lunch, come back later and apologize. Better still, call first."

They stood there, glaring at each other. John Rae's stare hardened.

Seb stood to one side.

"Right." John Rae stepped around. A few moments later, he was bounding down the stairs.

"Who the fuck was that?" Seb said to Maggie.

"Someone who could have thrown you through that wall." Maggie stormed over to the sofa, hauled the guitar case off the floor behind it. "Here. Take your damn guitar—that you still owe me for, by the way—and get the hell out of *my* apartment."

Seb's tone shifted down. "Maggs—I just want to know what's going on."

"This is what's going on." She threw the case on the floor in front of Seb, where it made more than a little racket. "Take your guitar, go pawn the damn thing and buy some more nose candy, I don't care. But I want you both out of here—*now*."

Seb blinked. "Hey, I'm sorry, *chichi*."

"Take it." She picked the guitar up by the neck. "Or out it goes." She headed to the open window.

"OK!" Seb dashed over, caught up to Maggie, put his hand on her arm. "OK!" He took the guitar, gently, went back, picked up the case, put the guitar away. "I think you might need to calm down."

Maggie folded her arms over her chest. "You're still here."

Seb stood, guitar cased, now in hand. "Where am I supposed to stay?"

"Why not ask the girl with the hot-pink lipstick?"

There was a pause. Seb looked down. "I'll call you?" he said quietly.

"Where's my key?"

"I lost it."

She'd have to get the damn locks changed. "Just go, then."

Seb nodded, turned, left.

When Maggie heard the front door finally slam downstairs, she shut the door to her apartment. Leaned against it. What was the matter with her taste in men? She needed to clear her head.

In the bedroom, she threw off her jeans and sweater and

donned her turquoise split-side wet-look running shorts, pink ASICS, and a cropped sleeveless foil tank top. She tucked a twenty-dollar bill and her apartment key into the shoe wallet woven into the laces of her right shoe. No socks. Didn't need them. The shoes had been through a recent marathon and were broken in just right, which meant they were about to fall apart. The right toe box was taped over with duct tape and the seams were pulling loose. Trail dust blackened the mesh. She remembered running through the Andes as a child, barefoot, and the feeling of the earth on her bare soles. She wished she'd had these when she ran through Quito a few days back, escaping the "accident" at the U.S. embassy.

Clasping her hair back in a ponytail, she tied her lucky Rockabilly red headband and headed down, taking the stairs three at a time.

Out on Valencia, the air was full of Spanish and the honking of traffic, although the telltale signs of gentrification were everywhere: high-end German cars parked next to beat-up jalopies, young hipsters waiting outside a new sushi restaurant that had opened last month, checking their smartphones, while an old Chicano selling oranges in string bags stood out in the middle of traffic. But if she closed her eyes for just a second, it was still the old Mission and she could almost be in Madrid, Buenos Aires, or Lima. She opened her eyes and broke into an easy stride. The savory tang of the *taquería* on the corner assailed her nose as she ran by.

Two hours later, dripping with sweat, Maggie reentered her apartment building on Valencia and jogged lazily upstairs to the third floor. She'd made it to Fort Funston, a former World War II gun emplacement on the cliffs, where hang-gliders hovered over the Pacific Ocean shining off a muted sun. Their freedom above the bluffs propelled Kacha and her cousin Tica to the forefront of Maggie's thoughts, because, unlike those hang-gliders, Tica was the opposite of what they were—free.

Before heading for the shower, she squeezed half a dozen oranges and drank a third of the pulpy juice down, set the glass on the hardwood floor in the hallway, while she got her yoga mat out and did her stretches. Long runs could turn you into a musclebound geek if you weren't careful. First Maggie did the splits, all the way down. Yes, she was still that flexible. She savored the long stretch and let her skeleton crack into it. Then she flipped over onto her back, legs all the way up, one ankle behind her head. Relaxed into that. Then the other, both ankles crossed behind her neck. The Yoganidrasana sleep pose. It felt good to let her entire body just release, as she stared at the Edwardian curlicues on the ceiling.

Drove Seb crazy, too.

Deep breaths and she unwound from her position, back on her feet.

Standing in the hallway now, guzzling more OJ, the 5x7 padded prepaid envelope on the stand stared her in the face. She'd forgotten all about it.

Setting her glass down she picked up the envelope, ripped it open. Peered inside. A blue flash drive. She retrieved it, checked the envelope again. No note. Just the drive.

She took it, along with her juice, to her office, which had an electronic keypad on the fire door that was molded to resemble wood. She typed in a ten-digit key code. The heavy-duty deadbolt gave an electronic whirr and the lock clicked open.

Maggie's office was a seven-by-nine room with dark burgundy walls, a high white ceiling, and hardwood floors. With escalating rents, most San Franciscans would have been ecstatic to share this room with another person who bathed once a week. But Maggie chose to keep her large flat all to herself. Even with rent control, she paid a pretty penny. Her sanity thanked her. And the need for security sanctioned it.

Maggie's 'puter lair was cooking with two machines chugging away under the desk lid mounted to the wall under a window that faced a dismal light well. Wires snaked here and there from a 650-watt power supply plugged into a battery backup. Router lights flashed blue and green. The one wall was adorned with handbills from her travels. Bullfights, which she wasn't crazy about. Flamenco performances, which she was.

Her cave. Sanctuary. Some might question her need for so

much computational power right where she slept, but if Hillary could get away with it, why not her?

There was a photo in a silver frame on her work surface: a black and white of Seb caressing his Les Paul—*that* Les Paul—looking like a lion onstage at El Rio, ripping out a solo. Maggie considered tossing it in the trash, but settled for turning it face down and shoving it back under the window next to a JavaScript manual. She pulled a wireless keyboard onto her lap, dialed into her server. Once she got past the two-stage authentication, she plugged the flash drive into a USB port in a standalone, non-networked machine. Her sanitizer box, used to shake out any suspicious files. She used two different virus checkers on the file before she examined the contents.

A single file: *dita.mpeg*. A movie. She opened the file with a movie viewer.

It began with outdoor footage in a jungle clearing. Parrots squawked in the distance as a group of men in hardhats stood around a white mechanical drill about ten feet tall. It was in motion, pumping up and down into the earth. The shakiness of the video and the distance of the group suggested that the scene was being filmed covertly.

A crude caption across the bottom of the video read: "Yasuni site 22A" and listed a date of approximately one month ago.

The engineers were primarily Anglo, with the red Commerce Oil globe emblems visible on their hardhats. The drill stopped and one man with a substantial paunch removed a three-foot long cylinder from the drill. The video cut to an engineer in blue plastic gloves laying the same metal tube on a field worktable. He opened the tube lengthwise to reveal a column of moist dirt a few inches thick.

"Let's hope this one finally gets it." A middle-aged man in a hard hat came into view, bending down to smell the soil sample. He stood back up, going out of view. "Petroleum city," he said. "Don't even bother testing it."

"That bad, huh?" an off-camera voice said.

"Let me put it this way—don't light a match."

A few men laughed.

"We'll have to move further on out to find a decent sample."

"Guys—there is no *further on out*. This is as far as we can go. This was supposed to have been cleaned up."

"Good luck with that," another voice said, mimicking SpongeBob.

More laughter.

"Now what?"

Another voice spoke. "We've been here for three days," the man who had been in the video said. "We're out of time. We need to have that cleanup verification."

"That's why you have us contractors." The video swerved to another man, in safety glasses and bushy white mustache, wearing a Commerce Oil hard hat. He grinned as he held up a ballpoint pen and clicked it. "You always have us to blame."

"No big. By then you'll be working on the Florim offshore well in Brazil. Making a grand a day."

"Don't forget expenses," Ballpoint said. "And hazard pay. I might get a blister on my thumb from signing papers."

Several men laughed.

A woman's voice spoke. "So you're just going to sign the verification that this site has been cleaned up anyway?" She was American, with an east coast accent, and she sounded young. Judging by the somewhat muffled sound, she was the one taking the secret video. Probably had a small digital camera with her, or even just a cell phone. The man with the mustache lost his smile and shook his head, as if she might be crazy. "Where the hell did we get *her* from? Of course we're going to sign the clean-up verification." He stormed out of camera shot.

The video turned to black.

Forging of oil clean-up verification by Commerce Oil, Maggie thought. Nothing new there. But this was actual video, unlike the note she'd received last year that had started Maggie off on the oil-worker-kickback investigation that led to the failed Quito op. And this had been shot in the actual Yasuni, a wilderness preserve where drilling wasn't to have begun yet.

She wondered if the woman speaking was the one who had sent her the two notes last year. The handwriting on the envelopes was the same. Maggie drank some orange juice as the video broke to footage of a group of natives in dense jungle. An older woman held up a glass of drinking water that was brown in color, like thin tea. She explained that though tainted with oil, it was the only water they had to drink. "We have no choice," she said in Quechua. A beleaguered man with heavy bags under his eyes said all of his livestock had perished. Another young man said, in an empty voice, that his three daughters had died of cancer. The same young American woman asked them, in good Spanish: "So, even though Commerce Oil was fined over nine billion dollars in 1993 and were ordered to clean up this site then, nothing has been done?"

They all nodded silently.

Maggie put down her unfinished orange juice. It no longer tasted quite right.

The video broke again and Maggie started to see and hear Indians demonstrating in a section of jungle that had been clear-cut. Bright red earth exposed a tract of land between two thick sections of trees. A dirt road of some sort. A hundred or more natives waved signs to stop the proposed drilling in the Yasuni. They were shouting in Spanish and Quechua, some shaking their fists. Their dress ranged from pure jungle—simple skirts or speedos—to jeans, T-shirts, and baseball caps. The camera pulled back to show the demonstrators blocking the path of a huge bright-yellow earthmoving machine with the word CATERPILLER emblazoned on its side. The video moved farther back still. More than a dozen soldiers waited with rifles, ready to enforce the progression of the giant bulldozer. It was clearly a standoff. Passions ran high.

The bulldozer roared. A blast of black smoke erupted from its upright stack. The machine clanked forward a few feet.

One young woman emerged from the crowd, throwing down her sign. She rushed up to the bulldozer and stood in front of its giant blade. The bulldozer ground to a halt. The girl was barefoot, wearing a light, billowy, native skirt and a colorful sleeveless top common in the hot Amazon. She had long glossy black hair and light skin. Maggie could make out the zigzag tribal tattoos under her eyes. She was about sixteen. A soldier in a cap, some kind of non-commissioned officer, came forward, waving a pistol, ordering the girl to move aside. She flinched at first, but stood her ground, arms straight by her side, mouth firm.

"Move or you will be arrested!" the sergeant bellowed.

The shouting of the crowd grew to the point where the camera microphone distorted, breaking up. Some called out the girl's name, urging her to stay strong. Maggie's heart pounded as she watched signs wave violently to and fro. Several other natives surged forward to join the young woman, standing alongside her now.

"Move!" the sergeant screamed, walking up and down the line of protesters. "Now!"

More natives joined the row of people, making it a double line.

The sergeant roared out orders. The soldiers readied weapons.

More protesters moved forward to join the line.

It was a complete impasse. The more the sergeant shouted, the more people joined the line. He became almost hysterical with anger, charging up and down the line of demonstrators. At one point, he turned, motioned for the soldiers to come forward. While the sergeant's back was turned, a big man with a beard knocked his cap off with a swipe of his hand, to much cheering from the protesters.

The sergeant swung back around, raised his pistol calmly, shot the bearded man in the forehead.

The big man dropped like a puppet whose master had tired of holding his strings. Most of the crowd turned and ran, screaming.

Only the young girl remained, standing there, flexing her fists, eyes clenched shut, visibly shaking. The dead man lay not five feet away from her.

The sergeant holstered his pistol, composed now, walked up to the girl. He placed his hands on his hips. "Move aside," he said.

The girl remained, trembling like a sick person.

More than a third of the demonstrators had dispersed. The rest had stopped shouting.

The sergeant turned to the soldiers. "Arrest her. And six more. Women. All ages. Quickly now."

Another third of the protesters ran off at this point.

The soldiers handcuffed the girl and selected others from the dwindling crowd. They led them aside.

The road was now clear, save for the body of the big man.

The sergeant waved the bulldozer forward as if he were directing traffic.

The machine blasted into action, smoke blowing out of its stack, and clanked forward, the dead man grinding under a tread, twisting, his head turning, then disappearing completely under the metal track with a pop.

The video went black.

Three minutes and thirty-nine seconds.

Maggie's heart punched in her chest.

The girl's name they had called out: Tica. Kacha's cousin.

Death in the Amazon, Maggie thought – *brought to you by Commerce Oil.*

For a moment, she wondered why the mysterious whistleblower didn't simply post this damning evidence on YouTube, where a million eyes and ears could hopefully see and hear. But then she realized: The woman would reveal herself. She was obviously a Commerce Oil employee. She would be easy to identify should Commerce get hold of this video.

So she was trusting Maggie. Just as she'd had trusted her with the oil worker taking kickbacks last year. Maggie had been selected to see this video.

That made her even more responsible to be the one to take care of this.

-10-

After the images had settled, Maggie logged onto Iggy, the private messaging network she and a few choice cyber-contacts shared for confidential communication. She'd written Iggy with another student as part of her master's thesis and it had proved secure enough that she was still using it herself—not that anything was one hundred percent safe. But Iggy was below the radar, because few people knew about it, and she knew every line of code, knew there were no compromises or Easter eggs. She took a slug of pulpy OJ while the program fired up, a black rose spinning as a chat widow opened.

Right now she needed to follow up on Kacha's cousin: Tica.

She typed a message to her old friend and co-conspirator: *@Enzo99 hola - ayt?*

No response. Maybe he wasn't online. It was close to midnight in Paris. She drank the last of her juice and flipped on the old desk radio, set to KRZZ, the local Latin station. A syrupy *bachata* came on, sad-sweet music with a couple lamenting their failed love in island Spanish.

At the bottom of the chat window, a text finally appeared.
enzo99 is typing . . .
hola, yes, I'm here, and how r things in the sister city?
a little grimier than Paris I bet
mebbe . . . + the big bad guitar player?
don't ask
lol - that bad?
yep – I have a huge favor to ask
i thot s much

is it that obvious?

Well, i like a womn who nos what she wants – so what can I do 4 u?

looking for a young woman named Tica...

Maggie went on to fill Enzo in with what little she knew.

How much time do you think you need? she typed

well, i have smthing for u rite now

ur 2 gud

this news isn't 2 gud tho' for your friend south of the border

Maggie took a breath and typed. *K, enzo, lay it on me dude*

10.147.121.193

An IP address behind a firewall somewhere.

merci beaucoup, she typed, *next time I'm in paree, dinner and drinks are on me.*

promises, promises

no I mean it...

It took one and a half songs for Maggie to hack the firewall to the server at the IP address Enzo had given her. She fired up her TOR browser, anonymous as it got for web surfing. And was presented with a web page in Spanish and an *ec* domain: Ecuador.

Carcel de Mujeres. A women's prison in Quito. She scanned the clickable links.

lista de presos. Prisoner List.

Further authentication was required. Monchy and Alexandria sang about their love flying away by the time Maggie confirmed that SQL injection was not blocked at *Carcel de Mujeres.*

Amateurs. So trusting. Yet they lock people up.

She built an https URL in the command line, added a default SQL admin userid and password, hit *enter*, and was taken directly to a "secure" page of confidential prisoners. She sorted them by date.

The first was a middle-aged Afro-Brazilian woman with a face like a bag of rocks. Certainly not Kacha's cousin.

The second was a thirty-something light-skinned Mestiza

with cropped hair and thick glasses. Her occupation was listed as teacher. Too old.

The next was a pretty soft-skinned Indian teenage girl. Long silky black hair. Eyes intense, a deer frozen in the headlights of incarceration. Her real name wasn't listed, but it didn't matter. She had the zigzag tattoos on her cheeks the girl in the video had. She was the same girl. She was simply given the name of Yasuni1.

Tica Tuanama.

Maggie scrolled down. Mixed in amongst the hard faces were prisoners Yasuni2 through Yasuni7. All Indian women, some old, some young, many with Kichwa tattoos on their faces. Maggie bet all the money she had in the bank and more that they were the other six women arrested with Tica.

She scrolled back up to Yasuni1.

Next to her id was a blue asterisk, which Maggie clicked.

Emergencia médica. It was dated four days ago, a day before Kacha helped Maggie escape Quito.

She sat back while Bianca Alejandra Feliz sang about needing to turn over a new leaf in her life. Her heart was thumping in her ears. She called John Rae.

"Imagine my surprise." It was clear he wasn't unhappy at all to hear from her.

"Can I change my mind about dinner?"

"It's a woman's prerogative."

"Like sushi?"

"See, that's good," he said. "Some people would assume a Texan would eat steak. But you're moving away from that stereotype."

"Does that mean you like sushi?"

"Uncooked fish? Are you serious?"

"Pick me up at eight," she said. "I know a place where the meat is bloody."

"I hope you're talking about the steak," he said and clicked off.

Maggie shook off the image of the Caterpillar rolling over the dead man, and a poor Yasuni Indian girl in a prison and her "medical emergency," then navigated her browser to Balou.com, where she created a free email address: JenniferLopezFan86.

She typed in the email address Kacha had given her in Quito. In the subject line, she wrote: Jennifer Lopez-*¡Qué Bárbara!*

Then she searched the net for Jennifer Lopez fan sites and quickly cut and paste a blurb promoting the artist into a makeshift email newsletter. It looked like junk mail, spam. Kacha would respond, per their agreement, giving her the coded contact info they'd agreed upon in Quito. Maggie sent the email. And checked her watch.

In the bathroom, she finally stepped out of her sweaty running gear and took a shower. A Long. Hot. Shower. Afterwards, she climbed into a fluffy white robe and dried her hair with a towel. Her limbs were warm and relaxed from the long run. She put on some Segovia and sat in the leather chair she and Seb had violated scant hours before and dug out an Acorn report she was supposed to be working on. Get that BS out of the way.

She studied the numbers until fresh fog streaked by the bay window and the incessant traffic on Valencia grew more incessant with frenetic San Francisco rush hour.

Then a *ping* from down the hall pulled her out of the report, although it didn't take much to make her put Acorn down. An alert from her 'puter lair. A second ding followed the first. She set her green-and-white printout on the floor and padded down the hall.

Two emails from KachaKachaEc re: Jennifer Lopez-*¡Qué Bárbara!*

Take me off this email list, spammer! Followed by a date and time to call. Maggie deducted an hour from the time, and a day from the date, per their agreement, so that anyone who might be watching would see a time well past the actual.

The second *take me off this email list* email had a phone number to call. Maggie subtracted 99 from that, another simple code she had told Kacha to use, for the added security that was in it.

Kacha wanted Maggie to call her late tonight. In a few hours, as a matter of fact. Kacha was obviously anxious for any news of Tica.

Hang in there, Kacha, Maggie said to herself.

She dressed in slim faded Cavalli jeans with a button fly, espadrilles, and a loose bottle-green sweater, pulled her hair back in a tail, and slipped on big gold hoop earrings and sunglasses to hide the puffiness around her eyes, threw on her favorite leather rock-n-roll jacket, and headed out.

Down Valencia into a local Mexican *checks cashed/phone calls made/letters written* office teeming with illegals calling home. She waited until the rush died down and approached an old codger filling a plastic chair behind the counter. She got out her credit card, sent $2,500 of her own money Western Union to the main office in Quito, care of Kacha. Then she purchased a throwaway phone that had been used by more than a few dishwashers and day laborers to call their respective homes and loaded it up with fifty dollars. She wiped off the grime with a Wet One from the packet she carried and slipped the phone in the pocket of her oversized leather jacket.

She had to keep going for a few more hours. On Mission she gulped down a *café cubano*, sweet and thick, at a stand-up coffee place, and thought about dinner with John Rae and his handler. She needed a new dress to replace the one she'd given Kacha. Something to guarantee an edge.

She walked the Mission, past the illegals trudging to their jobs in the restaurants and sweat shops, past the young *bohos* lugging laptop bags and mongo cups of coffee, chatting at sixty miles an hour on cell phones. The rapid changes taking over her neighborhood. She wound up at the alley-like Capp Street where she climbed the few steps to a door with bars galore and more than a few locks on it, with its sign: Entrance by Invitation Only. She rang a bell.

A buzzer over the door let her enter.

A security guard in need of a shave with droopy eyes and arms crossed leaned against the far wall. He had a wicked-looking magnum in a holster halfway down his thigh.

"Hey, Gus."

Gus nodded at Maggie's arrival. "Dimitri's in back."

She walked through rooms filled with rolling racks of garments hanging in plastic bags. Designer brands at a mere fraction of the price. Just don't ask for a receipt. Or tell anyone where you got those Cavalli Jeans that listed for close to a grand. Or that Alexander Wang Maggie was already eyeing.

~~~

At eight o'clock exactly the doorbell rang. Maggie examined herself in the hall mirror, her new little black dress almost as gorgeous as she was. She pressed her lips together to get the gloss spread just right.

¡Que wena!

She threw the red mid-length leather coat over her arm, grabbed her bag, and headed out. Clacking down the steps, she got to the front door soon enough.

And when John Rae, wearing a slim-fitting charcoal jacket and bolo tie, saw Maggie in the black cocktail dress, his eyes actually popped. "Wow, Maggie. You clean up pretty good."

"Why, thank you, sir." She put her arm out for him to take as they stepped down the stairs.

If John Rae was going to ask for her help, she was going to get the same in return.

And Tica and her compadres would stand a chance of being freed.

-11-

"Damn!" John Rae said, setting his oversized ebony-handled steak knife on his plate, parallel to the fork. The tines of the fork were pointed downward in the center of the plate. All that was left of his steak was a well-trimmed bone in the shape of a T. He wiped his mouth with a white cloth napkin and sat back in his chair.

"Where did you grow up?" Maggie asked, swirling a glass of Malbec.

John Rae gave her a wry, crinkled smile. The atmosphere in Lucinda's, an Argentine steakhouse on Mission, wasn't exactly quiet, but with the soft lighting and minor chords ringing gently from a piano in the corner, unobtrusive. Meaning that you didn't have to shout, like so many San Francisco restaurants anymore.

"Geneva," he said. "If you can believe it."

"I can," Maggie said, leaning forward on her elbows. "You may sound like a Texan, but you eat like a European. Why Switzerland?"

"Boarding school. My old man was too busy making money and my mother too busy spending it for either of them to waste much time on their kids." John Rae picked up a water glass, took a drink. "You don't miss much."

"I miss enough," she said, gazing around the full dining room. For all intents and purposes, she and John Rae looked like any other couple out on a date. "Where is this mysterious handler of yours anyway?" she asked. "This master behind the operation that's so damn secret I'm not even allowed to know what it is? He's over an hour late."

John Rae checked an old-school wristwatch on a black crocodile band. "He'll be here."

Their eyes met. Behind his carefully crafted devil-may-care attitude, with his longish hair swept back and designer stubble decorating his fine chin, John Rae was more intelligent than the law allowed, although he did his best to hide it.

"Whatever your decision, Maggie, you can't tell anyone. Not even Ed—that boss of yours that you trust so much."

"I trust Ed implicitly. But that doesn't mean I'm going to jeopardize everything I've worked for by telling him I'm going against a direct order. I'd like to stay out of jail if at all possible."

The busboy stopped by, cleared the table. Then the maître d', a young Latina in black pants and a crisp white cotton blouse, came over. "Your other guest has arrived," she said to John Rae.

"Well, it's about time . . ." Maggie turned in her seat and gave an involuntary gasp when she saw a dour-looking man in his mid-sixties, gray hair combed tightly back from a long aristocratic forehead. His slender worn face had dark bags under the eyes as if he'd been up for days, if not years. He wore a tweed jacket with leather patches on the elbows, blue oxford shirt with a button-down collar, corduroy slacks. He carried an ancient brown-leather satchel. He looked like a college professor who had just lost tenure and was taking it out on the bottle. His name and face were indelibly etched in Maggie's brain, although she hadn't seen him in person since she was a child. Back then, he reminded her of Nosferatu. She turned to John Rae with an open-mouthed look of disbelief.

"Please ask him to join us," John Rae said to the maître d'. She left.

"Sinclair Michaels is heading up this operation?"

John Rae gave a single nod.

"Why in the *hell* didn't you tell me?"

"I couldn't."

"You mean you knew I'd have turned you down flat if you had."

"Standard protocol. You'll learn more about that if you come over to the dark side. Which I hope you decide to do."

"I'm aware of protocol, John Rae. But Sinclair Michaels and I have a rocky past, to say the least. Not to mention that the Agency let him go."

"Retired."

"Is that what they call it now?"

"OK, so he was asked to leave. True enough. But Sinclair's got a genuine knack for getting things done south of the equator. He knows people, and he knows his way around. He was head of Ecuador Station. Back in the eighties . . ."

"I know all about it. My father reported to him." Before Sinclair Michaels fired him.

"Then I guess I'm just stating the obvious."

~~~

"It's been a few years, Maggie," Sinclair Michaels said.

He was sitting in the chair next to John Rae, across the table from Maggie. In his knobby hand he twisted a glass of amber liquor on the white tablecloth. He'd sunk half the moment it arrived. His drinking was the main reason he was no longer directly employed by the Agency. But his skill as a field op kept him on the contractor payroll and he was brought in from time to time, especially for clandestine ops with which the agency would rather not be associated.

"More than a few years," Maggie said coldly. "Try twenty-four. You had just sent my father back to the U.S. Released him from his assignment in Quito. One that he had worked so hard for. Because you didn't think it was appropriate for a State Department employee to 'shack up with an Indian whore'. I believe that was how you referred to my mother."

Sinclair Michaels pursed his lips, rotating his glass on the tablecloth. "I don't think those were the exact words I used."

"Well, that's *exactly* how they sounded when I listened to you berate my father in the next room of my mother's hut."

Sinclair looked up. "And you were what, Maggie—all of five years old at the time? How much can you possibly remember?"

Maggie returned a hard stare. "I remember just fine. I haven't been pickling my brains all my life. My mother and I were destitute after you sent my father back to the U.S. with his tail between his legs." Worse, her poor *mami* was heartbroken. And Maggie? Maggie had just been learning to love the gringo who came and went, but mostly went, leaving *Mami* and her alone while he attended to important worldly matters she didn't understand. All she knew was that he was always gone. And then he was gone for good.

John Rae stood up. "I'll go for a stroll around the block while you two clear things up."

"No, John Rae," Maggie said, putting her hand on John Rae's wrist. "You need to know exactly who's running your little renegade op."

John Rae glanced at Maggie, then over at Sinclair Michaels. "All right," he said quietly. He sat back down.

Sinclair Michaels cleared his throat before he spoke to Maggie. "When I was Ecuador Station Chief, we had strict guidelines about employees cohabiting with locals. Any relationship—from simple friendships on up—was thoroughly vetted. I don't need to tell you that South America Region was, and continues to be, a political hotbed. Under the circumstances at the time, with the Shining Path insurgency farther south, there was too much risk with your father practically living in an Indian community where terrorists came and went with ease and sympathies ran high. Simply too much risk."

"Despite the fact that he could have been gathering information on those activities."

"He wasn't tasked to do that."

"Do I have to tell you, the *expert*, that the Shining Path were Peru—not Ecuador?"

"The border between the two countries has always been porous. Terrorists came and went freely. Still do. I asked your father to show more restraint. He ignored me. In the end, I had no choice but to send him back home."

"My mother died a year and a half later. Malaria. We were

living in the slums of Guayaquil."

Sinclair Michaels drained his drink, waved his glass brusquely at the waiter.

"Another one of these," he said when the man arrived. "A double."

"Ah, yes," Maggie said. "The reason they gave you your walking papers."

"I've been keeping tabs on you as well, Maggie. You're an intelligent young woman. Brilliant, in fact. Undergrad from Stanford: mathematics. Master's degrees in finance and computer science, UC Berkeley. Star player in the newly minted Accounting Forensics team. But emotionally? Well, I would have expected a little more cool-headedness from someone with your analytical skills, someone who might want to make a name for herself." The fresh drink arrived. He picked it up the moment it was set down in front of him and took a controlled sip. "I sent your father home because he broke some basic rules. It was nothing personal."

Maggie had always suspected otherwise. When she was a little girl, it was simple bitter hatred directed at a man who shouted at her father in a drunken tirade, as if he were a child who messed his pants. As Maggie grew older and learned more about Sinclair Michaels, she saw the situation as one of a worried man looking over his shoulder, even envious of a potential rival, invoking a rule many Americans stationed in Latin America openly violated, as a reason to simply get her father out of the way.

But what bit deeper was the fact that her father went back home to the States with his head down, without putting up a fight. She remembered him leaving that day, mumbling his goodbyes, making empty promises to return. While her mother shed silent tears. So Maggie was really angry at two men: Sinclair Michaels *and* her father, an ambitious gringo who left an Indian woman and some half-breed child as if they were an embarrassment.

Anger had a way of spreading like a cancer. And which cancer had grown the bigger of the two? It wasn't hard to figure. She hadn't spoken to her father since her graduation. It didn't matter that he'd brought her back to the U.S. after *Mami* passed, schooled her well, gave her all the advantages an American had. That was his guilt at work.

But the other man she detested was sitting across from her, expecting her to help out on a clandestine project that could easily cost Maggie her career. The man who had helped shorten her mother's life.

"I was hoping you were as mature as your qualifications make you out to be," Sinclair Michaels said, drinking.

"Maybe you're wrong about a lot of things. Maybe the drinking has finally marinated that brain of yours. Maybe it was affecting it back when you let my father go—because you felt threatened and knew you were losing your edge as Station Chief."

Sinclair Michaels' face tightened. He polished his drink off in one gulp, set his glass down as if it was a hot pistol. "This is an opportunity for you to serve your country," he said through his teeth. "Not wallow in self-pity over some half-imagined childhood grudge." He turned to John Rae. "I hope we're not wasting our time here with your little prima donna, John Rae. She's as hot-headed as her mother was."

Sinclair Michaels turned back to face Maggie just as she stood up, pushing her chair back with a screech, drawing attention from the other diners. She grabbed a full glass of water and jerked the contents into Sinclair Michaels' face. The splash was audible around the dining room that broke out in murmurs before it fell into stony silence. The piano player stopped playing.

Sinclair Michaels looked as if he'd just emerged from a dive in a pool fully clothed. Water ran off his face and hair onto the tablecloth. He picked up a cloth napkin and wiped his face.

"When someone calls your mother a whore," Maggie said calmly, "you don't ever forget it. No matter how old you are. Consider yourself lucky. I should have used that steak knife on you."

Sinclair Michaels continued to mop his face, glaring at

Maggie. Outside on Mission a car horn blared.

The maître' d approached the table and stood back a good few feet, hands folded defensively in front of her. "Is everything OK here, folks?"

"Just fine," Maggie said, grabbing her red-leather coat. "Just taking care of something I should have done a long time ago." She flung the coat over her shoulder. "Good luck to you, John Rae," she said. "You're going to need it." She turned to go, wondering if she could still book a seat for tomorrow's flight to Quito. She could resume her search for Tica there, somehow.

Hushed whispers of conversation broke the silence as she headed for the door.

"Cell two-thirteen," she heard Sinclair Michaels say quietly behind her. "High Security Wing E."

Maggie stopped, her back still to the table.

"*Carcel de Mujeres*," he continued.

Maggie turned around, squinted at Sinclair Michaels. John Rae was blinking in apparent mystification.

"The women's prison on the outskirts of Quito," Sinclair Michaels said.

"I know where it is," Maggie said.

"But you didn't know the exact cell, did you? Or Tica's status."

"The question is: How do you know about her?"

Sinclair Michaels picked up his empty glass, held it out for the maître d. "What are you standing there for? Make yourself useful."

The woman took the glass and left, blushing. Maggie walked back to the table, stood behind her chair. In the background, the pianist began playing again, the chorus to "On Broadway."

"You think I didn't read your debriefing report?" Sinclair said, looking up at Maggie. "That girl in the slums of Quito took one hell of a chance when she helped you out of that devilish situation. You wanted the department to do something about her cousin, Tica. And her six accomplices—the Yasuni

Seven. The department, typically, gave you the cold shoulder." He shook his head. "But I can make that kind of thing happen. I've got thirty years' worth of contacts down there." He raised one eyebrow.

Maggie sat back down, dropped her voice.

"Tica's still alive."

"For the time being." Sinclair Michaels acted as if nothing had happened, even though his shirt and jacket were drenched down the front.

"You can get Tica out? And the rest of the Yasuni Seven?"

"Oil Minister Beltran certainly can. One phone call is all it would take."

"Beltran," she said. "The master of ceremonies at that shootout of a party? The one who appreciates women? Especially their asses? The one who tried to rip us off? You mean *that* Beltran?"

Sinclair Michaels gave a cynical smile. "Yes, Maggie. *That* Beltran."

"I'm not getting it."

"Beltran belongs to *us*."

So Beltran was another louse owned by the U.S. government. Bought and paid for. Typical that a shady old op like Sinclair Michaels would be his handler. His drink arrived. He didn't touch it for the time being.

"You can guarantee that Beltran gets Tica out?" she said. "And the rest of the Yasuni Seven?"

"If you help us."

Maggie gazed over at John Rae. "If Sinclair says it's going to happen, Maggie, it's going to happen."

"Yes, I believe that." She turned back to Sinclair Michaels. "But, just for grins, tell me why he should, in this case."

"Best fill her in, John Rae," Sinclair Michaels said.

Maggie turned to John Rae.

"Oil Minister Armand Beltran has been kidnapped," he said.

"Couldn't have happened to a nicer guy. Who did it? I'd like to send them a nice floral arrangement."

"Some terrorist group, calls itself Cosecha Severa. Right on the road not far from his palatial residence—where you jumped out of the window into the Olympic-sized swimming pool."

"And you're going to get him back."

Sinclair twirled his untouched drink. "In the wrong hands, Beltran knows too much. And he's in the wrong hands."

"And you need me to help you with the financial stuff again. A payoff. Only this time, it's to free him from terrorists."

Sinclair took a sip, toasted Maggie. "You do pick it up quickly, Maggie. John Rae, why isn't she one of us yet?"

"I'm working on it, Sincs."

"Now *I* need a drink," Maggie said, signaling for the waiter.

Fresh drinks eased the tension.

Maggie took a sip of Malbec and set her glass down and smoothed out the tablecloth in front of her. She looked around the room, where people were still staring at her. Meeting their gazes, they turned away.

"Cosecha Severa," Maggie said. "The name translates to: 'Grim Harvest.' Sounds a little . . ."

"Grim?" John Rae smiled. "Yeah, you could say that. They shot his driver in cold blood, left his body on the highway. Middle of the day."

Sinclair Michaels swirled his Scotch. "Grim Harvest have quite a reputation for doing environmental damage in the name of saving the environment. Blowing up oil pipelines in Colombia, that sort of thing. Tell me there's not some irony there."

"The end justifies the means," Maggie said. But she liked the irony of Beltran having to be paid off, not to line his pockets, but to save his miserable life, better.

"Grim Harvest have moved their operation from Colombia into the Ecuador rainforest," John Rae said. "Where your Tica is from. One of the last pieces of unspoiled Amazon the Chinese bought the oil rights to. Grim Harvest is holed up in the jungle somewhere. Headed up by some character who calls himself Comrade Cain. He's no joke. Ex-Shining Path. They've got Beltran and are ransoming him off or they'll send him back one body part at a time. Starting with a foot, ending with a head." John Rae took a drink of his sparkling water.

"Like I said, 'couldn't happen to a nicer guy.'"

"Beltran's a bum, Maggie," John Rae said. "But he's our bum. That's why I'm going down there to rescue him. And that's why I need your help again. On the money end."

"How much do Grim Harvest want?" Maggie asked.

"Two million," John Rae said. "Sound familiar?"

Maggie almost smiled. The irony was getting even better. "They must have heard there was two mil on the table—from Beltran. The money he didn't get from us when he tried to screw us."

"It's the way diplomacy works," Sinclair Michaels said. "Washington—and Commerce Oil—want Beltran out and back in office in Quito." He sipped. "ASAP."

"Where he can pave the way for oil exploration," she said. "But it means he'll do us favors."

"Exactly."

"It's nuts, Maggie," John Rae said. "But we have more say about what goes on down there with Beltran in charge. And we're playing with the house's money, anyway—the money you saved from Beltran. And Beltran can help you out. With Tica."

"When the op is completed and Beltran is returned," Sinclair Michaels said.

"And you're sure he's on board with getting her out of prison?"

Sinclair Michaels took a drink and nodded. "Beltran is going to be grateful. Grateful enough to place a phone call and have your poster princess of the Yasuni released. I've known Beltran for decades. From back when he was an officer in the military and I was Ecuador Station Chief. I groomed him and the Agency helped make him what he is. Although I haven't been able to speak to him specifically about this—because he's being held prisoner—I have no doubts, Maggie. No doubts whatsoever. We're engineering his release and he will do what we say."

Maggie took a deep breath through her nose.

"I'm in," she said.

"Excellent," Sinclair Michaels said. John Rae beamed.

"Under one condition," she added.

John Rae's face dropped. As did Sinclair's.

"That I'm going down there with you," Maggie said.

Sinclair and John Rae traded glances. Sinclair shook his head. "Out of the question."

Maggie said: "These money transfers look simple from a distance, but they're a can of worms. Banking hassles, authorizations, network problems. You need me there. Besides, I'm not leaving there until I see Tica walk out of that prison with my own eyes."

There was a pause while the pianist played the intro to "Bridge over Troubled Waters."

"I think she means it, Sincs," John Rae said.

"I think she does, too," Sinclair said. "But she's right. Banking in that part of the world is a dark art. And Maggie's our witch."

"I prefer the term *sorceress*," she said.

"You better tell her the bad part," John Rae said to Sinclair.

"Which is?" Maggie said.

Sinclair Michaels leveled his gaze at Maggie. "You leave for Colombia in the morning."

-12-

"Colombia?"

John Rae explained, "We meet a few of Comrade Cain's playmates in Bogotá, make the trade for Beltran, we're done. We hustle Beltran back to Ecuador, right next door, then we take care of Tica." John Rae turned, eyed Sinclair Michaels. "Back before the weekend."

"You'll do it in your sleep, John Rae." Sinclair Michaels reached down by his chair, came back with his satchel, set it on his lap. He unbuckled the strap, opened it, pulled a manila envelope, handed it to Maggie.

"Everything you need to set up the money transfers. Access codes, web addresses, all that mumbo jumbo. You'll have to get it all down tonight. You won't be able to bring these docs with you."

Maggie took the envelope. "Haven't you people heard of zip drives?"

"Leaves too much of a trail."

She didn't agree, but it didn't matter. "And the ransom money? The two million?"

"Sun Bank of Jersey."

A nebulous offshore bank off the southern coast of England. "OK," she said. "I'll start setting things up as soon as I get home. I can hopefully work on the way down on the flight as well."

"A car will pick you up at seven a.m. tomorrow," John Rae said. "You'll be given a passport, money, and further instructions. Get your things in order, Maggie. Most of all your trusty laptop. Otherwise pack light. Basically what you wear on your back. We'll be a couple of days. No more. Anything we need can be bought en route. Keep your receipts." He grinned.

"You make it sound like a business trip," she said.

"Not even," John Rae said. "It's a . . ."

"Milk run?" she said with a smile. "I think that's what you called the Quito op."

John Rae returned a smirk. "We're going to get more cooperation from Beltran on this one."

"Because he'd like to keep his head." Maggie stood, checked the time on her cell phone. She needed to call Kacha, per their email thread. "I'll be ready by seven in the morning."

"See you on the flight to Colombia," John Rae said.

"It's a pleasure to work with you, Maggie," Sinclair Michaels said with apparent satisfaction—and relief. "Your father, when he hears of this—and he will—will be very proud of you. I'm sure that means something."

She couldn't deny that. But the likely outcome of this op left her with mixed feelings. With Beltran free, the company that had laid waste to the Amazon for decades, leaving oil-saturated muck where once there was fresh water, expanses of lifeless swamp where once there was a rich forest teeming with life, pushed the indigenous tribes out of their homeland, endangered their lives, would continue business as usual. That wasn't good. But the mysterious Commerce One employee, the woman with the east coast accent—Maggie couldn't leave her by the wayside, not after the risk she'd taken to expose a company—an *American* company—perfectly willing to destroy one of the planet's lungs by falsifying reports, and bending the local authorities to kill people who stood in its way. People like Tica.

There was Maggie's promise to Kacha, to get Tica out of prison.

People like Tica were the ones in the front lines, fighting for change.

Maggie saw the sly look in John Rae's eyes as she got up to leave. He winked and she knew he was happy to have her along—and happy for her. She'd gotten what she was after: a guarantee to free Tica. Sure, her anger at Michaels was genuine, but getting what she wanted from the man made it that much sweeter.

But seeing the look before the wink, she couldn't help but wonder if John Rae had something up his sleeve.

~~~

At the corner of Mission and 24th, at the entrance to the BART station, Maggie parked herself in the corner next to a homeless man curled up in a sleeping bag grimy from outdoor life in the city. With all the people coming and going, a blanket of white noise covered her and she dialed the number in Quito Kacha had emailed her.

The phone was answered on the first ring. "*Dígame.*" It was Kacha. She sounded breathless, a little nervous. More than a little.

"*Hola,*" Maggie said, switching to Quechua, her native tongue—and Kacha's. "It's me—your long lost cousin. Are you well?"

"So-so."

Not good. "That's what I thought."

"It's safe to talk?"

"Yes. But no names."

"OK," Kacha said as the roar of a large vehicle thundered in the background on her side of the call. She was outdoors as well.

"Have you heard from your other cousin?" Maggie said.

"No. Do you know anything yet?"

"I do, but it's best not to tell you."

"She's in prison?"

"It seems that way. But she's alive."

"Which one?"

"If I tell you, and you try to do something about it, it will mess up my plans."

"That's your good news?" Kacha said, a little angry. "Now I just *know* I have to do something to help her."

"Sit tight," Maggie said. "Please." She didn't want Kacha getting her hopes up.

"No," Kacha said bitterly. "I'm going to check all the prisons. I don't care what happens. She's my cousin. You sit there in your safe country, keep your secrets to yourself. I helped you!"

"Listen," Maggie said. "I told you I'm going to straighten this out. And that's exactly what I'm doing."

There was a pause while a car honked somewhere in Quito. "How?" Kacha said, desperation creeping into her voice. "*How?*"

"Give me twenty-four hours," Maggie said. By then she would be in South America. "I'll call you. Is it safe to call you there—at the number you're at now?"

"Yes, it's on the Plaza . . ."

"Ah-ah-ah!" Maggie said, shutting her up, although anyone who traced the number could find out—eventually. "Be there tomorrow, this time. Does that work?"

"Yes."

"If you don't hear from me tomorrow, be there in forty-eight hours. If not forty-eight, then seventy-two. But I *will* call you at some point. Do you understand?"

There was a pause. "Are you coming here?"

"I can't say. Got it now?"

Now there was a long pause. "Yes."

"In the meantime, if you go down to the Western Union on Mariscal Sucre tomorrow, there'll be a letter waiting for you from your *norteamericana* auntie Ofelia Ruiz. Bring proper ID, so you can collect it, hmm?"

"*Que weno!*" Kacha said, her voice breaking. "Please thank her."

"There is a condition to your auntie's generosity, however. No more extracurricular work for your sister. She raises her baby, while you find a proper place for you to live. No more quick dates with men in the bushes."

"I don't think that will be a problem. Not at all."

"Things will be up in the air for a while. Stay tough, *chica. Añaychayki.*"

"*Imamanta,*" Kacha said.

Maggie said goodbye and clicked off the phone. She walked over to the trash bin overflowing with garbage and shoved the cell phone into a rancid milk carton sticking out.

She wondered what the normal people were doing, then looked over at the man in the sleeping bag.

What normal people?

-13-

You're the one who told me to take some time off, Maggie typed.

Ed's response was quick. *A day. Or two.*

She sat at the computer in her home office, poised over the keyboard, wearing her beat-up denim jacket over a red turtleneck sweater, faded bellbottom jeans, and Doc Marten shoes. Her scruffy Swiss Army rucksack, with its shock-absorbing laptop compartment, sat by the side of her chair, with a change of shirt, socks, and underwear, cosmetic bag, air sickness pills, all ready to go. *Back by the weekend. I need to take that vacation time stacked up anyway. I'm already at the max and losing it.*

There was a pause while the chat window flickered. *Fair enough*, Ed typed. *But this better not be time off for job interviews. I need to be the first to know before you jump ship and snag a slot with some high-paying multi-national.*

Going up to Lake Tahoe, Maggie typed. *Decompress. Go off the grid for a while.* As if she could ever do that. Even so, she didn't feel good, lying to Ed.

Just be back at work by Monday, Ed replied.

Plenty of time, she thought.

Maggie shut down her MacBook, stuffed it in the padded compartment, zipped up her bag, and stood up. Hands on her hips, she leaned back, cracking out her spine. She did a quick walk-through of her flat, making sure everything was turned off, thermostat down, windows shut. She cleared a few items in the sink, put them in the dishwasher, and set it to run. She walked over to the bay window in the living room and scanned Valencia Street. Early-morning San Francisco. Late-model luxury cars, the young and prosperous in hoodies, trendy clothes and flip-flops, heading to work at startups with laptop bags slung over their shoulders, sipping cups of Peet's from the place on the corner.

In a few short hours she'd be close to the equator once more. Life was more immediate down there and people lived closer to the ground, struggling just to survive. Kacha. Maggie's mother, bless her soul. Maggie thought again about Tica, in a prison outside Quito. A girl she'd never met, sixteen years old, already faced with the worst life had to offer. But a symbol for something bigger.

And then there was Beltran. And Comrade Cain of Cosecha Severa—Grim Harvest.

OK, so she was uneasy, too. But what was that phrase that kept coming up?

A milk run. That was it.

A yellow cab pulled up on Valencia outside her apartment building and double parked. A man in a turban hopped out and came jogging up to her front door in orange sneakers.

Maggie drew the blinds, grabbed her bag, locked the office, set the alarm, engaged the two deadbolts to her apartment. There hadn't been time to get the lock changed. When she got back. Hopefully, Seb had truly lost the key. She'd been ignoring his texts. And would continue to do so. She was leaving her phone behind.

On the way downstairs she knocked on Señora Rosario's door.

Slippered feet shuffled up on the other side of the door. "*Si?*"

"It's only me," Maggie whispered in Spanish.

"Is that *pendejo* Sebastian bothering you again, Magdalena?"

"Not today," Maggie said. "Just wanted to let you know I'll be off for a few days again. So if you see any moving men leaving with all my possessions, you'll know something is up."

"Ai. Be careful."

"I will. Thanks for keeping an eye out."

"You know it. Go with God."

"You too," Maggie said.

In the cab the driver—the man posing as a cab driver—handed Maggie a sealed envelope over the seat without looking back as he negotiated the Mission's already crowded streets and got onto 101 South. Inside the envelope, Maggie found a coach ticket to Bogotá, a U.S. passport under the alias of Alice Mendes, a Commerce Oil company badge for same, and a stack of used U.S. currency and a smaller one of Colombian pesos. Ecuador used U.S. currency, so she was fine if she wound up there.

The cabbie didn't look at her in the rearview mirror, didn't say a word, didn't collect a fare. He dropped her off at SFO's international terminal and left as quietly as he came.

~~~

"What do you mean you're out of vodka, sweetheart?" Maggie heard John Rae say to the flight attendant a few rows up from her in the packed 777. "Isn't this an international flight?"

She sat in the last row where she enjoyed the constant stream of passengers using the airplane lavatory. The middle-aged flight attendant behind the trolley cast a frown down at John Rae, sitting in an aisle seat. Her heavily sprayed blonde coif moved in one section when she did that. "An international flight *in coach*," she said.

"Got *anything* with alcohol in it?" John Rae said.

"At nine in the morning?"

"Just give me what the pilots are drinking for breakfast."

The attendant clanked bottles as she checked her supplies. "I have Jim Beam."

"Well, why didn't you say so, darlin'?" Maggie saw John Rae hold up two fingers. "Better make it a double. Might be my last chance until Bogotá."

"Enjoy your deregulated breakfast in a bag, hotdog." The flight attendant tossed a bag of peanuts at John Rae after setting him up with liquor. He caught the nuts on the fly and flipped them over to his other hand.

John Rae was playing the good old boy again, pretending to be the kind of guy who chugged RC Cola and ate moon pies.

His hair was back under a black ball cap. He wore light-tinted sunglasses and needed a shave. All of this helped tone down his Anglo characteristics. Once through customs, the two of them would look like a couple of hipster vagabonds off on a South American adventure. Maggie found herself studying the line to John Rae's jaw from her aisle seat. He looked like Brad Pitt in *Thelma and Louise*. And he knew it.

The toilet flushed through the wall behind her with a whoosh of suction. Ambience. But traveling coach was low profile. So much for Jayne Bond.

Out the oval window morning skies shimmered over the Gulf of Mexico.

A backup plan, she thought. Never leave home without it. Belt and suspenders. The heart of an accountant.

Maggie got up from her seat, worked her way up to John Rae's row, where he was sipping his drink. He looked up at her, caught her sly smile.

She gave him a wicked wink, nodded imperceptibly back to where the bathrooms were. John Rae's brief stare confirmed that he understood. Then he went back to his drinking.

Maggie headed back to one of the two toilets, let herself in. Locked the door. Waited. Leaning back against the sink. Picked a piece of lint off her jeans. Finally, she heard a light knock on the lavatory door.

"Avon calling," John Rae whispered.

She reached over, unlatched the door.

John Rae let himself through the accordion-style door, squeezed in, shut it, locked it. Turned to face Maggie. He was wearing a beat-up pigskin jacket. "I never would have taken you for the Mile High Club, Maggie."

"In your dreams."

John Rae shrugged. "Story of my life."

"Spare me."

"I'm glad you made contact. I was planning on doing the same. I need to talk to you. Before we land."

"OK," she said. "What about?"

"That emergency contact number? Should have been in

your little packet from Sinclair?"

She recited the number back to him.

"Not just a pretty face. But it's too bad you wasted your time learning it."

"Really? And why is that?"

"Because if something *does* go wrong, Maggie, on this op, which it won't, but if it does, then you're to hightail it out of town. Pure and simple. No heroics this time. Get out of Denver, baby, go. No looking back. Just get out anyway you can. No calling *anybody*, not even an emergency contact. Got that? Vamoose. That goat-truck thing you pulled in Ecuador? Gives me the confidence knowing you can do an encore. But you won't. Just go to the airport, buy a ticket, come back. No fussing around. Do I make myself clear?"

She blinked in mild confusion. "Yes, but the instructions clearly say to call . . ."

John Rae shook his head. "This piddly little op, which amounts to paying off some *terruco* so a dirty Ecuadorian oil minister gets to live another day, isn't worth worrying about if we hit a snag. Which we won't. I already feel iffy about you coming along, but you insisted, so if anything does go wrong—which it won't—you are to *promise* me that you'll turn around, make like a banana, and split. OK?"

"No. Because the instructions are to call that 866 number."

"Look, I'm a big fan of what I say goes. And it's telling me this. So I'm telling you."

Maggie nodded. "So *that's* how you do it in the big leagues. Bail at the first snag."

"Just promise me. I have my reasons."

"Reasons that boil down to you treating me like your kid sister."

"Doesn't matter. Once the op starts, it's Johnny's way," he said, pointing to his chest. "Am I in charge or not?"

"You know, I actually think Sinclair Michaels is."

John Rae fanned that away. "Oh, sure. But Sincs is sitting on his derriere, sipping a few fingers of Kentucky mash right now. I've done a shipload of these payoff runs and it won't be an issue. But if it is, I don't want you risking your neck. I say we bail if things get funny in *any* way, any way *at all*. Cool with you, *chica*? Did I say that right? Without sounding like a sexist pig?"

"You're being overprotective. Because I insisted on coming along. Because I'm a woman. You're worried. That's sweet. But that's actually pretty sexist, too, you know."

"Well, you know what I say to that? Johnny's way."

"*Johnny's way*? Seriously? I can't believe I'm having this conversation with a grown man in an airplane lav."

"*Something funny—run like a bunny.*"

"Wow. Sesame Street for field operatives. Are you *expecting* something funny to happen, *Johnny*?"

"Jesus Christ in a hammock, Maggie, Haven't you heard a word I'm saying? No. No, I'm not expecting anything but a clean payoff. But I don't tell you how to move a zillion bucks around. You don't tell me how to be a kick-ass field op."

"You're a cowboy."

"Now you're gettin' it."

A pretty sweet cowboy, she thought. But still. Never mind. Business. There were a number of body parts touching. She couldn't help but feel the heat coming off of him.

John Rae raised his eyebrows. "I could have pushed back on you coming along, you know."

"Maybe."

"So just do it."

"If you say so," she said.

"Yeah, I do. I did. And now I feel better. When it all comes down to it, this is just government work, like delivering the mail. And there's no need to get your knickers in a twist over something like that."

"I actually think the mail is pretty important."

"It is. But if the mail doesn't show up today, it shows up tomorrow. Anyway, you promised me. So we're good."

"OK, now let me tell you how we do it *chez* Maggie." She produced a folded-up piece of paper between her two fingers, proffered it. "It's called belt and suspenders."

John Rae gave a grin. "You're wearing stockings and suspenders under those jeans?"

"So sad." She shook her head. "No, it's my contact info on a site called Frenesi. Take it."

John Rae took the paper, opened it, read it.

Then he looked up. "IceLady69?"

"It's a dating site," she said. "A place to leave messages for each other as a last resort. You need to be a little creative with your handle, but I think you can actually do it. Pick a name. Sign up. Ping me. You got your phone with you, right?"

"Until I toss it once we get to Bogotá and make the call to meet Comrade Cain."

"Sign up for the rip-off airplane Wi-Fi service, create a logon for Frenesi, ping IceLady69. Then get rid of that piece of paper. You can eat it. That's the way they do it in the movies, huh?"

"A fallback communication plan. I like it."

"As a last resort, Frenesi is where we can reach out if everything else is unavailable. And no one else will know about it."

"But it won't come to that."

"A cakewalk," she said.

"Milk run," John Rae reminded her.

"It really is."

"And you're just gonna split if something goes wrong, right? Which it won't."

"Yep," Maggie said. "So what's your screen name gonna be? Give me an idea, so I won't be talking to some perv."

"MadDog."

"Not bad," she said. "But probably taken. You might have to play around with it some."

"What's MadDog in Spanish?"

"*Perro rabioso*."

"That sounds like 'rabid dog'."

"Well, it kind of is. But if the shoe fits . . ."

John Rae pocketed the paper. "You're a natural, Maggie."

The plane bounced, major turbulence, throwing John Rae

against her, mashing her back onto the metal sink, and John Rae onto her. It was quick, but memorable. They straightened back up quickly, brushing themselves off, looking away. The intercom crackled, the captain instructing passengers to return to their seats and fasten their seatbelts.

The plane jostled again.

"Where were we?" John Rae said, giving her a direct smile.

"You're going to set up that Frenesi account." Maggie winked. "See you in Bogotá. By the taxi stand."

John Rae smiled. "IceLady69?"

"Later, Mad Doggie," Maggie shuffled around John Rae without touching him too much, which wasn't a hundred percent possible, then let herself out of the airplane restroom.

The big-hair flight attendant was coming down the aisle, checking seatbelts, looking left and right. She noticed Maggie exiting the lav, then John Rae behind her. She frowned, then shook her head.

Maggie smiled to herself as she found her seat, sat down, buckled herself in.

As if . . .

-14-

"Alice Mendes?" the Colombian passport-control agent said, looking Maggie in the eye.

"That would be me," Maggie said, meeting his gaze.

The agent was about forty, fine-skinned, with an angular face and mean eyes. He wore a khaki uniform shirt with little red epaulets and a chunky watch that would probably be good to thirty fathoms if it hadn't been a knockoff. He reeked of strong tobacco. But the time he was taking, studying Maggie's forged passport, said something wasn't right.

In the Plexiglas passport-control booth next to her, in front of the yellow line where the other disembarked passengers waited not so patiently, Maggie heard the female agent continue to grill John Rae about the reason for his visit to Colombia. She had asked four questions so far. But John Rae was staying cool. *Vacation*, he had said—and *business*, adding that little lilt that seemed to work with the ladies. Maybe she could show him around Bogotá. When did she get off work anyway?

The agent scanning Maggie's passport didn't look up. *"¿Cuánto tiempo te quedas en Bogotá?"* he asked her. Rude bastard was using the familiar *tú* form. Talking down to her. Maybe it was a trick.

"*No ha-blow es-pan-yol,*" Maggie said in a nasal twang. "English."

He looked up, puckering his lips. A Latina who didn't speak the language. What good was she? Besides the obvious. He squinted at her breasts in her tight red turtleneck, then rubbed a long thumbnail over the corner of her passport photograph.

Maggie wasn't too worried about that. The passport was made by Agency techs, so it was probably better than an original. She'd studied the passport herself thoroughly on the flight down, memorizing her new temporary persona. The document had perfect wear and tear, smudged stamps that spanned the years, trips to England, France. Authentic-looking.

The agent worked his nail under the corner of her earnest-looking photo. Behind the yellow line on the floor, tired passengers gave heavy sighs. Children whined. John Rae stood at relative ease, asking the female agent about a good place to have dinner in Bogotá. She wasn't taking the bait.

Several pairs of feet came clomping up to the far side of John Rae's passport station.

Maggie tilted her head a notch and glimpsed, out of the corner of her eye, three people standing around John Rae. Without lifting her head, she saw two pair of black lace-up boots, uniform pants, and a pair of gray slacks ending in shiny pointed black loafers with buckles.

The agent in front of her peeled the corner of her photo up.

"Please don't do that," Maggie said to him.

He looked up, eyes narrowed, mouth tightened. A woman telling him what to do. Some jumped-up *Ladina* from the U.S., thinking her shit didn't stink.

"Me gustaría lamerte todo," he whispered between his nicotine-stained teeth.

So he'd like to lick her all over. Classy. If it was a test, she wasn't going to fall for it. She looked back in mock confusion. "I'm sorry? What did you say? Something important?"

He ignored her, flipping pages in her passport hard enough to pull one seam loose.

Next to her she heard the man in gray speak to John Rae in English. "Come with us, please, sir."

"Why?" John Rae said. "Is something wrong?"

"Just a formality. This way."

Maggie turned her head slightly, saw the man in the gray suit more clearly. He had a thick mustache.

"Whatever for?" John Rae said. "What have I done?"

"Just a few questions, sir."

"But I want to know what this is about," John Rae said. "I have an important meeting downtown. My associates from Brila Chemical are waiting for me."

"Just come with us, sir," the man said.

"Why don't you give them a call?" John Rae reached in his pocket, got his cell phone. "I've got the number plugged in right here . . ."

"What are you doing?" the man in gray said.

"Just texting my associate," John Rae said, quickly punching in keys, hitting enter. "Let him know I might be a few minutes late. Even though there's not going to be much of a delay, right?"

"Stop!" The man in the suit snapped as one of the uniforms slapped a hand on John Rae's arm. The phone flew out of John Rae's hand and hit the tiled floor, spinning.

John Rae lurched forward and stepped on the phone in a reasonable display of nervousness, crushing the device flat with a crunch of plastic and electronics.

"Now look what you made me do!" he said. "I just got that. 4G LTE and everything."

"You did that on purpose."

"I most certainly did not. Cost a frickin' bundle, I can tell you."

"Be quiet."

There was a clack as the other uniform, a chunky young woman with a solid figure and glistening black hair rolled in a tight bun, readied a small machine gun.

"OK, OK," John Rae said, raising his hands halfway. "Hold your horses, guys and girls. Let's just go straighten this out, then." He gave Maggie a quick *what-the-hell* look, almost indiscernible.

Maggie took a deep breath, which filled her beating chest like a drum. The woman with the machine gun caught her glance, stared furiously back, nodding for Maggie to mind her own business. Maggie looked away, fought another breath down into her lungs. She heard someone in line behind her say "Look. They're taking that man away."

"Probably drugs," someone else said.

"You don't bring dope *into* Colombia, knucklehead."

While the three officials marched John Rae down a brightly lit hallway off the main corridor that led to baggage claim, Maggie's agent was still leafing through her passport.

"Do you know that man?" he asked casually in Spanish.

"I already told you: *no hablo español,*" she said with more than a trace of annoyance. "How long is this going to take anyway?"

"Do you know that man?" he said in English.

"No. Why? What has he done?"

"Where are you staying in Bogotá?" the passport agent said in English.

"Let me just find the name of the place." Maggie slipped her rucksack off her shoulder. She dug inside, found her copy of Lonely Planet Colombia—complete with a U.S. hundred-dollar bill tucked inside the page listing Bogotá hotels. She handed the book over. "Here it is," she said, holding the page with her finger. "Casa Dann Carlton. It's downtown. Nice, is it?"

"We're going to be here all night," someone in line said behind her.

"Welcome to Latin America," someone else said.

The agent examined the guide. He handed it back, sans hundred-dollar bill. He found a page in her passport, stamped with it fanfare, then gestured impatiently for the next person behind the yellow line.

A simple shakedown. Common in this part of the world. But what about John Rae?

She dared not make a fuss. She might wind up in the same place.

"Next!" the passport agent hissed.

Maggie collected her passport and strolled down the corridor, trying to act casual. Peering down the side passageway where John Rae had been escorted. Nothing but closed doors. She cocked an ear. Nothing. She headed cautiously down the side hallway.

"Move along," a woman said in Spanish.

Maggie turned, saw the female soldier with the machine gun. Where had she come from?

"Restroom?" Maggie said. "*El baño?*"

"There!" the guard snapped in English, jutting her jaw toward the main hallway, where baggage claim was. "Go."

Maggie sighed, followed the signs toward baggage claim.

John Rae was a big boy. If anyone would know a way out of the jam like this, it would be him. This was probably child's play. But what if someone had been tipped off? Maggie thought it might be a genuine misunderstanding. Or more extortion. More than a few South American passport agents paid a "fee" for their lucrative jobs and were under pressure to produce. But it felt like too much of a coincidence—both of them being hit up.

At baggage claim, Maggie milled around the carousel, even though she had no checked luggage. The oval machine ground into motion as more travelers arrived. Luggage starting bouncing down a chute. She nonchalantly kept looking back the way she came. With any luck, sooner or later, one of the arriving passengers would be John Rae.

The guard with the hair bun and submachine gun arrived, along with another guard. The woman scanned the crowd, possibly looking for someone. Maggie turned abruptly and headed toward Customs, keeping her eyes straight ahead as she marched past two soldiers and a German shepherd. It felt like even the dog was staring at her. One soldier gave a low whistle as Maggie walked by.

At Customs, agents were opening luggage with gusto, burrowing through clothes to the consternation of the travelers. But no one stopped Maggie.

Crossing the last dozen yards toward the automatic exit door into the airport proper, Maggie knew what No Man's Land on the Berlin Wall must have felt like. As much as she wanted to, Maggie didn't turn to see if bun-and-gun and her friend were on her tail. But she acted as if they were, picking up the pace without actually breaking into a run. The electric doors whipped open and she was suddenly immersed in the dissonance of a big South American airport: people holding up cardboard signs with names on them, others barking out offers of taxis and ground transportation, vying for her attention. Maggie burrowed into the crowd, flipping her backpack down, unzipping it, pulling out a floppy beige knit slouch hat and dark sunglasses, quickly donning both and stuffing her long hair up inside the hat as she exited the throng hovering around the doors.

She passed through a second set of electronic doors, taking her outside, where a line of taxis pumped exhaust into the cool night air. She turned, looking around indifferently. The female guard with the machine gun was still inside, in front of the first set of doors, scanning the crowd.

A considerable line of people waiting for cabs greeted Maggie. A man with a paunch and cap was deciding who went where.

"Wait there," he instructed Maggie, pointing her to the end of a long queue of people herding luggage.

She moved in close, slipped a folded U.S. twenty-dollar bill into his rough hand. "My mother's in the hospital, *amigo*," she said in Spanish. "Her second stroke. I haven't slept a wink for days, just getting here." She dropped her tone to unabashed helpless female. "I'd be so grateful."

The money disappeared. "Right this way, miss."

"Her mother's in the hospital!" the man said as he pushed the businessman aside who was just getting into a rumbling little Daihatsu at the front of the line. Maggie dived into the back seat, yanked the door shut, handed another twenty to the stout driver in front.

"As fast as this fine vehicle will take us, uncle. Burn rubber, if you please."

Bald tires squealed on asphalt as the taxi peeled out of the clogged lane in front of the airport.

-15-

"You want to get out *here?*" the taxi driver said, blinking at Maggie in dismay from the rearview mirror. The rosary beads hanging from it vibrated with the uneven pinging of the tinny engine. They were on the outskirts of Bogotá, stars twinkling on a deserted stretch of country road. The perpetual coldness of the Andes blew steadily.

"I do," she said, peeling off bills, handing them over the seat. "*Muchas gracias.*"

The *taxista* took the money. "But it's not safe here, *señorita*. It is the middle of nowhere."

"I'm fine." She got out, waited for him to turn around and head back into the capital. He did, finally, giving a reluctant shrug before carving a tight 180 in the two-lane road, and setting off, the engine whining. She watched the red taillights disappear.

The sounds of night began to take over. Crickets. Wind. She was back in the world of her birth. An ancient world. Despite the bad turn things had taken, she felt its power.

She was safe enough to catch her breath and decide what to do next.

She recalled her cozy lavatory chat with John Rae. If something went wrong, he said, she was to get out of town, then Colombia, in that order. No hanging around. *Something funny, run like a bunny.*

She looked off into the distance, away from the lights of Bogotá. *Get out of Denver*, John Rae had said, pressed up against her in the airplane WC.

And that's what she'd been doing.

But now...

She had come too far to simply cut and run, based on John Rae's overprotective instincts. She knew her way around this part of world. Better than he, truth be told.

John Rae could have been stopped at the airport for no reason beyond the fact that the authorities just did that sometimes. They were *tombos*—cops—and that's the way they were. Maggie's harassment was your standard hit-up for cash. John Rae might even be out by now. An experienced operative, he'd know how to get out of most fixes.

Hitching her backpack up on a shoulder, she hiked off the main road, onto rocky ground, watching her step in the darkness. She headed up the hillside where she could watch the road and satellite access would be unrestricted.

Sitting on a rock, Maggie extracted the MacBook and fired it up, dialing into the Agency's IKON global network with the high-power network card plugged into a USB port. In the night gloom, the screen glowed blue. Up the hill, a lone bird gave a series of shrieks. Maggie clicked on her IP-masker app. A good surveillance tracker would get past that, but it would take longer and she wouldn't be online long. Long enough to call the emergency number. She pulled her headphones out of her knapsack and plugged them in as she started up Skype.

She dialed the contact number Sinclair Michaels had given her in his instructions, using the country code 57. It would appear to be an out-of-country call. Again, that could be unraveled, but it would take whoever might be watching more time.

The call droned on for several rings. A small beast shot out of the shadows from behind a rock, scampered down the hill toward the road, taking a few of her nerves along with it.

Her heart settled as the call finally connected.

The buzz of a call center filled the night air around her, surreal with the lonely hillside darkness.

"Authentication, please," a voice said.

"Solar Solar One," she said.

"And your password."

"Ivory nation."

"Turn off your IP masker. We need to verify your machine and GPS."

She did so. Green flickers lit up her network card as her machine was verified.

"One moment, please." Maggie was transferred to a quieter office somewhere in Langley.

"All in one piece?" Sinclair Michaels said.

"Yes. But I can't say the same for Jack Warren." She used John Rae's code name on this op.

"Don't worry about him. A momentary hiccup. Nothing a little payola won't take care of."

"So you're aware of what happened?"

"Yes."

"Perhaps you can clue me in?"

"Nothing serious. Where are you? Your GPS shows you're out of Bogotá."

"Just on the outskirts," she said, embarrassed for running. "So, what next?"

"Call Cain's people and let them know there's been a delay. Get things rolling. Jack Warren will join you in a few hours. He may even be out by now."

"You want me to call these people myself?"

"Yes. We need to keep them calm. I've dealt with Grim Harvest before and they can get antsy. We don't want them to take off on us."

Maggie and Grim Harvest. All by herself. "I'll need the number."

Sinclair Michaels gave it to her. Maggie repeated it back, making a quick rhyme out it in her head.

"I'm going to give you my direct Skype number," he said. "Just in case."

She committed that to memory as well.

"Just remember," Sinclair Michaels said. "This op is a textbook PE—" by which he meant prisoner-exchange— "No need to let it cause stress."

Undue stress, she thought. "I won't."

"Turn your IP masker back on," he said, hanging up.

Maggie turned the masker back on. Then she Skyped the number Sinclair Michaels had given her, adjusting her headphones. She realized that she was managing an op in her father's old stomping ground. What would he think, having been pulled from the action in the prime of his career?

Why did she care so much what that man thought?

"*Dígame,*" a woman's raspy voice said in a flurry of static as the call picked up. Horns honking. The woman was most likely on a cell phone outdoors in downtown Bogotá.

"I'm Alice Mendes," Maggie said in Spanish.

The woman spoke in a rough indigenous accent. "Where's your *jefe*?"

"Running late," she said. "Clearing customs. He had a wristwatch that caught the eye of one of the agents. You know how that goes."

"How late?"

"An hour or two at most."

The woman on the other end swore.

"We're still on to meet for a drink, though," Maggie said. "Where?"

She heard the woman take a deep breath before she responded using a dialect that had surfaced during the dirty war in Peru. Some words used reversed syllables. Others used heavy vernacular. It was the Latin version of Cockney rhyming slang, not understandable to most ears. The woman gave Maggie a location in central Bogotá, by the cathedral.

"I'll see you Monday," Maggie said. *Monday* meant one hour from now. Tuesday, two hours. "But it might be Tuesday."

"Tuesday is out of the question."

"Monday it is."

Maggie hung up, dialed into Frenesi, the online dating site that served as the secret rendezvous venue for her and John Rae. PerroRabioso had sent her a message a few hours ago, back when they were still airborne: *If I said you had a beautiful body, would you hold it against me?* John Rae confirming his screen handle. But nothing since. He might not be in a position to call yet. She sent a message back. *You bet. In fact, I'm going downtown to hang around with your thrill-seeker buddies and wait to hear you say it in person . . .*

That should be clear enough that she wasn't going anywhere and moving ahead with the op, in case communications with Sinclair Michaels were fouled up.

An ICE ping alert window popped up on the shimmering laptop screen in the darkness. Someone watching. Maggie closed the application and hit the MacBook's shutdown button, pulling the headphones and network card. She stuffed the laptop and accessories into the protected slot of her bag while it was still powering down. Then she stood up, dusting herself off.

A milk run, she reminded herself.

Sinclair Michaels had said all was settling into place. Just a delay.

And in the back of her mind was Tica, sitting in some godforsaken cell or worse; she wondered about the "medical emergency".

From the west a pair of headlights broke the darkness like flickering cat's eyes. A truck heading toward Bogotá. The groan of its engine drifted down the road.

Maggie hoisted up her knapsack, huffed it down to the road, crossed over. She stuck her thumb out as the truck came up behind.

The motor ground down a gear, the truck preparing to stop.

~~~

Cold night air whipped across the wide expanse of Plaza Bolívar as Maggie stood in front of the austere block-shaped Palace of Justice. Waiting. To her left, the cathedral's huge doors were closing for the night, tons of age-old wood groaning. A trickle of people had filtered out and were fanning across the broad stone plaza. Maggie fought the urge to check the time again. It wouldn't make anybody get here any quicker.

She scanned every car that went by, wondering what had happened to John Rae. Was he on his way? She'd feel a whole lot better when they rejoined forces.

A beat-up red Toyota with a gray-primered fender pulled over on Carrera 8, halfway up the plaza. Two people sat in the front. The driver wore a hat.

Maggie strode over. The car window rolled down.

The driver was a woman, wedge-shaped, wearing a fedora. Typical Quechua body type and garb. Maggie drew closer and looked inside the car. The woman wore a handmade cardigan, heavy Indian skirt, wool leggings that hugged her thick calves. She'd spent most of her life outdoors at high altitudes, judging by the deep wrinkles in her copper-colored skin. Her nose had the sharp profile of people who predated the Inca. She looked as if smiling was an extravagance.

"You must be Alice," she said in guttural Spanish.

Maggie dipped down to get a look at the woman's companion: a skinny Indian teenager not old enough for military service. He wore a faded black sleeveless Metallica T-shirt despite the cold. His head had been shaved a week or so back, but he had a sensitive-looking mouth with soft lips and a jacket over his lap, which concealed a pistol, but not very well.

"He can't be the person I'm supposed to meet," Maggie said in Spanish, meaning Cain. She didn't let on that she spoke Quechua. It could be an advantage.

"He's not," the woman said. "We're taking you to him."

"And Beltran too?"

"Yes."

"What guarantee do I have?"

"None at all," the woman said, looking straight ahead as she tapped the steering wheel. "But if that's a concern, you best leave now. You called us—remember? Now we're running late, thanks to you. And if we stay here much longer, we risk being stopped by the *tombos*. Now get in the car or be on your way, *princesa*."

With a squeal of rusty door hinge Maggie climbed in the back on a seat covered with a rough Indian blanket. The car lurched into traffic before she had time to pull the door completely shut.

The woman spoke to the boy in Quechua. "Check her bag. Make sure she doesn't have a *pieza*."

The boy turned around as the car barreled through an intersection, cutting off a bus, the woman leaning into the horn. Maggie's nerves responded appropriately.

"Bag," the boy mumbled in Spanish, gesturing with an impatient hand, which sported a death's-head skull ring and studded-leather wristband. Maggie handed him her knapsack as the woman maneuvered through traffic like a rally-car driver.

"What's your name?" Maggie asked the boy.

He ignored her and pulled out the laptop, seemed satisfied, put it back, then went through her undies and things with a blush on his face and his eyes down. He had delicate lashes. He put her things back carefully.

"Unarmed," he said to the woman driver in Quechua.

"She's a fool," the woman replied. "What about her papers?"

"There's a passport." He was leafing through it now. "*Estados Unidos*."

The woman reached a hand out as she drove. The boy handed her the passport. She slipped it in the pocket of her cardigan. The boy returned Maggie's bag to her.

"I need my passport back," Maggie said in Spanish.

"Yes, yes," the woman said.

"Now."

"Later."

What choice did she have? "No word from my companion yet?"

"No." The woman yanked the car around a horse and cart laden down with flattened cardboard boxes.

"You two are with Cosecha Severa?"

The radical group holding Beltran was one of many that popped up in this part of the world like pampas grass.

The boy made a fist and pounded his skinny chest with it. "Vengeance," he said, "is justice."

It sent a chill through her. "And Cain is your leader?" she asked.

"*Comrade* Cain."

"And I'm going to meet him, correct?"

"Enough questions," the woman said, jamming a sandaled foot down on the gas pedal as they swerved around a broken-down taxi with a driver gesturing wildly to a man in uniform. Some sort of accident.

The car sped away from the city center, onto rough streets, then higher onto dirt roads, into one of the largest slums Maggie had ever seen. She'd seen a few, grew up in one in Guayaquil. But at least fifty thousand people lived in Ciudad Bolívar. Houses built anywhere they'd fit, out of anything available. And people, dogs, pigs, noise, smells. Chaos. Life on the side of a mountain, connected by crooked stairways, dotted by haphazard, intermittent lights.

"Where are we headed?" Maggie said.

"She does ask a lot of questions," the boy said to the woman driver in Quechua.

"She's a *norteamericana*," the woman replied. "They think they own the world. But she'll learn. She'll learn."

~~~

High in the hills, the woman in the fedora turned around in her seat, facing Maggie, as she reversed up a narrow dirt road etched out of a steep slope overlooking the city. The car shuddered back toward a large shanty made of cinderblock, plywood, and tin. There was nothing to the left side of the car, just a stark drop-off, and the quivering lights of Bogotá through pollution and mist.

The woman stomped the brakes, twisted the car key, got out, and stood on the ledge where the land fell away. The boy in the passenger seat rolled his window down and climbed out with the gun in one hand. There was no room to open his door.

"Well?" the woman barked at Maggie, hands on her ample hips. "What are you waiting for?"

Maggie eased the door open with a pang, got out onto no more than a foot of dirt cliff. She looked down at a vegetation-lush precipice to corrugated roofs below lit by vaporous moonlight. Slinging her bag over her shoulder, she stepped carefully around to the rear of the car, clinging to the fender. The icy thin air only added to the precariousness.

"What did she expect?" the woman said to the boy in Quechua. "A handrail?"

"I thought *norteamericanos* lived in skyscrapers," the boy replied, the 45-caliber pistol dangling from his hand.

"They live in mansions, Gabby," the woman said, spitting over the side. "Come on, princess," she said to Maggie, switching to Spanish, nodding at the shack at the end of the road. The boy climbed on the bumper and sat on the trunk of the car, presumably to stand guard.

Maggie gazed out over Bogotá, the lights of the capital furry down below. The air was pungent with the smell of burning trash. Dogs barked in the distance.

A flashlight beam came bouncing out of the shack. A young woman walked behind it, the light in one hand and an automatic rifle over her shoulder. She wore a coarse black-alpaca jacket. Long dark hair fell over her shoulders. Even in near-darkness, it was clear she was striking. She had huge eyes and a white smile to match, which looked odd considering the circumstances.

The young woman showed Maggie and the Indian woman into a house that smelled of the wet earth it was built on and fresh sewage underneath. Here and there, hillside appeared in the gaps in the makeshift floor, but the shack was more substantial than most, with separate rooms and some cinderblock construction to keep it from blowing away.

Maggie was led into a lopsided room where a kerosene lamp on a table cast wavering light onto a poster of Chairman Mao. A stocky man with his back to her stood at a cracked dirty window someone had purloined from an old house that gave out onto a million-dollar view of Bogotá. He wore a loose camouflage jacket over blue nylon shorts and Teva sport sandals. The backs of his legs were scratched and mosquito bitten. He turned around.

He was in his mid-thirties, with frizzy dark hair that needed cutting. Intense brown eyes laid in wait behind gold-framed glasses and a fleshy scowl more than suggested an acute lack of patience. His fair skin was mottled by rosacea or some similar ailment and filmed with moisture, even though the room was cold.

From another room the cry of a baby startled Maggie.

"Can't you do something about him, Yalu?" the man snapped at the pretty woman. She huffed, disappeared into a side room where the infant was picked up, indulged, cooed.

"Are you Cain?" Maggie asked.

"It's *Comrade* Cain," he said. "And no, I'm not. I'm Comrade Abraham. Second in command."

Another biblical name. Like the Shining Path. Cain was ex-Shining Path, so he'd obviously adopted some of its conventions. "And where *is* Cain?" Maggie asked. "*Comrade* Cain? And while we're on the subject, I'll need to see Beltran as well."

"All in good time," he said, while the fedora woman stood back and leaned against an unfinished wall, crossing her arms over her bosomy chest. She shut her eyes and grew still, appearing to rest. Abraham went to the table. A map was spread out alongside papers, a little red book, and a blue-steel snub-nosed revolver. He pulled back the single high-backed wooden chair and dragged it to the center of the room. He twisted it around to face Maggie.

"Sit."

"I'd rather stand."

"It's not a request."

Maggie took a steadying breath through her nose and sat, knees together, placing her knapsack on the floor by her feet. Comrade Abraham stood directly behind her. The fedora woman watched her through slitted eyes, arms still crossed.

"What happened to Jack Warren?" Comrade Abraham asked Maggie. "Your companion?" Abraham spoke with an Italian lilt that made Maggie take him for an Argentine. From the next room, they could hear Yalu coaxing the baby back to sleep.

"He was delayed," Maggie said. "Shaken down by passport control for a payoff. He's on his way, so I'm told."

"Where are your papers?"

"Ask *her*," Maggie said, indicating the fedora woman.

"I've got her passport," she said.

"Well, Beatriz, give it here," Abraham said.

Beatriz didn't warrant a "comrade," it seemed. She pushed herself off the wall, sauntered over, handed Maggie's passport, along with a malevolent look, to Abraham, then returned to her spot on the wall.

Comrade Abraham flipped pages, standing behind Maggie. "Alice Mendes. San Antonio, Texas." She could feel his breath on her neck and smell the spices of what he had last eaten. "You work for Commerce Oil."

"I'm actually an accountant for Five Fortunes Petroleum, a subsidiary of Commerce Oil."

"They sent a bean counter. A paper pusher. A woman." It was as if he were insulted.

"A certified CPA. With degrees in math and computer science. Here to do the transfers, *once* we verify that Comrade Cain hands Beltran over in good shape—before we pay two million dollars. Where are they, by the way?"

"When your boss didn't show up, we took precautions."

Maggie let out an exasperated sigh. "Meaning Comrade Cain took off?"

"We don't like irregularities."

They'd already ditched the meeting down in the plaza. Now this. "What part of this do you call regular to begin with?" she said. "Holding hostages for ransom? People get delayed. It's part of everyday life in the *regular* world."

"An accountant with an oil company telling us how to do things. A *woman*. You don't impress men with guns, eating tree roots and living in the jungle. Fighting to save our planet. While you cook the books for some American conglomerate destroying it. Hiding shady deals your oil company wants done."

"Like paying ransom for someone you kidnapped?"

"An act you are ultimately responsible for."

"Perhaps we should just call it business and get on with it."

"This is why you Americans will ultimately fail, you know. You base your so-called free market on lies, corruption, and criminal payoffs. Yet you call it business. Free enterprise."

"You might have a point, there," Maggie said. "But I notice you aren't turning your nose up at two million *pavos*."

"Cosecha Severa will take your money if it furthers our cause."

Yes, they would. And it was her ace in the hole. A little ragtag paramilitary group wouldn't let two million U.S. slip away. Not even if the operation hit a snag. They were nervous and had backed off, but they wouldn't run. And they'd have to treat her reasonably well. "Are we going to discuss Marxist philosophy all night or am I going to meet Cain and Beltran at some point, make the transfer, and get this over with?"

"*Comrade* Cain." She heard Abraham flip a page in her passport. "When did you travel to France?"

Verifying her identity. "Three years ago. I believe it was April. Yes, April."

He turned another page.

"Italy?"

"A year or two before that. No, two years. September. Came back in October."

There was a pause. Comrade Abraham went over to the table, picked up the revolver, returned to stand behind Maggie. Her neck prickled when she heard the hammer ratchet back. When he pressed the barrel against the soft flesh of her neck, her nerves shot through the roof of her mouth. She told herself it was an act. They were playing tough. That was all.

"Why did you come here alone?" he said.

She sucked in what was meant to be a calming breath. "My partner Jack Warren was stopped at the airport. A bribe. *A little bite*. It's been taken care of."

"It better not be more than that."

"If it was, I'd be pretty foolish to let your people drive me up here, wouldn't I? An accountant? A woman? Alone?

Especially with the way Beatriz drives."

"You don't see why all of this would make us suspicious?"

"Absolutely," she stammered. "But it was simple extortion by minor public officials. I had to pay off the passport-control agent myself. It's not that uncommon, is it? Perhaps we should have factored that into the schedule." Her joke fell flat.

"Do you know what I think?"

"I suspect you're going to tell me."

"I think your partner better call us soon."

She steadied herself as the barrel of the pistol pressed into the vertebrae of her neck. "He will."

"Just as long as we understand each other," Comrade Abraham said. "But if I find out you're lying to us, or trying to trick us, do you know what will happen to you, Alice Mendes? Do you know what your fancy degrees will get you then?"

Maggie swallowed hard. "Why would I want to lie or try to trick people like you? That would be insanity."

"Yes," he said, pulling the gun away. "It most certainly would. But there are more than a few people who want to bring down Comrade Cain. My job is to make sure that doesn't happen."

Maggie gulped. "Understood."

"So we wait," Abraham said.

-16-

The door to the interrogation room opened.

John Rae looked up from the table he'd been seated at for some hours now and saw a tall well-built Latin man in his 40s, high cheekbones, wearing a white shirt, dark green tie done up to the top button. A shrewd look in his deep-set eyes. A higher-ranking official of some sort, didn't have to wear a uniform. Thick dark hair combed back, movie-star fashion. A lady-killer. Holding a manila file folder in his hand.

Overhead, a fluorescent light sizzled. It did that every few minutes. John Rae had used its pattern to judge time as they'd taken his wristwatch. It was past midnight. The beginnings of fatigue told him as well, as did the pressure on his bladder. No one had offered him anything yet, least of all a bio break, and he knew from experience this could be the start of a lengthy incarceration. If he didn't comply, things would worsen: moved to a grimy cell somewhere where he'd hear the cries of people helping the authorities with their inquiries.

He didn't really mind, as long as he didn't get kicked around too bad.

Things would go according to plan.

The room was nondescript, small, windowless, stuffy with the odor of his confined sweat. The walls were painted a light green meant to induce calmness, but a long time ago.

They were upstairs in a large building in Bogotá. The van ride from the airport had taken approximately a half-hour. Although he'd been hooded when he was brought in the back way, John Rae felt the big city around him. Traffic noises bounced off concrete.

"Jack Warren?" his interrogator said, reading from the file folder. But it was an act. He'd reviewed the file. He had a firm but patient voice. Confident. Didn't need a guard in the room with him.

"Yes sir," John Rae said, getting up, pushing his chair back with a screech, rushing round to shake hands, a gesture that wouldn't be returned of course. He was the frightened American tourist, wondering what this was all about, eager to set things right. When the handshake was refused, he said, "And who might you be?"

The handsome man ignored that. He smelled of expensive cologne. "Sit down." He spoke English well.

John Rae returned to his seat, sat on the edge of it. "So what seems to be the problem?"

His interrogator cracked an amused smile as he sat down opposite John Rae and crossed his legs. "Are we really going to start all the way back *there*—you pretending that you have no idea why you were detained?" He had the arrogant air of a senior intelligence officer well-versed with interrogation. Some ex-DAS guy probably, a Colombian agency disbanded due to – ah – irregularities.

"Where would y'all like me to start?" John Rae said.

The man tossed the file folder on the table. The corner of John Rae's passport stuck out. "Well, why don't we start with your real name?"

"What makes you think my real name isn't on my passport?"

"Please." He smiled. "Because it's a forgery. A very good one, yes, but a fake all the same. Of course, a man with a U.S. intelligence agency would have nothing less."

"Is *that* what I am? A secret agent. Like Jason Bourne? Wow. I only wish my life was that exciting. I work for Five Fortunes, an oil company."

"This is starting to get a little tedious."

John Rae sat back in his chair. It wouldn't do any good to play this hand any more. It would only piss him off. "You know, that's exactly what I was thinking."

"You weren't stopped just for the fun of it." The man gave John Rae a piercing look. "We knew an operative was coming to Colombia to meet Comrade Cain."

"Comrade *Cain*?" See how much he knew.

Ladykiller exhaled impatiently. "We were tipped off. Notified. Informed."

"Why was I supposed to meet this Comrade Cain?"

"Ostensibly to make an exchange for a hostage being held by a terrorist organization. Cosecha Severa. It translates to something like 'Harvest of Death' in English. Comrade Cain is the leader. The hostage's name is Armand Beltran. He's the oil minister of Ecuador."

Yeah, this guy knew plenty. "*Ostensibly*," John Rae said. "Your English is a whole lot better than mine. And I'm supposed to be a native speaker."

Ladykiller gave a shrug.

"But from what I remember, the word means 'supposedly'," John Rae said. "'On the surface.'"

Ladykiller pointed at him now. "Yes, that is correct."

"So what am I really doing?" John Rae said. "If I'm *ostensibly* doing all this other stuff."

"You're not really interested in Beltran," Ladykiller said as he sat back, one ankle over his knee, a relaxed chat with John Rae that was anything but. "A corrupt oil minister that an American oil company you pretend to work for wants to protect. No—it's Comrade Cain you're after. You were planning on taking him prisoner." He raised his eyebrows.

John Rae pursed his lips. Not many people knew *that* angle. He could count them on half of the fingers of one hand. And if Maggie hadn't taken off, left town, the way he had urged her to, had stuck around to see the op through, she could be in the shit. It was a good thing John Rae had sent his people an alert when he was nabbed at the airport. They knew what to do, but Maggie couldn't take the heat for it. He needed to get hold of the embassy. He sat back, folded his hands behind his head. "So what am I being charged with? Ostensibly?"

"All in good time."

"I think this is when you call the U.S. Consulate," John Rae said.

"And tell them what? That I have an individual with a forged passport posing as a U.S. citizen?"

"We both know I'm a U.S citizen, *amigo*."

"Do we? You could be Canadian. Irish. English. How do I know where you're from? I'm not a *native speaker*."

"When presented with a passport of the United States and a person of suspicion, you are required to contact the embassy. Standard diplomatic regulations between the United States and Colombia."

His interrogator consulted his watch. "Within twenty-four hours—give or take a few days." He looked back at John Rae. "And you just got here, *amigo*."

Yeah, the fun was yet to come.

Well, that was OK. As long as Maggie wasn't jeopardized.

~~~

Maggie watched Comrade Abraham pace the floor of the Bogotá safe house, back and forth, in the pall of the camping light on the table under the poster of Chairman Mao. Night winds picked up on the mountainside, blowing needles of cold air through the crack in the dirt-smeared window overlooking the city. Abraham pulled a cell phone from his shorts and stepped outside, slamming the door that caught the wind, and Maggie could hear him having another heated discussion out there. Beatriz, in her fedora, was still leaning against the wall, arms crossed, her hard features faded beyond the lantern's reach as she watched Maggie with a tired frown. She had Maggie's backpack, with the MacBook inside, by her feet. No computer use, Abraham had said, until Jack Warren showed up and they went to meet Cain.

Gabby was still posted outside in the car. Yalu, Abraham's wife, tended to the baby in the next room. Maggie sat on the only chair. For all intents and purposes, she was a hostage.

"I assume Abraham is calling Cain?" Maggie said.

"*Comrade* Cain," Beatriz said.

"I notice no one calls you 'comrade' around here." Maggie

said. "Revolution is just for the boys, isn't it?" Maggie shook her head. "You're just the hired help. Believe me; I know what that's like."

Beatriz didn't respond.

"So is *Comrade* Abraham calling *Comrade* Cain?" Maggie asked.

"What do you think, *princesa*? Your *amigo* isn't here yet."

John Rae should have been here by now, according to Sinclair Michaels.

Beatriz said, "It's not going to be good for you if he doesn't show up, you know."

Maggie knew that.

The front door opened and slammed shut, letting in a blast of garbage-infused air, and waking the baby again, who started to whimper afresh. Abraham marched in, running his fingers through his curly hair. He paced back and forth, pulled the .38 revolver, as if not aware of doing so. He stopped, glaring at Maggie in the lantern shadows. "We're tired of waiting," he said.

"I don't need Jack Warren to make those bank transfers," she said, eying the gun in Abraham's hand.

Abraham blinked as he squeezed the pistol for apparent comfort. "Keep going."

She needed to get hold of Sinclair Michaels. "But I do need to speak to my manager," she said. "Back in the U.S."

"Why?"

"Jack Warren has the access code. For the transfer. He was to give it to me once he confirmed Beltran was safe and that all was in order. A two-person verification, standard protocol. With Jack Warren out of the picture, I'll need to get the code from my manager. And I'll have to bring him up to date on what's happened as well."

Talk about winging it.

Abraham rubbed his face with his free hand. "I'll be back." He went back outside, a gust of trash air filling the room once again. The door slammed. The baby cried next door.

"He has to clear everything with Comrade Cain, doesn't

he?" Maggie said to Beatriz.

Beatriz stared at Maggie, impassive.

Presently Maggie heard Abraham in another intense discussion. She could discern the words *not take the risk, comrade.* Abraham was getting antsier.

The front door opened and banged shut. In the room next door the infant cried out again. Through the wall Yalu yelled, "Stop slamming that damn door!" Abraham came blustering into the room, gun in hand. Perhaps it made him feel more in control. He was blinking rapidly. "Call your manager in the States," he instructed Maggie.

"I'll need my laptop."

Without looking at her, Abraham snapped his fingers at Beatriz. Beatriz picked up the daypack, came over to Maggie, glaring at Abraham the whole time, dropped the pack with a thump by Maggie's feet. It was a good thing the laptop was in a padded sleeve.

Maggie pulled her chair up to the table underneath the poster of Chairman Mao, got out her MacBook, set it up with the network card, powered up, dialed into IKON with Abraham standing behind, breathing down her neck. She turned on the GPS and made sure the IP Masker was off. This was one time she didn't mind being tracked.

Opening Skype, Maggie dialed Sinclair Michaels directly. She enabled the webcam so that Sinclair might get a glimpse of where she was. As the ringing droned on, she tilted the screen up so that Abraham, over her shoulder, was hopefully visible. She hit the PrtScn key and her webcam snapped a shot of her with Abraham behind, the top of his pistol showing. Perfect.

The IP phone on her laptop continued to ring. It was well after 1 a.m. Same time in Washington, D.C., where she was calling.

On the sixth ring, the call finally picked up. Maggie breathed a sigh of relief. A blurry image flickered across the continents. As it settled she saw Sinclair Michaels, well-composed in a shirt with a collar, sitting in an austere office. With the operation in effect and the emergency of John Rae's arrest, or detainment—or whatever it was—impacting it, he wouldn't be lounging at home in his bathrobe.

Before Sinclair could speak, and use her real name, Maggie said: "Alice Mendes here, sir. Still no sign of Jack Warren."

Sinclair gave a slow nod and she could see him peering past her shoulder, where Abraham stood, gun in hand. "And what is the status there?"

"I'm proposing we go ahead with the exchange—without Warren. But I'll need the access code."

Sinclair nodded. "So you need me to give you the access code?"

"Exactly."

"Is Beltran there? Have you verified his well-being?"

"No."

"Where is he?"

"Good question." She turned, looked over her shoulder. "Where is Beltran?" she asked Abraham in Spanish.

She heard Abraham slip the pistol back in his pocket. "Safe and sound nearby," he said, stepping out of view of the web cam. "Can't you turn that camera off?"

"No," she lied. But it didn't matter. Sinclair Michaels had gotten a good look, no doubt recorded it, and had her GPS location as well. Maggie also knew Sinclair spoke Spanish and understood the interchange.

"I'm prepared to provide the access code, Alice," Sinclair said, switching to Spanish so that Abraham could follow along. "But not until we have Beltran. That was, after all, the original agreement."

Sinclair Michaels was playing his cards just fine. If Grim Harvest knew that Maggie had the code now, they could force the transfer without handing over Beltran. And besides, there was no such thing as an access code to begin with. It had been Maggie's invention to engineer a phone call back home, so that Sinclair Michaels and the Agency could pinpoint her location and get up to speed on the op, and learn that John Rae was still missing in action. Sinclair had picked up on the ploy.

There was a pause.

"I need to make a phone call," Abraham said, heading back outside. The door slammed. In the next room, the baby cried. Beatriz was left standing back in the shadows, watching Maggie.

"Do you speak English, Comrade?" Maggie said, not looking at Beatriz.

"What do you mean?" Sinclair Michaels said.

"Not you," Maggie said. "Someone else."

"Ah," he said. "I see."

No response from Beatriz. She couldn't speak English.

Maggie said to Sinclair Michaels in English: "The guy you saw is second in command. He just went out to call you know who. When he returns, I'll cough twice."

"Understood," he said. "Are you safe?"

"Yes," she said, opening a web browser in a spare window, one that Sinclair Michaels would not be privy to. "They're playing tough, but they're too eager for the money not to go along with a change in plans."

"Keep stalling them. I'll contact some people and cancel this op. But it might take twenty-four hours."

"No," Maggie said. "If I need to bail, I can make a run for it." While she spoke, Maggie logged onto Frenesi, the dating site. "These guys are motivated to keep things on track, so I'm not worried." Not too worried, anyway. "This can still work out. I say we go through with it." And get Tica out of her hellhole.

"I'm impressed," Sinclair Michaels said. "Good work."

Maggie flushed with pride as she logged into her IceLady69 account.

12inchesInDetroit wanted to buy her dirty underwear but there were no new messages from PerroRabioso. She'd leave him a message—just in case. She flipped to Google Maps, zoomed in on her location, got the coordinates: 4°35'53"N 74°4'33"W, copied them to a text scratch pad. She renamed the screen shot of her with Abraham standing behind her as 4_35_53_n_ 74_4_33_w.jpg. Outside she could hear Abraham raise his voice and say, ". . . Too much deviation from the original plan!"

She typed a quick message to PerroRabioso: *dude, u stood me up! I'm with ur buddies now, top of the hill, and weer all hot to trot . . . if ur the man u say u are, u better make it . . . peace out call me . . . xoxo heres a pic of me.* She attached the photo, with Abraham lurking in the background behind, the barrel of his .38 showing. John Rae was a clever boy and would understand—if he could get near a computer with online access.

She would have liked a picture of the exterior of the place too. Trying to find this shack in a rats' nest of slums would be a challenge, to say the least.

An ICE ping alert popped up on her computer. She closed the window, but left the computer running.

The front door slammed again and Maggie gave two deliberate, loud coughs. Sinclair said, "Got it." The baby next door was crying steadily.

Abraham huffed back into the living room. He came over to Maggie sitting at the computer, leaned in front of her, spoke directly to Sinclair Michaels. His body odor had been brewing for a couple of days. "We accept the new arrangement," he said in Spanish.

"And what does that mean, exactly?" Sinclair Michaels said.

"We will take Alice Mendes to Beltran. When she is satisfied, she will call you for the code and make the transfer there."

"Where is *there*?"

"A few hours away."

"Again: *where?*"

"I said: '*a few hours away.*' We're leaving now."

"Where are you going?" Sinclair asked again. "That's my employee there and I insist on knowing."

"Ipiales. Near the border with Ecuador. Don't worry. She'll be back in Bogotá with your precious Beltran by nightfall tomorrow. We're leaving now. This meeting is over." He stood back, the damn pistol in his hand again. "Shut that computer down," he instructed Maggie.

"Talk to you tomorrow." Maggie frowned at Sinclair

Michaels before she closed the Skype window. She left the IKON network up and her computer running. She accessed *system preferences* in the upper left corner and clicked the Agency override setting to disable hibernate. Then she folded the lid on the laptop, slid the machine with its card running into its protected pouch in her backpack, and fastened the Velcro strap. For as long as the battery held out, the machine would run and would be traceable via GPS.

"Get ready to leave," Abraham said, snapping his fingers at Beatriz again.

Beatriz came over, picked up Maggie's laptop bag, slung it over her shoulder.

"Jack Warren is out of the picture now," Comrade Abraham said to Maggie. "We deal with you. I hope you're up to it."

She would have to be. But she still had two million aces in the hole. Grim Harvest would bend over backwards to make this work. They could talk tough, but they'd already shown their desperation. She had the money. And she had her GPS broadcasting as well.

"What about Yalu?" Beatriz said to Abraham.

"She's staying here. I'm not having my wife ride in the back of an open truck all night. Not with her kid."

Maggie thought Abraham's phrasing a little odd. *Her* kid.

"Is that the only transportation we have?" Beatriz sighed. "A *camión?*"

"It's short notice," Abraham said. "Revolution doesn't pander to creature comforts."

"I see," Beatriz said. "Is there anything left to eat? Or did you finish it all?"

Abraham ignored that. "Beatriz, get someone up here to stand guard with Yalu and the kid. Should only be two days max."

"Isn't it late notice?" Beatriz said.

"Just do as you're told, please."

"Call me 'comrade'," she said, smirking.

"Just do it."

Next door, the baby started crying again and they could hear Yalu coddling it.

~~~

"She's in Ciudad Bolívar," Achic said, tapping the Google map on his tablet as he sat in the front passenger seat of the crew-cab pickup parked on the outskirts of El Dorado airport. He zoomed in on an undefined snarl of unnamed streets and incomplete roads, haphazard half-formed nothingness that defined the mongo slums on the mountainside overlooking Bogotá. The screen glowed in the darkness of the cab.

The *she* in question was Maggie de la Cruz. She was going by Alice Mendes for this op and, apparently, IceLady69 as well.

"Are you j-joking?" Marcelo said, drumming his spindly fingers on the steering wheel. He was a nervous little guy with thick dark hair combed over in a side part. Wiry little mustache. "We're talking about a n-needle in a haystack."

"A big-ass haystack," Clarence in the back said in his gringo surfer Spanish. "And a small-ass needle."

"Kind of like your *p-pinga*," Marcelo said.

"How did you know, Marcelo?" Clarence said. "You b-been p-peeking again?" Making fun of Marcelo's stutter.

Marcelo brayed with laughter, slapping the wheel. "Hell yes, *vato*. I can't take my eyes off your *p-pinga*. It's like a p-penis—only smaller."

Clarence broke down too, a booming guffaw filling the little cab, rank with men waiting all night in a small enclosed space.

The two of them were getting bored, ready to raid the safe house where Comrade Cain was. Grab him, tie his terrorist ass up, haul it back to Ecuador to face justice. They were amped up. They lived for this kind of thing.

Well, so did he.

But where was John Rae? The man in charge?

"Please, guys," Achic said, holding one hand up in the dark cab, hoping for silence. He needed to concentrate. The coordinates got him down to an area of within ten feet of the place. But they still had to drive up there.

They had been sitting in the beat-up 1994 Nissan Frontier

4x4 crew cab, with a camper shell on the back that would hopefully soon be holding a shackled Comrade Cain. They'd moved the truck farther away from El Dorado Airport after John Rae texted Achic the code that meant he had been apprehended getting off the plane: 999. Emergency. Then John Rae's cell phone went dead. No doubt he'd disabled it. But that had been quite a few hours ago.

Achic in the passenger seat, Marcelo at the wheel, Clarence in back, all dressed in dungarees, work boots, baseball and cowboy hats—looking like a bunch of *campesinos* who'd gotten off work, were cruising around. The truck was loaded down with firepower, machine gun and shotgun in tool boxes with blankets piled on top. Small arms in their jackets, waistbands, under seats.

Achic double-checked the coordinates—4°35'53"N 74°4'33"W—making sure he hadn't fat-fingered the numbers transcribing them from the photo file someone named IceLady69 had sent to someone named PerroRabioso on some weird site called Frenesi. John Rae had texted Achic the logon and site info prior to landing in Bogotá, saying his partner called it belt and suspenders. And right after the plane came in, John Rae had sent Achic the 999.

"I can't wait to m-meet this Alice M-mendes," Marcelo said.

"I hear you, bro," Clarence said. "Any lady looks like the female in that photo, takes a friggin' selfie with some *terruco* standing right behind her holding a damn gun to her head, *and* calls herself IceLady69 to boot . . . well, let's just say I'm gonna have to get on bended knee, forgo my errant ways, and beg her to marry me." Clarence, the big gringo from California, played a video game on his smart phone in the back. Tinny gunshots popped out of the speaker. Clarence was an ex-Ranger buddy of John Rae's, a freelancer. His blond hair was cut and dyed dark to blend in south of the border, and he'd removed his earrings and shaved off his hipster goatee. Marcelo was Achic's contribution to the team, ex-Ecuadorian Coast Guard—like Achic himself—with sharp eyes that twitched every now and then. But he was battle-hardened and just what you wanted when dealing with someone like Cain. Both men were hired guns on the covert-covert team John Rae had put together with Achic. To take down Comrade Cain. A side mission of John Rae's that, as far as Achic knew, no one else knew about. Not even IceLady69.

Problem was, it looked like someone else had found out. That wasn't good for the Ice Lady, Magdalena de la Cruz, whom he'd almost died working with a week ago, on the failed Quito gig with Beltran. She was up there with those *terrucos*. Alone.

Achic and his crew were to follow John Rae and her to where they went to exchange Beltran for two million U.S. And then they were going to grab Cain, shoot the *vato* in the leg if they had to, tape him up good, throw him in the back of the Nissan, take him across the border into Ecuador to stand trial.

Shoot anybody got in the way. Cosecha Severa members in particular. Preferably.

But now it seemed as if someone had found out about John Rae's little Easter-egg operation, his covert op within a covert op. Had him pulled aside at El Dorado airport. The surface plan to pay Cain and his Grim Harvesters for Beltran the *pendejo*, who'd tried to burn them all just last week in Quito, was unraveling. Achic was still hurting from the two bullets he took in that carnage, one in the leg, one in the shoulder. Numbed up with Kodon now, over the counter hydrocodone easily acquired in this part of the world, he was foggy and irritable waiting for this op to get rolling.

Did he mention irritable?

At almost losing his life.

Dirtbags like Beltran, selling out his country.

Angrier still at scum like Comrade Cain, thinking he could waltz into Ecuador, do whatever he and his *comunista* shitbag pals wanted to. To Achic's country.

All in the name of saving the Amazon. Please.

Sure, no one liked the big gringo oil companies tearing things up, but filth like Cain would send the country to hell faster than you could say Chairman Mao.

"What we goin' to d-do, *jefe*?" Marcelo said. "Sit here all friggin' night? Wait for your American b-buddy?"

"If John Rae doesn't show," Achic said. "We're supposed to bail. That's the rules."

"Say *w-what*?" Marcelo said. "Leave M-miss Eyepopper—who took a hell of a risk for us—up there with the *terrucos*? With a damn gun to her head?"

"She don't know John Rae was planning to catch Cain."

"Well, t-that almost m-makes it worse."

"He's right, bro," Clarence said. "Plus, you been itching to nail Cain since your coast guard days, when he was running into Ecuador like he owned the place."

Achic nodded. "Yeah, you're both right. Right on the money. I can't argue."

"Then let's get it on, already," Clarence said, still playing his video game in the back of the truck. "The Ice Lady wants me. I can sense it."

Achic checked the Google map on his tablet. Then he looked at the picture of the pretty woman, the same one who jumped out the window in Quito while he took a couple of bullets. Alice Mendes, the Ice Lady now, with some dickhead *terruco* standing behind her, gun in his hand.

She was smart to get that picture out to the Frenesi site.

Inside some cinderblock shanty, way up there in the slums.

She had *cajones*, to go up there alone.

Maggie, Alice Mendes, IceLady69, whoever, could be in some serious shit.

Fifty thousand hovels like that up in that slum. But with the coordinates she sent, Achic could find it. Ex-Coast Guard, man. No problem.

"Let's go, men," he said. "John Rae is officially a no-show. Which makes me in charge."

"*Cha cha time!*" Marcelo fired up the Nissan, the old engine chugging, like half the trucks did in this part of the world. "Cain, we come to crash your party."

"*You got it!*" Achic said in English, mimicking Johnny

Canales on TV. Reached under the seat, pulled his black Glock 18 automatic, the one with an extended magazine, adding a few inches in length to the handle.

"Now you're talking, homeboy," Clarence in the back said, thumbs punching, playing his stupid game, the truck bouncing around on the dirt road. "Let's go get us some *terroristas*."

Achic kept looking at the map, the red little pin on it moving, showing where their truck was, heading toward Ciudad Bolívar, getting closer.

Get Maggie safe and sound.

Get that Peruvian shitbag Cain.

~ ~ ~

Two-thirty in the morning Yalu awoke, thought she heard something outside the safe house. Maybe the wind. She'd finally fallen asleep, after getting little Ernesto back to sleep first, hugging him in the cot she was curled up in, in the bedroom, the door pulled shut. Just Ernesto and her, Comrade Iker standing guard out in the living room, although he was probably asleep too. Comrade Iker wasn't much, but he was better than nothing, so they said. And he was available.

The others had gone, taking the *norteamericana* who looked like a fashion model to make the exchange for Beltran. They'd left over an hour ago, headed off to the border. Yalu hadn't heard the old Toyota pulling back up into the dirt road. So it wasn't Abraham and the others out there, making noise. They had gone to meet Comrade Cain.

Cain.

How she wanted to see him again. More than wanted. But Abraham wouldn't let her. The last time was when she'd caught that dirty Beltran ogling her ass out on the road to his mansion. Not only was Yalu the bait in the trap, she offed his pathetic chauffeur.

Cain had been pleased.

Abraham didn't like her around Cain.

There it was again, a sound outside. A window? The outhouse door? Left unlatched and catching the wind again? Damn Abraham anyway.

"Hey! Iker?" she shout-whispered, not wanting to have to mollycoddle Ernesto back to sleep for another two hours. No answer. Iker was either asleep or in the outhouse. She needed to be sure.

Holding Ernesto in her arms, Yalu climbed out of her cot, quietly as possible, set the baby down on his back in his playpen. He murmured, eyes shut, dribble on his lips. Her son. And such a responsibility. The word *burden* came to mind. She scolded herself, touched two fingers to her own lips, pressed them dutifully against Ernesto's forehead. Then she stood up, glanced around the half-finished room ankle-deep in clothes and junk, searching for rats or critters who might feast on her son. All clear.

Wait. What was that? Inside the house.

She tip-toed to the door, picked up the Belgian FAL rifle leaning on the frame. Held the gun in one hand by the pistol grip, a light enough weapon for a woman. Pulled the bedroom door open with the fingers of her free hand, no doorknob, just a hole. She crept out, drew the door shut behind her.

"Iker?"

No answer. She gripped the gun in both hands, flipped the extended safety selector off and said, creeping to the front door, "Iker?"

Another two steps. The wind was blowing up a gale out there. Just her fears?

"Abraham?" she said. "Is that you?"

"Put the g-gun down, *chica*."

-17-

Yalu jumped, the voice right behind her—*right behind her*—in this very room. Not a meter away. She spun with the rifle, but knew she was too late.

There, facing her, a little mid-30s Latino with a bandito mustache, sharp eyes blazing in the dark, holding a submachine gun, small hand gripping the magazine. The gun's stubby barrel pointed at her belly, still a little soft from carrying Ernesto. He had one of those plastic battery-operated hiker's lamps on his head, an elastic strap around it, making his thick hair bunch up.

"D-down on the floor it goes, *chica*." He motioned with the machine gun. Casual. Confident.

She laid the rifle quietly on the rough floor, not wanting to wake Ernesto. If people knew who he was, who his father was, there would be hell to pay.

The little *vato* with the machine gun reached up, flicked on his forehead lamp. The light blinded her. "Sorry." He tilted it down. "Where are the others?"

"I'm the only one here," she whispered.

He cocked his head to one side. "So why are you w-whispering?"

"I'm the only one," she said, louder. Maybe she could get away with it. Where the hell was Iker anyway? Useless bastard. "No one else."

The little guy cupped a hand around his mouth, shouted: "Clear in here!"

The front door opened silently, telling her that it couldn't be Abraham, who always banged the damn thing. Another hiker headlamp appeared, on a dark-skinned smallish man, also in his mid-30s, with a Glock machine pistol. He moved silently. The beam of light from his forehead centered directly in Yalu's eyes. He came up close, making her blink. The front door stood open, some big guy with a military shotgun filling it. He had his back to them and was watching the front of the house. The wind blew through the open front door like wind in a tunnel. He had the door propped open with a cinderblock he found out front.

~~~

Achic stood, looking the woman closely in the eye under the light. She was hiding something. He saw her eyes dart down to an empty sleeping bag on the floor, a daypack next to it, then back up to him. Quick, but not quick enough.

"Clarence!" Achic shouted over his shoulder. "Did you check the outhouse yet?"

"Shit." Clarence's big frame thumped the ground as he hopped off the porch.

"Iker!" the *terruca* woman shouted, her hands cupping her mouth now. "Watch out . . ."

Achic struck her across the face with the gun, knocking her to the floor. He flipped the Glock to semi-auto. She howled, rolling. "Any more of that and you lose a kneecap," Achic said.

She looked up at him through gritted teeth, blood running down from her eyebrow.

She was hiding something all right.

~~~

Outside, Clarence marched to the outhouse, the big Kel-Tec KSG shotgun up and ready, like some badass weapon out of a video game he'd played as a kid.

He stood now, legs apart, stared at the little crescent moon in the top of the outhouse door. Yeah, he should have checked before. "Hello?" An eyeball appeared at the crescent moon. Big and worried.

"How's it going?" Clarence said, making sure to use the polite form, as he didn't know to whom the eyeball belonged. "I'm Clarence, your friendly mercenary. Come on out with hands up and all that good stuff. Because if I even *think* you have a weapon . . ." Clarence shrugged with the shotgun in his hands. "Hell, I'm being kind of a softie right now, compared to how you *vatos* carry on. Not to generalize or anything, but you *terrucos* do tend to be kinda fanatical."

The eyeball disappeared.

A second passed.

Two seconds.

Clarence sighed, fired the Kal-Tec twice at the outhouse door.

Twin *booms* reverberated around the mountainside. The outhouse door vanished, leaving a shredded suggestion on hinges.

Clarence strode up, pointing the shotgun into the ragged hole that had been a door.

A middle-aged Mestizo wearing a *chullo* hat sat on the floor in a crouch, pants and underwear down to his ankles. An automatic rifle lay on the floor. The man had been hit and was covered with blood, like he'd been through a carwash of it. He looked at Clarence with fearful eyes, wheezing. He didn't have much time left. His rifle might as well have been a mile away. A newspaper was tattered around the inside of the outhouse. Scrap of headline about Bogotá FC, winning 2-1. He'd been reading the sports section on the pot, fell asleep. Last newspaper he'd ever read.

He was going to bleed to death. That wasn't the way to go.

Clarence didn't want to fire again. Sure, it was the slums, but he'd already fired twice. Eventually, someone would notice, even in this part of town. He pulled his boot knife, stepped up onto the porch of the outhouse, shaking his head. "Should have come out when I gave you the chance."

~~~

Achic stood at the front door, watching Clarence return from the outhouse, wiping his dagger off on a piece of newspaper. He had the shotgun slung over his shoulder, hanging low, pointing forward. "How did we miss him, Clarence?" A little edge in his voice.

"My bad," Clarence said, slipping the knife back into the leg scabbard. "Almost three in the morning, I didn't expect some guy taking a dump."

"The woman told Marcelo no one else was here."

"Well, she didn't speak the truth, did she, *jefe?*"

"Stay here, keep an eye out."

Achic went back inside. Marcelo was tying the woman's hands behind her back to one of the rungs of the chair she was sitting in. Blood ran from above her eyebrow. He walked over to the closed bedroom door, pointed his gun at it, turned his head, gave the woman a questioning look. "What—or *who*—do I find in here?"

"Go to hell."

"If I find anyone, they're dead. You realize that, don't you?"

The woman spit on the floor, told him to go *straight* to hell.

Achic put two bullets through the door. Two holes appeared. One shot ricocheted.

Behind the door, a baby started crying.

Standing behind the woman in the chair, Marcelo's mouth dropped in surprise. "You put a child at risk?" Achic said to her, flabbergasted.

"She's got a *kid* in there?" Clarence said in English behind him, then must have realized his mistake, because he switched to Spanish. "*Tiene un niño?*"

The woman stared hard at the floor, grimacing.

Achic kicked the door open with a hiking boot, the Glock in both hands.

He could hear a baby gurgling away. He went in, the gun readied, searched the room. He came back out. "What's your son's name?"

"Long live the revolution!"

"That's a long name." Achic pursed his lips. "Clarence!"

"Yo!"

"Bring our little terrorist out here. Support his neck when you lift him."

"I know what to do, *jefe*. I got nieces and nephews."

"Marcelo, go out front and stand guard."

Marcelo gave a single nod, headed out the front door with his machine gun hanging in one hand.

Achic strolled over to the scowling woman, while Clarence went into the bedroom. They could hear him going, "Come on, little buddy," gathering up the kid, the child's voice full of sleepiness.

"Where's Cain?" Achic said to the woman.

"I don't know who you're talking about."

"Try again." He adjusted the beam of light into her eyes. "You can end this as soon as you like. It's up to you, not me."

"I don't know anything," she said, squinting.

Achic looked around the room, the light on his forehead sweeping across, settling on a poster of Chairman Mao. He turned back, blinding her again.

"Isn't this all some big mistake, Comrade? Should you *really* be here? With a child? Where's the American woman who was here? The one who came to meet Cain?"

Clarence stood next to him now, holding the baby in his blanket, jiggling him, giving him a little smile.

Achic continued: "Are you turning this moment over in your mind? Are you saying to yourself, 'What have I done? What have I risked? My *son*?'"

She looked down.

"I asked you a question," he said.

"I don't know anything," she said.

"Let me ask what your people do in this position. Are you reasonable? With a prisoner who has a child? No. I've seen what you do."

She looked up. Her eyes grew dark. "Vengeance is justice!"

He nodded. "When I was in the mountains fighting the Shining Path we cornered a woman *terruca*. She had a rifle in her hands and her baby strapped across her front, like a big bandolier. She knew we wouldn't shoot children. I just stood there like a *boludo*, watching her sink back into the jungle. She had a smirk on her face."

"Then you have your answer," she said. "Don't you?"

"So what do I do?" Achic said. "Throw your baby out the

window? No, because you definitely won't tell me anything then."

She smiled. "You won't do it anyway," she said. "You don't have what it takes."

"You're wasting my time," Achic said, while Clarence played with the baby. "You know you're going to tell me where Cain is, where Beltran is, where the *norteamericana* is— eventually. The more you delay, the more of my time you waste. It's a shame, because you *are* going to tell me. You know how this works."

She sneered. "You can't do it. You have no conviction."

"Who are you protecting? Cain? It's certainly not your baby. Your baby is in danger. Cain isn't. What does that make him? A man who hides behind babies, lets infants fight his war?"

She stared him in the face. "Now you're wasting *my* time. Look at you. Pussies! You don't have the balls." She laughed. "You're pathetic."

"It's Cain you're protecting," he said with genuine admiration. "How does one gain loyalty like that?"

She spit in his face.

Achic wiped it off, nodded. He turned to Clarence, holding the infant. "Have you ever had to kill a child, Clarence?"

Clarence's face grew tense and solemn. "A kid in Afghanistan, *jefe*. Boy about six. Mentally retarded. The Taliban tied explosives to him, made him into a suicide bomber. Only he didn't know it. That's how they roll. It bugged me for a long time. Hell of a long time. It still does. Yeah." He shook his head. "Still does."

Achic took a deep breath, his chest thumping. Then he reminded himself. Maggie. Cain. "You never told me that before, Clarence."

"I never told anyone, *jefe*." Clarence looked down as he jiggled the baby. "That's the first time."

"I understand," Achic said. "I understand."

Clarence frowned as he jostled the baby. "I'm hoping it doesn't come to that today."

"Yes, me too." Achic inspected his gun. "She thinks we have no conviction. That we're weak."

"Yes, she does, *jefe*." Holding the baby. "But you just have to think about something else and get it done. You need to think of the worst thing that could happen, to your mother, whoever is important to you, and think how this is going to prevent that from happening."

Achic shook his head. "But a child?"

The woman laughed, but it was brittle.

Clarence said to Achic: "If it were easy, *jefe*, anyone could do it. This isn't some game we play. This is what we do. *Must* do. We're warriors. This is war. It's why we're here. To do any less would betray our mission. Then the people we're supposed to protect aren't being protected. Then we've lost."

Achic took that in. "You said it well, Clarence. We need to do what it takes to find Alice Mendes. And this woman here is standing in our way. She could easily tell us what she knows. Save her child. So if anything happens, it's her fault. She could stop it."

"Exactly, *jefe*."

"Put my son down, you bastard!" the woman screamed. "Shoot *me* if you have any guts."

Clarence was looking nowhere, still holding the baby. The baby babbled, the surreal sound drifting in and out of wind blowing around the room.

"You're a brave woman," Achic said to her. "You *do* have conviction. But let's see who has the most, shall we?" He turned to Clarence. "Hold the child's leg out, Clarence."

Clarence unfolded the blanket, revealed two chubby little legs sticking out of a disposable diaper. The baby shouted with glee. He was the center of attention.

"Go ahead!" the woman shouted, breaking into tears.

"Hold him up, Clarence. Away from you. You don't want his blood all over you."

Clarence did as he was told. Her son dangled in midair, legs bouncing playfully. He let out another little happy noise.

Achic pointed the gun at the child's foot. His heart was a

hammer.

"Well?" he said, turning to look at the woman, while he held the gun on her child. "Do you think I have the conviction?"

She sucked in air, seemed to recover, shook her head wildly. "You don't. You don't have it." But her voice wobbled.

There was a pause. "You're right." Achic lowered the gun and gave a sigh of frustration.

"Here," Clarence said, the baby under one arm now, reaching out for the gun. "I'll do it."

"No, Clarence. I can't ask you to do what I should do as leader."

"I'm already down for one, *jefe*. I'm damaged goods. I think about it every day. And it's not like we're going to kill him—right?"

"No, Clarence," Achic said. "Of course not—not if she tells us what we need to know."

"Just give me the gun, *jefe*."

"No, it wouldn't do any good anyway. She doesn't care. Isn't that a terrible thing? Is there anything more abnormal than a mother forsaking her own child?"

"We have to, *jefe*." Clarence's big hand moved in, agitated. "I'll be careful as I can. I promise."

Achic gave a sad nod. "Very well, then." He handed the gun to Clarence, who took it expertly, flipped it in the air single-handed, caught it. "It's on single-shot, right?"

"It is," Achic said. "Try to be careful. We don't want to cripple him for life."

The woman's eyes flickered madly as she gasped. She was fighting to hold onto her sanity.

"Semper fi," Clarence whispered, pointing the gun at the infant's foot. Then he closed his eyes.

"I can't watch," Achic said, turning. "I'm going outside."

"God forgive me," Clarence said, holding the barrel over the baby's foot. "God forgive me."

"They're taking the American woman to Ipiales!" the woman shouted. "But Cain isn't there. He's staying at a safe house in Coca. They're taking her there. Over the border. To Coca!"

Achic turned and looked at her blankly. "What is the address of the safe house?"

"Two-twelve Espejo. Please put my Ernesto down! *Please!*"

Clarence sniffed, made a face. "I think Comrade Ernesto here needs a diaper change." He turned to Achic. "Nice performance by the way, *jefe*."

"I think it was an ensemble effort, Clarence."

"I'm going to contact the motion picture association, have you nominated for best actor."

"Oh, come on, Clarence. Best supporting actor if anything. You were the star of the show. Your sense of pathos. Irony."

Jiggling the kid again. "My dad used to own a video store. Before they all went belly up, that is. I watched a ton of old flicks as a kid. Those old black-and-white movies?" Handing the Glock back to Achic, who took the gun.

"Did you really shoot that boy?" Achic said, putting the gun away. "In Afghanistan?"

"Hell, no!" Clarence said, grinning. He gave Ernesto a bounce. "I'd rather pound my balls flat with a wooden mallet than shoot a kid."

"That was a very good touch."

"Did you ever do any community theater?"

Achic laughed. "I honestly didn't know what we were going to do next."

"Oh, you would have thought of something, *jefe*. That's why you're in charge. You go with your gut. And it works for you, nine times out of ten."

Achic gave a smile of relief. "I learned that from my *grandpapi*. Go with your gut."

"You tricked me," the woman said, her voice rising. "You fucking tricked me!"

Achic gave her a weary smile. "But you'll never really know for sure, will you? And now I know how much conviction *you* have."

While Marcelo stood guard, Clarence bound Yalu's ankles in electrical wire while she lay on the cot in the bedroom. But when all was said and done, she was looking at the playpen where Ernesto was jabbering away.

Clarence slipped a bottle of formula into the child's hands. "I followed your instructions," he said to her. "Not too hot."

"*Gracias*," she whispered.

Achic entered the room, stood by the cot. "Where is your cell phone?" he said to her. "Don't tell me you don't have one."

"In the kitchen," she said. "In a pot on the stove. There's a lid over it."

"Clarence, get her phone."

Clarence did.

"What's the number?"

"In the call log. The first number. It belongs to Abraham. My husband."

Achic found the number, dialed it, put the phone to his ear, winced as a shrill piercing noise came, followed by a woman apologizing for not being able to connect the call.

"Out of range," he said. "But we can still beat them there." He spoke to Yalu. "Clarence is staying here with you and your son. When Beltran and the American woman are free and safe, you'll be released." He handed the phone to Clarence. "If anyone calls, hold the phone up to her, so she can speak." Then he focused on Yalu. "You will say everything is fine. No problems. Got that?"

She nodded. She was defeated.

And then he was gone.

Clarence settled down against the wall, leaned back, started playing a game on his cell phone. Little gunshots came.

"What are you doing now, *ese*?" Marcelo said, starting up the Nissan truck, the out-of-tune engine rumbling, making the view of Bogotá vibrate, a million shimmering lights below. They had parked up the hill, away from the safe house. To keep that element of surprise when they approached.

Achic dialed into his Nexus tablet, logged into Frenesi, the swinger site. He used the ID PerroRabioso, the one John Rae had texted him before he went offline.

No new messages. John Rae was well and truly out of circulation, as the 999 code suggested. Probably in some cell somewhere, courtesy of the Colombian government. And nothing from Maggie aka Alice Mendes aka IceLady69. Achic typed a message to IceLady69 anyway.

He didn't have a clue what kind of code she might be using, so he wrote his note in Quechua. He remembered her speaking it to him at Beltran's party. And he had yet to meet an American operative who could speak it, let alone the slang version he was using, full of reversed words and street dialect.

John Rae is disappeared. We're coming to Coca. We know where you are. If you can, escape. If not, sit tight. We'll get you out. Achic. He hit Send.

"Step on it, Marcelo," he said, powering down his tablet. "With any luck, we'll get to Coca before they do. Abraham's wife said they're taking a truck. We can move faster, even in this relic. And we have Ecuadorian passports. We'll get through border control without a problem."

The pickup bobbed down the hill. By his thigh, the gun smelled faintly of nitroglycerin, from shooting through the door to the child's room. If there was ever a time to be grateful for not hitting a target.

But he would see the American woman freed.

Shoot a baby? The *terrucos* could do that. Maybe that was the price of revolution.

-18-

The International Harvester truck ground to a halt at the top of the ascent outside the last major town before the Ecuadorian border, where they were to meet Comrade Cain and Beltran. The ancient chassis resounded with the recoils and thumps of a timeworn engine and decades of rough roads. Several hundred miles of Pan American Highway had shaken Maggie's teeth loose, while she sat in the back along with the members of Grim Harvest. She remembered riding in trucks like these with her mother as a child, bouncing through the Andes. This vehicle was older than she was, most likely twice as old. Maybe she'd even ridden in this one as a girl.

Dust swirled through the side gates as Maggie stood up, gazing out over the canyon that the twisting road had followed for the last hour. The valley was lush, deeply gouged by a river cascading down its twisted chasm. A delicate-looking gothic-style cathedral nestled between the folds of the gorge, spanning the ravine, caught her eye. It sat on tall stone piers, reaching across the rift with a footbridge that led to its entrance. Early-evening mist climbed the emerald canyon walls, rising up to reflect against the church.

"The city of green clouds," Beatriz said, getting to her feet and straightening her *pollera* skirt. The boy with the shaved head—Gabby—and Comrade Abraham got up from the truck bed as well, dusting themselves off. There had been a heated argument when Abraham told Yalu she wouldn't be coming along—an argument that turned into a shouting match, with Maggie suspecting Yalu of being just a little too enamored with Comrade Cain.

Soon they were all on the dusty ground, Beatriz with Maggie's knapsack slung over her shoulder.

Maggie sensed something was up. "Where's Cain?"

"*Comrade* Cain," Abraham reminded her. "He's over the border."

Maggie let out an angry gasp. "He was supposed to meet us here. With Beltran."

"Comrade Cain has every right to take precautions. Too many things have changed."

"Do I need to remind you that *I'm* the one with access to the funds?"

"If Commerce Oil wants its precious Minister Beltran back, it's going to have to meet Comrade Cain where he demands."

Maggie gave it some thought, ire roiling inside of her. She still didn't know the situation with John Rae. And then there was Tica and her comrades, even now under arrest as far as she knew. If they were entering Ecuador to meet Cain, Maggie was just that much closer to seeing them freed. On the other hand, she was a hunted woman in Ecuador, with her photo on the bulletin boards of police stations from the Oriente to the costa. Still, when she got right down to it, what choice did she have? "So where are we meeting Cain now?" she asked Abraham.

"Not far."

"Name of the town. Location. Specifics."

"Coca," Abraham said. "We're meeting Comrade Cain at a safe house there."

"Beltran is there?"

Abraham nodded.

Coca was the last main town on the Napo River before the Amazon proper. John Rae had told her that Cain and other members of Grim Harvest were hiding out in the jungle, wreaking havoc on the oil companies. "I need to clear this with my boss," she said.

"Very well," Abraham said, snapping his fingers at Beatriz.

Beatriz came over, handed Maggie her backpack.

Maggie pulled her laptop from the pack, squatted, rested the computer on her thighs. She flipped the top open. The screen was blank. The machine was cold. She'd left it up and running with the GPS on so that some ally might track her. A long shot.

"The battery's dead," she said, standing back up, closing the computer, putting it away. She suspected there wasn't much Sinclair Michaels could do anyway, not at this very moment. She'd continue on with Grim Harvest through to Coca and see what transpired. She'd come this far.

She could always make a run for it, if need be. Even Gabby, a teenager, posed no problem; he didn't clock five miles a day and look forward to it, miss it when it didn't happen. And they wouldn't shoot two million dollars. Not just like that. "I hope you didn't know about this all along," Maggie said to Abraham. "I don't like being jerked around."

Abraham said nothing.

Beatriz was watching her with what Maggie suspected was muted admiration. "Come on, *princesa*," she said, gazing up at the sun slipping below the summit. "It's getting late. We still have to hike over the top of the mountain—around border control."

An hour later at the top of the mountain, the four of them stopped, puffing. Humidity saturated the air, even with the rainforest a good hundred miles away. No one was talking.

Despite the anxiety of the situation, the view of Ecuador sent powerful emotions through Maggie. Mountainous and verdant, with grand araucaria trees swaying amongst ferns and exotic plants, she felt the bond yet again. She'd been born here and she was as much Quechua as she was gringa. The Andes never let go.

The four of them trekked down, leaving Colombia, staying well away from the main highway that connected the two countries. At a narrow mountain road forking off the main highway, its potholed surface a reminder that it had once been paved, a white panel van mottled with rust sat under the trees. Its doors were open, obviously to let some air through. The driver was sitting back, arms crossed, a straw cowboy hat pulled down over his eyes.

"That must be our ride to Coca," Beatriz said to Gabby in Quechua.

"I hope this one has seats," Gabby said, hitching up his baggy jeans with one hand. His pistol swung in his right hand as he walked. "My *culo* is raw from riding in the back of that dang truck all morning."

"You kids have it easy. You just don't know it."

"Just because you've got a padded arse that can handle it."

"Show some respect!" She tried to cuff his head, but Gabby quickly dodged her and spun, waving the gun, pretending to take aim.

Beatriz laughed, a loud roar. "Better not shoot me, boy! I'm the one looking out for you."

"If that's the case, then I'm in real trouble, aren't I?"

Beatriz rubbed the back of Gabby's stubbled head as they got into the work van. It had bench seats.

Abraham gave Maggie a squint as they climbed in and set off for the Amazon town of Coca.

-19-

Coca flanked the Napo River, the last main town before the jungle. With the oil boom, the once-sleepy backwater had burgeoned to over forty thousand people and even late in the evening, the streets were full, mostly young men looking for excitement. Harshly lit bars were going full tilt, shouting and music creating a din that spilled out into Chimborazo Street along the riverfront. Hastily built structures took up all available space. Stores were just closing, many displaying household appliances and televisions, all the conveniences and creature comforts people moving from the city wanted. Cars and motorbikes jammed the road. Out on the water, a huge barge loaded down with two gasoline tanker trucks headed upriver.

Progress, Maggie thought.

Their van crawled down Chimborazo and took a dim side street that quickly turned into unlit dirt road, passing rundown houses, many in a permanent state of incompletion, rebar sticking out from rooftops like wild whiskers.

They passed a house with red lights, thumping with noise that seeped through heavily curtained windows. A couple of *vatos* in dungarees and yellow hardhats were just leaving, one lighting a cigarette, both keeping their eyes down. A woman in a short revealing robe shut the front door. A whorehouse.

A couple blocks beyond, near the end of the dirt road, they stopped at a one-story stucco house, silent and dark. The few houses down this way were interspersed with vacant lots, and all of them were dark. Maggie took a good look at the empty house in front of her. Someone had dumped an old car seat under the window. There were no vehicles parked anywhere.

"Doesn't look like anyone's home," she said drily to Abraham.

Abraham frowned, heaved the side door of the van back with a bang, climbed out, marched off, pulling his cell phone from the pocket of his shorts. Maggie watched him make a call, gesturing excitedly. Gabby turned to Beatriz, sitting in the bench seat in front of Maggie, and the two exchanged looks.

"What do you make if it?" Gabby said in Quechua.

"I think Cain isn't coming."

"*Comrade* Cain," Gabby said, grinning.

Beatriz smiled back.

Abraham returned to the van, looking more stoic than before. He stood by the open door for a moment, then placed both hands on the top of the doorframe.

"So where are Cain and Beltran?" Maggie said.

"We're going to meet them. Tomorrow."

"Where to now?" Maggie said, although she had a pretty good idea.

"The Yasuni," Abraham mumbled.

The Yasuni. The heart of the Amazon jungle. Where the oil exploration was going on. Where the heart of Grim Harvest were rumored to be holed up. Where the Yasuni 7 were from. Tica. Where that hideous video Maggie had watched was made.

It made sense Cain would be there. But it made her nervous. "I need to confirm this change of plan with my manager," she said.

Abraham ran his fingers through his frizzy hair. "Yes. OK. Inside."

"No," Maggie said. "I'm not going into that funhouse without talking to my boss first. We'll go somewhere. A café. A bar."

"We don't have time."

"Make time."

"I'm getting tired of your demands."

"*My* demands?" She laughed out loud. "Who exactly is taking *who* on a scenic trip halfway across South America in the hopes of meeting the elusive Cain? Oh, I'm sorry—it's *Comrade* Cain, isn't it?"

"Comrade Cain has every right to take precautions."

"Yes, you've mentioned that. Well, so do I. I'm calling my boss. Or it's no deal."

Abraham glared into the van. "I'll have to clear it," he said.

"Of course you do. God forbid you make a decision on your own."

Abraham stormed off, making another fervent phone call. Beatriz and Gabby watched Maggie closely. Abraham returned, climbed into the van, yanked the door shut with an angry slam. He produced his cell phone, held it out to Maggie. "Call your boss."

"I'm not calling him on that," she said. "Do you really think my boss wants a verifiable connection to a terrorist group? Drive down to the main drag. Along the river. I'll call from one of the bars or *cabinas* there."

"This is getting ridiculous."

"That's exactly what I was thinking."

"*¡Mierda!*" Abraham pulled the .38, waved it in the confines of the van. Maggie reared back. Beatriz and Gabby watched. The driver was noticeably quiet, staring straight ahead. "Enough!" Abraham shouted. "We're staying here for a few hours, then heading off to meet Comrade Cain to complete the arrangement. That's it!"

Maggie looked at the gun. "You know what? I've had enough of your bullshit. Let me out, *amigo*. The deal is off."

Abraham laughed through his nose. "Wouldn't you like to think so?"

"Get out of my way."

Abraham shook his head, gave an ugly smile.

"You won't get a single penny out of me," Maggie said.

"More talk. Words."

"Words that equal no money for you losers. Let me out. Now."

Suddenly the gun blurred through the air and smacked Maggie in the side of the head, making her skull ring like a broken bell.

"Want to keep talking?" Abraham screamed. "Keep at it!"

Maggie held the side of her buzzing head. Her vision shook out of control.

"Comrade," Beatriz said quietly to Abraham. "Please. She is just . . ."

"Shut up!" Abraham yelled at Beatriz, waving the pistol. "Who's in charge here?"

"You are."

"That's correct. So just do as you're told." He glared at Gabby. "You too."

"What did *I* say?"

The driver didn't look back, didn't say anything.

Quietly, Beatriz said: "Things are getting out of hand, Comrade."

Maggie wished she had something made of metal, something she could smack Abraham's head with. Something sharp. Something that cut flesh. Or something that fired bullets. She held her head, waiting for her senses to settle down. For the ringing to stop.

"We're staying here until morning," Abraham said. "Then we're heading upriver. The deal will be completed there. That's all there is to it."

Maggie said nothing. What else could she do? She'd overplayed her hand.

"Gabby, where's your gun?" Abraham said.

"Right here, Comrade."

"Keep your eye on Alice Mendes here. Beatriz, you have your machete?"

"Yes."

"Good. Keep up the rear. And now, if there are no objections, we're going into the house. That fine with you, Alice? Or do you need to clear it with God?"

Maggie bit down on her tongue.

They got out of the van then, approached the darkened safe house. The driver took off in a hurry. Abraham was on Maggie's left, Gabby on her right. Both men had their guns down by their sides. Beatriz brought up the rear and Maggie saw the big fish head of a machete swinging behind on the periphery of her vision. Her head was swimming.

At the front door Abraham reached up, got a key from a hole in the molding, unlocked the door. He pushed the door open, stood back. "Gabby, you know the procedure. Check the place out."

"Yes, Comrade." Gabby threw a who-cares shrug and entered with the big .45 in his hand. He reached for the light switch, flicked it up. No light.

"Someone needs to pay the damn power bill," he mumbled, going into the house, blinking rapidly to adjust his eyes to the dark. The place was the usual pigsty, chairs pushed up against the wall, mattresses on the floor, blankets twisted on top of them. Half-eaten tins of food here and there.

Springing over the mattresses into the darkness of the hallway, he scanned for intruders. He had yet to find one. He'd love to. He was eager to get into a firefight.

He was a good shot. *A good shot.* Comrade Cain had slapped him on the back during target practice once and called him a *pistolero,* right out of a spaghetti western. Well, Gabby knew that. He practiced and was good to begin with. But the compliment stayed with him, considering its source.

He *was* a *pistolero.* It was in his nature. And you couldn't deny a man his nature.

The *militares* would pay for killing his father. Pay with their lives.

Gabby moved into the kitchen, the sink bulging with dirty dishes, floor littered with more tins, stove full of pots thick with sludge. The core members of the group treated this place like a rubbish tip. Cleaning up was too good for them.

Then the bathroom. The old claw-footed tub sat full of scummy water. Cold as a witch's tit. Moonlight through the pebbled window reflected off the filmy surface.

A rat scurried out from under the tub, scratching nails and making Gabby jump like a little boy, taking aim to shoot the thing. He didn't. He was glad no one was there to see that.

Then a bedroom, ankle deep in old clothes and more mattresses. He stood back, surveyed the dump of a room, moving the gun with his line of sight. The closet door was wide open, flat against the wall. A pair of empty coat hangers hung next to a large camouflage field jacket on a wooden dowel.

Then the second bedroom. Junk everywhere.

A poster of a girl in a bikini in the light from the window caught his eye. Whoa. She was new. Normally, it was Chairman Mao or nothing at all in these places. Someone had taste. This *chica* was illuminated by moonbeams that set her alight. She was holding up a can of motor oil, right in front of her boobs, in case you didn't notice that she had a *perfect* set. They were exceptional. You could see the sheen on the tops of them, swelling out of her bikini top a size too small. Her full lips were parted, the tip of her tongue licking the upper one. Eyes sly and smiling, and her long dark hair was tousled and wild, like she was waiting to be thrown over your shoulder and taken off into the woods. Not very revolutionary. But inspiring. Gabby thought of the *norteamericana*, Alice Mendes, at the front door now with Abraham and his mother. He hadn't engaged her in conversation. It wasn't easy with your *mami* around. And he was shy to begin with. He needed to work on that. Alice Mendes was *fine*—she put even this poster girl to shame. She made Yalu look like his toothless aunt. And Yalu was nothing to turn your nose up at . . .

"Gabby?" Abraham shouted from the porch. "What's going on in there?"

"All clear!" he yelled back.

He heard them come in, Comrade Asshole telling the *norteamericana* not to try anything funny. He had her covered.

"They left this place like a bombsite again," Gabby's mother said.

"Yes, Beatriz," Abraham said.

"You really need to talk to them, you know."

"Yes, yes. Where's the damn lantern?"

"Over here. They could have at least paid the power bill."

Gabby saluted the oilcan *chica* with the barrel of his .45 and turned to join the others in the living room, tucking the pistol into the back of his waistband.

The closet door creaked.

Gabby snapped to attention, spun back around, reaching behind him for the gun.

A machine gun was already pointed directly at him. A pair of hard little eyes stared into his. "Forgot to c-check the closet, d-didn't you?" the man whispered.

~~~

"*¡La venganza es la justicia!*" they heard Gabby shout as a machine gun opened up in the back bedroom. It was followed by pistol shots, Gabby returning fire.

"Gabby!" Beatriz shouted, running toward the hallway with her machete raised.

Abraham sunk back to the front door and squatted, holding up the .38. His eyes were wild and nervous.

Unable to get out the front door, Maggie pressed herself against a wall cloaked in darkness, becoming part of it.

In the bedroom more automatic-weapon fire popped amidst a struggle. A man screamed, Beatriz called him a *bastardo*, then more automatic fire, then the continued brawl.

Outside the front door now, a man shouted in accented English: "Alice! If you're in there, get the hell out of the way! I'm going to open up! Then I'm coming in! Move—now!"

The voice knew her code name. It was Achic, from the Quito op. Maggie dived for the shadows, half of her landing on a mattress, an elbow smarting when it hit an open tin of something.

Shots tore through the front door amidst the chatter of automatic fire, random holes appearing in old wood, holes filling with streetlight. Big splinters sprayed across Abraham crouching. He leapt up and landed on a mattress. Scrambling around, he got into a squat, fired the .38 at the door. A single shot went wild. He hunkered back down.

The bedroom where Beatriz had gone was pure pandemonium, Beatriz attacking someone with the machete.

Rounds ruptured though the front door, one of the panels disintegrating. The tinkle of shell casings rattled on the porch outside.

"Alice!" a voice shouted in English again. "Stand back!"

"He's got a gun on you, Achic!" she yelled. "*You* watch out!"

Abraham raised his pistol in both hands and aimed at the front door. The gun shook visibly.

Maggie charged across the room, knocked Abraham off the mattress. Abraham rolled, staring up at Maggie with panic-stricken eyes. He brought the .38 up in one hand, into her face.

Her heart leapt as she kicked the gun out of his hand. She heard the pistol smack the far wall. Abraham swore as he gripped his injured wrist. She kicked him hard, connecting with his torso, a blow that vibrated through her boot. Abraham's hands covered his head as she kept at it, gritting her teeth. Out of the corner of her eye, she saw Achic's arm reach into the shattered front door panel and unlatch the lock.

"He's unarmed now, Achic!"

Maggie rushed to the far side of the room where a divot in the plaster indicated where the gun she had kicked out of Abraham's hand had struck the wall. She scanned the floorboards below and, behind a tattered wing-backed armchair, found the .38. She grabbed it and squatted down behind the chair. She pulled the hammer back with her thumb and waited.

The front door opened.

The house had quieted down; all they could hear was the nonstop party going on up the road at the whorehouse.

"Alice?" Achic said.

She dragged her hair out of her face, but stayed put. Her heart was pounding audibly.

"I'm OK," she said. "I'm OK."

Achic crept through the front door, holding an automatic pistol with an extended magazine. He saw Abraham on the mattress, gripping his head. Achic leveled the gun on him. "No sudden moves, Comrade."

"No," Abraham panted. "Don't worry."

"Who's the guy in the bedroom?" Maggie said to Achic in English.

"My partner." Then he shouted, in Spanish: "You in there, Marcelo?"

Out of the hallway came a small Latin guy with penetrating eyes, a pencil mustache and thick hair. He had a machine gun slung over one shoulder, and one hand gripping the other arm with a rag. Even in the dark, it was easy to see that it was soaked with blood.

"That d-damn woman put up a fight," he said, wincing. "Got me with that m-machete before I could put her away."

"She dead?" Achic said.

"Lights out. So's the kid. That leaves this one? Comrade Abraham, is it?"

"Last one alive," Achic said.

"How's the revolution going for you today, Abe?" Marcelo said, squeezing his wound with the rag, dripping blood.

Abraham held his head.

"How did you find me?" Maggie said to Achic, standing up, woozy.

"Three of us were supposed to meet up with you and your partner after you two landed in Bogotá. But you know what happened to him. Detained. He sent me a login and password to the site you told him to sign up for while your plane was still in the air. I saw your message with the map coordinates to the safe house in Bogotá. We headed up there, found out these guys had left, and were bringing you here."

A good thing, as it turned out. Maggie thought she had things under control, until Abraham took her hostage. How quickly things could change. "What about Yalu?" she said.

"We're holding her," Achic said. "Her kid, too. To make sure these shitbags let you go."

"What?" Abraham cried, rising up from the mattress. "What have you done to my wife, you animal?"

"I thought I said *no sudden moves*." Achic struck Abraham across the side of the head with the pistol, sending him back down to the floor. "Any more of that and I lose my temper."

"Please don't hurt my wife!"

"Do as you're told," Achic said. "And no harm comes to little Ernesto."

"What have you done to Yalu?" Abraham said. "Have you hurt her in any way?"

Maggie took in Abraham's words with interest. She stood up, slipped the .38 into the side pocket of her denim jacket. "Help me find the lantern," she said to Achic. "It's around here somewhere."

Achic did so, fired it up. He went over to the window, pulled the blind back an inch, checked for anyone walking by. No one. That was one of the few benefits of a derelict neighborhood, no doubt a reason Grim Harvest was drawn to a house like this. Achic came back, held the lantern while Maggie found a stray piece of rag, tore off two small sections, wadded them into ear bungs. She knelt over Abraham, plugging both ears. Cloth stuck out like fuses. Now they could talk freely.

"Now you can tell me what in the hell John Rae had planned with you mad dogs in the first place," she said to Achic. "Because he never mentioned a damn thing about it to me."

-20-

"So John Rae was planning to *capture* Comrade Cain?" Maggie said, shaking her head in disbelief.

"That's why he put this team together," Achic said, gently cutting Marcelo's bloody shirt away from his shoulder as Marcelo sat on a chair, gnashing his teeth, the knife in Achic's hand drawing painfully close to a blood-soaked patch where Beatriz's machete had found its mark. After the firefight, Achic had sprinted back to his truck, returned with a backpack of supplies. Marcelo pressed a rag on the wound to stem the bleeding while Achic worked around it to cut away the shirt sleeve. "We were planning on taking Cain back to Quito. To face justice. My country has had more than enough of terrorism, let alone gangs of *terrucos* coming in and wreaking havoc."

Even as the oil companies inflicted their own mayhem, Maggie thought—damage sanctioned by governments, probably far more lethal to humans in the long run than any band of radical idealists. Almost nothing about the modern world made sense anymore, which side to take. The only person who seemed to have any kind of answer to this situation was sitting in a prison cell in Quito, along with her six allies.

"I would have appreciated knowing that," Maggie said to Achic. "I was led to believe we were doing a simple money exchange for Beltran."

"John Rae didn't want you along in the first place," Achic said, cutting the bloody arm of the shirt away at the shoulder seam, around the cloth Marcelo held in place. "But you insisted. It was the only way you would agree to help."

True enough. Both John Rae and Sinclair Michaels had tried mightily to dissuade Maggie, hoping she would enact the cash transfer from the U.S. John Rae told Maggie to bow out if anything out of the ordinary transpired. Had he been expecting something like his detainment at the airport? Her near abduction by Grim Harvest? And how much did Sinclair know about John Rae's plan? Was he in on the thing as well? Being in the dark came with the territory in this line of work, even in the field, she was learning.

"Better let me help you with that," Maggie said to Achic, indicating Marcelo's wounded arm. "What can I do?"

"*Quikclot.*" Achic nodded at his backpack, open on the floor. "Side pocket."

Maggie kneeled down and dug through Achic's pack, pulling out a fat roll of gauze, medical tape, safety pins. She found what she was looking for: a blue and yellow plastic bottle of combat blood coagulant. Pulling open the top, she moved over to Marcelo's upraised arm.

"Move your hand away, Achic."

Marcelo winced as Achic pulled the soggy sleeve down and over his wrist. He dropped the bloody cloth to the floor with a soft splat. A gash ran diagonally down most of Marcelo's upper arm, a slice deep and ugly, flesh hanging from the wound. Uncovered, blood pooled quickly, running down Marcelo's forearm, over a tattooed snake coiled over the word *Defendemos.* We Defend.

"*¡C-cingada!*" Marcelo stammered, wiping the blood off the snake with his hand. The abrasion collected again and dripped anew.

Maggie poured a good four ounces of fine gray powder into the laceration, wincing at the exposed white bone. She filled the wound. The powder rapidly absorbed blood and swelled to seal the incision. Within fifteen seconds, the bleeding had stopped. Turning away for a moment, she suppressed a twist of nausea in her gut.

She noted that Abraham, face down on a mattress, was

silent, his hands cinched tightly behind his back in a plastic tie Achic had applied. He had a black hood over his head now and appeared still, like a corpse, in the cold glow of the battery-operated camping light on the table cluttered with junk. Upon closer inspection, it was obvious Abraham was vibrating with fear, though whether for himself or Yalu, she couldn't discern.

"That arm looks better," Achic said to Marcelo. "Not good, but better."

Ripping open several medicated gauze squares, Maggie placed them strategically over the gash, while Achic held Marcelo's arm up and steady. Marcelo, for his part, stayed motionless, gritting his teeth, studying the effort. Maggie unrolled a few feet of Medica combat bandage and soon had his entire upper arm wrapped, safety-pinning it securely. When she was done, his padded arm stuck out from his skinny torso like a chicken wing.

"Beltran was only part of the larger plan," Achic continued. "Yes, the Ecuadorian government wanted him back, but that was primarily the oil companies talking. The government would only authorize the operation if we brought Cain in as well. He's been a thorn in our side for years."

Two birds with one stone, Maggie thought. It would have been nice to know about bird number two: Cain.

"How long has John Rae been after Cain?" Maggie asked Achic.

Achic gazed away in thought. "John Rae was with U.S. Army Intelligence in the mountains, helping us root out Shining Path. We actually caught Cain once. John Rae started to interrogate him, but Cain's guerillas overran the camp and freed him. John Rae never forgot it. Neither did I."

Maggie rose, went over to her own bag, discarded by the front door where Beatriz had dropped it, and found her skull-and-crossbones rock-and-roll headscarf. She unfolded and refolded it into a makeshift sling as she came back over to Marcelo and, with Achic's help, got Marcelo's forearm through it where he could rest his arm without having to lift. He gave a muted sigh of relief.

"That'll have to do for now, Marcelo," she said.

"Thanks, *ch-chica*," Marcelo said, examining her handiwork with an appreciative nod. "As good as new."

"Not by a long shot," she said. "You need to see a doctor. And soon. Or learn to shoot with your left permanently."

"It's f-fine."

"No, it's not."

"She's right, brother," Achic said.

"What are you planning to do now?" Maggie asked Achic, standing up.

Achic retrieved his Glock 18, ejected the extra-long magazine that extended several inches from the handle of the gun. "Number one, get you to safety," he said, going through his pack. "Get Marcelo to a doc when day breaks. Find out what the hell happened to John Rae. Plenty to do. But the op itself, to swap Beltran for two million *pavos*—and capture Cain—is history." He pulled a fresh 33-round magazine from another side pocket in the bag, slicked it into the gun. "I hope you realize that."

Maggie thought about that. "What are you going to do with Comrade Abraham here?"

Achic shrugged as he aimed a pretend shot against a poster of Chairman Mao on the wall. "Take him along. He's not Cain, but he is second in command. After he goes through interrogation, what's left of him can rot in Latacunga prison. Standing room only." He raised his voice so Abraham could hear through the ear plugs. "Glad you came to mess with my country now, you scum?"

Abraham said nothing, moved little. Marcelo shifted in his chair, shuddering.

"I have some Kodon," Achic said to him. "It'll help kill that bastard pain until we can find a doc."

"No th-thanks."

"Going to tough it out?"

Marcelo grimaced. "It's part of the package, *jefe*. War. Others are dead. Not me. Pain is proof I'm still kicking. I won't mask reality. I'll live with it, as long as I can. If I can't, then I'll take your disco pills."

"Old school," Achic said, giving Maggie a weary smile.

Marcelo was some kind of modern-day Latin Samurai, steeped in his warrior code. Maggie didn't pretend to understand, just knew that men like him were necessary.

"You ready to go?" Achic asked her. "I'll drive you to Coca Airport. Hopefully you can still buy a ticket to Quito. With the oil boom, every flight is packed, and there's nothing more than puddle jumpers that land here anyway. You'll have to pay a 'special fee.' But in Quito, you can get a flight back to the U.S. You got your new passport?"

She nodded.

"Even so, you'll have to change your appearance. They'll still be on the lookout for you. Need cash?"

Maggie ran her fingers through her hair, blinked away the chaos of the last day plus. She hadn't slept since the flight into Bogotá. Over a day ago. She hadn't bathed. She hadn't eaten. Her teeth had what felt like a layer of fur on them. "I'm going to find a shirt for Marcelo," she said. "There's got to be something." Walking off, she headed down the hall, really just to get away for a moment—think things over.

Stopping at the first bedroom, she saw the bodies.

Knowing and seeing were two different things.

Beatriz lay sprawled unnaturally in a death run, legs splayed, on the floor. Her rugged Indian features were smeared with blood. She'd been shot more than once. She lay over Gabby, curled up, a dead boy, never to be a man now, Beatriz' big arm in its cardigan over him, as if she could somehow save him from his fate.

She had heard him call Beatriz *Mami* when he thought no one else was around.

Maggie hung her head in grief.

A lot of blood had been spilled over this milk run. Too much to simply walk away.

And if she were going to have any effect on the insanity taking over the country of her birth, getting Tica and the rest of the Yasuni 7 freed would be a good place to start.

She pulled an old blanket from the bed, musty and reeking of mildew, and gently laid it over mother and son, wondering what had prompted them to join the *terrucos*. Everyone had their own reason, and it was always personal.

She pulled the window blind down, shut the door on them, leaving them in silence.

In the first bedroom in a closet she found a camouflage jacket. Size large. But it would do nicely. Back in the living room, she handed the jacket to Marcelo. He looked up with gratitude. His shirt lay in bloody shreds on the floor around the chair. He was clearly in serious pain. His bare shoulders shivered.

"Thanks, *ch-chica*."

"Thank you for saving me from those madmen."

He gave a fatigued nod. "*Defendemos*," he said quietly.

"Yes," she said. "You do."

There was a pause.

"You ready to go now, Maggie?" Achic said. "Back to the U.S.?"

"No," she said, meeting his gaze. "No, I'm not."

-21-

"What the hell are you planning, Maggie?" Achic said, squinting. "If not going back home to the U.S. straight away?" Marcelo looked up from his chair. He had the camouflage jacket draped over his shoulders. His eyes were glazing over, no doubt from shock and pain. Abraham still lay on the mattress, a hood over his head, hands tied behind him.

"The transfer," Maggie said, standing up to face Achic. "Beltran for the money."

Achic stood there, frozen. "No."

"Yes."

"Are you s-sure about that?" Marcelo said. "It m-means meeting with Cain."

"That's what I came down to South America for," Maggie said.

"Too dangerous," Achic said, shaking his head. "I can't let you."

"With all due respect," she said. "It's my decision."

"John Rae would *not* authorize it."

"And where *is* John Rae?" Maggie looked around the wreck of a living room in a theatrical manner. "Oh, that's right—he's in jail. Or somewhere else. He's certainly not here. So he doesn't get a say. I'm going ahead with it." She raised her eyebrows. "And after all the effort and misery that has gone into this operation, it would be a sin to do otherwise."

"But capturing Cain . . ."

"No concern at all to me. That was never part of anything I signed up for."

Achic nodded. "I've got to get Marcelo to a doctor. Then

I've got to find John Rae . . . get him freed . . ."

"Then I suggest you get to it."

"What I'm saying, Maggie, is that I can't go with you—hold your hand."

"No one is asking you to."

"You think you're going out there alone?" Achic said. "The Yasuni? The middle of the Amazon jungle? With Cain and his Maoist maniacs?"

"I was born in Ecuador, just like you. I'm not scared of the jungle. In fact, I'd like to see it survive a little while longer. Who am I dealing with? Some two-bit *terruco* whose only real concern is probably two million bucks. Money I understand. It's what I do best."

Achic frowned. "How do you think you're going to get there?"

"I'll hire a boat and skipper. Down at the dock. Won't take more than a couple of hours to get up to the Yasuni." That would also be a good way to avoid the authorities keeping an eye out for her in public places, like airports.

Achic shook his head. "Too dangerous."

"Think about it: You've got Abraham. You've got his wife. The *kid*. Right?"

"Right . . ."

"If Cain gets out of hand, I'll lay it out for him. He'll be pretty receptive to any prisoner exchanges. You've got three people he wants." Well, two, Maggie thought. "On top of the two million dollars, he's in my pocket. I'm not worried." OK, that was an overstatement, but she did indeed have the upper hand. "I'll also make contact with the op manager, before I head to the jungle, get some support."

"John Rae never told me who that was. Best to keep it that way."

The old mantra about one cell knowing as little as possible about another. Ignorance *was* bliss. Or safety. "I'm covered, Achic," she said. "When I talk to my op leader, I'll make sure you're kept in the loop. You may even get pulled back in at some point."

Achic rubbed his chin and she could tell he liked the idea that the operation still had legs. "So," he said. "What next?"

"We call Cain. Or rather, we get Comrade Abraham here to make the call." She looked down at him. "We'll arrange the meeting between Cain and myself. I'll meet Cain, establish the ground rules. Then we'll make the exchange in a safe place. Any problems, I'll let Cain know we're holding three of his key people."

"Fair enough."

"And I'll need one task from you," she said to Achic.

"And what is that?"

"You said you're holding Yalu? And her son—Ernesto? At that safe house in Bogotá?"

"Correct."

"You'll need to move them. Somewhere safe."

"Why?"

"Because if Cain learns about it, he's likely to come straight for them."

"Why?"

"You'll find out soon enough."

Achic seemed to think that over.

"Once Cain knows the situation," she said. "He'll be more than happy to play along."

"I'm not sure Cain is ever happy about anything," Achic said. "Unless it's destroying something. But I think your plan could work."

"*Cajones, j-jefe,*" Marcelo said, giving Maggie an appreciative nod. "This lady's got some big ones."

"Let's call Cain now." Achic stood over Abraham, pulled back the hood long enough to remove the ad hoc earplugs. Twisting the metal dial up on the upper left side of his pistol, Maggie knew he was putting the gun into semi-automatic mode.

He knelt down, pointed the barrel of the Glock into the back of Abraham's knee.

"Feel that, Comrade?"

The black hooded head nodded.

Achic moved the gun alongside Abraham's knee, fired into the floorboard. There was a *pop*, the clang of an ejected shell, and a puff of dust as the 9 mm bullet drilled through the floor. "Next bullet is through the back of your knee—if you don't cooperate one hundred percent. Do we understand each other clearly?"

"Yes," Abraham croaked.

"Don't forget that we have your family."

"I haven't forgotten."

Achic stood up, turned to Maggie, waved his open hand. "It's your show now."

Maggie walked over, stood over Abraham.

"Where's your phone?"

"Pocket," Abraham gasped.

Maggie bent down, dug into the pocket of Abraham's shorts, came out with a greasy cell phone. She scrolled through the call log.

"This number, the one that's been called the most? That's Cain?"

"Yes, yes."

"There's got to be some kind of coded exchange between you two to authenticate. What is it?"

"A simple index based one we both know. Cain says a number; I reply with a matching phrase."

"OK, You're going to get me through to him." Maggie spent the next couple of minutes outlining what Abraham was to tell Cain. When she was done, she said: "Any questions?"

"No."

"And if I think you're trying to use any kind of a secret code to alert Cain, beyond the authentication? If I even *suspect* that's what you're doing, then you can look forward to your wife getting deported while you sit in prison—along with Achic's promise to rearrange your knee."

"I understand," Abraham said.

"Lift your head now," she said.

Abraham complied and Maggie pulled the hood off. Maggie punched the cell number from the call list and listened to it connect, then start to ring. She pressed the speaker button, putting the cell phone into conference mode, and set the phone down on the floor not far from Achic. Abraham turned his head in the direction of the phone, ready to talk.

After several rings, the phone picked up and the sounds of birds squawking blended with static and the wind. Finally, a man spoke. His voice was cultured and businesslike. Not what she expected. He uttered two numbers: "Two. Two."

Abraham said: "In class society."

"Go ahead."

"My status report, Comrade Commander," Abraham said.

"Yes, yes."

Abraham continued: "Another change of plans, I'm afraid."

"What is it, this time?" Cain said, more curtly than before.

"Alice Mendes is planning to come upriver to meet with you. She doesn't want an escort."

In the jungle, a bird shrieked. "No escort?"

"A directive from her manager. It should be fine, Comrade. In fact, it creates a much lower profile, doesn't it? One woman traveling alone? As opposed to having all of us bring her? One of the women in the cathouse down the street said the military circled by this place once or twice last week. That could be nothing. On the other hand, it could mean the *tombas* are onto us."

There was a pause.

"It does sound as if Alice Mendes traveling alone might be better," Cain said. "And you're fine with this change, Comrade? You are my eyes and ears."

"Absolutely," Abraham said. "Beatriz and Gabby have come down with a dose of food poisoning, so we would only have to wait for two replacements anyway if you thought she needed an escort."

"I think it should be fine if Alice Mendes comes alone."

Cain was getting itchy fingers. He wanted that two mil.

"Very well, Comrade. Alice Mendes plans to leave early morning. As soon as she can make arrangements for a boat up to the Yasuni."

"Tell her to meet Gauman at the lodge when she arrives."

"Comrade—Gauman isn't one of us."

"Exactly. That's in keeping with low profile. More soldiers have been posted and are checking everyone's papers. Make sure Alice has hers in order, by the way."

"Will do."

"Have you spoken to your wife? Everything good there?"

There was a pause. "Yes, Comrade. All is in order."

"Call me if there are any issues."

"I'm hoping to get some rest now. We have been on the go for many hours."

"I understand."

"Vengeance is justice," Abraham said, signing out.

Pocketing the phone, Maggie turned to Achic. "What are you going to do with Abraham?"

"He's coming with me," Achic said. "Once I've gotten Marcelo to a doctor. In the meantime, he can stay here. He's not going anywhere."

"I need your assurance that Abraham will not be harmed."

"Why do you care? After what they did to you?"

Her head was still ringing from where Abraham had pistol-whipped her. "I just need your word that you are turning him over to the authorities and won't be harming him further."

"I have no further need for him."

"Good enough."

Achic picked the hood up from the floor. "Lift your head, Comrade."

Achic re-hooded Abraham, and dug out a roll of duct tape from his pack. "Legs together now. We want you nice and still, until I get back."

Maggie slipped on her denim jacket, collected her backpack, walked over to the cluttered table. A copy of the *Quotations of Chairman Mao* was open, face down, the red cover splayed. She picked it up.

The little red book. How many wars had it started? How many lives had it ended?

Maggie opened the book to Chapter 2, quotation 2. "In

class society everyone lives as a member of a particular class, and every kind of thinking, without exception, is stamped with the brand of a class." Abraham had said: *In class society*.

A simple but pure authentication system. Give the caller an index to the book of Mao's quotations. He or she needs to respond immediately with a few words that begin the quote. It requires the caller to have memorized the entire book. Something only a devotee could do.

She turned back to the group. "I'll be in touch," she said. "Somehow."

"Just one thing," Achic said, wrapping Abraham's ankles with duct tape. "You were going to tell me why you're so sure we have so much leverage over Cain."

"It took me a while to figure out," she said. "But at the Bogotá safe house, and here, it dawned on me that something wasn't right—the way Abraham spoke about Ernesto. His concern when captured was for his wife—but not his child. Don't you think that's odd?"

"He loves his wife," Achic said.

"She looks fairly easy to love," Marcelo said drily from his chair.

"You don't think it's unusual that a man's first concern wouldn't be for his child?" Maggie said.

Achic shook his head. "Terrorists are hard to figure out. They don't think like you and I."

"Terrorists are no different than you or I," Maggie said. "They're just people." She addressed Abraham. "Tell us why you and your wife fight with each other. Tell us why you really didn't want her to come."

"Go to hell," Abraham growled, face down.

"Because Ernesto isn't your son."

Abraham said nothing.

"If he isn't Abraham's son," Achic began. "Then who . . ." He stopped as soon as the words escaped his lips.

"We don't know how Cain feels about Yalu," she said. "But we can assume there's some passion for his son. And that's why you must move both of them. Immediately."

"My G-God," Marcelo said, grinning. "We've g-got him, *jefe*. We've got Cain. By the short-and-c-curlies."

Achic said: "It does look that way, doesn't it?"

They heard Abraham breathing heavily then. It almost sounded like weeping.

-22-

It was well past midnight as Maggie headed down Chimborazo, the main drag along the wide Napo River. Plenty of signs of life still prevailed, mostly in the form of drunken exchanges wafting out of bars and clubs.

She found a cheap hotel room that wasn't particularly cheap above a discotheque throbbing with techno pop. Next door to her room, a couple bounded in the throes of passion, or at least one of them did. The woman was putting on a command performance with exaggerated sighs and moans.

Half a dozen empty beer bottles filled a metal waste can by a sagging twin bed. A lone bottle with an inch of beer and sodden cigarette butts lining the bottom sat on the sticky nightstand. Picking up the bottle with thumb and forefinger, she set it next to the wastebasket.

Mildew and grime mottled the bathroom, where a sharp urine scent lingered. As much as she needed one, Maggie decided against a shower in the wretched stall. She unlaced and kicked off her dusty Doc Marten low-rise shoes and stripped down, opting for a sponge bath with Wet Ones, slipping on her clean pair of underwear and white T-shirt. Then she brushed her hair 100 times, her teeth twice, feeling fortified. She rinsed the other pair of panties out in the sink and hung them on a hanger by the open window where they fluttered in the night air. Hopefully, they would dry by morning.

The bed screeched when Maggie sat down on it. She wasn't about to get under the soiled covers. She opened a bottle of cold sparkling water she'd purchased in a *tienda* next door and fired up her MacBook, plugging it in to a wall socket to charge.

Three emails from Ed, one dated the day she left the U.S., two today. Yesterday actually, because it was now past midnight.

Just checking in read the subject line of the first. She skipped that.

Where are you? read the second.

Need to talk to you ASAP was the third. It requested an acknowledgement receipt, but she declined, opening it anyway. Ed, she thought, you are such a newbie sometimes.

Maggs-

I just heard a scary rumor about that cowboy you worked with last week. I actually swung by your place tonight but you weren't home. Please tell that woman who lives downstairs I'm not a stalker. I know you said you were going to take off for the mountains but now I'm hoping those mountains aren't the Andes. Don't do anything foolish. We've been friends a long time and you can always talk to me. Give me a call as soon as you get this. Notice I didn't use the word 'please' there.

Maggie took a drink of fizzy water. She needed to contact Sinclair. Donning her headphones she Skyped his number in Alexandria, Virginia.

Sinclair Michaels answered, looking groggy and ruffled. He was sitting in a home office, wearing a robe. The green shade of a banker's lamp cast light on a Redskins pennant pinned to the wall behind him.

"I'm clean," Maggie said. *Safe to talk.*

"Hello, Maggie," he said in a voice clotted with sleep. Or Scotch.

She brought him up to speed. Sinclair nodded from time to time, hands folded in front of him on his desk. He seemed to take her news in stride, even the part about the Coca safe-house rescue and the deaths of two *terrucos*, and the arrests of Abraham, Yalu, and Ernesto, although she could see that he was aggravated. Most likely because the op had derailed and been taken over by Ecuadorian intelligence. *They'd* scored well enough. Sinclair Michaels, for his part, hadn't delivered. It was results that mattered, especially for a contractor.

She didn't mention Ernesto being Cain's son. That

information she would keep to herself for the time being.

"And where are Yalu and her son now?"

"Achic is going to have them moved."

"Where?"

"He didn't say. I didn't ask."

Sinclair frowned. "It's unfortunate we weren't able to complete the transaction," he said. "But good work."

"Not exactly."

"Never mind," he said. "Can you get to Coca airport? I'll have a ticket waiting and a diplomatic letter to speed you through to Quito and then out of the country. You still have your Alice Mendes ID?"

"I do," she said. "But I can make my own way to Quito. I know the country pretty well."

"Of course you do."

"And I'm not ready to come back yet."

He gave a squint. "No?"

"I'm meeting Cain," she said.

Sinclair Michaels eyed her sideways in the webcam.

"I'm going through with the transfer," she said. She told him about the phone call she had Abraham make to Cain.

"And Cain is willing to follow these new measures?"

"Why not? He's changed gears on us three times so far. He *wants* this money. It's within his grasp. He has no idea his people were arrested. He thinks it's business as usual and that we just want to keep a low profile. So the operation continues. Simply another change of venue. One that that benefits him, actually."

She watched Sinclair pick up a glass with an inch or two of amber liquid in the bottom and take a slug. He set it down, out of sight. For the first time ever, she saw him smile. Not much of one, but still.

"Are you really prepared to go through with this, Maggie?"

"I want Tica out—remember? And the rest of her cohorts. I need Beltran back in Quito where he can get that done."

"I'm not sure I can get anyone there in time to assist you."

"I don't need anyone. Don't want anyone. No more

cowboys. We just need to make sure the actual trade takes place somewhere safe."

"Most definitely."

"I'm thinking Quito. National Bank of Ecuador. Main branch."

"Good choice. Our part of the world. On the plaza, so we can cover it from multiple angles."

"I'll be in touch," she said. "Probably within the next twelve hours. Right after I meet Cain. How's John Rae? Or rather, *where* is John Rae?"

"Bogotá. But I'm told he's going to be released. You know South America. They have fifty terms for the word *delay*."

Yes, she knew all about that. "Where, exactly? What facility?"

"Just a moment," he said, clacking away on his keyboard, reading from a screen to the side of the webcam. "*Penal Corporativo*. But he's being processed. It'll just take longer than expected."

"That's great news," she said.

"John Rae's going to be impressed when he sees how you've held up. And with what you're about to do—single-handed."

"It's a milk run."

Sinclair gave up another tight smile. "Performed by someone who has just shy of three operations under her belt. Who weathered a serious firefight. Two. You've got quite a career ahead of you. If you want it."

Did she? She'd think about that later. For now, she was focused on the op—and springing Tica. "I better sign off."

"Good luck. Not that you need it."

Yeah, she would. But she felt lucky enough.

She could also smell something. Something that bore the hint of *rat*.

Once Maggie logged out of Skype, she opened Iggy, the chat client she wrote back in grad school with her *compadre* Enzo, and pinged France.

@Enzo99 hola - ayt?

It was late afternoon in Paris. She knew Enzo lived in an electronic cave where lights flashed and screens flickered 24/7. He never went outdoors. He was a cyber-vampire.

A reply began to appear:

Enzo99: Hey, *ca va?*

Magdalena: looking for some info on a friend

Enzo99: aren't we all

Magdalena: so true ☺

Enzo99: is this the one that disappeared? – nothing new sori to saye

Magdalena: no, another one

Enzo99: oh, sori to her that

Magdalena: 'Bogotá international airport, American, arrest, Jack Warren, Penal Corporativo' – there are your search parms, bro

Enzo99: Got it, 1 sec . . .

Magdalena: he was supposed to have been released this am, FWIW

Maggie waited while the bed next door banged against the wall amidst the horrendous overacting on the part of the female.

Finally, a response came back.

Enzo99: not Penal Corporativo - La Picota Prison - Bogotá

Magdalena: not Penal Corporativo - u sure?

Enzo99: y wud I lie to u?

Magdalena: not intentionally – at least I hope not ☺ *is he being released, can you tell?*

A few seconds passed.

Nothing here about that. hes in max security

Huh? Maggie thought. Huh!

Magdalena: muchas gracias, eh?

Enzo99: de nada

Magdalena: ciao

There was a silence before Enzo responded.

Enzo99: u know, one of these days . . .

Magdalena: Yes, I know. We have to meet in person. But how r u going to keep a brave ☺ *on your face when you see i weigh 300 pounds? That's 140 kilos to u BTW*

Enzo99: lol - I no u r a fether. I cn tell by the liteness of your kystrokes.

Dude was talking about her strokes now.

Magdalena: ic. well, i think u might be dee-luded, mon

Enzo99: I think you're beautiful.

She took a deep breath through her nose.

Magdalena: You don't really know me. I am not so nice.

Enzo99: disagree

Magdalena: I'm so sorry, Enzo—this is a really bad time. I'll ping u when I get back, k, and we can chat up then?

There was a pause. A long pause. She felt a pang inside for hurting his feelings.

Enzo99: My bad. I am the 1 sori. I will kep look for your friend. friendz. Check with me in a day. b safe.

An ICE ping alert popped, startling her with its warning window.

ciao she typed again and hit the shutdown button post haste.

Yes, she could definitely smell a rat from her earlier call to Sinclair.

Or was it a mole?

Next door the bed was starting to squeak again. Maggie checked the time. A few hours to go before she would head to the dock and find a boat to the Yasuni.

She could try for sleep, but sleep didn't seem likely. She lay back and shut her eyes.

-23-

Early morning, the moon still shining overhead, Maggie strode down to Coca's boat dock, her backpack slung over one shoulder. The air was cool and fresh. Even with all the questions racing through her mind, it **was** calming.

On the way, she dumped the pistol she'd taken from Abraham in a fifty-five-gallon drum overflowing with trash. She wouldn't get away with bringing a gun to meet a terrorist group that would be armed to the teeth. They would search her and the gun would only make matters worse.

She still needed to talk to Ed. But she wasn't going to risk another ICE alert just yet and give away her location to whoever might be watching.

Long narrow riverboats bobbed idly on the piers, all but one of them unmanned. At the end of the dock two Indians in bare feet and baggy shorts were provisioning a boat. One young man lugged a huge red Jerry can of gas across the boards, while an older man hunched over the motor with a long screwdriver. He looked up as Maggie approached, cigarette dangling from his mouth. His face was bronzed and deeply lined from sun and water.

"Are you for hire?" Maggie asked him in Quechua. The Indians in this part of the Amazon spoke it as well. Even though the sun had rendered the man's face to look much older, he was probably just shy of middle-aged.

"Booked," he said in voice thick with phlegm. "Taking a group of Germans up to Napo at nine."

"Napo—the Yasuni. That's where I'm going. Maybe I can ride along. I'm willing to pay. Cash."

"Private party," he muttered. "Eco-tourists." He gave a frown, apparently not aware how such travelers were keeping people like him alive.

"How much are they paying you?"

He told her.

A peacock sauntered up to watch the interaction curiously.

"I'll pay double," Maggie said, pulling out a roll of U.S. dollars, peeling off bills. "It's just me—no one else. I won't get drunk, ask a lot of stupid questions about the wildlife, or make you stop so I can take photos. I won't get sick or fall out of the boat. All I want to do is get to Napo as soon as possible. Have your boy run to the Germans' hotel now, before they get up, and tell them to relax, lie in, that your boat needs some part and you'll be ready by this afternoon. You can be back by then, I'm sure. But we leave now." She raised her eyebrows.

He eyed the wad of money in her hand.

The peacock's feathers splayed.

The driver gave a single nod.

~~~

The long motorized canoe chugged upriver, water splashing over the wooden hull when the boat hit a swell. The torn green awning flapped in the early-morning breeze with its sweet scent of rich wet earth. The sun was rising over the rainforest in a rush of orange. Birds picked up their singing, echoing across the water.

Maggie couldn't help but wonder how many such mornings were left in the Yasuni.

In front of them, a huge barge came into view, slogging upriver, stacked high with 36-inch thick lengths of pipe. To carry away the black gold. Destined for one of the two last pristine remnants of Amazon rainforest. The report of the canoe's engine popped off the giant metal hull of the barge as they swept by and Maggie saw the name stenciled on the sides of the pipe: Commerce Oil.

Halfway to Yasuni, they stopped at a *tienda*, the last store before the jungle, to gas up, where there was cell-phone coverage. Maggie helped the driver lug a can of fuel to the boat and he accepted her offer of a cold drink.

Inside the store, originally built decades ago by nuns who ran a nearby mission, when all that lay beyond here was unspoiled jungle, Maggie found numerous shoppers, oilworkers stocking up on beer, cigarettes, and other luxuries, although traveling water-bound shops would fill in—at a handsome markup. The inane musical drone of a video game and ringing cash register, along with the thumping of the generator outside, killed what had once been relative silence.

She purchased a couple of dripping Inka colas, a sandwich roll stuffed with ham, and a pack of American smokes for the driver, a tube of toothpaste, and two large bags of boiled sweets she would jam into her knapsack. There would no doubt be children where she was headed.

Over at a grubby dairy case popping with fluorescent light, two men in dungarees examined a stringy slice of red monkey meat dripping blood out of its homemade cellophane wrapper onto the wood floor. Illegal. The sisters would never have allowed it.

Back out on the river Maggie drank neon yellow soda as the manmade breeze of the boat heading upriver helped erase the stickiness of the coming day.

Back in San Francisco, Ed would be up by now. She wasn't going to risk another logon just yet. She got out Abraham's mucky cell phone as she chewed her stale sandwich, wiping the phone off with a paper napkin. The phone was a preload, so nobody would be tracking it.

She called a number in San Francisco, California.

On the second ring, Ed answered.

"Did you order a pizza?" It was a standing joke between them and a quick and dirty way to give Ed a head's up to assess the situation before giving a name. Static crackled across the virtual wires as the boat bounced off a surge of water.

"Last night before I went to bed, I did," he said. "Extra-large Hawaiian. With extra pineapple. Where the hell is it?"

"I'm eating it now." She tore off a hunk of dry roll and not-so-fresh meat with her teeth. She was starving. She pulled the phone away from her ear while the screech of a PJ–pocket jammer–was plugged into the phone on the other end. Ed was cleaning the line.

Then: "It's good to hear your voice, Maggs."

"Ditto." Chewing.

"But it sounds a little in and out. I'm going out on a limb here and guessing it's not coming from your apartment. Mostly because I keep stopping by your place and you're not there."

"These South American cell-phone providers are less than excellent."

"Christ," Ed said. "That's what I was afraid of."

They passed an open gas flare in dense jungle, burning high above the tree line, a byproduct of oil production. Left uncapped, it scorched the last dark blue of night away.

"Better lay it on me, Maggie."

She did. When she was done, she heard Ed light a cigarette, take a deep suck of poisonous smoke, and say: "Turn that damn boat around. Now. That's an order."

"You're not exactly a 'that's-an-order' type, Ed. Nice try, though."

"How about 'please'?"

"Sorry, Ed," she said. "I've got to see this through."

Even with the splashing of the river, she could hear Ed's deep sigh of exasperation. "You know I always go to bat for you, Maggs, but do you have any idea what this is going to do to your career? If you survive, that is?"

"It might sound glib," she said. "But career is the last thing on my mind right now. Perhaps it should be. But it's not. There are other things taking priority—people. Seven of them. Tica and her six compadres. Maybe they can do something about this insane, illegal, oil exploration."

She heard Ed take another puff of cigarette. "Yeah," was all he said in a tone that made her realize he understood completely. "So I can threaten you and it doesn't make any difference?"

"You're just not that scary, Ed. It's one of the many reasons I like you. You've survived in a pack of people who care about nothing—except starting wars all over the globe. You're head and shoulders above the rest of the Agency."

"Great. Will you put that down as a recommendation in my LinkedIn profile? When I have to go looking for another job?"

"Sure." Maggie chewed some more dehydrated sandwich. It was a good thing she had strong teeth. "So I guess it comes down to this. You're duty-bound as my friend to help me in any way possible. Since I would do the same for you."

"That's pretty low, Maggie."

"Yep. But I am going to see the Yasuni Seven freed. And you might as well be part of it. You know how fickle the Agency is. When it happens, they're going to be pushing each other out of the way to take credit. So you might as well be first in line."

"You never used to be this cynical."

"I need you to get John Rae out of jail. Something funky is going on there. But with your connections, I bet you can pull it off. I also need you as a contact point, because I'm not trusting Sinclair Michaels anymore, so you get to be de facto leader of this op now."

"Come on, Maggs."

"Admit it," she said. "It makes total sense."

"Yeah," he said. "I'm going to end up working for you in a year or two. Where's John Rae being held?"

"La Picota Prison," she said. "Bogotá. Maximum-security wing. He's going by the name of Jack Warren."

She could hear Ed scratching it down old school on a pad of paper. "What else?"

"I'm meeting Cain out here in the Amazon, planning to do the exchange in Quito. Beltran for the two mil. By tomorrow."

"You got the money transfers all set up, ready to go?"

"Does the pope shit in the woods?"

"I'll get a team of goons together to monitor the transfer. Doesn't give me a lot of time."

"Ai-yi-yi."

"I insist, Maggs. You're my responsibility. Don't worry. Cain won't even know they're there, unless he tries to pull a fast one."

If anyone could do such a thing, it was Ed. "K," she said.

"Anything you read on my work email is going to be bullshit from now on. Disinformation. Play along."

Ed wasn't trusting the powers that be. Interesting.

"I thought it was all bullshit anyway."

"Ha ha," he said, puffing. "Give me a word. For Quito."

Maggie thought for a moment. "Moshi's."

"Got it. Call me later."

"If not later, then tomorrow. You got my number, but who knows about coverage. And these Grim Harvest guys tend to get weird about making contact with the outside world."

"Maybe because they're terrorists?"

"Maybe."

"I don't want to tell you how worried I am."

"Then don't." The cell phone startled to crackle as the boat swerved around a wide bend of muddy river. "Time to go, bud."

"Stay safe, Maggs. I'll do my best to get your cowboy out ASAP. Hopefully, we'll be sitting around a table at Moshi's—that's the real Moshi's—in a couple of days, patting ourselves on the back and looking forward to commendations. Or at least, keeping our jobs."

"Just don't eat all my calamari this time."

"You're too slow."

"Ciao."

She clicked off and powered down the phone. When the driver bent down to light a cigarette, out of the wind, she slipped the old-style cell phone down in her cleavage. Not super comfortable, but she could get away with it. She'd smuggled how many baggies full of Bacardi into music concerts as a teenager?

Truth was, she didn't know exactly what to expect next. Everything she suspected told her Cain was just another dissolute ex-revolutionary who would sell out to the highest bidder. For some of his ilk, that meant working as security for the drug cartels. But Cain seemed to have gone one better and found himself an even bigger opportunity: trading hostages with the oil companies. Shipping cocaine to the Western world was small potatoes compared to that.

They arced around a sunken tree poking up out of the water as they continued their journey upriver.

~~~

Not long ago, a boat under motor wouldn't have been allowed so far back into tribal areas, but the onslaught of oil had changed things.

It started to rain just as they headed into a tunnel of trees, shortly before ten a.m., which meant a torrential downpour that thrashed the jungle canopy and awning of the boat with ominous strokes. Rain in the Amazon wasn't the civilized showers found elsewhere, or even volleys of water—but vertical floods beating down unmercifully, soaking everything despite whatever measures were taken. Nothing man-made stayed dry. The bottom of the boat was inches deep in water and Maggie had to lift her feet and prop them on the gunwale. It was a reminder that this was still, for the time being, the wilds.

And then, as quickly as it had arrived, the rain was gone. Billowing clouds parted for emerging sunshine. Steam rose from the river. Monkeys reappeared, shaking branches overhead, letting water fly down. The boat headed upstream on the narrow passage, then they pulled out from under the trees into a lake. A dozen thatched huts sat just across the water that shimmered with bluing sky.

On the far shore, where the village once had an unobstructed view of unblemished jungle, numerous non-pleasure boats and barges now crowded a small dock. Pickup trucks and jeeps were parked anywhere there was room. Construction workers came and went, and a bright yellow Caterpillar was firing up its motor, blasting black smoke into the air. It had a huge blade on the front and was towing a trailer loaded down with lengths of pipe, identical to the ones Maggie had seen on the barge. More pipe was stacked nearby on the docks.

Maggie saw several soldiers, looking bored, standing around the dock with rifles shouldered.

"How long have they been here?" she asked the driver.

"A state of emergency was declared a week or so ago. After the attacks on the oil work by the terrorists. It all started with the arrest of a sixteen-year-old girl and half a dozen villagers from the interior just over a month ago. A minister was kidnapped in Quito. They're getting worried in the capital. Have you got your papers ready?"

"Yes."

As the boat approached the dock, Maggie saw a wide clearing, cut in what had once been dense jungle, coming into view. She heard the Caterpillar groan.

Her driver pulled the long canoe up on the shore amidst the squawking of rust-colored pheasants. Prehistoric-looking, the Indians called them "stinky turkeys," as the taste of their flesh made them inedible. Nature had a way of protecting her offspring. Maggie hoped that adage applied to the Yasuni as well.

A youngish woman in a loose handmade skirt and thin white blouse approached, with two children, a girl of five or six, who wore tattered shorts and a faded T-shirt with robots on them, along with a little boy who sported a mop of jet black hair. The woman was pretty in an exotic way. Blue zigzag tattoos on each cheek accentuated her gentle features.

Maggie gathered her backpack, hopped off the bow onto the beach. The driver spun around, took off with a lazy wave. One of the soldiers came sauntering up, a young guy with knock-off aviator glasses and a sheen on his slim face. He gave Maggie the once-over, like she was a sight for sore eyes.

"Sorry, do you need to see my papers?" Maggie said in Spanish, retrieving her Alice Mendes passport. "It's not very interesting. You guys must get bored to death stationed out here."

"You don't know the half of it, *chica*." He examined her passport. "San Antonio, Texas? I hear half of Mexico lives there."

"Only a third." She smiled and fluffed her hair out with her fingers. Flirting could open doors. "Ai, it's hot. How on earth do you guys have any fun?"

"It's not easy." He smiled. "You're *norteamericana*. What are you doing here? Tourist season is over." He looked around at the construction. "Maybe for good."

"I'm an accountant with Commerce Oil." Maggie got out her forged company badge. "Five Fortunes, actually, but it's all the same thing. We're doing an equipment audit."

The soldier examined her company ID, gave it back, along with the passport. "I'll need to see inside the bag, I'm afraid."

She let him. It was a good thing she'd ditched the pistol.

"Are you here because of the truck that was attacked?" he asked, once he'd finished.

"Yes," Maggie said, playing along. "It's not a huge thing, but we do need to follow up, so we can file a claim. Those things cost some serious cash."

"I imagine they do. Your Spanish is excellent."

"*Gracias.*" Maggie winked. "Maybe I'll catch you later."

He walked back to the dock like a man who'd just received a check in the mail.

"Are you Alice?" the woman with the tattooed face said in a soft voice.

"Indeed. And you are?"

"Gauman's wife." She turned to the boy and told him in Quechua to go get his *papi*. He scampered off with purpose.

"Gauman," Maggie said. The name Cain had mentioned.

"He's taking you inland." The woman gave Maggie a shy smile, took the girl's hand, and said, "This way, please."

Maggie followed her to a hut.

Villagers peered out of their shelters as Maggie walked by. There didn't seem to be much for anyone to do but stay inside, away from the soldiers and construction. Maggie pulled a bag of candies from her backpack as she walked, tore it open. Children gazed out of huts with interest. She shook the bag.

"Any takers?"

One or two brave kids ventured out. One child came up

with his mother. He dipped his arm deep into the bag and extracted a small fistful.

"Come on!" Maggie shook the bag.

More children appeared, along with a few adults, helping themselves to sweets.

A man emerged from the hut, sun-beaten, wearing threadbare baggy shorts, and a washed-out green ball cap with a long brim. He needed a haircut in the worst way and looked exhausted. Even so, he had the stoic, expressionless face of an Indian who knows better than to make his presence too well-known.

"Gauman?" she said.

"Yes," he said. "I've been waiting for you. Follow me." He turned, headed off toward the jungle. Maggie had to pick up the pace to keep up.

The clearing turned out to be a section of rainforest that had been obliterated for a wide road. The surface was red mud, deeply rutted, and unwalkable after the recent downpour. Water still ran in gurgling rivulets and formed deep puddles. The remains of a truck sat at an odd angle a hundred or so meters down. Black burn marks were visible around the cab, signs of a fire, or worse. The bulldozer was attempting to forge the road, but its treads were tearing deep gouges into the wet earth, filling the air around it with flying sticky red mud.

"Let's get away from this," Gauman said. He and Maggie headed off into the trees.

"How long ago did they cut the road?" she asked in Spanish. She wasn't going to let on that she spoke Quechua. It had been a handy ruse so far. Who knew what she might learn?

"Two months ago," Gauman said as he walked, looking straight ahead. "It's temporary—so they tell us."

"Certainly doesn't look that way."

"No."

Her mind was cast back to Tica and her allies, arrested for protesting the bulldozers.

"Are you with Grim Harvest?" she said quietly. She didn't see a weapon on him.

He shook his head *no*. "They frighten me. But they say they will save our land. So I help them sometimes. In small ways. They give me food to feed my family. I used to take tourists deep into the jungle. Otters. Birds. Monkeys. I know them all. Since I was a boy. No more. I have no work, but Grim Harvest."

"Have there been any more arrests?" she asked casually.

"For the truck you saw?" Gauman shook his head again. "No. But there have been skirmishes."

"I heard something about some demonstrations a while back. A teenage girl . . ."

"Tica," he said, without looking at Maggie. "My neighbor's cousin. A teenager. She was quite active in getting people to protest what is happening to our land. But now people hide in the jungle. They don't want to be taken away."

"*Taken away*?" she said. "That doesn't sound good."

He gave Maggie a quick sideways glance. "We told Tica not to protest. But her mind was full of justice. She is young. She thinks the world is one where her voice will be heard. Instead, she was taken by the soldiers. To set an example for the other young people."

They marched through the more navigable rainforest, heat rising as the sun baked the tree canopy fifty meters overhead. Howler monkeys boomed, their throats dispensing warnings to the human invaders.

They had gone well inland, away from the road, when two guerillas appeared out of nowhere. Only Maggie seemed surprised at their arrival; Gauman gave the pair a silent nod.

One was a woman about forty with the thick hair of an Indian cut into a sensible short length. Her face was angular and her cheekbones high. Her eyes were almost Asian. She had light-colored skin and wore denim cutoffs, hiking boots, and a shiny nylon shirt with vertical green-and-white stripes bearing a patch with the letters "AN" on a small embroidered tower. A Colombian soccer team. Although she was tomboyish and affected no feminine behavior, wearing no jewelry, earrings, or nail polish, she was lithe and had a way of holding herself that would easily turn men's heads. She gave Maggie a tight squint, accentuated by flat unsmiling lips pressed together. "Alice Mendes?"

"Yes. And you are?"

"Let's go," she said without warmth, turning to lead the way. The bulge of a small pistol was prominent in the waistband of her shorts under her soccer shirt.

Her companion was an older man, probably in his 60s, although life outdoors often made that difficult to judge. He wore a battered baseball cap, Speedos, and Teva sport sandals, and a huge sweat-soaked cotton T-shirt with the name of an auto-parts store on it. He had an old bolt-action rifle slung over his shoulder and a machete in his gnarled hand. He gave Maggie a warm smile, waved the machete for her to go ahead of him.

Gauman turned, disappeared the way he had brought her.

The three of them set off further inland, Maggie in the middle.

The man and woman spoke Quechua. Maggie learned they were northern Colombian U'wa Indians from land that the Colombian government had appropriated for oil drilling. The woman was referred to as Comrade Lita. Maggie knew that when the fighting in Colombia had grown worse after the U'wa had blown up an oil pipeline, many of the Indian revolutionaries had come down to the Yasuni, recruited by Comrade Cain for Cosecha Severa. Lita mentioned Comrade Cain several times, in the same tone of voice a priest might utter the Lord's name.

"Any more repercussions?" the man said to Lita. "From the truck attack?"

"Willy finally died," Lita replied, as if talking about the weather.

"Is Comrade Cain here?" Maggie asked Lita in Spanish.

"Oh, yes. You've got the ransom money."

"And Beltran?"

"*Chat-chat-chat.* What are you—a doll with a pull string on her back? You look like a doll. A pretty little doll."

Maggie took a breath and continued on, ignoring the unease that was building.

A milk run.

~~~

They trekked until late afternoon, their clothes soaked with perspiration. Maggie had stashed her jacket in her knapsack long ago. She wished she had a pair of light hiking pants and not the jeans she'd put on in San Francisco which had now molded to her in the sticky heat. The sun and humidity so close to the equator were oppressive, even though the group stayed under the tree canopy much of the time.

They passed several settlements, two of them deserted. One small village had been bulldozed, the huts pushed aside and flattened to make room for a secondary road. In the wreckage Maggie saw a dog's corpse, buzzing with flies, and a child's toy drum, crushed and broken.

"This was Tica's village," Lita said in Spanish to Maggie. "You probably don't even know who she is, do you, little doll?"

"I know who Tica is."

"And why would you even know about the little people your company treats like so much garbage in your way?"

"Not all *norteamericanos* are the same."

Lita laughed and turned back to face the trail. "Just the ones that want our oil. Which is all of you."

"Tica's long gone by now," the tall older man said behind Maggie in rough Spanish. "She won't be coming back. Gone."

Tica would be getting out, Maggie told herself. She just didn't know exactly how yet.

Finally, they arrived at a clearing below a mammoth kapok tree. Tall grass waved in a welcome breeze that was tantalizingly false. Out in the sun, it was even hotter.

A glint of light flickered from atop the kapok, flashing across her face. Maggie looked up. Again, something reflecting sunlight. A mirror.

"Cain says to approach," Lita said.

They set across the clearing.

-24-

The narrow wooden stairs that began at the bottom of the giant tree and wound around its trunk up past the tree canopy were rotted out in places and completely missing in others. The stairwell to the observation deck, used in better times by ecotourists, had fallen into disuse and was in serious need of repair. Looking up, Maggie saw more than a few steps gone, many in sequence. Anticipating the climb tickled her armpits in a disagreeable way.

"Comrade Cain isn't going to come down to you," Comrade Lita said, stepping up on the first plank, turning to give her a smirk. "You should be honored you're allowed to go up to him."

"Honored I'm willing to transfer two million dollars your group needs."

"So you can get your precious oil minister."

"While we're on the subject, where *is* Beltran?"

"I think you forget who is in charge. Watch the first step." Lita jumped up onto the second stair. It creaked under her slight weight.

The older man with the rifle and machete stayed back, where he disappeared through a secluded opening in the bushes. Maggie was startled when she noticed a Caucasian woman in granny glasses and fatigues sitting on a log there, reading a paperback. An automatic rifle was propped up next to her. Maggie hadn't seen her earlier. Then again, she wasn't supposed to. The woman looked up, smiled at Maggie with obvious amusement.

"Come on, come on!" Lita sprang up the groaning steps,

disappearing around the first bend of the kapok.

Maggie followed. The first stair crunched ominously.

The original 150 or so steps to the top had been reduced by a fifth, no longer in existence or completely unusable. One section of stairway hung entirely away from the tree, bridged by a yellow rope ladder tied to stairs at either end of the gap. The ladder wavered in the breeze, stronger above the canopy. Even Lita, who had been making quick work of it, took care climbing the rope ladder. Maggie tried not to look down as she stretched out onto the rope. Her weight felt like an impossible burden and, try as she might, she couldn't help but glance at the treetops and bushes below. For a moment, she thought she must have taken leave of her senses to pursue this journey. She pushed the thought from her mind, body perched on a web that moved with her and the wind. Finally, she made the other side, grabbed the wooden stair with one arm and pulled herself up, trying not to kick frantically.

The worst was over. Except for the trip down.

Fifty vertical feet later, they reached the top of the weather-beaten observation deck.

What had once been intended to provide an unobstructed view of the Amazon rainforest for miles around had grown into a natural tree house of sorts. Fast-growing branches sinewed around the railings, taking over, permitting intermittent views of stunning wilderness that appeared to have no end.

Appeared to.

"What took you so long, Alice?" a man's voice said, with a hint of playful mockery.

It was the cultured voice Maggie had heard on the phone call with Abraham.

She stepped up onto the deck, brushing slivers and leaves off her jeans.

Standing before her was the reason for this risky jaunt in the first place, the reason John Rae might still be sitting in some South American prison, the reason Maggie had gone AWOL. The reason the U.S. government was prepared to hand over two million dollars, so that Commerce Oil could destroy this primeval jungle.

Comrade Cain was not at all what she expected.

-25-

What Maggie had expected was a grizzled *terruco* with a dirty beard and hard criminal stare, the kind of man you'd see on a street corner in the worst part of town in the worst city on the continent, someone who feared no one, even though many would be trying to take him down. Some *vato* whose front teeth and conscience were missing, whose bulk would easily intimidate.

But before her on the observation deck high above the jungle was a relatively slim man, mid-40s, with an unassuming way about him that belied who or what he was—the leader of a terrorist group about to trade a hostage for two million dollars.

Comrade Cain was light-skinned, with distinguished features, his short dark hair combed back over a high forehead, and a few days of designer stubble to take it all down a notch. His soft brown eyes could convince you that the outcome of your pap smear was nothing, that you would live forever. He had a fine mouth that looked like it was kept closed more often than not and opened only if it had something important to say. If not for the olive-green fatigue shirt, open, exposing a slim hairless torso and the black handle of a pistol sticking casually out of the front of his khaki shorts, Comrade Cain could be working in a branch bank, tallying up daily figures.

Maggie found herself staring. "Comrade Cain," she said.

He gave a wry smile. "Cain is good enough."

He put his hand out. "Alice Mendes. You made it to the Yasuni. And the top of this beautiful old kapok. One which we are trying to save—along with the rest of the rainforest. You obviously have a lot of determination." He spoke formal

Spanish and clearly was well educated.

His friendliness disarmed her. Maggie took his hand. It wasn't gnarled. No missing fingers. He had a gentle but firm touch. It seemed absurd, as if she had suddenly been dropped into one of her meetings at the Fed and was shaking hands with a colleague.

Over Cain's shoulder, Maggie caught Lita drinking from a canteen and watching Maggie's interaction with Cain closely. Lita quickly glanced away.

The green-eyed monster. There was no hiding jealousy.

"Does everyone who wants to meet you have to climb up here to prove themselves?" Maggie said.

"Only if I need to be here myself for some reason."

Maggie followed Cain's eyes as he glanced over at Lita, who had gone to the railing and was scanning an expanse of trees across the clearing in the distance with a pair of binoculars. Two yellow-tailed orioles spun off from the lower branches of the tree next to them and flew into the sun.

"More progress on the road, I see, Comrade," Lita said to Cain, adjusting the field glasses.

Cain said, "They've completed their measurements on sector four. They are ready to start the pipeline."

Maggie recalled the barge on the Napo River loaded down with three-foot thick lengths of pipe.

"We'll have to strike quickly," Lita said.

"Yes." Cain gave Maggie an uneven glance. "And once we have the funds, we'll strike again. And again. Until they desist."

"Where is Beltran?" Maggie asked Cain.

"Not here."

Maggie shook her head. "There'll be no money transfer until I see him in the flesh—safe and sound."

"You seem very sure of yourself."

"I have every reason to be."

"Don't fret. There's too much value in Beltran being alive."

Maggie placed her hands on her hips. "So where is he?"

"There's no harm in telling you now. He's in Quito. *Safe and sound.*"

Not far from where he was kidnapped. A man like Cain went for the simplest solutions. It was no doubt part of his success.

Maggie saw Lita's head cock slightly to the right in an artificial movement as she pretended to view the jungle and not eavesdrop on their conversation. That little motion gave so much away. She suspected that Comrade Cain had that effect on most of his female followers.

"Fine," Maggie said. "Then Quito is where we're doing the money transfer."

Cain narrowed his eyes. "I never agreed to that."

"I'm not really giving you a choice. When do we leave? Now seems like a good time."

Cain came in close, his face inches away. He had a scent that was animal and captivating and she could see him the way many women no doubt saw him, but underneath the charisma was a whiff of rage. His smile gone, his face became a tight grimace. "Americans—so sure of yourselves. You think you have so much power. But you're deluded as to what you can achieve."

Lita was smirking, looking sideways.

"Perhaps we should head down and leave for Quito," Maggie said, about to turn.

Cain seized her wrist, like a lizard grabbing an insect. He held it like a vise.

"That hurts," she said, not struggling, a battle she would only lose.

He cocked his head to one side. "Do you really think you're above being a prisoner yourself?"

Maggie dropped her voice, so that Lita couldn't hear. "We have Ernesto," she said very quietly, raising her eyebrows.

Cain's eyes flinched. His mouth dropped. His grip lessened.

"Let go of my wrist now," she said.

Cain obliged.

"Get rid of Lita."

Cain glared at Maggie.

"I said *get rid of her.*"

"Lita," Cain said. "Go down and gather the group for our meeting."

Lita turned. "But that's not until later tonight, Comrade."

Cain didn't take his eyes of Maggie. "Do it now."

A look of hurt crossed Lita's face. Her head dropped. "Yes, Comrade." Lita glanced once more at Maggie before she crossed the deck and descended the stairs. They creaked as she made her way down.

"Where is my son?" Cain said, when Lita was out of earshot.

"You'll find out. When I have Beltran. In Quito."

"How do I know you're telling me the truth?"

"I know enough to know he's your son."

"Perhaps you're bluffing."

"Call Yalu. Put the phone on speaker."

Cain got out a beat-up Nokia, hit speed dial, pressed the red speaker button. He held the phone up in the palm of his hand.

Someone answered on the fifth ring.

"Hello," Yalu said mechanically.

"It's just me," Cain said in an intimate tone of voice. "How are things?"

"Everything is fine," she said perfunctorily.

"Are they really? It doesn't quite sound like it. How is Ernesto?"

"He's fine."

"Are you sure you're all right?"

"Yes."

Maggie said: "Tell *her* to put the phone on speaker."

"Please put the phone on speakerphone," Cain said.

The phone clicked and the other end of the line echoed. They could hear Ernesto babbling.

Maggie said, "Clarence? Alice here. Kindly tell Cain what you were told to say by your *jefe*."

"*Hola*, Comrade Cain," Clarence said. "*Cómo está?*"

"Who the hell are *you*?" Cain growled.

"Just your friendly American mercenary," he said in fluent Spanish. "I'm at an undisclosed location here with your lovely wife or whatever she is and your little boy. He really is a kick in the pants. You know, it makes me want to find a nice girl, settle down, and get me some bambinos of my own."

Cain grimaced. "If you so much as . . ."

Clarence hung up the phone. The dial tone was jarring, juxtaposed with the twittering of the birds at the top of the ancient tree.

"I take it we're both on the same page now," Maggie said.

Cain scowled at her. "What makes you think I'm not willing to sacrifice my son for the cause?"

"It's a gamble. But Yalu wouldn't. And she means something to you."

Cain ran his fingers through his hair desperately. "Are they really safe?"

"Yes." She watched a flurry of emotions cross Cain's face. But one emotion dominated. Anger. Controlled fury. The raw fuel of a revolutionary.

"If anything happens," he said, "don't think it will go unpunished."

"You brought this on yourself," Maggie said. "When you took Beltran. Murdered his driver. It's a shame, really, because I hate to see what's happening to the Amazon as well."

Cain gave a bitter laugh. "What does someone like you understand about the problems here? Or even care? All your people do is create them."

"Tica," she said. "The Yasuni Seven."

He nodded, seemingly surprised. "I'm impressed. And how does a *norteamericana* even know about Tica?"

"Enough to know that if Beltran is released, she might be set free."

He thought about that. "Really." It wasn't a question.

"Maybe we want the same thing. Maybe I wouldn't be here if I didn't think this would help the Amazon and its people in some way."

"They told you Tica would be freed?"

"More or less."

"You're being used."

"Aren't we all? But in this case, I'm willing."

"Very well," he said, exhaling deeply. "But I don't operate in a vacuum. I have my followers and they have a say in everything. Lita—you saw her—has a say. And a sway over the troops."

"Poor Comrade Cain," Maggie said. "So many women to juggle. Shall we head down now?"

Cain gathered a small machine gun, a black-and-olive INDEP Lusa, slung it over his shoulder. He nodded at Maggie's knapsack on her back. "Your computer." He put his hand out. "It stays with us for the time being. Until the transfer."

She unslung the bag, handed it to him. "Lead the way."

Cain's eyes met hers, looking deeply into the windows of her soul. She worked hard to pull the curtains.

"Do I trust you, Alice Mendes?"

"As much as I trust you."

Two streaks of red, blue, and yellow flapped by the observation deck. Macaws, a meter long apiece. Without their precious jungle they would cease to exist. Maggie reminded herself that this was what it was really all about.

And she wondered, with two million dollars at stake, how much Cain truly wanted the same thing.

-26-

The cell door creaked open, ambient light cutting across the darkened windowless cement floor, coming toward John Rae sitting up against the cinderblock wall.

He'd heard two pair of shoes marching down the hallway in unison, the lady-killer interrogator's gleaming loafers and a heavy pair of guard's boots. They'd stopped outside. Then the fumbling for keys.

John Rae hadn't been sleeping. Not since San Francisco, two days now. It wasn't the aching in his jaw that kept him awake, where they'd belted him a few times with a phone book when he'd told them to go do what was biologically impossible in answer to their questions. That was simply collateral damage. He'd had worse. And this incarceration, in La Picota, just outside Bogotá, wasn't as bad as some. Add it to the list. Sure, there was the other prisoner crying out for his mother down the hall during a fervent questioning that turned ugly, then the man-on-man sex two cells over, not exactly consensual. But John Rae had his own cell, all five by five feet of it. No bed, of course. Not even enough room to lie down and stretch out. No overhead light. No food. No water. But that was kid's stuff. Did they really think a little sensory deprivation was going to break him?

Especially when he was where he wanted to be.

No, it was wondering what was happening to Maggie, whom he'd put at risk when he'd engineered own his arrest at El Dorado Airport. Achic, Marcelo, and Clarence, they were big boys, could fend for themselves. They knew to dissolve the op if John Rae didn't show.

His arrest had to look like the real deal. But Maggie, if she didn't have the good sense to walk away after she witnessed him being taken into custody, could be in some deep yogurt by now. And like him, she didn't always seem to have that kind of sense. Had to like her for that—among her many other attributes, though her taste in men was, perhaps, questionable. But he should have never let her come along.

Now, however, it was time to play along with Ladykiller, answer the questions, get his ass on out of here. Go find Maggie, wherever she was. In case she didn't go home, the way John Rae had told her to. Make sure she was OK. He'd stalled long enough.

The door opened completely, a block of harsh light coming to rest on John Rae sitting, shielding his eyes now.

"I think I'm ready to talk," he said.

"Doesn't matter," Ladykiller said, in another crisp white shirt, tie up to the top button, holding his file folder on Jack Warren. Looking like a Hispanic George Clooney working for some shady national security agency in Colombia.

"*Doesn't matter?*" John Rae said, climbing to his feet, using the wall to support. Feeling a tad woozy. "What do you mean, *doesn't matter?*"

"Someone back in your country played a trump card, *amigo*." Ladykiller smiled. "Got you out. Too bad."

"No shit, Sherlock?"

"No shit, Sherlock," Ladykiller said, feigning John Rae's Texas drawl. The guard, for his part, stood behind like a wooden statue, looking stoic. Didn't speak English.

"Mind if I ask who?" John Rae said.

"No harm in telling you, I suppose," Ladykiller said. "Someone in your San Francisco office."

Maggie got his ass out somehow. Goddamn. Now that was actually kind of embarrassing. Not to mention unnecessary. He'd had the key all along. She just didn't know.

"Mind if I know your name?" John Rae said to Ladykiller.

"Mind if I know yours?" Ladykiller said, smiling. "The real one—no more of this Jack Warren nonsense, please."

John Rae shrugged. "Sorry, Charlie."

"I as well."

"I was just about to tell you too."

"You can't win them all," Ladykiller said. "Isn't that what you people say?"

"Your English is pretty damn good, *amigo*." John Rae put his hand out. "No hard feelings, eh?"

Ladykiller took his hand, gave it a single shake. "Until next time."

~~~

Night fell quickly in the jungle. The buzz of katydids replaced the sticky silence of the waning day, while howler monkeys settled in the canopies, booming out the boundaries of their territory for the night.

A band of guerrillas gathered around a stream with a view in either direction, but still concealed by trees overhead. Finishing up an ad hoc meal of stale crackers and tinned sardines, they had dessert: *cupuaçu*, a coconut-like fruit split open with a machete, its moist pulp tasting of chocolate.

There were eight of them, including Maggie: Comrade Cain, Lita—never far from Cain—the woman in the grannie glasses who had been standing guard at the base of the kapok tree, the older man with the straw hat and machete, and several U'was from northern Columbia, who faced a similar battle in their own homeland with the invasion of the oil companies.

Amidst the rustle of leaves, wafting through the trees at ground level from different directions, figures appeared, rifles slung over their shoulders, machetes hanging from their hands. People of all shapes and sizes: Mestizos, Indians, even a purebred Caucasian with horn-rimmed glasses who spoke with an Argentine accent. Soon, more than thirty people total. They stood silent.

"The meeting will come to order now, comrades." Lita took her place in front of the semicircle. Comrade Cain waited off to one side, a hand in the pocket of his cargo shorts, matter of fact.

Lita read from the group's manifesto: a rousing passage

about injustice and the rights of the people tending to their land being trampled by the moneyed masters. It was simple and passionate and hard to disagree with. She shook her small fist from time to time. Breathing hard, she was clearly swept away, almost like a woman in the throes of sex. Her face shone. The group cheered every fervent point.

Ovations reverberated through the trees when Lita finished.

"Our comrade and commander!" Lita announced, voice soaring with emotion. She stood aside as Cain approached, stopped in the apex of the semi-circle.

Voices dropped to a muted hush.

Cain spoke, low, unassuming, but in a tone that carried.

"If you leave me in peace, I leave you in peace; if you strike me, I will strike you." He looked around the group. "Simple words that sum up how we have no choice but to strike back at those who would strike us, strike our comrades, strike our land. *Your* land. The land that the Kichwa have guarded since the beginning of time."

The group was silent again. Eyes were tightly focused on Cain.

"I'm a man of few words. Words are precious, yet at the same time worthless—if not backed up with blood. Words mean nothing without action."

Murmurs of agreement.

"Today we saw proof that the corrupt government, funded by the Americans and Chinese, is ready to begin building their pipeline through this sacred ground. Despite the petitions that the people have signed and dutifully delivered to the fraudulent politicians. Despite the peaceful protests that end with arrests and disappearances." He gazed around the semicircle. "Tonight some of us will strike another blow. The rest of you will return to your posts and take reassurance in the knowledge that you played your parts. The next meeting will be in two days. I will be elsewhere, comrades, but I will still be here—with you—in spirit. I could not ask for finer companions in this hour of justice."

He scanned the rapt faces, nodding silently.

"*La venganza es la justicia,*" he said quietly.

"*La venganza es la justicia,*" Lita said, thumping the area just above her heart with the ball of her fist.

The group roared the same.

Vengeance is justice.

~~~

Cain requested candidates for the mission. The challenge seemed to be turning down the many volunteers. Maggie eyed her backpack leaning against a tree. Lita had placed it there during the meeting. While Cain, Lita, and several others crouched around a map on the ground, Maggie wandered over to the tree. As the unselected volunteers filtered off, Maggie swept up her backpack, stole off into the bushes with it. She went around a toppled tree, out of sight, undid the top button of her jeans, sat down and fired up her MacBook, quickly plugging in the network card. Although she'd charged it last night in Coca, the machine was already down to 81 percent booting up and getting onto the IKON network.

She turned on the IP masker, logged onto Frenesi, and opened her messages. She continued to be a hit with middle-aged digital stalkers proclaiming they had open marriages. Then she saw it, a message from PerroRabioso. Rabid Dog. Maybe it was John Rae, finally out of prison in Bogotá.

It wasn't.

In cryptic slang Quechua, Achic informed her that Yalu and Ernesto had been moved to another location. That was a relief. But still no word from John Rae. Achic was hoping to rejoin the operation once Maggie got to Quito.

She checked her email from the Fed. One from Ed.

"Maggs:

Just so you understand, you are treading on some thin ice. Really need to talk to you. Our friendship is in jeopardy, to be perfectly honest. Unless you contact me on my cell phone by end of day. This is no joke."

She connected the capital letters. JR OUT. And she suddenly felt a whole lot better.

She responded to Ed's email, using a simple Perl script and

SMTP protocol to create a mail header, plugging in a fake "from" address and other properties to resemble a message from a popular U.S. free email domain. That's where it would look like her email originated.

"Hey Ed –

I'm so, *so* sorry. Something came up, with Seb, if you can believe it. Yeah, you probably can. ☺ I know, I know, I really have to get my personal life under control. I *promise* I will sync up with you tomorrow. I'm going to take care of things. I'll be at Moshi's for dinner the way we planned. I'm *so* sorry.

Maggs."

Ed would know she was headed to Quito and should be there by tomorrow. She started up Iggy.

Magdalena: no time to chat, ami, - i need a trace on a couple of phone numbers – if poss

Enzo99: k, go

Maggie got out Abraham's phone that she had liberated in Coca, and gave Enzo Cain's number, as well as Yalu's.

Enzo99: cn tll u rite now, num 1 blocked

Cain was blocked. Figured.

Enzo99: bt 2nd on nother srvc, cn b snffd

Yalu's number was traceable with Enzo's sniffer.

Magdalena: do it, plz

Maggie started as she heard boots marching through the tall grass toward her hidden spot.

Magdalena: gtg

She pulled the USB network card and powered down quickly, slipping her MacBook into her knapsack while it was still grinding. She got up, fastening her jeans, making a show of it, and pretended to just notice Lita streaming toward her, an ugly look across her face.

"What are you doing here?" Lita growled.

"What does it look like?"

Lita stormed around the tree, saw Maggie's knapsack on the ground, gave her an angry stare.

"You think I'm going to let it out of my sight?" Maggie said. "The authorizations, the transfer, none of that will happen without this laptop."

"You were not to use it until the time came."

"And I didn't. But you left it sitting against a tree. While you were waxing poetic over the People's Fight. Besides, I needed these." Maggie held up the packet of Wet Ones. "Some of us are into hygiene. Call me decadent."

Lita eyed Maggie coldly. She put her hand out. "Give me the backpack."

The cheeping of cicada bugs filled the air.

Maggie picked up the backpack, held it out. Lita took it, put it down to one side. She turned away, then spun back at Maggie, her arm coiled like a spring. A punch flew like an incoming rocket.

Maggie deflected the punch, but caught the next one and went down with a buzzing jaw. Lita piled on top of her, kicking and punching like a demon. Maggie was no match for a battle-hardened guerilla. It was all she could do to cover her face from taking too much damage.

"If you're planning something against him!" Lita bellowed, punching systematically. "Well, you'll have to deal with me!"

"We have an arrangement!" Maggie gasped, fending off blows. "What's the matter with you?"

Lita seized Maggie by the collar with both hands, straddling her. "If you so much as think of hurting him, I will kill you with my own hands. And it will be a pleasure. Do you hear me?"

"He's all yours, sister," Maggie panted. "Lighten the hell up!"

"What is going on over there?" Several pairs of boots came running through the grass. *Thank God*, Maggie thought.

"Whatever you've heard," Lita said to Maggie. "It's lies. All lies."

Numerous faces peered over the fallen tree at Lita on top of Maggie. One was Cain's.

"What the hell is going on?" Cain's voice was one of surprise more than anger, almost apologetic.

"Nothing." Lita threw Maggie down with a thump, getting

up, wiping her hands on her shorts. "A disagreement over the backpack." She picked it up. "She was *not* to touch it."

"You left it against a goddamn tree," Maggie said, sitting up, feeling her jaw.

"We need to be on our way," Cain said, looking at Lita, then Maggie, then back at Lita.

Maggie stood up, brushing herself off. Her jaw throbbed.

"We're ready to leave for Quito," Cain said. "The funds will be ready?"

"Ready. And Beltran?"

"He'll be in Quito. We'll make the trade there."

"Then what are we waiting for?"

"We need to make one stop before we leave the Yasuni."

"This mission you were talking about?" Maggie said apprehensively. "At the meeting?" She had enough to deal with.

Cain gave a curt nod. "You're coming along. Then we'll go make the transfer." He turned and left.

-27-

They moved ahead, silently, Lita leading the way through night jungle. The other guerillas followed, Maggie and Cain at the end of the line. In the darkness Maggie had to focus to keep up with a tall man lugging a large knapsack in front of her.

"Where are we going?" she asked Cain.

"You'll find out soon enough."

"No flashlights?"

"There are patrols."

Her nerves ratcheted up. The incessant squealing of cicada bugs was broken from time to time by the hoot of an owl. They pressed on until they got to the kapok tree Maggie had climbed earlier that day. Her muscles were still sore.

Just past the tree, the group stopped in the clearing where tall grass waved in the moonlight. Two small green disks of light appeared as Lita brought a pair of night-vision binoculars up to her face. Lowering the field glasses, she turned to the group and made a cranking motion with her hand. *All clear.*

They crept across the field, the thick grass brushing their legs. More dense rainforest lay ahead. Maggie's eyes had finally adjusted to the light.

A gap in the darkness appeared, filled with moonlight: the road that had been carved out by heavy equipment, slicing into the Yasuni. Lita turned to the group, her left arm extended in front of her body, her right hand toward her chest, then away, in a repeated motion.

Fan out.

They did so, moving to where the road was clearly visible.

Lita made a V sign, motioning for the rest of the group to

stop, then proceeded ahead, silhouetted against the ambient light from the road. She stopped, raised the field glasses to her face again. She turned and turned a thumb down.

Enemy seen.

Sounds of weapons being racked into firing position echoed through the trees. Maggie's heart rate quickened. A tap on her shoulder made her start.

Cain motioned for Maggie to stay put, giving her a stern look.

Where would she go? In the middle of the jungle at night?

Cain caught up to Lita, on the edge of the trees. The other guerillas followed, guns ready. Maggie tailed them, despite Cain's warning.

Through the trees, she saw the bulldozer that had had such a difficult time getting started earlier that day at the lake. Attached to it was a trailer laden down with sections of three-foot-thick oil pipe. The equipment was most likely left there to continue the next day, rather than slogging back to the village. A crisscrossed stack of pipe stood by the side of the road.

A lone figure sitting in the open cab took Maggie by surprise when it moved, turning to stare into the trees where Lita and the others hid. "Who goes there?" A guard. A soldier.

He climbed out from under the metal awning over the driver's seat, picked up a hand-held radio. Looking around, he stepped down onto the metal track.

He flinched as Lita, armed with a pistol, and two *terrucos* charged out into the road, their automatic rifles pointed at him.

"Drop the radio!" Lita barked.

The guard's head jerked from side to side. He saw he was outnumbered and tossed the radio off the earthmover into the mud. His hands rose into the air.

"Don't shoot!" he said. "Don't shoot!"

He was the same guard who had checked Maggie's passport.

Cain strolled out into the dirt road.

Lita brandished her pistol. "Down from the vehicle."

The soldier jumped down, staggered, caught his balance,

arms out.

"Hands up."

His hands went back up, trembling.

Lita swaggered up, struck the soldier across the side of the head with the butt of her gun. He yelled and went down into the mud.

"Was that necessary?" Maggie shouted, dashing out from the trees.

"On your knees!" Lita shouted at the soldier. "Close your eyes."

"I want no trouble." The soldier climbed to his knees in the mud, clamping his eyes shut. "No trouble."

Lita kicked him in the side and he grunted, falling over, throwing his arms out to break his fall.

"What the hell are your people doing?" Maggie said to Cain.

Cain turned. "You thought we were playing games? That all we wanted was money?"

"I never thought that at all. But this is not part of any deal. It ends now."

Cain's teeth showed as he spoke, "Now that you understand what I am capable of, perhaps you'll think twice before trying anything besides making that transfer."

"Why would I want to try anything?" she said. "I came here alone."

"Lackey!" Lita roared. "Hands on the back of your head."

The guard obeyed. Lita stood with the gun pointed at the back of his head. She nodded at the tall guerilla with the backpack.

The lanky man moved to the bulldozer, slipping off the pack, setting it gingerly on the ground. He unfastened the top, got out a large coil roll of what appeared to be electrical wire, followed by rolls of duct tape, and a box that, once opened, produced a dozen sticks of what had to be explosive. He unsheathed a knife, cut off a strip of tape, and fastened two sticks underneath one of the sections of tread on the bulldozer's continuous track. He attached wire to the charges, unrolled the spool a couple of meters, looking up at the other grunts. "You two," he said. "Give me a hand."

The two guerillas slung their weapons and went about assisting him, although it was clear they were reticent working with explosives. In minutes, the bulldozer and stack of pipe were wired with multiple charges. The tall man ran wire to a safe point in the trees, joined every ten meters or so with blasting caps.

"A wall of fire," one of the guerillas called it.

Lita had taped the soldier's hands behind his back and his ankles together. He lay face down in the road.

"No," Maggie said to Cain. "I will *not* allow this."

Cain ignored her. "Everybody back into the trees." They all drew back into the jungle, all except for Maggie. The guard lay struggling on the ground.

"My grandmother was Quechua," he gasped.

Maggie marched over to the soldier, the sludge sucking at her Doc Martens. She turned to Cain, by the trees. "He'll be blown to pieces."

"As will you," Cain said. "If you don't get to safety."

"I understand your anger, Cain," she said. "But let me tell you something—and you best listen. If you're going to blow up a few hundred thousand dollars' worth of equipment to prove you have muscle and can push Commerce Oil around, there's not much I can do about it. But if you think you're going to kill this man in cold blood, you can forget our deal. Commerce Oil is *not* going to have this murder on their hands."

Cain walked over to Maggie. "Even though they have the murders of thousands of our people on their hands already? Through the black death they leach into the ground?"

"Let me rephrase that," Maggie said. "*I'm* not going to have this man's murder on my hands." Her eyes locked with Cain's.

"You're in no position to bargain."

She placed her hands on her hips. "Actually, I'm in a pretty damn good position. I have your precious money."

"You won't die for oil."

"It has nothing to do with oil," she said, dropping her voice so only Cain could hear. "But if this man dies, I can't vouch for your son's safety."

"You're bluffing."

"You willing to take that chance?"

"Do you really think you can tell us what to do?" Cain said. "You Americans think you own the world. Well, not this part."

"Call my bluff," she said. "See where it gets you."

"Leave her, Comrade," Lita said, coming up on them. "We don't need their filthy money. We never did."

Cain frowned then. Perhaps he thought she would buckle. But revolution didn't run on spirit alone. It needed cash. And if Cain had any human feelings, his son might factor in as well, although Maggie was beginning to question that.

Not even thirty and possibly about to die. Well, there wasn't much she regretted. Except for not reconciling with her father. Her damn father.

"Let the oil company see what we can do to *her*, Comrade," Lita hissed. "Their precious little doll. That will make them think twice."

"Be quiet," Cain said.

Maggie saw Lita balk with anger—and a trace of hurt. But her gamble had to pay off. Had to.

Cain and Maggie stared at each other.

"Let him go," Cain finally said to Lita.

"What? Are you serious, Comrade?"

"Another death doesn't further our cause right now."

"It delivers vengeance!" Lita said. "*Vengeance is justice*—or do you forget your own words?"

It was then that Maggie saw the tightrope Cain walked. One between appeasing the madmen he needed to follow him and those with the money to advance his mission.

"Let him go, Lita," Cain said. "He's a simple soldier. Like you or I."

"Are you becoming ambitious?" Lita said. "Are you going to move to Quito and be a politician now?"

Cain jerked his head toward Lita. His pistol, holstered by his side, rested an inch from his hand. "And do you forget who is in charge, Comrade?"

A howler monkey bellowed up in the tree canopy.

Lita was first to look away. "Very well, Comrade," she whispered, her voice devoid of its passion. She drew a knife from the scabbard on her belt, stepped over in the slurping mud, cut the soldier loose, roughly, staring Maggie in the eye.

Freed, the soldier rolled over, scrambled to his feet, winded with relief. His uniform was caked with muck.

Cain spoke, "Tell the others how I let you go," he said. "How I showed mercy. Tell them it's not too late to join the people's fight."

"Yes," he panted. "Thank you. *Thank you.*"

"Off you go now," Cain said. Turning, he headed back into the trees.

The soldier turned to Maggie, his wet eyes connecting with hers. "And you most of all." He spun and ran down the road, lopsided and breathless as he headed toward the village.

The blade of Lita's knife suddenly glinted in front of Maggie's face. Maggie lurched back.

Lita smiled, put her knife away. She turned, marched angrily back into the trees as well, but stood away from Cain.

Shaking out her nerves, Maggie joined the guerillas in the trees.

The tall man picked up the wires that had been bunched together, their bare ends twisted collectively into two points. He dug into his bag and came out with a large square nine-volt battery. He touched the ends of the wires to the terminals. One. Then the other.

The flash of the blasting caps popped down the wires, a chain reaction, toward the earthmover.

Thunderous explosions hurled the track off one side, followed by billowing orange blossoms of flame and the clanking of heavy metal. The engine compartment flared white, ripping open like tin foil, before the bulldozer blew over on its side, dozens of tons of steel groaning. A meter-long section of tread came heaving down into the road, smacking into the mud at the spot where the soldier had lain. Smaller pieces of track followed, clanging off the earthmover. A section of pipe flew through the air like a missile and snapped a palm tree in half, mid-trunk.

Through the trees birds squawked. Monkeys thrashed and screeched.

The guerillas jumped, hooted, slapped each other's hands in a victory dance—all except for Lita, who simply hoisted Maggie's backpack onto her shoulders, turned, and trudged back into the darkness of the jungle, head down.

-28-

In early-morning darkness, Gauman backed the eighteen-foot aluminum fishing boat into a secluded inlet dripping with vines. Maggie, Cain, and Lita climbed aboard. Once out on the Napo River, equipped with a 90-horsepower outboard motor, they skipped past barges and transports like a giant skeeter bug, hitting a swell now and then that knocked the boat sideways, but it was momentary; they barely touched the water all the way back to Coca.

Gauman let them off in the back of a boat yard, where a guard dog straining on a chain barked nonstop at their arrival. Under severe lights by a fence topped with barbed wire, Lita and Cain hustled Maggie into a rusted Chevy van, a '70s' throwback with mag wheels and faded stripes on its side.

And soon they were on Highway 20, shooting toward Quito.

Maggie sat shivering in the back seat by the window in her denim jacket soaked with river spray, over her mud-caked jeans and once-white T-shirt. Next to her, keeping a watchful eye out, sat Lita, with Maggie's backpack, and her right hand resting on a Beretta perched on her thigh. Cain sat in the front passenger seat, wearing a throwaway plastic poncho that had left pools on the floor mats. Underneath, he carried a small Lercker pistol that looked like a cap gun. The larger firearms had been left back in the Yasuni; in populated areas, the last thing Cain and Lita wanted to look like was militia. Gauman drove.

No one spoke.

Toward Mulauco the sun rose, a gray haze casting first light across the windshield.

Maggie needed to get hold of Ed. After last night, the situation was edging out of control. She needed backup. Soon.

Lita had her laptop.

As they approached Mulauco traffic turned sluggish, lines of trucks from the countryside funneling through the small town.

Maggie leaned forward, gripping her belly. She gave an Academy-worthy groan.

"What?" Lita said.

"I need the toilet."

"When we get to Quito."

"With this traffic? It'll take over an hour."

"Cross your legs, like the rest of us."

"I'm not going to make it. You want a mess all over this seat? Because that's what we're talking about."

From the front seat, Cain turned and eyed Maggie. His tongue moved under his bottom lip, as if he were trying to determine whether she was telling the truth.

"I'm serious as a heart attack," she said. "I've been trying to hold it."

Cain frowned, turned to Gauman. "Pull over—up ahead."

The driver slowed, guiding the van into a vacant lot with weeds cracking the asphalt.

"Lita," Cain said. "Go with her."

Maggie said: "If you think I'm squatting in the back of this damn parking lot with a ton of traffic going by, you've got another thing coming."

"La-de-da," Lita said. "We do have a real live duchess on our hands."

"What you've got is someone who is going to have a real live accident any minute now. I don't know how old those anchovies were, but they went right through me. Can I make it any clearer?"

"Tough shit, lady."

"And that's exactly what it'll be." Maggie noticed trucks up ahead, pulled up under an orange-and-yellow Primax sign with a jagged chunk out of the corner, a bare bulb burning away the remnants of night. "Stop there," she said. "That truck stop."

"Go ahead," Cain said to Gauman. "Lita. Go with her."

"Give me your pistol," she said to Cain. "This one's too big."

Cain and Lita traded guns. Lita slipped the smaller Lercker into a jacket pocket. Gauman hopped out, ran around, heaved open the sliding side door.

"Let's go, little doll," Lita said to Maggie. "You *are* in a hurry, aren't you?"

The two of them headed back behind a restaurant closed for the night. Filthy wasn't the word. The woman's toilet had no lights and the floor was a good inch deep in the kind of stuff that should never cover a floor.

Next door, the men's toilet was only slightly better off. But at least there was a bulb lit and places where you could step that didn't involve used toilet paper adhering to your shoe. Maggie entered, Lita right behind, hand in her pocket, clutching her pistol. The smell was less than captivating.

Two truck drivers stood at a long encrusted urinal, relieving themselves. One did a double take when he saw Maggie and Lita walking in.

"The woman's room is out of commission," Maggie said, rushing over to an empty stall, going in, slamming the door. She pulled her jeans down, sat on the pot.

Maggie coughed as she got out the phone and pretended to do her business. Shifting the volume down, she quietly tapped out a text to Ed:

on my way to Moshis. Beltran hopefully there. things getting dicey. cant talk. need backup. will ping u later

Lita's hiking shoes appeared by the stall door. "What the hell are you doing in there?" Lita said. "Hurry up already."

Maggie hit send, hoping her text would go through. But in the middle of nowhere, who knew? She watched the spinning blue circle, then saw a message pop.

UNABLE TO SEND. BALANCE IS 0. PLEASE TOP OFF YOUR ACCOUNT. THANK YOU FOR USING

AGUILA CELLULAR.

Goddamn!

She saw Lita's eye through the side crack in the door.

"What the hell is that?" Lita said. "Are you on a fucking phone in there?"

Maggie jumped up, shoved the phone back down her bra. She flushed, yanked up her jeans, exited the stall. Lita grabbed Maggie, spun her around, slammed her against the tiles. *Hard.* A big man in a ball cap standing at a urinal turned his head, mouth agape.

"All better now?" Lita screamed, shoving her sharp nails down the front of Maggie's shirt, ripping out her phone. "You damn *puta!*" She hurled the phone against the far wall where it smacked the tiles a foot from the pissing man's head. He spun around, a stream of urine following.

"What are you looking at, *boludo?*" Lita growled. "Get lost before I beat your ass!"

He zipped up as he fled the bathroom.

Lita pulled her gun, about to strike Maggie.

Maggie said, "You're in love with him."

Lita stopped, pistol midair. "What the hell do you know? What do you know about *anything*? Money—that's all you know!"

"Yeah," Maggie nodded. "And I thought love was a no-no with you revolutionary types. But he's not your regular commie with BO and a scratchy beard reading Chairman Mao, is he?" Maggie gave a knowing squint. "Come on, look at him."

Lita blinked back, her gun arm dropping to her side.

"Yeah, he's something all right," Maggie said. "Any woman with one good eye can see that. Who wouldn't want to go a few rounds with Comrade Cain? And he's got that fire burning inside to boot. What a combo: looks *and* passion. But do you really think he's gonna be happy with some trigger-happy *revolutionista*, eating sardines out of a can in the jungle for the rest of his life? You think he's gonna hold your rough little hand when he's got two million *pavos* itching away in the other?"

Lita took a deep breath, the gun by her side forgotten. "That money is for Grim Harvest."

The stiffness and openness of her reply let Maggie know she'd hit a direct target.

"It's meant to be," Maggie said. "But he doesn't buy that Marxist mumbo jumbo. I've never seen anyone look so bored at your little meeting. And he didn't much like your attitude out on that road last night, did he? You two sure have your differences when you get right down to it. He doesn't want to give the money up either—like you do. Why is that?" Maggie raised her eyebrows. "You're right—I do know about money. It's the heart of everything. And two million U.S. buys a lot of everything. Especially around here." She saw her words sinking in.

"You don't know anything about him," Lita said.

"I know he's a got a woman in Bogotá who wrenches necks when she walks down the street. Yeah, you know who I'm talking about. In your gut, you sensed it. You're not alone. I've got a guy back home who cheats on me *right under my nose* and *still* want him." Maggie shook her head. "You think Commerce Oil didn't do their homework on Cain? He's going to take that money and run, babe. Leave you high and dry with your band of dreamy revolutionaries. Because that *chica* in Bogotá has an insurance policy. His kid. Oh yeah." Maggie gave a sympathetic frown. "All those hushed phone calls he makes? You'd be an idiot if you didn't suspect. And you're not an idiot. Not by a long shot. No, you're just *in love.*" Maggie patted Lita's cheek. "Poor Comrade Lita. In love with the wrong guy. Join the club, sister."

Lita looked up, blinking. "Ernesto."

"If it makes any difference, he'll leave her too. His type always does. But not for a while. Not with his kid sucking on her tit. And definitely not for you. It'll be someone new."

Lita gave a heavy sigh, nodded, put her gun away, the look of anguish vanishing back under a veneer of tough *terruca*.

"I have my mission," she said. "We need to get back to the van." Lita stormed out in a huff, turning the corner to exit the restroom.

Maggie saw her cell phone—Abraham's cell phone—lying on the floor in front of the urinal. From where she stood, she could see the glass was cracked, one side hanging loose, but it still looked more or less intact.

"Come on!" Lita shouted from the door.

Bending down swiftly on her way out, Maggie scooped up the phone, gave the power button a quick press, and saw it flicker red. Slipping the phone in her left jacket pocket, where it would be obscured from view by the rest of the van when Maggie resumed her seat in the back, she followed Lita.

-29-

Late-morning sun clawed its way through low clouds as the van ascended into a bad part of town, of which there were many in Quito. This one was north of the old airport, up along the mountainside where the few sidewalks were broken up and overgrown with wildflowers. Metal bars obscured every window. Graffiti made an urban camouflage across the desolate buildings.

Gauman pulled the van over next to an open space where an abandoned car without wheels lay in the weeds like a metal skeleton. Maggie watched Cain and Lita as they got out of the van, waiting for that precious second or two when their backs might be turned. Cain pulled his poncho off and Lita helped him with it. Gauman was checking his phone for messages.

No one watching.

Maggie pulled the shattered cell phone from her jacket pocket, out of view from the open van door. She stuffed the phone down the crack of the bench seat behind her. She would bet the thing was still functional, capable of sending a GPS signal if nothing else.

"Let's go!" Cain said, turning around to glare at Maggie as he threw the crumpled poncho onto the passenger seat. He was getting nervous. She didn't know if that was a good thing or not, but she suspected it wasn't.

Maggie climbed out. Gauman drove down to the end of the dirt street, making a 180, then shut off the engine.

Outside the thin air bore the metallic tang of pollution.

"This way," Cain said. He and Lita flanked Maggie, practically pressing her in between them, hands in the pockets of their jackets where they gripped unseen pistols. Lita carried Maggie's backpack. They guided her across the street toward a multistoried apartment building with outdoor stairwells, a structure that looked more like a jail spray-painted with slogans and obscenities than anything else.

Lita hadn't said a word since her confrontation with Maggie in the highway restroom. Maggie hoped that meant her "revelation" about Cain had taken hold. With any luck, she'd begun to drive a wedge between Lita and Cain.

Cain and Lita hustled Maggie to the third floor up to a red door. It had a silver swirl of graffiti across it. From within, a television brayed with canned laughter.

Lita knocked four times. The volume of the TV dropped. Footsteps approached the door. "Who's there?" an older woman said.

"Justice," Lita said matter-of-factly.

The door opened partway. A pear-shaped woman in her sixties wearing a blue housedress and floral apron gave a frown at the dried mud on the cuffs of Maggie's jeans before she stuck her head out, looked around, then stepped back and held the door open. "Tell her to brush that off," she said to Lita. "I don't want it in the house."

"It'll give you something to do," Lita said, pushing Maggie past her. The woman sighed as she stood back, letting them into a tiny living room. She jumped with surprise when Cain appeared. "Oh, Comrade Cain! I'm so sorry. I didn't realize."

Cain nodded deferentially. "Think nothing of it, Comrade."

All the blinds were drawn. An intense-looking man, about thirty, with a long gleaming braided ponytail, wearing a black-leather motorcycle jacket, had risen from an armchair where he scrutinized the arrivals from behind thick framed glasses. His eyes glistened behind them. Another guy, a lanky teenager wearing a reverse ball cap, loose black T-shirt and baggy jeans, lay on the floor, head propped up in one hand, flipping a remote control with the other. He settled on cartoons. A .38 lay by his unlaced sneaker. Otherwise, the small room was neat, with twin doilies positioned equal distances apart on a table pushed next to the wall by the door.

"Get up!" the man in glasses hissed to the boy, who turned, saw Cain, immediately jumped up, almost at attention.

"Comrade, it is always an honor," the man in the glasses said to Cain, bowing. The heavy bulk on one side of his jacket suggested a weapon.

"Where is the prisoner, Paavo?" Cain said.

"This way." Paavo extended a rough hand toward the back of the apartment.

Maggie followed Cain and Paavo down a narrow hallway painted bright blue, with a wooden crucifix on the wall. Lita stayed behind with Maggie's backpack. At the end of the hall were two doors, one with a pickax handle leaning next to it. The key was in the doorknob. Paavo unlocked the door, picked up the pickax handle, and stood to one side, on guard. Cain went in, followed by Maggie.

The small room's single window faced the stairwell outside, but was boarded up with thick plywood, well-secured. The cramped size of the room and lack of air amplified Beltran's sour body odor and the urine smell that drifted from a plastic bucket in the corner. A single bulb burned overhead.

Beltran sat on a single bed. He stood up. He wore soiled gray suit pants and a shirt that was wrinkled beyond belief. A half-empty Styrofoam container on the floor held the remnants of a messy meal. Although he tried to remain composed, it was obvious Beltran was scared. His pockmarked skin looked sallow and his signature pompadour was disheveled, dirty and devoid of hair product.

"You're Cain?"

Cain nodded once and Beltran glanced nervously at Maggie. "Am I getting out of here?"

"Soon," Cain said. "This woman needs to make sure you're who we say you are. She's making the transfer payment."

"Thank God," Beltran muttered. His demeanor was a far cry from the night of the party when he'd marveled at Maggie's derrière.

Then he blinked at her in recognition. Before he could

speak, Maggie said: "I work for Five Fortunes Petroleum," squinting to shut him up.

"Ah," he said, getting the drift of things quickly. "And Five Fortunes is paying my ransom?"

"On behalf of Commerce Oil," she said, giving a dry smile. "Don't worry. You'll get the opportunity to return the favor. Many opportunities."

"I understand," Beltran said. "I have no issue with that."

Of course he didn't. "Have they been mistreating you?"

Beltran eyed Cain, then looked back at Maggie. "No."

Maggie wasn't so sure. "When I get you out of here, you're coming with me. To the American Embassy. You'll be sent back home after debriefing, but the first thing you *will* do is to get a girl named Tica Tuanama and six other prisoners out of Carcel de Mujeres prison. Is that clear?"

Beltran nodded. "I know the girl you mean. And the others. The Yasuni Seven."

"Commerce Oil doesn't want that kind of publicity. They've been all over the news. We want them out. Immediately."

"Fully understood," Beltran said.

Cain interjected, "But there are some things you won't be talking about." He gave Beltran a friendly pat on the arm. "We always know where to find you."

"Of course," Beltran said quickly.

"Good enough," Maggie said. "I'll authorize the funds transfer." She turned and left the small room, with its smell of misery and confinement. Cain followed. The wedge-shaped woman was waiting outside. She went in, then came out carrying the bucket. It sloshed.

To her annoyance, Maggie found Lita sitting at the small square table in the living room with Maggie's laptop out and powered up. She waited, pistol to one side.

The television had been turned off and the teenager was gone.

"What do you think you're doing?" Maggie said.

"Aren't you going to make the transfer now? Oh wait, let

me rephrase that: Are you ready to show me how to make the transfer?"

"Don't be ridiculous."

"I'm going to drive."

"Why wouldn't you trust me? I want out of here as much as you want me out."

Lita gave an impatient sigh.

"It's not Facebook," Maggie said. "There are quite a few steps to the authorization. Get one wrong and access will be revoked."

Lita gave a shrug. "I'm anxious to learn."

"Comrade . . ." Cain began.

"I'm doing this," Lita said with a steely voice, glaring at Cain. "She might pull some trick on us."

Cain exhaled. "Very well."

There was little Maggie could do. After the restroom incident Lita was watching Maggie closely. And Perhaps Lita wanted to know the true destination of the funds, to see if they might be going directly to Cain. The seed of doubt Maggie had planted might be bearing unwanted fruit.

Maggie couldn't let it jeopardize what she had in mind. With Lita at the keyboard, it would be trickier to pull any sleight of hand. She'd have to think of a way. And fast. But she was tired and cold and hungry and beat up—and surprised at her revulsion on seeing Beltran in his current state.

From the back of the house they heard the door to the cell room being locked. A moment later, Paavo emerged from the hallway.

Maggie sat down on the hard-backed chair next to Lita. "You're not going to get far unless you plug the network card into the USB port," she said. "It's in the zipped pocket of the bag."

Lita found the card, plugged it in.

"Now you need to enter the password," Maggie said.

"I'm all ears," Lita said, fingers poised over the keys.

Maggie told her.

"Interesting," Lita said, tapping in the password, gaining

access. The computer desktop appeared.

"Log onto the secure network." Maggie pointed at the IKON network client symbol, a globe with interconnected lines. Lita clicked it, typed in the ID and password. The little green light on the USB device flashed. She smiled, obviously pleased with herself.

"Now we have access," Maggie said.

Almost immediately an ICE alert popped up. A small exhilaration thrilled Maggie. Whoever was trying to track her might find her this time. And in this case it might just get her out of a jam.

"What is that?" Lita said, pointing at the pop-up window.

"Nothing to be concerned about," Maggie said.

"Then why is it there?"

"It happens all the time. It's called a false positive. Just ignore it."

"Why?"

"Look, I don't have time to take you through Computer Basics one-oh-one. Or years of the Bank's security policies. It's just part of the protocol."

"Yes, but why?"

"Because this is a highly secure system. Are you going to ask questions nonstop or can we get on with it?"

"How would you like the back of my hand across your face?" Lita said through her teeth.

"Just do as she says, Comrade," Cain said to Lita with forced patience.

"Don't tell me what to do, *Comrade*," Lita replied. But she clicked the pop-up away. To Maggie, she said: "Warning disregarded. What next?"

"Before you can make the transfer, you must notify the system administrator."

"Why?"

"Because there's always a manual step to these procedures."

"Why?"

"Because nothing fully automated can remain secure."

"That makes sense to me," Cain said.

"It would," Lita said. Then to Maggie: "How do I get hold of this server administrator?"

"*System* administrator—sysadmin for short. Open that window there." Maggie pointed to a white "I" icon.

"What is that?"

"The bank's internal messaging application."

Lita opened the Iggy client window to the app Maggie had written with Enzo, back in graduate school. "Iggy?"

"The admin ID is enzo99. You'll have to send a message, telling him you need authorization for the Quito bank transfer. You'll have to do it in English. Do you speak English?"

"A little." Lita pushed a pad of paper and a pencil over. "Write it down."

Maggie brushed her hair out of her face, picked up a pencil, and wrote:

"@enzo99: request confirmation for the preauthorized bank transfer in Quito. Please notify ED. Have verified that the merchandise is safe and am ready to move forward."

Lita and Cain read over the message Maggie had written, translating it.

"Who is ED?" Cain asked.

"*What* is ED," Maggie said. "External Deposits. The account Commerce Oil uses to stage money transfers. Looks very benign on the reports."

Cain pursed his lips. "As long as I get the money."

"*We*," Lita snapped, eyeing Cain. "Cosecha Severa."

"That's what I meant, Comrade."

"Of course you did."

Maggie noticed Paavo eyeing Lita, then Cain. Did he sense the tension? But her ruse seemed to be working. She watched Lita type the message to enzo99, check it, then hit Enter. Her heart pounded while they waited for the reply. She'd known Enzo a long time—digitally. Enzo knew her boss's name. About her search for the woman's prison in Quito. All of that gibberish about transfers and authorizations would hopefully trigger a huge alert in his big suspicious brilliant brain.

Finally, the response came.

Enzo is typing...
Will process the request through ED. But first I need your bank access location and confirmation.

Maggie wrote on the pad of paper: "National Bank of Ecuador, Quito Main Branch. Access code: UIO593."

Lita typed it all in.

Very good. ED notified. Please stand by.

Maggie breathed a sigh of relief. Enzo was a genius. She made a mental note to fly to Paris at the next opportunity and take him out to dinner and marry him, if he wasn't too hideous.

"Stand by for *how long?*" Cain said.

"Ten-fifteen minutes," Maggie said, winging it.

"It takes that long?" Lita asked.

"People think everything with computers takes nanoseconds," Maggie said. "That's Hollywood. When people are involved, it's much different."

"Oh," Lita said. "Just like everything else."

"Just like everything else," Maggie said.

Another ICE alert popped up. Lita clicked OK, ignoring it.

They waited for close to ten minutes before the reply came from enzo99.

Transfer is pending. Proceed to the main branch to complete authorization in 24 hours.

Maggie had a pretty good idea what Enzo had set up with Ed. The 24 hours would give Ed time to get a team together, back her up.

Lita divulged a smirk, suddenly jumping up from her chair, whooping, before she high-fived Paavo. She even gave Cain a high five, which seemed to irritate him. "Don't you know what this means, Comrade?" Lita asked Cain.

"It says go to the main branch in twenty-four hours," Cain said, looking unevenly at Maggie. "I thought the transfer was supposed to be immediate."

"No," Maggie said, ad-libbing again. "Although the authorization process *is* complete, the actual funds transfer to Beltran's account can take anywhere up to forty-eight hours. In some countries, depending on the bank, even longer. So twenty-four is actually pretty decent."

"You told me last night that the funds were ready."

"Ready, yes. But transferring them still takes time. We're talking about two million dollars here."

"Why in the hell didn't you tell me this?"

"I told Jack Warren," Maggie said, meaning John Rae's alias. "Several times. I thought you understood the procedure."

"Damn it," Cain said. "Goddamn it."

"Don't worry, Comrade," Lita said. "By tomorrow we'll have our money."

"The money is going into an account under Beltran's name," Maggie said. "So he'll need to sign it over to you." That was BS, too, but the only way to ensure that Beltran was at the signing, to make sure he wasn't "forgotten." "Do you have an account to transfer it to?" Two million in large bills easily filled two suitcases, so she knew they wouldn't be taking it all in cash. Besides, few banks were prepared for a withdrawal that large. It would take hours just to count it. And think of the unwanted attention.

Cain nodded. "Yes, yes."

"We need to get hold of some decent clothes." She motioned at her own muddy getup, then at Lita and Cain in their well-worn shorts and jeans. "Beltran looks like he's been sleeping on the streets. We can't walk in a bank to transfer that kind of money looking like vagrants."

Cain said to Lita: "Send Señora Gomez out to find some clothes."

"I'm a small," Maggie said.

"Whatever." Lita powered the laptop off by hitting the button. It ground down and rattled before it died.

"What did you do that for?" Maggie said. "Are you trying to ruin the damn thing?"

Lita folded the laptop shut. "If we need your precious little *computadora* again, doll face, you can always charge it up then."

Christ. Maggie shook her head.

"What do we do for a day?" she said.

"We wait," Cain said. "We wait."

-30-

After a night sitting up against the living room wall in the safe house, dozing intermittently with one eye half-open, watching the tall geeky teenager and Paavo watching her while they took turns sleeping in armchairs, it was finally time to get moving and make the transfer. Cain had slept in another bedroom, Lita in a room with Señora Gomez, Beltran in his cell-room. Señora Gomez had gone out to the shops early and returned with a transparent pink plastic bag full of bread rolls. She seemed to be the busiest terrorist of the bunch. She had fetched presentable clothes last night at Maggie's suggestion, but nothing for Maggie, which gave her pause.

Now she drank watery coffee and chewed a roll with no butter or jam—Señora Gomez had bought day-old bread—sustaining herself with the hope that Ed was putting together a team to monitor the handover at the National Bank of Ecuador down on the Plaza de la Independencia. Making sure Beltran was released without any nonsense, that Maggie made it out unscathed.

And soon, with any luck, Tica and the rest of the Yasuni 7 would go free as well.

It had been a harsh few days but it was looking like it was actually coming together.

"The van's here," Lita said, slurping from a cup as she pulled the curtain back an inch to check the street down below. She let the drape fall back into place, drained her coffee.

Lita was practically unrecognizable in a loose blue synthetic pants suit that had seen much better days, over a cream-colored blouse with a bow at the collar, and black flat shoes.

Her outfit bore a hint of thrift shop, but with her hair combed back and held in place with a black headband, and large lightly tinted sunglasses, she looked much more at home in a bank than the jungle madwoman that she was. A large beat-up leather shoulder bag lay on the table, empty, and Maggie assumed it was intended to carry some of the money away after the transfer.

Lita instructed the teenager to do a perimeter check of the building. Meanwhile Cain had slipped on a nondescript black jacket and was checking his gun, which made Maggie wonder. He wore laundered jeans and a shirt. No suit, or tie.

Maggie still wore her mud-caked jeans and grubby T-shirt. Something was up. "Why the gun? We're going into a bank."

Cain didn't reply.

"What the hell is going on, Cain?"

Lita set her cup down on the bare coffee table, nowhere near a doily. "It's your turn in the back room, princess."

Maggie started, her heart thumping. "I followed through on my end," she said in a controlled voice to Cain. "You're going to get your money. You need to let Beltran—and me—go."

"Of course," Cain said. "But first I have to make sure everything is as you say it is."

"We have Beltran," Lita said brightly. "The money is in his name. And he will sign anything. No one is going to argue with him. He's the oil minister. What do we need you for, doll face?"

Maggie's head reeled. "You think Commerce Oil is going to put up with this?"

"We *will* let you go," Cain said. "Once the money is transferred into our account."

Bullshit. Cain and Lita would be halfway back to the jungle. Maggie would be the guest of Paavo and the creepy adolescent who couldn't take his eyes off her.

"Do you expect me to believe that?"

"Believe what you wish," Cain said.

"You won't get through that transfer without me," she said between her teeth.

"Let me just put it this way," Cain said, narrowing his gaze. "We *better* get through it. Because if we don't, we'll be right back here to find out why."

And then the shit would hit the fan.

"And what makes you so sure I don't have someone to back me up?" Maggie went up to Cain, looked him directly in the eye.

Cain shook his head. "You're a rogue. No one really knows where you are, or what happened to you—except that you transferred money without your partner. What were you doing? Trying to use the opportunity of his disappearance to impress your bosses? Well, you took a chance, didn't you? No one to protect you. Without the cash as leverage, you're just another gringa who was swallowed up by South America."

She lowered her voice. "What do you think it means for little Ernesto. Hmmm?"

Cain frowned. "It's a risk. But I'm a little better at risk-taking than you. Unlike most, I thrive on it. I still have Beltran. I still have you. An American citizen? An employee of a large oil corporation? The kind of money they have? I suspect they'll pay for you, too. And, if not . . ." He shrugged.

Cain was prepared to throw Yalu and his son to the wolves. She'd miscalculated. "How do you know the transfer wasn't bogus?"

"Because I don't think it was. But if, for some reason, it fails, I'll be back. And that won't be good for you."

"I'm going to make sure you pay for this."

Lita came over, gave a little smirk. "Come on, doll face, time to trade places with Beltran. I hope he kept the bed nice and warm for you. Do you know how to use a bucket? I'm so sorry there's no bidet for your pampered fanny."

Maggie sucked in a breath. She needed to think.

Cain said to Paavo, "Get Beltran ready. Lita, take Alice back. Make sure she's well-secured. *Well*-secured."

Maggie eyed the revolver on the arm of the chair. About ten feet away. But with a good chunk of Cosecha Severa in the same room, ten feet too far.

Paavo came out with Beltran in his suit that had been pressed. His tie was askew, but he'd been put together. He blinked his eyes, looking meek and hopeful.

"He's going to make a great impression signing over two million bucks," Maggie said.

"Money talks," Cain said. "You should know that better than anyone."

"Let's go," Lita said to Maggie. She had plastic cable ties in one hand, her Beretta in the other.

Maggie's eyelids flickered with rage as Lita guided her past the crucifix in the hallway to the cell-room. Señora Gomez was on her hands and knees in the bathroom, her heavy bottom waving in the air as she scrubbed the toilet. Lita shoved Maggie into the room, followed, shut the door. The room reeked of Beltran's sweat and worse.

"Turn around," Lita said.

"Do you really think you're going to get away with this?"

"Turn around, I said."

"You don't think it's going to look just a little bit weird, some guy who needs a bath transferring two million dollars to a couple looking like you two?"

"If I have to ask again, you are going to get this pistol across your face."

Maggie turned around to face the bed, Beltran's dirty rumpled sheets awaiting her. "Cain is sending you into the bank with Beltran to manage the transfer, while he waits outside in the van, isn't he? Where it's safe. That's why he didn't bother with a shirt and tie."

"Hands behind your back, bitch."

"Ah, that's it." Maggie put her hands behind her back. Lita tied them. Maggie turned her head, caught Lita's eye while Lita cinched her wrists down. "You're going in without Cain. Yeah, it would be pretty difficult for Comrade Cain to walk into a bank, wouldn't it? His face is on quite a few wanted posters. Not you, though. Can't send any of the other Grim Harvesters in with you either. Now that would look odd, a bunch of *terrucos* accompanying Beltran. So it's just you." She caught a flinch in Lita's eyes, confirming her suspicion. "Has he explained why you have to take the risk and he doesn't? For the good of Grim Harvest, is it?"

Lita tightened the cable tie even tighter, but Maggie could tell she was listening.

"That's when you need me along," Maggie said. "Bank transfers in the millions are a can of worms anywhere, but especially in this part of the world. You'll probably have to pay someone off. Do you know who, and how? I do this kind of thing for a living. You did okay on the computer out there, but that was with me telling you exactly what to do. You need me. Any suspicions and they'll call the *tombas*. That's way too tight, by the way. My fingers are already numb."

Lita examined her work.

"And if you get nabbed," Maggie said. "Do you think he's going to wait outside for you?"

"You think you know so much. You and your fancy job. *College degree*. Where did it get you? Right in this room. A room where we make the rules."

Lita spun Maggie back around. Maggie's fingertips pulsed ominously.

"But he's going to take off on you anyway," Maggie said. "As soon as he gets those two million smackers. With Miss Hottie and his baby. I wonder where they'll go. They can't stay in Ecuador. Or Colombia. Brazil maybe. Until things die down. Copacabana? Kids love the beach. I bet she's a knockout in a string bikini. But she'll go topless, of course. He'll like that."

"Shut up."

"Long afternoons making love, while little Ernesto snoozes away, contented. Sucking on his pacifier while Yalu sucks on something else."

"Didn't I just tell you to be quiet?" Lita grabbed Maggie by the collar, wound up her right fist, and punched Maggie square in the nose. Pain shot through her face and head and she saw stars as she fell back onto the bed with a bounce. She lay there in anguish on top of her bound arms, head hanging over the side of the bed, spinning.

"You don't like me and I don't like you," Maggie gasped. "But we're both alike. And we both fell for his lies."

"You did, perhaps."

"Don't kid yourself, girlfriend. He's playing both of us, so he can have what he wants. He's going to screw you, and not the way he screws her."

Lita blinked at her, as if in doubt momentarily, then left the room and locked the door.

Shit, Maggie thought. *So much for that.*

A warm trickle of blood ran from her nostril down her cheek. Maggie rolled over, making the bed squeak, and landed flat on the floor on her side, puffing for air. She didn't know which hurt more, her nose or her wrists.

She heard a knock at the front door. The teenager was back. Instructions were mumbled to Paavo and him before she heard Cain and Lita leaving with Beltran. The door shut and several pair of footsteps hastened down the outside stairwell. Maggie gasped as blood ran off her chin onto the green carpet inches away from her face. Her wrists ached. Her hands were starting to deaden.

Twisting her neck, she saw the sliding mirrored closet door. Could she somehow break it and use an edge to cut the hard plastic tie binding her wrists? Not without making a hell of a racket and tearing up her arms. She rolled up quietly, landing on her feet in a crouch. Thank God she did her yoga. She peered under the bed, hoping to find something sharp, anything, to cut her loose.

Then she saw it, right in front of her: the corner of the metal bed frame. It would take an age, but she had time. She just had to be quiet.

The front door opened again and Señora Gomez said she was going out. The door shut. The TV volume ratcheted back up.

On her haunches, Maggie waddled over to the corner of the bed, turned her back to it, positioned herself so that the cable tie around her wrists caught the bottom of the corner of the metal frame. Her hands buzzed.

Steeling herself, she started to rub, trying to avoid skin. Even so, it hurt her hands more than any effect it had on the plastic. She also had to prevent the bed frame from squeaking or moving around and thus attracting attention. Several minutes passed and all she had to show for it was that her arms were killing her. Her thighs were burning too. She was making zero progress.

She rubbed harder.

The metal frame squeaked. She froze.

Someone in the living room got up, came pounding down the hallway. Her nerves shot into overdrive. Quickly, she stood up and lay back on the bed. Her arms rang out in pain and her whole face throbbed.

The key twisted in the lock. The door opened. Paavo's thick shadow blocked the hallway light. "What's going on in here?"

"My damn wrists are killing me. That she-devil tightened the straps way too tight. You've got to help me. Please."

"They'll be back."

That's what she was worried about. "Come on, man," she pleaded. "I'm going to lose circulation pretty soon."

Somebody else came lumbering down the hallway. The kid looked in over Paavo's shoulder, eyeing Maggie in a helpless position. His narrow face split into a wicked smile. "What are you doing, bro?" he asked slyly.

"Not what you think. Now go back out there and stand guard."

"*Stand guard?* While you do what? As if I didn't know."

Maggie breathed through her mouth, one nostril plugged with blood. If there was one thing she never wanted to experience, it seemed like it was about to happen.

"Get back out there," Paavo said to the kid.

"Why? She looks pretty hot tied up like that."

"If Cain heard you, you'd be in serious trouble."

"I thought it was *Comrade* Cain. Besides, he's got Lita. What do we have? Señora Gomez? Maybe you like it big and stanky, but I think Alice Mendes here is much more my type."

"I'm going to pretend we never had this conversation,"

Paavo said, pulling the door shut and locking it.

"I'm going to lose my hands in a minute!" Maggie shouted.

Both men padded back to the living room.

Think.

Then she realized how dense she could sometimes be.

Yoganidrasana sleep pose.

She stood up, kicked off her low-rise Doc Martens.

Lying back on the bed, she lifted her legs, bending her knees, brought her right foot all the way up to her ear. Razors of pain circled her right wrist and she knew it was bleeding. She breathed deeply and got the foot behind her neck. *Yes.* Then, slowly, she brought the other foot up, hoping the guys in the front room weren't coming back anytime soon. The TV was still going. It took a while, but finally her ankles were crossed behind her neck, her head resting on them. Not bad. With her butt lifted, she pushed her hands down as far as they would go underneath her behind and rocked, which sent stabbing pains through her wrists, but on the second try, her bound hands popped under her rear. Her hands were now in front of her.

Maggie, you flexible bitch.

She gritted her teeth, raised her hands up, up over her head, jammed her eyes shut while she fought them past her feet, then unhooked her right leg. Worked it down. Her hip cracked. Then the other leg. Stretching out. She lowered her hands in front of her. It was done. Her right wrist sang with pain and dripped with blood.

But you couldn't beat the results.

With her hands clasped together in front of her, she rose up—quietly—pulled the blanket off the bed, wrestled the mattress off the frame, which took some doing, but it wasn't rocket science. Just clumsy. Tipping it up on end, walking the mattress over to the door, she leaned it against the entrance. A barrier. And noise cover. She stepped back into her shoes and went to the mirrored closet door, looking for a good place to kick the damn thing in. Get herself a good long piece of glass to use as a weapon.

"Three people leaving that apartment on the third floor," John Rae said.

Through the high-powered binoculars from the back window of the delivery van, he saw a Mestiza dressed like a Jehovah's Witness, carrying an empty shoulder bag, and Comrade Cain, leading Beltran in a suit out into an open stairwell. "Right on the GPS coordinates Maggie's friend passed to her boss."

Two days in solitary confinement with no sleep, plenty of hostile treatment, and no food or water had left John Rae bruised and more than annoyed. But when all was said and done, he was here, thanks to Maggie's mysterious web buddy calling Ed with her location. Now John Rae was back where he should have been originally.

What was ironic was that he didn't particularly want to be released from the brig just yet. But Maggie had changed the equation. And now he had her to worry about. It was cool, though. He still had his part mapped out. Two birds. One stone. It was doable.

"It's him all right, *vato*," Achic said with excitement, next to John Rae in the back of the van, watching through binos as well.

John Rae raised his binoculars again. Last time he'd seen Cain was in a skirmish in the mountains between Peru and Ecuador. Cain was still fit, but a few lines had appeared on his chiseled face. He wore a loose black jacket, the pocket on one side heavy. Where the hell was Maggie? "Beltran's looking a little worse for wear," he said. "But I don't see Maggie."

"Maybe she's already at the bank," Achic said.

"No. We checked."

"Maybe she's on her way. Maybe we missed her."

"We haven't seen anyone looks like her leaving," John Rae said. "Just that tall kid, doing a check of the building." That was John Rae's first clue this was a safe house. "And that plump woman." He focused his binoculars back up to the apartment with the red door. "They could be holding her."

That made more sense.

"Cain must be heading to the bank," Achic said.

"Got to be. That woman with him's got an empty bag."

"Shouldn't we be following Cain then?"

"Yes," John Rae said. "But I bet you five beers Maggie's still up there in that safe house with those dirtballs."

"Not taking that bet," Achic said. "But if she is, she'll still be there *after* we grab Cain."

John Rae heard the urgency in Achic's voice. "Not necessarily," he said. "They could move her." Or worse, John Rae thought, but didn't want to give voice to *that* thought.

"So what do we do?" Achic said hurriedly. "They're getting into that van."

So they were. Some old '70s piece of shit. Mag wheels. It fired up quick and took off.

"You guys follow them." John Rae opened his heavy gabardine jacket, pulled his Glock 18C, checked it. "I'll catch up with you if I can. I need to make sure she's not still up there."

"After all this?" Achic blinked in disbelief. "You're going to miss the glory? Arresting Comrade Cain?"

"All yours, little brother," John Rae said, reholstering the gun, but leaving the snap undone for quick access. "You might find it in your heart to give me a side mention when you're telling the arrest story on TV and to the newspapers. And when they pin the National Order of San Lorenzo on your scrawny chest."

The man in front of the van said something rushed in Spanish to Achic. Getting antsy.

"Alert the rest of the team." John Rae pulled down his dark knit hat and slipped on his sunglasses. It was hard not to look like a gringo, but the scroungy three-day beard was helping.

Achic produced a small red walkie-talkie, with its bold letters: Motorola Talkabout. John Rae had one too. "Radio us when you get in range. Maybe you can still make the party."

"*Adiós, amigos*," John Rae said, opening the side door of the van as the guy in front started it up, gunning it like a wild man.

They couldn't wait. Lucky bastards. "Kick that mother in the nuts one time for me." Especially if he'd hurt Maggie.

"You got it." Achic doing his Johnny Canales impression.

John Rae hopped out, heaved the door shut. The van squealed into a tight half-circle, leaning out, then barreled off down the street after Cain.

He looked up at the red door on the third floor. Yeah, he bet Maggie was still up there.

~~~

Maggie examined the mirrored closet door, turned her back to it, cocked her knee up to her chest, kicked back hard. The door cracked under her heel but didn't shatter. OK. A little harder. Again. A squawking crunch. Hopefully, the mattress she'd propped up against the door of the room was muffling most of this.

Again.

Success. Smashing the door without putting her Doc Marten all the way through. She didn't need to lose a foot. Glass crashed to the floor in a high-pitched clink and jangle. She turned back around. Shards of mirror everywhere. A two-foot section jutted up menacingly from the bottom of the mirrored door, vibrating as if to vie for her attention. *Pick me. I'll do the most damage.* Bad luck? For someone else.

~~~

"Can't you turn that damn thing down?" Paavo said out in the living room.

The TV interviewer wearing the red clown's nose had just blasted his guest with a seltzer bottle and the audience was screaming with laughter. The teenager in the baggy gangster get-up ignored Paavo, digging into a huge red bag of chips.

"Are you kids deaf?" Paavo said. "Why does everything have to be so loud?"

A knock on the front door caused him to turn his head.

"It's Señora Gomez," Paavo said. "Back from the shops. Turn it down already. You know *she* isn't going to put up with that racket. Or those chips. You're spilling them everywhere."

There was another knock on the door.

"What was that?" the kid said.

"I just told you, moron. The front door. She's back. Now turn that down already. She's going to give you a ration of shit."

"No—back there." The kid nodded back to the cell-room, where they were holding the *norteamericana*. "I heard something." The kid put the chips down, got up, picked up his .38, marched down the hallway.

"No funny stuff!" Paavo shouted, grabbing the remote, shifting the volume down to half its former level.

Another knock at the front door.

"All right, all right." Paavo pushed himself up from his chair, went to answer the door. Then he remembered. *The password.*

"Who is it?" he said.

"Cain," someone on the other side of the door said.

Cain? That wasn't the password.

~~~

In the small darkened room, Maggie heard one of them striding down the hall, muffled by the mattress she'd shoved upright against the door. She shifted around the corner in front of the shattered closet door with a two-foot long length of jagged mirror in her bound hands. The thicker end she held wrapped in a blanket that trailed on the floor.

Along with the din from the TV and the two *terrucos* arguing, they hadn't heard her until the door was in pieces. Then the TV volume had dropped.

Now she heard someone unlocking the door to the room.

Maggie raised the glass sword in her tied hands, ready.

~~~

"*Who* is it?" Paavo said again at the front door. The answer was simple. *Justice.*

"Cain," someone on the other side of the door said again.

No, not right. Paavo pulled his pistol.

~~~

The bedroom door opened a few inches, hitting the mattress.

"What the fuck?" the teenage *terruco* said, pushing against it.

"Why are the lights . . ."

Maggie turned, stood, raised the glass blade, her heart pumping like a fist. She watched the mattress fall back into the room and bounce off the metal bed frame, clanging up a storm.

The teenage kid came in, stepping over the mattress, gun up. He turned toward the smashed closet . . .

Maggie swung the glass blade, caught him across the throat. A giant razor slashing open his neck, cutting his scream short. The air in front of him filled with a spray of blood, hitting her, sticking to her face. The gun fell from his hands as he grasped his throat and gawped at Maggie with round-eyed shock. The pistol bounced off under the mattress, into the corner.

She kneed him in the groin. Hard. He doubled over in a gush of blood and she kicked him onto the lopsided mattress, knocking everything awry. The .38 lay in the corner under the bed frame. She stepped over the metal frame and got down, fumbling for the gun, both hands still girded together. Just out of reach.

~~~

Paavo turned from the unopened front door when he heard the noise from the back of the apartment. He headed back, past the crucifix, his 9mm raised.

Then he heard the *vip-vip-vip* of an automatic pistol behind him at the front door.

He spun back around, saw a diagonal of bullet holes through the front door, leading up to the lock. Another rapid salvo of shots blew the doorknob out.

He raised his weapon in both hands and waited for his intruder.

~~~

Outside the blasted front door, John Rae stood back, the Glock up, and jammed the heel of his cowboy boot onto the weakened door. It crunched, gave way, opened a foot into the apartment.

Just some crappy furniture, a coffee table with an open bag of chips on it, and a TV on the wall to the left, some inane shit with dancing girls.

But a man in there had wanted some kind of password from him. He knew that much.

~~~

"Hey there!" the girl they called Alice yelled.

In the hallway Paavo whirled back around. Things were coming at him from both sides.

The *norteamericana* was standing there with a .38 aimed coolly at him. Hands still tied together. How the hell did she manage that? He started to raise his gun, but knew he was too slow. He just hoped she was a bad shot.

~~~

Maggie fired into Paavo's chest, her tied hands bobbing with the shot. Paavo bolted back, looking down at the blood blossoming across his chest in amazement.

She fired again. And again. All hits. He was popping red all over.

Paavo went down on his back, flat, the back of his head smacking the floor and bouncing, making her wince. He lay eye-open dead in front of the open front door, the gun still in his gnarled hand.

The open front door was riddled with bullet holes.

Someone was out there, waiting. They'd shot the lock off the door, kicked it in. She pointed the .38 at the door. She figured she had three more shots.

Friend or foe?

"Want what he just got?" she yelled in Spanish, her hands buzzing around the pistol. Then, in English, for good measure, because she didn't know who was out there. "This gun's loaded!"

"Maggie?"

"John Rae?" It hurt her head to speak, her nose full of blood from Lita's fist.

Behind her she heard the teenager. She swiveled around. He was staggering out of the room, holding a blood-soaked pillow to his neck.

-31-

"I've seen worse," John Rae said, pulling back the blood-soaked pillow on the teenager's neck just enough to inspect the gash Maggie had inflicted with her length of glass. Maggie jerked back in disgust. A crooked slit, twice as wide as a mouth, dripping without the pillow. John Rae let the teenager squeeze the pillow back into place. "He'll probably live."

The kid, for his part, was now a creature owned by fear. Speechless and terrified, he gripped the cushion tightly to his neck.

"Got a cell phone?" Maggie asked him. Her voice sounded strange to her and she pinched her nose, painfully pushing it this way and that to see if it was broken. The boy got his phone out of a pocket with a trembling hand that immediately went back up to clasp the soggy pillow. Maggie took the phone, her right wrist hastily bandaged with torn sheet, growing red where the plastic tie had cut into it. She dialed 911, Quito's emergency number, instructed the operator to get an ambulance there quick, while John Rae knelt down, went through the pockets on Paavo's lifeless, bullet-ridden body. She hung up, kept the phone. She didn't need the teenager calling anyone.

"Nice shooting, Maggie," John Rae said, standing up, holding Paavo's phone. "We don't want to leave this around for him to use."

They heard neighbors talking excitedly downstairs, no doubt alarmed by the gunshots. But no one was out on the landing, or on the stairs. In a neighborhood like this, people minded their own business. They probably had a pretty good idea that an apartment with as many unsavory types as Cosecha Severa milling around was to be avoided to begin with.

Maggie guided the boy over to an armchair. "An ambulance will be here soon." Christ, she needed a box of tissues and a painkiller.

His lips moved, the words tortured and strained. "You can't just leave me here," he rasped.

"And what were you going to do to me?" Maggie said, raising her eyebrows. "I reckon you're getting a bargain, *amigo*." Trembling, he sat down, clasping the pillow.

Maggie didn't see her laptop bag anywhere. She didn't have time to look for it. She'd have to disable it when she got a chance.

"We need to get out of here, Maggie," John Rae said. "Before the cops show up. We can still make the bank. I'll call and have backup send someone out to pick us up."

"From downtown? In Quito traffic?" Maggie shook her head. "It'll take forever. Besides, you need your manpower down there to grab Cain. And they're not too far ahead of us anyway. We can grab a taxi. I hope you have cash." Maggie was already on the liberated cell phone dialing 105—operator assistance—as they pulled what was left of the front door shut. She got the number for a radio taxi and started punching in numbers as they descended stairs. As Maggie predicted, no other residents were out. Just eyes at windows, looking through cracks in blinds as she and John Rae hustled.

She jumped when she saw Señora Gomez trudging up with sacks of shopping. She was more than a little surprised to see Maggie as well. "*Buenos días, Señora,*" Maggie said, flashing a brilliant smile as she and John Rae tore by. "There's a bit more cleaning for you to do up there now, I'm afraid."

Señora Gomez stood on the stairs, mouth open, watching the two of them dash out into the unfinished street.

Within a few minutes, an old yellow cab trundled up the dirt road, puffing exhaust.

~~~

"There it is," Maggie said. "Cain's van." On the ride into Old

Town, she'd cleaned up as well as she could and her nose felt a little less congested, but her words were still coming out nasally and painfully.

From their vantage point in the taxi on the adjacent side of the palm-tree-lined square in the Plaza Grande, Maggie and John Rae watched the Chevy van parked on the south side of the plaza, across the street from the National Bank of Ecuador. They couldn't see the driver.

Scratchy music seeped from the taxi's radio.

"Chevy van," John Rae said into the red walkie-talkie, the device now in range. "South side of the plaza."

"Check," Achic replied, he and his team positioned around the plaza, ready. "The woman went into the bank with Beltran about fifteen minutes ago."

"No sign of Cain?"

"Must be in back of the van, if he's here."

"He's here," John Rae said. "He's not going to let that money get too far away."

"Could take quite a while," Maggie said. "If Cain's account isn't set up right. And especially if they're planning to take some cash with them. Which I bet they are."

"She had an empty shoulder bag."

"Well, they can't take all of it. Not even close."

"How much can she carry?"

"In a shoulder bag like she has?" Maggie gave it some thought. "A million, if it's shrink-wrapped and packed tight. But that would take the bank quite some time. Hours. They'd have to put a couple of people on it, supervise it. It would also create a huge alert if she attempted to collect that much in one visit without prior notice. And what is Grim Harvest going to do with a million cash in the jungle? Guard it round the clock?" Maggie shook her head. "So she might grab a hundred K or so. That wouldn't raise a red flag. The rest will be transferred to an account. Which Cain will control."

"So we could be here a while," John Rae said.

"Maybe." But not likely. Maggie smiled to herself with grim satisfaction. Cain didn't know what lay in store. None of them did. She'd made sure of that.

"And there are my guys," John Rae said with a note of pride, nodding at operatives stationed around the plaza. One sat on a park bench, in dark sunglasses, pretending to read a newspaper. Another stood outside the tourist office next to the bank, daypack over one shoulder, browsing artisan crafts in the window. Achic was somewhere unseen. "As soon as Lita and Beltran appear and head to the van, that's when we move in, make the arrest."

"Is this is a milk run?" Maggie said wryly.

"Not quite the one I planned."

"Why not just arrest Cain now?"

"For what? Sitting in a van?"

"Sitting in a van, running a terrorist organization."

"The guys upstairs want to do it this way, make sure Beltran is freed, make sure Cain doesn't have any recourse whatsoever in a court of law. We need to catch him with the money—or attempting to get the money. Proof positive."

Maggie nodded.

John Rae ran a thumbnail along his bottom lip. "Hurry up and wait."

"Any idea who turned you in?" she asked. "Back at the airport?"

He gave a soft laugh, followed by a frown. "No."

"Me neither," Maggie said. "But I think whoever did it has a hand in running this op."

John Rae squinted. "I'm reserving judgment."

"Sinclair knew of your plan to capture Cain."

"Hell, no. I kept that on the down low."

"I'm sure he could have found out easily enough."

"Found out from who?"

"Sinclair knew all your movements."

John Rae frowned. "He also knew yours. *You* weren't turned in."

"Because he wanted Beltran freed. But he didn't want Cain arrested. Once he found out about your covert op to capture Cain, you were conveniently sidelined."

John Rae seemed to mull that over. "Why would Sinclair want that?"

"Because he's protecting Cain."

"Why? You may not like Sinclair, Maggie, but his patriotism is not in question."

"Sure it is. Everyone believes in the convenient fiction that this is all just business, but it's anything but." Maggie flashed on Yalu and Ernesto and Lita, all pawns on Cain's personal chessboard, even Abraham, his second-in-command. Just as she and John Rae and Ed were all pawns on someone else's chessboard. "Everyone's playing their own game in their own way for their own ends." She paused, then said, "The Agency let him go."

"So his fondness for applejack made him a target with the suits back in D.C. They gave him early retirement. I can't tell you how many times that's happened. The Agency takes it out of you. But Sinclair is highly respected and still in demand as a contractor. He's also invested most of his career in this part of the world."

"Yes, I know." Did she.

"He's committed. Why would he foul up an op?"

"Who knows what he's thinking? But I'm going to find out." She still wondered who her mysterious driver had been, back when she first escaped Quito. That was connected too, somehow. Not to mention all the ICE pings.

"Well, find out, then." John Rae let out a breath. "If anyone can, it's you. You contacted Ed, got me popped from the brig. You're a rock star. When you leave that boring desk job of yours, I better be the first person you call. We need more like you."

"You don't know how fondly I'm thinking of that dull desk job right now," she said. "I can't wait to get back and look for a few missing cents while I sip my nonfat latte and think about where to go for lunch. If I still have a job. And my freedom."

"I'm just glad you got word to your mysterious friend and he got word to Ed. And the access code you made up: UIO593—the combination of the Quito airport code and the area code—just in case they couldn't pinpoint the GPS."

She smiled. "Thanks for covering my back there at the safe house. I got past that kid, but wouldn't have made it past Paavo without you blowing in the front door and creating a diversion."

"And you were supposed to head straight back home right off the bat if something went wrong."

"It's about Tica," she said. And a promise she'd made.

"I haven't forgotten."

Maggie just hoped Tica was still alive. "You'll probably have to remind Beltran, since I was left back at the ranch for MIA."

"As soon as we nail Cain and his psycho girlfriend," John Rae said. "First order of business." John Rae's radio crackled. He picked it up post haste. Someone spoke in his ear. He pulled the walkie-talkie away. "You can stop your frettin', darlin'. They're on their way out."

Maggie stared across the plaza: Lita and Beltran leaving the bank. Beltran's dazed frown and Lita's empty shoulder bag did not bode well for either of them, or Grim Harvest.

"She doesn't look too happy," John Rae said.

"She shouldn't," Maggie said.

"Her money bag is empty."

"That's right."

John Rae turned to Maggie. "You seem to know more than I do. They just got a two-million-dollar payday— didn't they?"

Maggie shook her head slowly.

"They didn't?" John Rae said.

Maggie smiled.

John Rae turned to Lita, then back to Maggie. "What are you up to, Maggie?"

"There is no money."

John Rae blinked in apparent confusion. "And why is that?"

"Because I never set up the transfer in the first place."

"Say what, Maggie?" John Rae said, mouth open. "You never set up the money transfer?"

"Afraid not."

"But *why*?" John Rae's voice conveyed the most surprise she'd ever heard from him.

"Because I started to distrust this whole setup—and Sinclair in particular." She nodded at Lita and Beltran, about to cross the street to Cain's van. "Shouldn't you be keeping track of those two?"

John Rae turned back quickly, bringing the walkie-talkie up to his ear. "The deal was a bust, boys," he said, hand on the car door handle. "But let's grab Cain and Lita, and whoever else is in that van. Achic—separate Beltran from the rest, make sure he's safe."

Excited chatter popped from the walkie-talkie.

All of a sudden, a puff of smoke billowed out of the Chevy van's tailpipe. The boxy vehicle squealed out into traffic.

"Cain's taking off!" Maggie yelled, though she wasn't really surprised. "He must have gotten a signal that the transfer didn't happen. He's bailing, leaving Lita for the wolves—just like I predicted."

"Christ!" John Rae flung open the car door as he shouted into the walkie-talkie. "Cain's pulling a runner! Grab Lita and Beltran. Backup unit—follow the van." John Rae jumped from the taxi, narrowly avoiding a speeding car that veered around the open door, horn shrieking. He yelled into the walkie-talkie as he tore across the street toward the plaza.

The cab driver turned around in his seat and eyeballed

Maggie suspiciously. "Now what?"

The cab wouldn't make any headway in this traffic, already ground to a halt with all the commotion. But she was damned if she'd let the man who held her hostage get away scot-free. "We're good, *vato*." She tossed a hundred-dollar bill over the front seat and threw open her door. Just that small motion sent shivers of pain through her injured wrists.

Out on the street, she dashed across the plaza, taking a diagonal path in front of the cathedral. She looked around and saw the two ops who had been waiting for Lita and Beltran hustle toward them, guns drawn, along with John Rae. Lita jerked her head from side to side, watching the men close in. Beltran broke away, but was caught by Achic, appearing out of a doorway.

"Hands in the air!" John Rae shouted, gun leveled at Lita.

Lita hesitated, her left hand holding up the hem of her bow-collared blouse, right hand reaching down her blue pants.

"Don't do it!" John Rae barked. "Slowly raise your hands!"

The van was speeding up Venezuela, dodging cars, hitting one with a loud *pang* before it pulled into the opposing lane and an onslaught of traffic, forcing vehicles out of the way. Maggie followed on foot, exiting the plaza onto Venezuela.

Maggie turned her head as she ran, saw Lita shaking a fist in the air.

"*¡La venganza es la justicia!*"

John Rae kicked her legs out from under her and she fell to the ground, shouting. The other ops converged on her. Achic moved Beltran to one side.

"It's about time!" Maggie heard Beltran yell.

Maggie charged up the hill after the van. Oncoming traffic had stopped. Horns exploded. People packed the sidewalks, but were staying a healthy distance from the action. Even with her fatigue and pain, and at the nearly two-mile elevation, Maggie moved like a greyhound. She was coiled up like a spring and it felt good to air out her lungs and stretch her legs and *sprint*.

The van disappeared over the rise. Maggie raced after it, but hit a wall of onlookers. She shot out into the street, weaving between stopped cars, reaching her legs out further as she followed the yellow line up the hill.

A cacophony of car horns pulsated from the other side. The sparse air forced her to breathe deeply, but she was keeping pace and knew the van would have to hit traffic sooner or later.

She crested the top.

In the middle of the street just over the hill, a blue pickup truck seemed to be trying to negotiate a three-point turn, effectively blocking traffic in both directions. Cain's van had cleared it, though, and was speeding away in a lane freed up of immediate cars.

Damn!

Maggie breathed thin air and found a reserve, the one that got her across marathon finish lines in less than two hours, the same one that got her across Quito a week ago. She lengthened her stride and pumped her arms. And found she was able to pick up speed. Eventually, Cain's van had to slow down, if not stop, in Quito's congestion.

Two blocks passed by in a blur, the back of the van getting closer. She pressed on.

Her heart pounded as the Panecillo came into view, the virgin on the hill looking down with her mournful stare. Blood rushed in Maggie's ears. The clots in her nose gave way and she tasted blood. She must have been a sight to the drivers and passengers in the cars she kept passing. Gray morning fog billowed around the bottom of the incline. Maggie hurtled down what was left of Venezuela, to where it split around the base of Panecillo hill. Cain's van made a screeching left, disappearing from view.

But traffic was building. Maggie fought to maintain her pace. The road was slippery with the fog. *Come on,* she told herself.

Nothing like a few days without sleep, a firefight in a safe house, another in the jungle, a couple of punches, to take it all out of you, make you feel your almost thirty years. Add on a pair of Doc Martens instead of ASIC Gels and 9,000 feet above sea level at high speed.

But finally, *finally*, around the next bend, Cain's van got stuck behind a blue city bus. *Yes!* Traffic in the opposite direction blocked it from passing.

Gasping for air, Maggie jogged up to the van, drawing her pistol. She climbed up on the rear bumper, gun up in one hand, hanging on with the other, peering in through the window.

A man in a ball cap at the wheel. Cain, in the bench seat behind him, turned around, looking directly at her, Maggie looking back at him. Staring into each other's eyes.

She jerked down on the rear door handle. Locked. Pounded on the van with her fist.

Cain raised a small pistol, the Lercker, resting his gun arm on the back of the bench seat to steady his aim.

Maggie flinched down, hanging onto the door handle.

Two shots ripped through the back of the van, one right through a door window inches above her head. The window cracked into a web of shattered glass and she swore she heard the other bullet zip by her ear. The van lurched forward, and she lost her grip, the van throwing her off and she landed, skidding back, arms out for stability, slipping on fog wet road, trying to regain her balance but losing the battle, flat on her butt in the middle of the street.

That hurt.

Cars behind her. Honking up a storm.

Sitting on her derriere, raising the .38 in both hands, her bandaged wrist smarting, blood still running from her nose, she fired into the back of the van, punching a hole the size of a nickel.

Return fire popped from inside the van, two more much smaller holes peppering the back doors. Twenty-five millimeter. Small, but deadly. She cringed down onto the asphalt. Near prone, gripping the .38 in both hands again, Maggie took aim, fired. Another hole was punched into the back door.

The van's side door screeched open. The driver's door followed suit.

Both men fled the vehicle at the same time, one each side, leaving the van to idle in traffic, tail pipe puffing. The driver skewed off to the left, ball cap flying off his head, into a throng of people across the street from a white church where a crowd was ballooning out through the tall doors. Forget him.

Maggie scrambled to her feet, gun in hand, unsteady. She lumbered around to the right side of the van. Cain was running away, black jacket flapping. She saw the small pistol in his right hand.

Crowds of people in front of the Mission-style church. Men in suits. Women in gowns. A wedding. Church bells rang out.

Winded, she kept after Cain, ducking in and out of the multitude, pocketing her pistol. It wouldn't do to be seen with it. And she couldn't fire, not with all these people.

Cain was fresh. She wasn't. "Stop!" she yelled, breathless. "Stop that man!"

Cain ducked behind a clump of churchgoers. Then he leaned back out, gun pointed at her. Fired off a round.

Maggie ducked, which slowed her down. She heard screams as people bolted, tripping over one another. One man in tails tumbled, taking a woman in a blue chiffon dress down with him. But no one seemed to be hit.

It didn't bother Cain, who grabbed an old woman in black by her gray hair—generating more screams. He brought the gun up to the terrified woman's head, jerking her temple to the tip of the barrel. "Don't make me do it," he growled at Maggie.

More screams. The old woman's face became a mask of terror.

Maggie froze in place.

To Cain, the woman was collateral damage. Nothing more.

Maggie raised her hands in the air.

"Let her go, Cain," she said, puffing. "I won't follow you."

"On the ground! Now!"

Maggie got down on the sidewalk.

"Down flat! Hands behind your head."

She did.

Cain gave a smirk as he tossed the woman loose. The woman sprang away, toppling, then crying out in fear.

Cain snarled: "Follow me and the next person dies. No question."

"I won't follow." Maggie didn't move.

"Head down!"

She obeyed.

And heard Cain's feet beating the pavement.

And then he was gone.

Someone helped Maggie up, then beat a hasty retreat.

Gone.

Cain was gone.

-33-

Maggie stood in front of the church, shaking with residual adrenaline, wiping blood off her face onto her sleeve, cursing herself. Wedding guests eyed her guardedly in her mud-caked jeans and improvised blood-soaked bandage. No one offered any words, just distance. She realized how off-kilter she looked.

She'd best leave now, before the police arrived. If they even would. Quito could be a lawless city, overwhelmed by crime.

Shaking her head, she turned, headed back to the plaza.

When she got near the Panecillo, the brown Chevy van was gone.

Hardly surprising, a perfectly good vehicle, albeit marred by a few bullet holes, left running in the middle of city traffic. It was probably already being ransacked in a nearby alley or garage.

She had done her best. It just wasn't good enough.

But with Beltran freed, Tica and the Yasuni 7 would hopefully soon follow.

She let out a sigh of frustration and walked back toward the plaza.

~~~

They sat at one end of a polished conference table in a windowless room in the American embassy in Quito: Maggie, John Rae and a man named Fisher, who sported a crew cut, crisp white shirt, and a striped tie from some prestigious east coast school. On the flat screen monitor on the wall in split screen mode were Sinclair Michaels, dour and severe, and Ed, hair disheveled, shirt wrinkled.

Maggie's wrist stung through the antiseptic and fresh

bandage and she had a wad of gauze up her nose.

"All in all," Fisher said, tapping the eraser end of his pencil on a pad of paper, "a success. Beltran freed. Two high-ranking terrorists in custody: Comrade Abraham and Comrade Lita. Considering how this operation began, with Agent Hutchens being detained in Bogotá, I'd say: an excellent outcome." He tapped his pencil again. "Well done, Agent Hutchens."

Fisher didn't need to say what *hadn't* been achieved: Cain was still a free man.

John Rae sat back in his chair. He'd pulled off his knit cap and his long dirty-blond hair was twisted and askew. He looked about as worn out as Maggie felt. "Let's not forget Forensic Accounting Agent de la Cruz," he said. "There wouldn't even have *been* an outcome if not for her. Not to mention she managed—yet again—to save the Agency two million."

Fisher cleared his throat. "Absolutely."

"Yes," Sinclair Michaels said gravely from the screen. "We could *not* have done it without you, Maggie."

"I wish I'd known about the operation to begin with," Ed said in a tone that tried mightily to deny disappointment. "We might have been able to put a bigger team together and capture Cain. But it goes without saying how impressed I am, we all are, with you, Maggie. I'm going to do my best to see this gets the proper recognition."

The proper recognition. She'd be lucky to keep her job. The fact that Beltran had been rescued and Commerce Oil could push ahead with their plans to drill the Amazon meant she might not be charged with anything. But there wouldn't be any promotions or anything that even smelled like a commendation. The Agency didn't operate that way. You go against the system, you're done. No one forgets. Especially the suits in Washington. She'd be double-checking data entry in a basement office until she was old and gray—or quit in shame.

"Truly excellent," Fisher said.

"What about the release of Tica Tuanama?" Maggie asked, her question focused primarily at Sinclair. "And the rest of the Yasuni Seven?"

A taut brief silence followed.

"Well?" Maggie asked.

Sinclair cleared his throat. "We are certainly going to request that Minister Beltran look into Tica and the alleged prisoners," he said. "But I've no doubt he has quite a few things to do first. He just spent many days in captivity himself."

"I was assured it would be taken care of," Maggie said between her teeth.

"I'm not sure I said that."

"I am."

"You're just going to have to be patient." Sinclair spoke to her as if she were a surly teenager. "We're doing the best we can."

"Now wait a damn minute," John Rae said to Sinclair. "We made Maggie a promise."

"That was before you planned to grab Comrade Cain, Agent Hutchens. Without telling me."

"I don't report to you, Sinclair. You're a contractor. I don't need to tell you squat."

"Perhaps not. But you will need to explain to your superiors why you failed to catch Cain."

John Rae frowned at Maggie. He was no doubt in hot water, too, despite the acceptable aftermath.

When no one spoke, Ed said: "I want everyone in this room to know that I'm not going to let the Yasuni Seven slip through the cracks. I think it's shameful—no, let me rephrase that. I think it's *criminal* that this kind of thing happens just so Commerce Oil can tear up the Amazon for the sake of profits."

"And we tend to agree with you," Fisher said. "But there's nothing to be done for the time being. Enquiries have been made. The Ecuadorian government won't even acknowledge that Tica or anyone connected to her is under arrest at this point. We're stuck at an impasse—for the moment."

"Who is *we*?" Maggie said.

"The State Department," he said.

"How about getting someone a little higher up involved?" Maggie said. "In Washington."

Fisher tapped his pencil. "Commerce Oil is here at the courtesy of the Ecuadorian government. We can't tell them how to run their country."

"Courtesy?" Maggie laughed. "Commerce Oil is getting filthy rich. Along with all those who put them there. While Indian girls disappear in clandestine prisons. There's nothing courteous about it. This is an example of a flagrant abuse of human rights."

"I do understand how you feel, Maggie," Sinclair interrupted, clearly wanting to end the discussion.

"Do you? A few days ago, I hit a server with Tica's prison information on it. She and the others are being held in Carcel de Mujeres—right outside Quito. Now, if I can get that much information with the help of a friend who plays more Angry Birds than he hacks, think how much your techies from Langley can find out. Especially since they already told you Tica's cell number. Want me to help them? I'd be glad to."

"It's not about where the prison is, Maggie," he said. "It's about how we proceed. We're in a weak position. Without Cain as an offering—a bargaining chip—we're asking, not demanding. So we have to ask nicely. Diplomacy is a dark art."

"And that's obviously not going to be enough to help Tica." Maggie stood up, biting back on the disappointment. "Not today." She'd been a fool to trust them, Sinclair in particular. But she couldn't let them win. Tica and her compadres would have to come later. Somehow. She'd just have to make it so. "If we're all done here, I'd like to get to my hotel and into a shower and a change of clothes."

Then she'd be going up to the slums. To deliver the bad news to Kacha. But first she had a few things she was going to look into.

Because something wasn't sitting quite right with Cain's escape.

~~~

Early evening, Maggie climbed out of the taxicab up in the

pueblos jóvenes where Kacha lived with her sister and her sister's baby girl. The approaching cold night sharpened the air. Maggie was refreshed, having abandoned herself to an endless steaming shower, washing her hair three times, cleaning and rebandaging the gash on her wrist delicately and working on her bruised face. Her nose had stopped gushing blood. She'd pulled on new black gabardine trousers, a white cotton blouse, and black flats she picked up in a boutique on Sucre Street near the hotel. She'd topped off the outfit with a rough alpaca jacket, black, with rich orange-and-red embroidery on the shoulders.

But she really didn't feel much better inside, having to say the words she had to say.

She walked up the dirt street to the girls' shack, carrying a plastic bag that contained two large Styrofoam containers full of roast chicken and rice. Dogs barked and swarmed around her, hoping for a scrap. A boy ran by with a stick, whipping the air that was alive with music wafting out of open windows. The smell of cooking, stews with meat and spices, made her salivate, taking her back to her own days with her mother in the slums. In a place much like this.

Did she miss it? *This?* Who could say what one missed? One missed what one knew. She missed the innocence of childhood. She missed her *mami*, who kept so many bad things in life away from Maggie as a little girl.

With a heavy heart she stepped up on the rickety porch. She could hear the baby crying, and Kacha's soft voice, coaxing it back to sleep.

The door opened. Kacha stood there, in a robe, cradling her niece swaddled in a fuzzy blanket. Kacha's face lit up in a hopeful smile, causing Maggie's to stiffen before it could crumple. As much as she fought it. Her look immediately alerted Kacha that she wasn't bringing good tidings.

"Oh," Kacha said, her smile quickly fading. "You better come in." She stood back, jiggling the baby.

It was a dismal meeting. The food lay untouched.

"Where is your sister?" Maggie asked, once the news had

been delivered. "Suyana?"

"She's out . . ." Kacha said.

"Turning tricks? Why? Didn't you get the money I sent?"

"No. The man at the office said there was a delay."

Maggie saw red. "I'll take care of it tomorrow." She dug into her pocket, came out with a wad of bills John Rae had given her. She peeled off several hundred dollars. "Here. No more walking the streets."

Kacha took the money with a sigh of relief. "Thank you."

"She's lucky to have you look after her little girl."

"I have the easy part," Kacha said.

"I want you to understand something, Kacha. I'm not going to stop. I'm going to get Tica out. And the rest of the Yasuni Seven."

Kacha nodded slowly in acknowledgement, but her disbelief in Maggie's abilities was apparent.

"There's more to do," Maggie said, to herself as much as Kacha. "I *will* resolve this."

"You've already done so much."

Maggie left, walking down the dirt road toward the Plaza San Francisco, her head hung low, full of darkness, like the night. But she wasn't finished. Not by a long shot.

Down the hill, where the paved streets began, she found a hole-in-the-wall electronics shop wedged between a produce market closed up for the night and a cheap restaurant harshly lit with fluorescent overheads, teeming with diners, heads bent down over steaming bowls. She bought an unlocked moto e phone for less than a hundred U.S. and a prepaid micro SIM card. The clerk had her up and running in minutes. She'd seen techies back home struggle with similar tasks.

In the noisy restaurant, she ordered a bowl of spicy bean soup, which the cook loaded up with cilantro. She spooned a few scoops of bright orange *ají* into it and found a spot at the counter where mountain music screeched from a radio. The aroma of the place had her salivating and the good cheer of the clientele made her homesick once again, even though she *was* home. Technically. But this home was a long time ago.

She didn't really know where home was.

She ate a mouthful of *locro de habas*, fired up her phone, downloaded a TOR browser for anonymity, then searched and downloaded Phone Tracker Plus. It was installed by the time she was halfway through her soup.

She had a head for numbers and didn't forget them. Not once she'd committed them to memory.

She turned on GPS and plugged in the number for Abraham's cell phone, which she'd jammed down the bench seat of Cain's van. She set her new phone on the counter while she ate more soup. The red pin moved on the map of Quito and settled near the Panecillo. And stopped there. Less than a mile away.

Too excited to finish her soup, she got up, used her phone to call a radio taxi, went out into the cool night air, and waited on the cobblestones.

A tinny Daihatsu soon came whining up the street.

~~~

"Stop right here," Maggie instructed the cab driver, an emotionless young man who wore sunglasses at night and had his radio set on a classical station. The red pin on the map hovered on the phone in her hand, showing this to be the place. And down the end of a dirt cul-de-sac, silhouetted against the deep valley of the city pockmarked by twinkling lights, there it was: Cain's van. A couple of men in shadows moved around it stealthily. The beam of a flashlight bounced.

"Wait for me and keep an eye out, please," she said to the driver.

"You need to pay me first. This is not the best part of town."

She paid him. "I'll need a ride back to my hotel."

He nodded, but she wondered how much help he would actually be if she got into a scrape.

She exited the car and walked into the alley. The snort of a pig caught her attention. She stepped back, let it cross her path, to avoid getting her new shoes trampled by hoofs. The pig trotted by.

A couple of kids were playing in the van. The men had the front doors open and were busy removing the dash. She approached. "Excuse me," she said.

"What do you want?" one man said, one eyebrow higher than the other. A crowbar dangled menacingly from his hand.

"I know who this van belongs to," she said, getting her money out. "And it doesn't belong to you."

"It does now," the other man said, lighting a cigarette.

She unfolded a U.S. twenty, let Crooked Eyebrow follow it. "But I don't care. I just want to know what you found inside. That's all I want to know." She held the twenty out. It fluttered in the chill night air, then disappeared.

"Not much," the man said, nodding back at the van. "Just the radio."

"You're going to sell the van for parts?"

He shrugged.

"Can I look in the back?"

"Why?"

"I have my reasons. I'm not going to take anything. I promise."

Cigarette Smoker looked at her bandaged hand, as if waiting for it to produce another bill. It did. Now each man had one.

"Help yourself," he said. "But if you find anything, it's ours."

She went through the van. There was nothing left but an empty cola can, some crumpled napkins. She found Abraham's broken mobile in its hiding place and left it there. Well, it was worth a shot. She climbed out, stood up, dusted herself off.

"*Bueno*," she said with a sigh.

She noticed an overweight little boy, a striped shirt stretched over his round belly, standing in the shadows. Something in his hand caught her eye. It looked like a radio.

"What have you got there, *amigo*?"

"It's mine!" He hid it behind his back.

"I know it's yours, *chico*. I just want a look. I won't even touch it. You hold it out in front of you just so I can see it. OK?"

"What will you give me?"

She came over, reaching into the pocket of her jacket, pulling out a ballpoint pen with her hotel's name on it. She held it up, clicked it, raised her eyebrows.

"OK," he said, reaching for the pen.

"Ah, ah, ah," she said, holding it back. "Show me your radio first."

"Oh, OK." He held it out with both hands, so she couldn't take it.

A Motorola Talkabout. Red. Identical to the one John Rae had been using in the plaza waiting on Lita and Beltran. Before Cain had so very uncannily gotten away.

Because Cain had been in on that entire conversation. Listened to everything. Knew it was time to run.

Because John Rae had planned it that way.

-34-

"There's a red-eye to Quito from Houston," Maggie told Ed on the phone, looking out of her hotel window at the plaza. Night had descended over Old Town and the glistening lights through the mist softened the harshness of life and the reality of what was happening in this city. This country. The country of her birth. "You can grab a flight from SFO and make it by morning. I'll meet you at the airport."

"You really sure about all this, Maggs? Because we're both cutting our careers short. Maybe worse."

"Yes, Ed," she said. "Very sure. I need your help on this one. I don't want to meet John Rae alone."

"OK," Ed said. "Are you going to set up the meeting? Or am I?"

"Leave it to me," Maggie said.

"Fine," Ed said with a sense of finality in his voice. "See you when I get to Quito."

She hung up, ran her fingers through her hair, thought about hitting the minibar, decided against it. She was close to exhaustion. She didn't want alcohol in her system. She didn't want anything in her system. She wanted to climb into a clean bed, under crisp sheets, and disappear.

She called John Rae's hotel room, in New Town.

"I was hoping to hear from you," he said, with that telltale flirtatiousness in his voice. There was a time it would've excited her. "I didn't know where you were staying."

"I prefer it here in Old Town," she said. "You can keep your plastic Hilton glitz."

"Maybe you can show me around. Up for a drink?"

"Sorry," she said. "I'm beat."

"No doubt. Rain check? When we get back home to the U.S.?"

"Sure," she said. And she wished it could have happened that way.

"I'm heading back first thing in the morning," he said. "I've done all the damage I can do down here. Been called back to D.C. to get my bottom smacked but good. But I'm not hanging my head on this one."

"I'm afraid you're going to have to reschedule your flight, John Rae."

"And why is that?"

"Because we need to meet."

"Sounding pretty final there, darlin'."

"Yeah," she said. "I guess you could say that."

"I don't think so," John Rae said. "I've had about enough of South America for the time being."

"You're not getting a choice." She eyed the red Motorola walkie-talkie on her nightstand she'd paid the chubby boy twenty dollars for. "I've got you, John Rae. I know what you did. And you owe me."

There was a pause. "So what is this all about?"

"I think you know," she said. "I'll leave directions to the meeting place at the front desk of your hotel in the morning. Don't you dare stand me up, John Rae. Not unless you want to be on the wrong end of an investigation. And no funny stuff. Got it?"

There was a pause. "Got it," he said quietly.

She clicked off her phone and undressed, hanging her new slacks up on a wooden hanger, smoothing them out. She still had the .38 she'd taken from the safe house. She clicked the latch, opened the cylinder, checked for rounds. One left.

She set the alarm for three a.m. so she could get up to meet Ed's flight. It would be another night with little sleep, but in the grand scheme of things that was nothing. Kacha was sleeping in a slum. Tica was sleeping on the floor of a cell, if she was sleeping at all. Maggie engaged the security bolt on the hotel room door, climbed into bed, put the pistol on the bedside stand. She left the light on so that she could see the gun as she drifted off.

-35-

To say that the view of early morning Quito from the top of the Basilica was stunning was an understatement. Fog drifted through the long narrow valley nestled in the Andes that held a city of two million at an altitude of close to two miles.

Ed was still gasping for air as he hung over a stone parapet, the gargoyles practically mocking him. A severe drop to the slates of the church's roof lay far below. The steep iron ladder they'd climbed was almost vertical. They couldn't get any higher.

"How do you ever get used to this damn altitude?" Ed said.

"Takes time. Did you remember to take that medication I told you about?"

"Yeah, yeah," he panted. "But it still feels like I'm going to have a heart attack."

"With all due respect, dear boss, you need to drop a few pounds."

"What I need is a bottle of oxygen."

Maggie patted him on the back. "Climbing up here didn't help." But she needed somewhere safe to meet, where she could see whoever was coming from a distance. When you were dealing with Field Ops, anything was possible.

"Where the hell is John Rae?" Ed wheezed. "He's late."

Maggie checked the time on the twin clock towers opposite. "He'll be here," she said.

"You better hope he's not on that flight back to Houston. Setting us up."

"He'll be here."

Ed caught his breath as best he could as the wind whipped

through the tower. "I've got some bad news," he said.

Maggie's stomach dropped, as much as she might have been expecting it. "Director Walder is going for the gusto? I'm facing legal sanctions?"

"Not quite," Ed rasped. "Not if you agree to one concession."

"Ah," she said. "There's always a concession."

"Lucky for you there is."

"And what is it?"

"The two million you so valiantly saved the department?"

"Twice now," she said. "Money destined for Beltran. Then Cain. Does that make it four million I saved?"

"Not in this case," Ed said. "Because if you'd handed it over in the first place, the second might not have happened."

"Debatable," Maggie said. "But what about it?" As soon as she said it, she realized. "No. Don't tell me we're giving it to that bum anyway. Not after we just saved his worthless skin without paying off the ransom."

"Afraid so, Maggs."

"And why on earth are we doing this?"

"Because Beltran is valuable to us," Ed said, pulling out a pack of Winstons from his jacket pocket, shaking one out.

Maggie laughed through her nose, still stuffed on one side, then shook her head.

Ed placed the cigarette between his lips. "And because we need to placate the Ecuadorian government. After two lopsided missions."

"You mean Beltran is valuable to Commerce Oil, and Commerce Oil wants to placate the Ecuadorian government. So they can drill in the Yasuni. And this is how they do it—with taxpayers' money."

Ed found a book of matches, lit one up, but it blew out in the breeze. "As I said before, Maggs, half of Washington is getting their pockets lined by Commerce Oil." He tore off another paper match. "The other half are waiting their turn. We're in hot water—meaning Forensic Accounting is on the chopping block. They don't like the way we play with their best buddies."

"So I should have just given Beltran the damn money in the first place. When Grim Harvest kidnapped him, he could have paid them out of that. Then everybody would have been happy."

"It's called irony, Maggs." Ed struck the match, tried to get it up to his cigarette before it went out. He didn't make it. "Christ."

"You're a sad bastard, Ed. Are you sure you should be doing that? Because the way I'm feeling right now, you're not a candidate for the kiss of life."

"I got your cowboy out of jail, didn't I?"

"OK, so you come in handy now and then."

He squinted. "Where is the two million anyway?"

"Bitcoin," she said. "In a dark net account. It's actually worth two point two right now."

"Unbelievable." Ed shook his head. "Well, it goes into Beltran's Amazon Wildlife Restoration Fund—by tomorrow. Got it?"

"Or I face a panel, go to jail, and you lose Forensic Accounting. Maybe your job."

"I don't give a shit about Forensic," Ed said. "Losing it would be a blessing. And I can always come back and contract, just like Sinclair. But I'm kind of fond of you, Maggs. You don't need to suffer. Not for the Agency. They're just not worth it. It's pin money."

"Do I keep my job?"

"Hell, yes."

"Not sure I want it."

"Don't blame you, there."

"Fine," she said. "But I don't have a secure laptop."

"We'll be home tomorrow," Ed said. "Worse comes to worst, I'll get you another day. But I need your promise. They're waiting to hear."

"Nothing really *works*, Ed. Not the way it should."

"Tell me about it." He finally got a paper match lit, brought his face down to it, got the cigarette going with a sizzle of beard. He came back up, smoke escaping his mouth into the breeze.

Maggie reached over, pulled the cigarette from Ed's mouth, dropped it on the gravel of the roof, ground it out with the heel of her flat.

"That's the only satisfaction I get anymore, Maggie."

"I'm kind of fond of you too, Ed. And you really need to start taking better care of yourself."

Ed's face collapsed into a deep frown. "What for?"

Then they heard, echoing from the rafters in the Basilica below, footsteps negotiating the scaffolding going from one end of the roof to the other. A high precarious walkway.

"More than one person is coming," Maggie said. She reached into her jacket pocket, felt the .38 for the reassurance that was in it. She had one shot and one shot only. But one could be enough. Maybe she was getting used to this life. But her nerves were still bumping together.

And then they appeared, on the roof below: John Rae, in a lightweight beige suit and sunglasses. And another man, wearing a newsboy cap, in dark slacks and a tweed jacket. He looked up.

Sinclair Michaels.

"Looks like John Rae brought backup, too," Ed said.

~~~

When the two men had climbed the ladder to the top and caught their breath, Sinclair was the first to speak. "I think I need to know what this is all about, Maggie."

"I believe you already have a pretty good idea," she said, "or else you wouldn't have taken the red-eye down from Washington to meet me with John Rae."

"Do I?" Sinclair Michaels gave a cutting smile. "Maybe I'm just trying to show a little respect, considering everything you've done for us. I also need you to know that you can't threaten my people."

Maggie reached into her other pocket, brought out the red Motorola Talkabout. "This was in Cain's van. Because he was in on the arrest conversation yesterday between John Rae and the agents."

John Rae did a double take when he saw the walkie-talkie.

Maggie put it away.

Sinclair glared at her. "That doesn't prove anything."

Maggie looked at John Rae. "My suspicions took a radical shift when Cain first took off after the failed transfer. Sinclair wasn't close to the action. But *you* were. And then, you instructed the backup van to follow Cain. But there was no backup van," she said. "Just a pickup truck blocking Venezuela—making sure that Cain got away. That's who you were alerting."

John Rae grimaced, but kept silent. It was hard to argue with the evidence. "John Rae is protecting a terrorist," she said to Sinclair. "Funny, because at first I thought it was you."

Sinclair said, "I've had my eye on Cain since Ecuador—a long time. But I was never ordered to do anything more than have him release Beltran."

"That was all you wanted. Even if I had to take a risk. You coaxed me along, lied to me, said John Rae was getting out—when he wasn't. All designed to make me think it was just a milk run. You couldn't afford a failed op. Not a contractor with a drinking problem."

"I am not in the habit of releasing terrorists like Cain."

"But John Rae is," she said. "Unbeknownst to you. He was ordered to capture Cain. During the Beltran trade. You weren't in on it. You were just the floater agent to front it, to make it look genuine."

"You need to learn that you play a part, Maggie," Sinclair said drily. "Even if you don't like the part. Even if you don't know you're playing it."

"You were put in charge of the second op—a milk run—but the Agency wanted a little more for their two mil, especially after the embarrassment of the first one: They wanted Cain. You didn't know that. They asked John Rae and he arranged it. So that no one else could take it and make it happen." She turned to John Rae. "But you had your own agenda—covert within covert within covert. You derailed

Cain's capture, faking your own arrest. You needed Cain to stay free. You urged me to run if anything went wrong. Your team was told to back off if that happened as well." She zeroed in on John Rae. "The question is: *why*? Why are you protecting Cain?"

"Let me tell you something, Maggie," John Rae said. "Cain is mine—make no mistake. And he will pay for his transgressions. But not until the time is right, not until I'm done with him. Not until he's got *all* the info we need. ISIS? The Islamic State? Cain has connections to people who fund those boys. *That's* who I want. Grim Harvest are the Keystone Kops in comparison."

Sinclair pursed his lips, pulled his hat off, brushed his thinning hair over, put his hat back on. "John Rae explained everything to me, Maggie. As he said, he does have his reasons. Reasons you don't need to concern yourself with."

"Beltran is willing to set up the Yasuni rainforest for Commerce Oil. Commerce Oil is going to get what they want. Cain's not going to be able to do much about that now."

John Rae spoke. "Rest assured that our relationship with Cain is going to play out much better than you think."

"I'm not assured about anything you guys do anymore," Maggie said. "But I will be guaranteed one thing."

"Ah," Sinclair said. "Here it comes, John Rae, my boy. What does she want? Recognition? A promotion? A 'bonus' of some sort, funneled into an offshore account?" Sinclair shook his head. "The idealistic ones are the most hypocritical."

"No," John Rae said, staring at Maggie. "I don't think she wants any of those things, Sinclair. I think you're reading her all wrong."

"Tica," Maggie said. "The Yasuni Seven. Out. Now." She held up the walkie-talkie, wiggled it. "Or I go to the *New York Times*. And the *Manchester Guardian*. And *Der Spiegel*. And whoever else likes to keep tabs on the American intelligence machine. It does sell newspapers."

John Rae said, "You'd do that? Compromise national security?"

She put the walkie-talkie back in her pocket. "If I have to."

John Rae nodded, serious now, his accent all but gone. "I don't blame you for being upset, Maggie. I thought it was going to work out a little differently, though. I thought the Beltran trade was going to happen that first night in Bogotá. That you were going to see it through, then be on the next flight out and it *would* be a milk run." He laughed sardonically. "Everyone was going to be fat, dumb and happy. But Cain got jumpy when I didn't show. Took off, gave you a wild goose to chase. But you didn't stop chasing! Well, that's to your credit, I suppose. But I'm sorry. Sorry as hell."

Maggie said, "Then you can make it up to me."

"Tica."

"And the rest of the Yasuni Seven."

"How on earth are you going to do that?" Sinclair said, turning to John Rae. "Beltran will never agree to such a thing. Never."

"Beltran." John Rae laughed. "Talk about the tail wagging the dog, Sincs. Beltran owes us his damn life. Or Maggie, rather. Cain is a loose cannon and she played him like a pro. And yet Beltran still calls the shots. What's wrong with the picture you painted, Sinclair? All the years you spent down here, making 'friends.' Beltran was the best you could do?" He shook his head. "Now I hear that he's going to get the two million after all."

"Commerce Oil paints the pictures, John Rae," Sinclair said. "Better get used to it. Or find another line of work."

"I'm not sure I'll be doing either one of those things, Sinclair," John Rae said, eyeing Maggie now. "I'll see that Tica's taken care of, Maggie. It's time to call in an IOU."

"How?" she said.

"I got this covered. Don't sweat it."

Somehow she knew John Rae would deliver.

She patted Ed's arm again. He'd finally caught his breath and was frowning as he took everything in.

"Come on, boss," she said. "It's a long way down. And we've got a flight to catch."

-epilog-

Maggie's door buzzer rang just as she was slipping into her black jacket, half of a stylish new two-piece by Akris Punto she'd picked up for a song at Dimitri's illegal emporium on Capp Street. By invitation only. Don't tell your friends. Carefully, she pulled the cuff of her crisp blouse over the minor bandage on her wrist. Not too noticeable. Her bruised nose was faded now too. She walked over to the window of her living room on Valencia Street in her new Lanvin pumps, pulled the curtain aside.

Her limo was here. Delta Financials was doing its best to woo her. Two hundred K a year. Stock options. A parking spot out front with her name on it. Free coffee.

Big deal, she thought. The money meant nothing to her, especially in the face of letting everyone down. Tica. Her cohorts, still in prison. The woman who'd sent her the Commerce Oil video. Ed. And Kacha. A few hundred-dollar bills for her trouble. Maggie was still fighting with Western Union to free up the couple grand she'd sent. Beatriz and Gabby weighed heavily on her as well. Even the driver who'd died in Quito. The only one she'd helped was the pig, Beltran. How was that for consolation?

Her cell phone chirped with an arriving text. She pressed a button and saw, first, a previous message from Seb: Rehearsing all day, gig tonight. Wanna come? If only to talk? She deleted it.

Then she saw the message from John Rae: Is your TV on?

Check out CNN.

She grabbed the remote, tuned in, and was startled to see a very familiar face.

Comrade Cain. Wearing jungle fatigues and looking like the world could get out of his way or die. She popped up the volume.

"A daring prison break outside of Quito, Ecuador, early this morning resulted in the escape of seven prisoners, all from a group called the Yasuni Seven, members of the Kichwa tribe who live in a part of the Amazon being taken over in a controversial play by Commerce Oil. The escapees, all of whom belong to the Save the Yasuni Movement, are believed to have been arrested and incarcerated in the clandestine women's prison months ago. One of the prisoners is a sixteen-year-old Indian woman named Tica Tuanama, who has risen to notice as the front person for the Save the Yasuni Movement. A statement released afterwards by a rebel group known as Grim Harvest has taken responsibility for the breakout. Several of the prisoners were near death and it is reported that various surgical procedures were performed, including the harvesting of organs."

A grainy photo showed a defiant Tica, zigzag tattoos on each cheek.

"The leader of the rebel group, who calls himself Comrade Cain and has long been wanted by the international community for crimes of terrorism, is reported to have led the attack. More news to follow as we get it."

Maggie saw rough photos of Grim Harvest, taken from surveillance-camera feeds, in the streets of Quito, weapons raised as they shepherded prisoners into two vans. There was Yalu, with a stunning smile as she held an assault rifle in one hand, shaking a fist at a camera.

And off to one side, John Rae. Maggie took a quick second look. Sunglasses and Chullo cap with the ear flaps down and a bandana tied around his face. But it was him all right. The pointed toes of his cowboy boots were a giveaway. Holding a wicked-looking machine gun.

Well, boys will be boys.

But delivering on his promise after all.

Maggie turned off the television. And felt just a little better.

And stopped worrying about the mysterious driver who picked her up that day in Quito, and who might have ordered it. And who might have been tracking her. And the woman who exposed the corruption and violence in the Amazon. And what Commerce Oil was doing to the Yasuni and how the Agency and half the world condoned it. Soon it would all be behind her. Wouldn't it?

The door buzzer rang again, three successive bursts this time.

She gulped the last of her espresso, put the demitasse cup in the sink along with the saucer. Picked up the red Motorola Talkabout sitting by the coffee maker, tossed it in the trash under the sink.

Her MacBook on the countertop was soon open to the account belonging to Beltran's bogus Amazon Wildlife Restoration Fund. One point nine five million still left.

So trusting. To leave it there. He thought she was toothless now. In the end, it really was pin money to the Agency.

She transferred all of it to the Save the Yasuni Movement fund after first converting it back to Bitcoin. Untraceable.

Tough luck, Beltran. It's probably chump change to you too—with the number of people paying you off.

She pressed Enter, completed the anonymous transfer, watched it go through, logged off.

Picking up her briefcase, she turned off the lights, headed out to her interview.

###

-about the author-

Born in the wilds of San Francisco, with its rich literary history and public transport system teeming with potential characters suitable for crime novels, it was inevitable that Max Tomlinson would become a writer.

He is also kindred spirits with a dog named Floyd, a shelter-mix who stops and stares at headlights as they pass by at night. There's a story there, too. If only Floyd could talk. Then again, maybe not. Who really needs to hear what a dog wants to eat 24/7?

Perhaps he's channeling the demons of Jim Thompson, Elmore Leonard and Patricia Highsmith, like his owner, and trying to make some sense of them.

http://maxtomlinson.wordpress.com/

CPSIA information can be obtained
at www.ICGtesting.com
Printed in the USA
LVHW041758210523
747621LV00002B/226

9 781522 995975